Nightfall

NORAH WILSON

Nightfall

PUBLISHED BY:

NORAH WILSON

Cover by Kim Killion, Hot Damn Designs
Book Design by Michael Hale, Hale Author Services

Acknowledgements

I wish to thank everyone who critiqued and proofed this book, including many members of the Domino Divas, the most talented and amazing support group a writer could ask for.

A very special thank you to Rita Bellinger, a goddess among Beta readers. A writer herself, Rita is a speed reader with a photographic memory. Her vigilant eye caught a handful of typos, extra spaces and an unintentional name change even after I could have sworn it was pristine. You rock, Rita!

Note re Bonus Material

Please note that bonus material in the form of an excerpt from GUARDING SUZANNAH, Book 1 in my Serve and Protect Series, appears at the end of this book. That bonus material will make this book appear several pages longer than it actually is. Bear that in mind as you approach the end and are anxiously trying to judge how much story is left!

Chapter 1

AIDEN AFFLACK HUMMED to himself as he lifted the brass doorknocker to summon St. Cloud Police Chief Weldon Michaels to the front door of his Carrington Place residence. Rapping twice, he stepped back.

What *was* that tune running through his head? It had been with him since he'd risen this evening.

Audioslave? Nope.

Queens of the Stone Age? Un-uh.

Collective Soul? Yeah, yeah, that was it. Definitely. He cricked his neck one way, then the other and felt the satisfying crack. *Ooh, I'm feeling better now.*

The curtain in the bay window twitched, but Aiden feigned obliviousness. From inside, he clearly heard Michaels jam a clip into an automatic weapon. Aiden rolled his eyes. Nobody trusted anyone anymore.

"Who are you and what do you want?"

The voice came through the door. A very cautious man indeed.

"I'm a friend of your wife's," Aiden called. "Well, more a friend of a friend, actually, but I have a personal message for you, from her."

"Nice try. Now move on, before I call the cops."

Aiden thought about knocking the door in. It was solid oak with a good deadbolt on it, but it could have been made from cardboard and paperclips for all the challenge it would present. On the other hand, there was no reason to get messy.

He cleared his throat, did his best to summon a puzzled tone. "Well, hell, I thought you *were* the cops. Do I have the wrong address? I'm looking for Chief Weldon Michaels. Got a message for him from his wife Lucy. Pretty woman, 'bout an inch over five feet, brown hair and eyes? Oh, and a real cute little daughter. What's her name? Devon? Any of this sounding familiar?"

Silence for a few heartbeats. "What kind of message?"

"She wants to come home, but before she can see her way clear to doing that, we need to have ourselves a talk."

Another pause, then the sound of the deadbolt retracting. The door cracked open, and Weldon Michaels peered out past a security chain.

God save me from fools. Growling, Aiden pushed the door open. The hardware anchoring the security chain tore free from the wall. Before Michaels could cry out, Aiden stepped inside and closed the door behind him. In the next heartbeat, he seized Michaels' right wrist and squeezed until the other man screamed and dropped the pistol he held. It hit the hardwood floor with a clatter but didn't discharge.

"A gun?" Aiden released the other man's hand. "Now I ask you, what kind of a greeting is that?"

Michaels — clearly a slow learner — reached for a second weapon jammed into the waistband at the small of his back. Before he could get to it, Aiden had Michaels face down on the floor with his right hand way closer to his right shoulder blade than God ever intended it to go.

"Jesus, my arm. You're breaking it!"

"Not even close. You develop a feel for these things," he said conversationally. "It's sort of like braking when you're driving on ice. You gotta find the threshold."

"No, my shoulder! It's gonna pop! I swear to God!"

Aiden reefed Michaels arm a half inch higher, eliciting a scream, followed by a stream of curses.

"See? Still plenty of play. It's a feel thing. Now are you gonna behave yourself if I let you up?"

"Christ, yes! I'll do whatever you say."

"Atta boy." Aiden helped the other man to his feet. "Now, let's go plug the code into the alarm, shall we? And don't fuck with me. If the alarm company or the cops call in a minute to ask if everything's okay, things will be very much *not* okay for you. Understood?"

"Understood."

Aiden "helped" Michaels to the alarm panel, where he keyed in a five-digit number. The winking red light went out.

"Good man. Now we're going to need your handcuffs. I know they can't be far away, since you laid hands on that pistol fast enough. So be a darling and let's go fetch them."

Michaels swore again.

"I know, I know. It's gotta sting, getting cuffed with your own bracelets, but look at it this way: they'll be a helluva lot more comfortable than the alternative if you force me to improvise."

Michaels sagged. "In that drawer."

A minute later, Chief Weldon Michaels sat cuffed in one of his own kitchen chairs, a sturdy-looking oak proposition. Michaels somehow managed to look both scared and pissed at the same time.

Aiden took a seat at the table, placing both guns — one retrieved from beneath the telephone table in the entryway and the other from the small of Michaels' back — on the gleaming wood surface. "Okay, Weldon — may I call you Weldon? — we need to talk."

Michaels glared back. "You're wasting your time. I don't keep anything of value of here, at least nothing portable enough to carry off. And damn you, you've already scored both my guns. I suggest you just let yourself out and get while the getting's good."

"You think I was bullshitting earlier, don't you? You think I was feeding you a line about your wife to get inside?" Aiden leaned back in his chair and kicked his feet up to rest on the table. "That's rich."

Fear flashed in the other man's eyes, which he quickly attempted to hide with bravado. "Look, mister, if you have a message for me, let's get on with it."

"Afflack."

"What's that?"

"If you're gonna call me mister, you might as well make it Mr. Afflack. Or Aiden, if you prefer."

Another flash of fear. Aiden could almost hear the wheels turning in Michaels' head. *He's shown me his face, given me his name. There can only be one reason for that …*

"Not to worry, Weldy. I think I'll call you Weldy."

Michaels tensed. Testing the cuffs and the strength of the chair's spindles, no doubt.

Aiden sighed. "For Chrissakes, I'm not planning to kill you. I'm just going to spend the night here chatting, much like we are right now."

Michaels blinked. "Spend the night?"

"Forgive me. It's probably horribly uncomfortable with those cuffs on. Let me just deal with these nasty guns. Then I'll take the bracelets off so we can talk all civilized-like."

Aiden picked up the SIG 9mm with his left hand, grasped the barrel with his right. Closing his eyes, he slid his hand up and down the barrel a few times to attune his mind to the metal. Then he bent it effortlessly.

"Jesus Christ!"

Aiden placed the ruined pistol back on the table, picked up the .22 and repeated the process on the gun's short barrel.

"What the … how'd you do that?"

Aiden shrugged. "A parlor trick. You should see what I can do with a dinner fork." He stood and extracted the handcuff key from the pocket of his worn jeans. "Now, about those cuffs …"

Michaels shrank back.

Aiden lifted his eyebrows. "What? You'd prefer to keep them on after all?"

The other man collected himself, embarrassment staining his cheeks. "Of course not. Please remove them."

Aiden obliged.

As soon as his hands were free, Michaels immediately started massaging his sore right shoulder.

"Ah, yes, the shoulder. Sorry about that." Aiden gave him his best *aw shucks* smile. "But I couldn't have you putting bullet holes in me, could I?"

Michaels said nothing, but the stiffness in his face spoke volumes. *Good. Get brave, you miserable little wife-beating worm. Get angry. Give me a reason to hurt you again.*

Michaels cleared his throat. "So, this message from my wife?"

"She wants to come back to St. Cloud. In fact, she'd like to move back into this very house, seeing as she put so much sweat equity into it." Aiden glanced around at the tastefully appointed kitchen. "I must say she did a great job."

"Of course she can come home. That's all I've wanted since she left."

"Ah, but there's a catch, Weldy. You can't stay."

Michaels made a choking sound, but quickly found his voice. "She thinks I'm just going to clear out of town?"

"That would be ideal, but no, I don't think she expects that. It will be sufficient if you leave this house and never darken the door again."

Michaels started to bluster that he owned the goddamned place and no one could put him out of it, yadda, yadda, yadda.

"Save it," Aiden commanded. "You see, I know what you did to her, Weldy."

A pause. "I don't know what she told you, but —"

"You systematically isolated her from her friends and pressured her into quitting work. Then, when you got her where you wanted her, you escalated the abuse. You *terrorized* her, Weldy. You threatened the life of her child if she tried to leave you. Is any of this sounding familiar? No? Well how about this: you used your position and power to convince her that escape was impossible."

Michaels leapt up, his face wreathed in fury. "You don't know the first fucking thing about my family."

Aiden swung his feet to the floor, but remained in his chair. "Oh, I know quite a bit, Chief Michaels. For instance, I know you've been abusing the police resources at your fingertips to search for her, ensuring she had to stay on the run, unable to stay anywhere for any length of time. I know she's terrified for her life and that of her daughter."

"If she'd just —"

"Shut up, Weldy, and listen. I'm the messenger, and the message is that it's over. She's coming back, and you, my friend, are going to become the most obliging, most accommodating, most *respectful* ex-husband on the face of the planet. Oh, and you'll relinquish any rights to the child."

"Fuck you." Powered by rage, Michaels gripped the table's edge and overturned it, then bolted for the door.

Grinning, Aiden swept the table away as if it were constructed of matchsticks and gave chase, overtaking his quarry in a blur of speed. By the time Michaels reached the door, Aiden lounged against it, the picture of indolence.

"Going somewhere?"

"Jesus!"

Michaels' face suddenly looked like it was stretched too tightly across the underlying bones. Shock did that to some people. With others, their faces went slack, as though —

"Who are you?" Michaels rasped. "Dear God, *what* are you?"

Aiden allowed his smile to spread, noting the precise moment when Michaels caught the first glimpse of his grossly elongated cuspids. This time, Michaels' face slackened.

"I'm glad you asked."

Sam Shea burrowed deeper into her denim jacket and shifted her legs yet again. The August night was soft, and three hours ago she would have called it warm. Now, however, dew was beginning to form on the blades of grass around her. Only the patch beneath her butt and outstretched legs remained dry as she sat propped against the base of a gargoyle statue.

Yes, a frickin' cement *gargoyle*. Unfortunately, she didn't have a lot of choices about where to pitch her tripod. It was the only spot in the vicinity where she could get far enough away from the ubiquitous streetlights to see even the brightest stars in the sky. Rural shoots were so much easier.

Of course, it was anybody's guess what she was here to capture. It might have nothing to do with celestial bodies. On the other hand, what else could it be?

Well, okay, ninety minutes ago, she'd have laid bets that she was here for an electrical storm. The flashes of lightning had started to the south, illuminating the suburban landscape in an eerie purplish light. Counting the seconds between flash and boom, she tracked the storm from nearly ten miles off. She'd pack up and head for the car when it reached six miles, the safety zone. No photo was worth getting killed for, especially when she could get a decent shot from the relative safety of her rented Acura. But the storm had veered off at the last moment, making a retreat to the car unnecessary.

So if it wasn't a fantabulous light show, what the heck had drawn her here?

For the first time in a very long time, she wondered if her vision had let her down. Right place maybe, but the wrong time? Or maybe there was another Carrington Place in St. Cloud, and she'd camped at the wrong one. But what were the chances of that in a city of just over 100,000 people? Of course, maybe there was another Carrington Place in an entirely different St. Cloud.

Except she knew she wasn't wrong. She was never wrong. She'd thought so once, six years ago. After five hours of nothing more dramatic than the occasional distant meteor streaking across the night sky, she'd given up her post in disgust and gone back to the dubious comfort of her motel bed. The next morning, she'd found the local coffee shop abuzz about the dishwasher-sized meteorite that had crashed to earth in a pasture eight miles out of town. The same pasture where she'd abandoned her vigil at 4:00 am. If she hadn't bailed out, it would have made a hell of a photo.

No, she wasn't wrong. Despite the boredom of the past few hours, the raw energy that had drawn her here still persisted. *Something* was going to happen here, dammit.

For the umpteenth time tonight, she flicked on her hand-held infrared spotlight, lifted her infrared binoculars to her eyes and did a ground-level scan. Two houses down, a skunk made its leisurely way across the front lawn, oblivious of the surveillance. Nothing else stirred. With a sigh, she lowered her binoculars and flicked the light off.

No light show in the sky. Nothing interesting on the ground.

She leaned back again, wriggled her butt into a more comfortable position and glanced up at the leering griffin's massive head. "Don't let me nod off, okay? I'd hate to miss the fireworks. Or whatever we're going to have."

Predictably, the griffin made no reply.

"Okay, be like that," she muttered. "See if I —"

The sound of a door closing — specifically, the door of the two-story house directly across the street — cut short her one-sided conversation with the gargoyle. Automatically, she reached for the floodlight and the binoculars.

There! A man — rendered slightly greenish, thanks to the infrared technology — gliding out the flagstone driveway.

Quickly, she traded the binoculars for the tripod-mounted digital camera, flipping it to NightShot mode. A quick look through the viewfinder confirmed the target was out of range for the camera's infrared illuminator. Dammit. She squeezed the trigger switch on the spotlight again, locked it in the on position, planted its legs in the soft earth and trained it on the adjacent driveway. This time when she found her subject through the viewfinder, her mouth went dry.

Dear God! If she could give the fiercest storm a corporeal human body, this is what it would look like. Beauty and violence, all rolled up in one gorgeous, terrible package.

Zoom, focus.

God, what a face!

Hard zoom, focus, click.

Without conscious thought, habit took over as she snapped picture after picture.

She watched him draw out a cigarette and apply a flame to it. Fascinated, she watched him inhale deeply, remove the cigarette from between sensual lips, then exhale. Then he lifted his lids and looked directly into her camera lens.

Sam pulled back, shrinking closer to the gargoyle's cold cement base. *He can't see me. Not from this distance. He's standing in the light and I'm buried in shadow. And he sure as hell can't see my spotlight.*

Carefully, she leaned forward again to peer through the viewfinder. And there he was, still staring straight into the camera. And then — holy mother of God — he smiled at her. A knowing, toe-curling, sex-drenched smile.

She jerked back again, but this time, she failed to suppress a gasp. Not that it mattered, because he was gone. Vanished. She searched the sidewalks for his retreating form, but he'd melted away as completely as the smoke from his cigarette had dissipated in the night air.

She exhaled the lungful of air she'd been holding. Whew! That was ... interesting.

But even more interesting was the dawning conviction that nothing more was going to happen here. As she sat there bringing her heartbeat under control, she realized that the muted anticipation that kept her rooted to this spot for half the night had dissipated. Interesting, indeed.

Well, no point hanging around now. She got to her knees and packed her gear. Before stowing the camera, she flipped back through the pictures she'd captured to make sure she hadn't imagined the last minutes. She hadn't. There he was. Even frozen in greenish miniature, he emitted an improbable dynamism. She frowned. Could he be the force that had called her here? A shiver lifted the hairs on her arm. It didn't seem very likely. Of course, the alternative to that scenario was that her vision had been just plain wrong, which was even less palatable than the thought that a man might have drawn her here.

Sighing, she shut off the camera and tucked it carefully in the carry tote. With a last glance around the empty streets, she headed for her car. Ten minutes in a hot shower and a few hours sleep on the pillow-top mattress at her hotel would fix her up. She'd figure this thing out in the morning.

An hour later, she turned on a lamp and crawled out of bed. The dream would just keep coming back if she didn't write it down. She found a pen and hotel stationery and scribbled the words *St. Cloud, riverbank under the bridge, tomorrow night. Call and postpone your flight!*

There. Maybe now she could sleep.

Three hours later, after a poached egg and a cup of room-service coffee, Sam uploaded the images from her camera's flash card onto her photo viewer, a task she would normally have done last night. Backup was critical in this business. But since she hadn't captured anything saleable, she hadn't bothered. Now, she breathed a sigh of relief when she saw confirmation that the upload was successful.

She paged quickly through the first few photos, which she'd taken merely to fine-tune her settings. The house across the street with its foot lighting, the row of streetlights marching west, the retaining wall behind her. Then she reached the first shot of the man.

Ugh. Monochromatic green. NightShot was useful for surreptitiously framing your shot, but you then had to switch modes to get a normal-looking color shot. Of course, that required using a visible flash, which in turn required her to be considerably closer to the subject. It was great for photographing small critters in darkness, but not so great for capturing people. It just wasn't socially acceptable to creep up on a stranger and blast their night vision away with a blinding flash.

Especially this stranger.

She bent closer to the display to inspect her work. She'd zoomed in on the guy, but it was a full-body shot rather than tight to the face. He looked taller than she remembered, but the wide shoulders and narrow hips were the same, as was the longish, wavy hair. He wore what appeared to be a leather jacket over a dark shirt and dark pants.

She pulled back, feeling oddly disappointed.

He had the kind of body that would make any woman look twice, no question about it. But she just wasn't feeling that same gut punch she'd felt last night. Guess she could chalk last night's reaction up to jet-lagged giddiness and the late hour.

She toggled up the next photo, and *oh, baby*, there it was, that thrill low in the belly.

A high forehead pleated in a frown, and a straight nose. Several strands of curly blond hair spilled forward to graze high cheekbones, partially obscuring his eyes. At least, she thought his hair was blond. It was too pale to be otherwise. The light also illuminated lean cheeks, a strong chin and an unsmiling mouth. Beautiful. Stern. Forbidding.

She advanced the next photo, and sucked in her breath on a hiss.

His face was tilted toward her to better reveal a sinfully gorgeous male mouth, but that wasn't what set her heart to pounding. It was his attitude of sharpened senses. She could swear he was scenting the night breeze through those flared nostrils, his head cocked to catch the slightest sound, eyes searching the darkness. She leapt out of her chair, overcome by the sensation that she was about to be discovered.

God, woman, get a grip. She snorted at her own panicked reaction. He couldn't see her. Not now, and not last night, either. At most, he may have suspected he was being watched and played to a possible audience, but standing under the streetlight like that, looking into the deep shadows ... No, there was no way he could have seen her.

She seated herself in front of the viewer again and toggled up the next photo. Despite being prepared this time, her heart still jolted in her chest.

He was looking straight at her!

And oh yeah, he'd known he had an audience. An appreciative audience. Unlikely as it seemed, he must have sensed her. Awareness was written there in his face, in the lift of an eyebrow and that sensual, full-lipped smile.

Sam expelled her breath. "Well, aren't you all that?"

The unknown man smiled back from the photo, his NightShot-glowing eyes maddeningly unreadable.

Magnetic.

The word slid into her mind, making her lips tighten. Last night, she'd allowed herself to contemplate the idea that this man might be the force that drew her here. The idea was no more palatable in daylight than it was in the dark of night. To think she might have delayed her return to Sioux City after the Montreal gallery opening, extending her Canadian trip to come to St. Cloud, New Brunswick, to take a photo of a mere *man*?

No. No way. It didn't bear thinking about. She'd been mistaken about the time and location, that's all. There was a first time for everything, right? Besides, last night's vision had rectified the mistake. She now had a very clear idea where she needed to be and when.

She toggled the cursor, but there were no more images. Sam moved backwards to the final picture, the one where she was sure he knew she watched him, and shivered.

Maybe she'd do a little research, for curiosity's sake, starting with finding out who lived at that Carrington Place address she'd camped outside of last night. Maybe something would surface to explain why she'd been called there.

Four hours later, she had a fix on the owners, a couple by the name of Weldon and Lucy Michaels. A Local Google search revealed that Weldon was the chief of police here in St. Cloud, but turned up nothing on Lucy. Well, that let out anything nefarious going on inside that house, him being the chief of police and all.

She pushed thoughts of Michaels and his late night visitor to the back of her mind and turned her attention to preparing for tonight's stakeout. After studying maps at the library, she drove unerringly to the downtown, parked in a parking garage, and set out on foot with her camera bag slung over her shoulder. A four-minute walk connected her with the riverfront walking trail, and another ten minutes put her practically in the shadow of the bridge. The grass was tall here, with a couple of distinct trails leading down the embankment toward the river. This was it. This was the place. She fished her digital out of her bag and took a couple of shots.

The sound of crunching gravel alerted Sam to the presence of another pedestrian. She glanced up to see a young man approaching from the west. As he neared, she noted industrial facial piercings and a faux-hawk.

She lifted a hand. "Excuse me, could I —"

"Sorry," he said, side-stepping her. "I don't pose for tourists."

As if. Before she could correct his assumption, he'd walked on. She jogged to catch up.

"Hey, if I wanted to take your picture, I wouldn't want to do it here. I'd want to do it in a studio, or at least with the proper lighting equipment to do you justice. But that's not why I stopped you. I just have a question."

He slowed. Apparently flattery worked. "Whatcha wanna know?"

"Those paths back there, the ones leading down to the river. What's that all about?"

He shifted the bag he was carrying from one tattooed shoulder to the other. "Homeless."

Sam felt the truth resonate inside. Yes, that fit with the feeling the dream had left her with. "Is anyone down there now?"

Judging by the look he gave her, she expected him to say, *What am I? Kreskin?*, but what actually emerged was, "Dunno. Maybe. Or maybe they'd be out hustling for handouts this time of day."

Sam chewed the inside of her lip. "The police don't object to them living down there?"

"The cops?" He snorted. "Don't imagine they give a rat's ass where they sleep at night, long as they're outta sight. All they really care about is keepin' the panhandlin' under control." He glanced up the trail, obviously wanting to be on his way.

"Thanks for your help."

"No problem." He hiked his bag up and walked off.

She lifted her camera and took a few shots before crossing the neatly mown green to the taller grasses. She picked the closest path, which also happened to be the most well-worn, and descended the embankment, pausing occasionally to take more pictures. Passing through a thin belt of trees, she emerged to find a hard-packed footpath paralleling the river's edge.

The smell assailed her immediately. There was the usual pungent river smell that made you think of mud and fish and silt and organic rot, but underlying it was the unmistakable odor of human urine. Ugh. She snapped another picture.

She turned west and walked toward the bridge. Before she got twenty yards, she spotted the first makeshift shelters. Made from a mishmash of plywood, corrugated cardboard and blue plastic tarpaulins, the flimsy structures huddled just inside a thin belt of trees she'd just come through. No wonder none of this was visible from the walking path. For that matter, it probably wasn't terribly visible from above either, save perhaps for a few flashes of blue through the canopy of leaves.

Briefly, she thought about following the path all the way to the bridge and out the other side of the copse of tree. The riverbank appeared to be deserted, but she couldn't bring herself to go further. Deserted or not, there was something invasive and ugly about wandering past these squalid refuges like a sightseer, camera in hand. Plus, frankly she was scared. These people couldn't or wouldn't be integrated into normal society, often due to chronic mental illness. It was the same in cities all over North America. Bursting at the seams, psychiatric hospitals everywhere disgorged their long-term residents into their streets to make do the best they could.

She retraced her steps and continued west along the trail until she found another path in the tall grass. As she expected, it led down to the river, then back toward the treed area that concealed the tent community. Again, she ventured only far enough down the path to spy where flashes of blue tarp began to reappear.

Though less plentiful on this side, she counted six structures, some of them no more than lean-tos.

She turned and looked west. Less than a mile away, tall condominium buildings and a handful of old brick office buildings rose up against the skyline. Sighing, she retraced her steps up the incline, through the tall grasses to the manicured green bisected by the graveled walking trail. Just like that, she was back in the shiny clean St. Cloud of the tourist brochures.

She turned back eastward and followed the trail for a hundred yards or so before veering off toward the concealing ribbon of brush and trees that shielded the shelters. A handy thing, that little green belt. It kept the homeless out of sight and out of mind for the tax-paying, job-holding, upstanding citizens of St. Cloud. That same invisibility kept the ire of the police off the backs of the vagrants.

She followed the tree line with difficulty. The grass here was knee deep, and without benefit of a beaten path, it conspired to trip her with every step. But just the other side of the bridge, she found what she was looking for — the perfect vantage point for surveilling the area later tonight.

Tucked just inside the tree line, it afforded enough cover for her, and offered the best view she was likely to get of the encampment below. Also ideal was the positioning of the streetlights on the four-lane bridge above and the towering light standard that illuminated the walking trail behind her. With any luck, there should be sufficient light to monitor goings on without having to constantly sweep the area with her infrared equipment. Likewise, it was close enough that she could step out of the tree line quickly if the commotion tonight turned out to be a light show in the sky.

Satisfied, she trekked the short distance back to her car. Just one more task and she could go back to her hotel and catch a few hours sleep. Stashing her equipment in the trunk of the rental, she walked half a block to Queen Street and found a payphone. She located the general number for the St. Cloud Police Department, plugged a quarter into the phone and dialed it.

When the receptionist answered, Sam instructed the woman to put her through to Chief Michaels, employing the tone she'd learned in her first year in business-for-self. The trick to obtaining cooperation was not to demand it, but rather to simply take that cooperation for granted. Faced with such easy, inherent authority, most people gave her exactly what she expected. The St. Cloud PD receptionist was no exception.

The phone rang twice in Michaels' office before it was answered. "Chief Michaels," a voice clipped. "Who am I talking to?"

"Good afternoon, Chief. I'm a reporter for —"

"Whoa. You can stop right there, lady. We have a communications officer who handles press inquiries. Call the switchboard again and they'll route you —"

"You had a visitor last night. Is that right, Chief Michaels?"

A pause. "I'm going to transfer you to my personal line. Please hang on."

She heard him make the transfer. Before his personal phone could manage a full ringburst, he'd picked it up.

"Dammit, what more do you people want from me?"

You people?

"I'm sorry," he said, rushing to fill the silence. "I'm just a little tense. The moving company is there right now, packing up my belongings. I'll be out by nightfall, just like I said."

Sam blinked, listening to his ragged breathing. What the devil was he talking about? Channeling that voice of authority again, she went fishing: "Very good. And the rest?"

"I won't hurt her again, I swear it. I won't even make contact. She can move back tomorrow. I'll give her a divorce, full custody of Devon, the house … whatever she wants."

Holy crap! What had she stumbled into?

"Hello? Hello?" The chief's voice rose on a note of panic. "Are you still there?"

"Relax, Chief. I'm still listening."

"You have to believe me! I'll never lay a hand on Lucy again. On either of them. God, I won't even breathe in their direction. You'll see. You can watch me as closely as you like."

He'd been abusing his family? *Bastard*. "You can bet we'll be watching," she said in her silkiest voice. "Need I tell you what we think of recidivists?"

"No, ma'am. I'm sorry. Jesus ... my ulcer. I have to go. I'm sorry."

The line went dead. Slowly, Sam hung up the receiver. Well, well, wasn't that interesting? Chief Michaels' late-night visitor had been a friend of Mrs. Michaels. And a very persuasive one, by all appearances. What could he possibly have said or done to reduce the chief of police to the jabbering wreck she'd just talked to?

She thought about the photos back in her hotel room and the peculiar energy that had emanated from Michaels' caller, and decided he was probably quite capable of decimating stronger men.

No matter. It was none of her concern. Michaels was still alive and well, and presumably newly embarked on the straight and narrow.

But who was the mystery caller? The estranged wife's new boyfriend? Hired muscle? Some vigilante out to avenge victims of violence? Random whack-job?

Well, she wasn't going to solve that mystery here, standing in a phone booth.

Correction — she wasn't going to solve that mystery at all.

Stepping out of the phone booth, she headed for her rental and the promise of a nap back at her hotel room. She had to be fresh, had to focus on tonight. Whatever the reason she'd been called to St. Cloud, it would all become clear tonight.

Chapter 2

SIX HOURS LATER, she stood in the spot she'd scouted out earlier, slapping at mosquitoes. Blood-thirsty beasts! How had she managed to forget insect repellant? Sighing, she bent and dug through her pack yet again, pulling each item into the light cast by the towering light standards. Fully-charged cell phone, spare battery pack for her spotlight, bottled water, protein bars, sunscreen, extra sweater, windbreaker, sweatpants, even dry socks and an extra pair of runners. But no bug spray.

"Dammit." She smacked a mosquito on the side of her neck, feeling the warm wetness of blood beneath her fingers. "Let that be a warning to the rest of you," she muttered, but the high-pitched whine of more hungry mosquitoes closed in on her.

A sudden cry, cut off almost before it was born, and the mosquitoes were forgotten. Heart bumping, she scanned the riverbank. Nothing. But that sound … An owl, maybe? She swept the area again.

Wait! Right there. Two men locked in combat. She hit the infrared spotlight and peered through her binoculars. Yup. Locking the trigger on the spotlight, she grabbed her camera, framed the scene and started shooting.

Okay, maybe not combat. It looked more like …

Oh, God.

She pulled back from the tripod.

Freaking wonderful. Last night, a thug putting the fear of God into a wife-beater, and tonight, a homosexual tryst by the river. What in bloody hell was happening to her?

She glared at the entwined figures, but suddenly something about them didn't seem right. The smaller one … was he trying to push the other away?

She lifted her camera again, found her target and zoomed in. And oh Christ on a bike! The big guy was … oh Jesus, he was *biting* the smaller guy's neck. On one level, she was stunned, but on another level, she went to work. *Click, click.* Please God, don't let the batteries on the spotlight fail. *Click, click, click.* Back off the zoom. *Click, click.* The victim was swatting frantically at his attacker now, but the bigger man hung on like a pit bull. *Click, click.*

It struck her then, the inappropriateness of what she was doing. She was watching an assault, for God's sake. *Photographing* an assault. Or worse.

She lowered the camera and yelled: "Hey! You there. Stop it!"

He did stop, but not because of her shout. Another man appeared as though out of nowhere and dragged the big man off the victim. Sam fumbled for her binoculars, clapping them to her eyes in time to see the victim going down. And oh Lord, was that blood spewing from his neck? Yes!

She shifted her focus back to the combatants in time to see the newcomer twist the original attacker's neck savagely. The pit-bull biter guy went down like a sack of cement.

Cursing, she dropped the binoculars and rummaged through her bag until she found her cell phone. Taking a look to get her bearings, she broke out of the tree line and started down the hill. Eyes scanning the ground in front of her, she moved as fast as she dared on the rough, ill-lit terrain. Half way down the hill, it occurred to her she should call 9-1-1 sooner rather than later.

Skidding to a stop, she flipped her phone open and dialed with shaking hands. As she waited for the 9-1-1 operator, she glanced up again. Her stomach lurched. Not a dozen yards away, the man she'd thought was the victim's savior was now bent over the fallen man, having taken up where the first attacker had left off, at his neck!

"9-1-1. What is your emergency?"

"Stop it!" she cried, lurching forward again. "Get off him!"

The second assailant lifted his head from the wounded man's neck, and she jerked to a stop again. And oh my sweet gentle Jesus, it was him! The one who'd conducted the forcible re-education of Chief Michaels last night. And his face, the face she'd thought so beautiful, was smeared with blood.

"Ma'am, what is your emergency? Where are you?"

"Get away from him! I have the police on the phone right now."

His lips curled up in a devastating smile. He stood, fixing her with his intent blue eyes. No, wait. It was dark. She couldn't see the color of his eyes. *The photos*. No, that wasn't it. They'd glowed green in the photos. Why did her mind insist she could see vivid, day-bright blueness?

The 9-1-1 operator's tinny voice came over the cell phone again, asking once more about the nature of Sam's emergency. Sam blocked her out. "Just back away from that man. The police are on the way."

His smile grew wider. "Nice try, but I can hear that operator from here. And if you're thinking they can instantly pinpoint your location from that cell phone, forget it."

She lifted her chin and spoke into the cell phone: "I just witnessed an assault on a homeless man, here in St. Cloud. I'm on the river's edge, south side, just down river of the Merrill Bridge. The cops shouldn't have any problem finding me. I'm less than a hundred yards below the main cluster of tents."

He sighed. "Well, that's torn it. If the cops are coming, I guess I'd better be on my way."

Sam stiffened as he moved toward her. "Stop right there! Don't come any closer."

"Or you'll what? Throw your phone at me? Relax. It's him I'm after, not you."

Her heart pounded as he strode past her, close enough for her to feel his energy brush her. On the line, the operator urged her to hang in there; the police were on their way. As though on cue, she heard the distant wail of sirens. Please God, let them be responding to her call!

The stranger bent and picked up the body — and from the impossible angle of the man's neck, there could be no doubt it was merely a body — of the first attacker. Shouldering the weight like it was nothing, he turned back to face her.

"Can I give you a word of advice?"

She blinked. *A word of advice? From this killer?*

"Do yourself a favor and keep the ... um ... specifics of this incident to a minimum. Trust me, it'll go better for you."

The sound of the sirens swelled behind them. Definitely headed this way. Emboldened by the cavalry's imminent arrival, she drew herself up. "You can't intimidate me. I'll tell them exactly what I saw."

He grinned. Grinned, dammit! "So be it. But don't say I didn't warn you."

She opened her mouth to damn him for the psychotic monster he was, but he'd disappeared.

No. No, that wasn't right. He didn't *disappear*. Not poof and gone, like a magician. She'd actually seen him go. She'd unquestionably seen him adjust his burden, turn, and run off. But he'd done it so damned fast, she'd perceived it as little more than a blur.

Fast. Oh shit, oh shit, oh shit. *Inhumanly* fast. No one could move like that!

"Ma'am, are you there?"

She pressed the phone to her ear again. "Yes."

"The police are almost there. Can you see them?"

She turned to see the reassuring strobe of blue and red lights racing toward her. "Yes, he's slowing down. Oh, he's climbing the curb with his car, right onto the grass. Now he's driving on the walking trail ..." She lifted her arm and waved wildly. "Over here!"

The vehicle — a 4×4 SUV of some kind ... maybe an Expedition or an Explorer — swerved off the graveled trail and plunged down the grassy slope, its bouncing headlights evidencing the roughness of the terrain. It came to rest about twenty feet from where Sam stood. She started toward the vehicle only to be stopped in her tracks by a sudden blast of blinding light. Shielding her eyes, she squinted toward the vehicle. Roof-mounted lights. They had to be halogen. Nothing blinded like ...

Both front doors of the vehicle flew open. Although she couldn't see anyone, she thought it was safe to assume two officers slid into position behind those doors.

"Drop your weapon and put your hands way up where we can see them."

Weapon?

"I said drop it!"

Oh, God, the phone. They thought it was a gun. She threw it to the ground and lifted her arms. "That was my cell phone. I'm the one who called it in."

"Kneel down on the grass," continued the officer, as though he hadn't heard her. "Cross your feet at the ankles and lace your fingers together behind your head."

They had guns trained on her, she realized. Not that she could see them, but she could sure feel them.

"Okay." She knelt as instructed and linked her hands behind her head. "But you're making a mistake. A man's been attacked. See for yourself. Over there." She gestured to the left with her head. "He needs care urgently. He's bleeding badly, from the neck."

One officer, the one who'd been driving, approached, gun and flashlight trained on her. Silhouetted as he was by the lights behind him, she couldn't make out his features, but she saw him turn his head right to left, left to right, doing a visual sweep.

"You're too late," she said. "They're gone."

"You'll forgive me if I check for myself."

Sam wanted to scream her frustration, but she bit it back. They had to take care of their own safety first. Stupid to do anything else.

The cop—the tall one who'd been driving—moved in and patted her down for weapons. Though he was brisk, efficient and impersonal, it was all she could do not to smack his hands away. They were losing precious time! She'd seen the way the victim's blood had spurted. He couldn't last long. "Please, that man could be dying."

From the corner of her eye, she saw the other cop go to the aid of the victim. Thank God.

"Male Caucasian," he called to his partner. "Approximately fifty years of age, smelling strongly of alcohol." A pause while he knelt for a closer inspection. "Unconscious, but I'm getting a decent pulse, and he seems to be breathing okay. But she's right about the blood. There's quite a bit of it on his shirt and on the ground, or at least what looks like blood."

"See? I told you. It's his neck. I know it sounds crazy, but the attacker bit his neck." She started to get up, but the officer turned his light on her.

"Stay right there," he directed, then started speaking into his radio.

Though he spoke in the code of cops, Sam followed the gist of the exchange easily enough. He confirmed that a man had been assaulted as reported, and that in addition to that ambulance, they needed the K9 unit, pronto. He slipped his radio back into its holster and joined his partner over the sprawled victim. She heard them murmuring together, but couldn't make out the words. A moment later, the first cop came back.

"You can get up, ma'am." He bent to pick up her cell phone and held it out to her.

With the unmistakable wail of an ambulance siren growing closer, she got to her feet and accepted her phone.

"Sorry to put you through that," he said, "but as I'm sure you can appreciate, we come into these things blind."

"Forget it." She waved off his apology. "How's that guy?" She glanced around the officer to get a better look at the victim, only to see the other cop sitting back on his heels, doing nothing in the way of first aid. "Um, shouldn't he be applying pressure to that man's neck wound or something?"

"Ma'am, that man doesn't have a neck wound. Nor any kind of wound, as far as we can tell."

"That's impossible! I saw the attack. I saw blood! Spurting, spewing blood."

"There's plenty of blood, sure enough. But what we don't have here is a wound."

"But I saw —"

"Spewing blood. Yeah, I got that. But I'm guessing he musta vomited it up."

Vomited? No. No way. It was arterial blood, spurting from his neck. The way he'd lifted his hands to try to stop it ... "No, I'm sure it was coming from his neck."

"That'd be a helluva trick, seeing as he doesn't have so much as a hickey."

Lord, was she losing her mind? "Let me take a look at him."

Again, he stopped her. "That won't be necessary. The paramedics just rolled up."

"Omigod!"

He raised an eyebrow, waiting for her to elaborate.

"I can *prove* it. I took photos. God, why didn't I think of it sooner? Let me go get my camera and I'll show you."

He blinked. "You took photos at night? In the pitch dark?"

She gestured to the streetlights. "There's a difference between low light and no light. But as it happens, my camera also has infrared capability. That's what I was using to shoot the attack."

"You just happened to be standing around at one o'clock in the morning and caught the attack on an infrared camera?"

"I'm a photographer. I take all kind of nature shots. Mostly freaky weather. You know, lightning, meteor showers, that kind of thing."

"Wouldn't think you'd need infrared for that."

"No, but when I'm moving around in the dark, it's nice to be able to see what else is out here with me."

He glanced around. "So, where is this fancy camera of yours?"

She pointed toward the trees. "Up there on the hill. When I realized what was happening, I dropped it and came running down here. I'll just fetch it and come right back."

"I'll go with you."

"It's okay. It'll just take a minute."

"That was not an offer."

Oh, criminey. Did he think she was gonna bolt, like some teenager who'd placed a mischief call to 9-1-1? She shrugged. "Suit yourself."

Two minutes later, she picked up her camera triumphantly. "See!"

"Digital?"

"Yes."

"So you can show me the shots?"

"Of course. Here's the one I was taking when I realized what was ... Oh, shit."

"Let me guess. The picture didn't come out."

Sam swore again. Pungently. "That bastard. He took it."

"He?"

"The guy who knocked the first attacker away. He took my flash card."

"First attacker? There was more than one?"

"Yes. There were two."

"And the guy who intervened after the first attack? What happened to him?"

"He actually turned out to be the second attacker. I mean, I thought he was trying to save that old man, but then he starts right in where the other attacker left off."

"Where he left off?"

"Yeah, biting the victim's throat."

Even as she said the words, in the back of her mind, Sam heard that amused, warm-whiskey voice again, warning her it would go better for her if she avoided specifics. He'd known there would be no evidence left, no wound on that poor man's neck. But how was that possible?

Screw *how*. How didn't matter. In fact, a self-healing artery or vein or whatever the hell it was made about as much sense as anything else she'd witnessed tonight. Hell, the first attacker, the one her blue-eyed stranger had killed, was probably up and walking again with nothing more than a kink in his neck. And maybe she'd wake up in a moment and be in her bedroom in the hotel.

"Ma'am?"

She blinked. "My medication ... I can't remember when I took it last."

His eyebrows shot up again. "Your medication?"

"Yeah, my ... um ... lithium." In the background, the paramedics headed down the hill with a wheeled gurney. She looked at the cop again, fixing him with what she hoped was a weirdly intent gaze. "Can I go? I really think I better go lie down now."

She watched the expressions chase across the officer's face as he mentally moved her from reasonably credible, if confused, witness to full-fledged crazy. She held her breath as he weighed the situation. Standard operating procedures would no doubt demand he take a full statement, but what use could she be? A crazy woman who'd probably seen nothing more than the vic making out with a John, then puking up blood from a stomach ulcer caused by too many years of swilling rotgut whiskey.

"Okay," he said at last. "You'd better get along, then. And take that medicine, you hear?"

Yes! "Thank you, officer. I will."

Before the cop could change his mind, she gathered up all her equipment, shoved it willy-nilly into her camera bag and set off briskly. Her car was parked upriver from the scene, but she angled slightly downriver so she could intersect more closely with the paramedics, who were making their way across the grass to the ambulance waiting at the curbside. She didn't veer too close — no need to give that cop a reason to change his mind — but she got close enough to see that the victim was conscious now and talking to the ambulance attendants.

She chewed her lip. Just because he was conscious didn't mean he was okay. He could still be in serious —

Laughter erupted between the two EMTs. "No, you *cannot* have a drink for medicinal purposes," the short one said.

Okay, if he was asking for booze, the man was going to be fine. Time to get the hell out of here.

Twenty minutes later, Sam let herself back into her room at the Lakeview Inn. She turned the deadlock and flipped the security bar, then turned to lean against the door. Made it.

It had been a close thing. Four blocks from the scene, she'd come within a heartbeat of running a red light with her shiny rental car. She'd jammed on her brakes at the last moment to avoid T-boning a taxi cab, who'd blared his horn at her. Shaken, she'd forced her attention back to traffic, mainly by chanting *don't think about it, don't think about it, don't think about it* all the way back to the motel.

Okay, time to think about it.

In just a minute.

She pushed away from the door, dropped her camera bag on the bed and reached for her suitcase. Unzipping a side compartment, she found what she was looking for — her flask of Grand Marnier. She wasn't much of a drinker, but she always packed an emergency supply of GM. On the road like this, with her schedule turned upside down, it could be invaluable helping her get to sleep. But tonight she wasn't looking for a sleep aid so much as something to keep her sanity from coming unglued.

She grabbed an old-fashioned glass off the desk, peeled the protective wrapper off it, and poured herself a healthy belt. Then she swallowed a mouthful of the orange liqueur and plunked herself down on the bed. Okay, *now* she could think about it.

Jesus. What had she seen?

You know what you saw. And it wasn't a homosexual tryst, dammit, and that man didn't vomit up that blood.

The telephone on the nightstand rang. Sam lost her grip on the glass, but caught it before it hit the floor. Shit, shit, shit. Liqueur on the bedspread. And for what? Probably the front desk telling her she'd left her car's lights on or something. And when they got a whiff of this room tomorrow, they'd for sure think she stumbled in drunk. Ugh.

She put the glass down on the night table and grabbed the phone on the third ring.

"Hello." She wiped her sticky hand on the coverlet, since it was already doused.

"Hello, Samantha Shea."

Sam's hand flew to her mouth. Him! Oh Jesus God, how had he found her? *Why* had he found her?

"Ah, I've frightened you. Not to worry. As I told you earlier, I mean you no harm. If I did, you'd know it."

"How did you know my name?"

"How do you think?"

Of course. The tag on her camera bag. The tag he'd clearly seen when he'd stolen her memory card. A sliver of anger wedged its way into the fear. "I want those photos back."

"I'm afraid they've been erased."

"Bastard!"

A low chuckle. "You are a brave thing, Ms. Shea. You haven't even asked how I found you here, at this motel, among all the bedrooms for rent in St. Cloud."

Fear supplanted anger again. Her eyes flew to the window. "You followed me."

"I did."

To have done that, he must have stashed or otherwise disposed of the body while she was talking to the cops, made it back to the scene in time to steal the memory card from her camera and be in position to follow her when she'd left. "Why?"

"Because I want to make you an offer."

Sam's heart took another leap until she could hear her own pulse pounding in her ears. "I can't imagine what you could offer that I might want."

"You might be surprised, Samantha."

She'd been about to say, "It's Sam," her automatic response to hearing that detested name, but bit it back just in time. The last thing she wanted to do was to let this creature think she was inviting intimacy. "I doubt it," she said.

He laughed, and she felt a hum start up in her chest. Not good. "Look, say what you want to say."

"Very well. People generally have one of two reactions when they're confronted with evidence of vampirism."

Sam's breath caught in her lungs. *Vampirism. Vampires.* There it was, out in the open, the word she'd refused to allow her mind to form.

"Most of them want to forget. They want to go back to the safe, comfortable world they knew before that unwelcome knowledge got foisted on them."

"Well, I can understand that reaction."

"Do you want to forget, Samantha Shea?"

She forced a laugh. "You make it sound like I have a choice."

"You do. I can give you that."

Her heart rate, which had been lulled back into something approaching normal by the hypnotic warmth of voice, jolted into the stratosphere again. "I'm trying to imagine how you could make me forget, and the only scenario that comes to mind involves me also forgetting to breathe and have a pulse."

Again the laughter. "Nothing like that, I assure you. Once more, I remind you that had I wanted to destroy you, I'd have done it already."

"Then ... how?"

"Hypnotic suggestion, for lack of a better word. If you wish, I can send you off to sleep and you'll wake with no memory of the experience. It would be as though it never happened."

"Right." Was he insane? "So I open my door to you and you come in here and —"

"Well, if that's an invitation ..."

"It was not!"

He sighed. "I thought not. But before you get too bent out of shape, I should mention that I can actually do it over the telephone. There's no need to open your door."

Over the phone? Oh, Christ, was he doing it now?

"No!" She gripped the receiver tighter. "I mean, I think I'd just as soon not muck around with anything in my mind, thanks."

A slight pause. "Now why do I get the idea you said more than you intended to with that statement?"

Sam sucked in a breath. "I meant just what I said. I don't want you or anyone else mucking around in my brain. Understood?"

"Perfectly. Goodnight, Samantha Shea."

"Wait!"

A pause. "Yes?"

"You said people reacted one of two ways. What's the other way?"

"Why, they want to know more, of course. Now, if that's all —"

"Wait! Don't hang up. I ... I want to understand."

"And perhaps one day you will. Goodnight, Sam Shea."

"But —"

A dial tone sounded in her ear.

"Well, hell!"

Sam Shea. Aiden terminated the phone connection with his own words echoing in his head. Samantha Shea meant nothing, but *Sam Shea ...* That definitely rang a bell.

He leaned on the hood of his rented Sedan de Ville and opened the Internet browser on his iPhone. Within a minute, he found what he was looking for. The online gallery he'd visited a dozen times or more to buy the prints that hung on the walls of all his residences.

Sam Shea — *his* Sam Shea — was a woman. A *beautiful* woman. *Huh.*

Somehow he hadn't anticipated that. Not that he recalled ever having given it active thought. He'd just presumed the renowned nature photographer was a man. Weren't most of them guys, especially the storm-chasers?

He paged through the website, looking for a picture of her or a hint of her sex. Nothing. Out of habit, he checked for his favorite print, the one of the thunderstorm over the Alps in northern Italy. It was nowhere to be found, which was exactly what he'd paid so handsomely for. Exclusivity. It was his and his alone.

And well worth the price. In the middle of the picture, a deep stack of thunderclouds boiled, while below, a jagged bolt of lightning forked to the earth. But above the fray, in the upper third of the photo, sprawled the placid night sky. The remote coldness of the stars stretched so indifferently over all that violence below appealed to him. So much so that it was the focal point in his Vancouver penthouse.

Not that she took only storm photos. Clearly, they were her bread and butter, but she took all manner of other eerie, other-worldly looking landscape pictures, quite a few of which he owned. Mostly morning twilight. There was something about the way the atmospheric particles scattered the light of the sun before it cleared the horizon. The one she'd taken in Tibet, with the dream-like haze bathing the mountains ...

Now evening twilight was another story. He never could bear to watch the day dying, even when —

Aidan cursed. What kind of a stupid-assed thought was that? He killed the Internet connection, shoved the phone into his pocket and got back into the rental.

He'd pay Miss Sam Shea a visit some time soon, he decided, as he keyed the ignition. His lips curved in a smile as he remembered how she'd faced him down over the unconscious body of Justin MacKellar's last — and very, very fortunate — victim. She'd been scared as hell, but she'd also been determined to save the vagrant from what she'd obviously construed as a second attack. He really should have explained that he'd been saving the derelict's life, and that the vampire he'd just dispatched to hell probably had a kill total in the thousands. He could have told her the truth back there on the riverbank, or just now on the telephone. But where was the fun in that?

Humming to himself, he pulled away from the curb and into the all-but-deserted lane. Yeah, he'd definitely call on the beautiful and foolhardy Miss Shea. But in the meantime, he had that wife-beating piece-of-shit police chief to check up on. A guy like that, if you didn't show him your follow-through, he'd get brave again. Aiden had promised his friend Delano Bowen that he'd clear the path for Lucy Michaels' return, and he planned to keep that promise. Which meant sticking around St. Cloud long enough to make sure the Chief's new resolutions stuck.

And in the meantime?

He grinned, thinking of the night clerk at his hotel, a delectably innocent-looking young lady. Except when she'd checked him in two nights ago, she'd made sure he got a good look at the tattoo on her neck. The strategically placed dots would be taken for moles or beauty marks by non-vamps, but even a day-old vamp would recognize them for what they were. Simulated bite marks. Simulated because the real thing healed almost immediately, leaving no trace behind. He'd held her gaze a few seconds too long to be polite, and when he passed her his credit card, she made sure their fingers touched. When she finally handed him the swipe key for his room and breathlessly instructed him on where to find the elevators, he'd given her a smile with the merest hint of fang. God, he'd thought she was going to orgasm right there!

If she was working the desk again tonight when he got back, he'd be calling for some … uh, room service. Or elevator service or behind-the-counter service or on-a-desk-in-the-business-office service.

Smile widening, he cranked up the volume control on the car's radio and hummed along with The Killers' *Mr. Brightside*.

Chapter 3

AIDEN WOKE THE next evening with one thought in his head. Okay, two thoughts, but *blood, blood, blood* didn't really count.

No, the thought clanging like a Klaxon for his attention was this: *Sam Shea had been the unseen presence watching him two nights ago as he'd left Chief Michaels' house.*

It was her scent that gave her away. An expensive bottled fragrance with notes of white flowers, musk and powdery spices, underlain by the unmistakable smell of female flesh, shampoo and soap. Dammit, he should have put it together the next night on the riverbank. The scent signature was exactly the same. Of course, he'd been a little preoccupied, what with her calling the cops and him needing to get rid of a body before they arrived.

But how could it be? He threw the covers off and sat up naked on the edge of the bed. She couldn't possibly have tailed him. He'd been on foot that night, and it would have taken another vampire to keep up to him. And Sam Shea was no vamp. Even if she somehow had the speed, no way would he have been oblivious of a tail. He'd lived too long among things that killed to relax his guard.

Aiden strode to the mini-bar, took out a unit of whole blood and regarded the remaining supply. Damn, he was going to need more. He'd used an extra unit last night before hooking up with the lovely Julie from the front desk. The problem with fang-bangers was they'd have you drain them in their ecstasy. So the vamp had to be mindful enough for both of them. It helped to take the edge off the blood lust first. Good thing he had. Young Julie had gone up in flames. Smiling, he placed the bag of blood into the blood warmer he'd set up on top of the mini-bar.

Okay, back to Sam Shea. How, on back-to-back nights, had she managed to get herself to the only two scenes where Aiden happened to be operating? It damn sure wasn't coincidence. He'd bet his pearly white cuspids on it.

He padded to the bathroom, turned the shower on and stepped under its warm spray. As he shampooed his hair, he turned the problem over in his mind. When he stepped from the shower minutes later, he was none the wiser.

He'd fix that soon, he decided. The moment he could get away from St. Cloud, he was going to track Ms. Shea down and have a word with her.

Sam closed the door behind her, plunked her bags down on the tiled floor and headed straight for the alarm panel, punching the code in carefully. When the blinking light went off, she released a sigh. Thank God. She'd set the damned thing off twice last week by forgetting her code. The alarm company had assured her it would become second nature, but so far, it still required conscious effort.

And she still hated the damned thing. It was a baleful, blinking reminder that *he* had put this fear in her head. In her gut. Granted, it made her feel safer, especially on nights like this when her flight didn't get in until after dark. As did the brand spanking new compact 9mm pistol sitting in the gun safe in her bedroom closet. But until her brush with him, she hadn't felt the need for either.

Goddamn, a *gun*. Never in her wildest imagination would she have seen herself owning one. And now that she did, she honestly had no idea if it would stop a vampire. For all she knew, the bullets had to be made of silver or something. Hell, if Joss Whedon was any authority, she didn't even need that security system she'd spent so much money on, 'cuz he couldn't cross her threshold without an invitation.

That was the worst of it. All this expensive security wasn't even buying her a good night's sleep. Too often, her dreams were invaded by vampires. Nightmares where hideous creatures leapt from the darkness to savage her. But even more disturbing were the other dreams, the ones where he — *dammit she wished she knew his name!* — whispered outrageous promises in her ear while he peeled the clothing from her body with his big, hard hands and —

Oh, for Pete's sake. She had better things to think about. Like her growling stomach. She hadn't had anything to speak of since noon.

Leaving her bags in the entryway, she marched to the kitchen and inspected the contents of her refrigerator. What she found put a smile on her face. "God bless you, Marlie. You're worth every penny and then some."

Taking a plate bearing a stuffed pork chop, mashed potatoes, green beans and a dollop of turnip, she popped it into the microwave and hit reheat. Then she headed for her office, where she found the message light blinking on her answer phone. Flopping into her chair, she hit the button to play the messages.

The first was from Marlie, hired cook and goddess of the kitchen, suggesting a Shiraz or a Bordeaux-style red with the roast pork. And oh, she hoped she'd rearmed the alarm properly when she left. *You did it perfectly, Marlie, just like you do everything else.*

The second was a hang-up. *Fine. I didn't want to talk to you either.*

The machine went on to play the third and final message, and Sam's straightened her spine as the magazine editor identified himself. *Hot damn! A sale.* A batch of catastrophic weather pics, no less. She did a little spin-a-rama with her chair.

About bloody time. In the wake of Hurricane Katrina, the market had gone soft. It was as though the public had hit its saturation level for images of destructive — or even *potentially* destructive — natural phenomena. Oddly, though, even as the frequency of tsunamis, hurricanes, earthquakes and wildfires surged, the market was starting to come around again. The more people were subjected to violent weather, the more their fascination seemed to grow. But for a while there, it had been dusty sunrises on the Mojave Desert and gorgeous arroyos and eerie petroglyphs. Standard nature photography, served straight up.

Not that she was complaining. As long as she could subsidize her travel, sock a little money away, and never have to cook for herself, she was happy.

And lucky thing for her the traditional nature market was there to fall back on, because *not* going wherever she needed to go to take those pictures didn't seem to be an option. When the demand for the wild stuff had gone soft, she'd tried ignoring the voice in her head that told her where to go and when to get there. Why chase something down if there was no buyer for it? But the result had not been pretty. She'd morphed into such a bitch, she couldn't stand living with herself.

Of course, she'd figured it would get better with practice. The voice could be subdued.

Not so much, as it turned out.

So she wound up going wherever the next big tornado or sensational lightning storm or falling meteorite was going to be, and took the bloody pictures. Then she'd hang around for another day to take pretty sunsets or sunrises or whatever struck her as marketable. So far, that approach was getting her through.

Except for that trip to St. Cloud. She chewed the inside of her lip. After that phone call from Lestat, as she'd dubbed him, she hadn't hung around long enough to take any landscape shots. In fact, she'd been so creeped out, she changed her ticket, flew into South Dakota, where she paid cash for a bus ticket and rode home to Iowa.

Of course, she'd had the whole flight and subsequent bus ride to reflect on how melodramatic — not to mention pitifully, stupidly ineffectual — her attempt at evasion was. The man had her name, and if he'd given her bag even a cursory search, he also had her coordinates. Even if he hadn't memorized the tag on her bag or found her stash of business cards, he could still run her to ground in a matter of days — hours, probably — with her name alone, unless he was illiterate and completely without resources.

The microwave dinged. Sam pushed herself out of the chair and headed back to the kitchen, where she found and opened a bottle of Australian Shiraz and set the table for herself. *That* she could do.

She made short work of the meal, and was just leaning back to sip her wine when the telephone shrilled from her office. Only the business line rang in there. Another sale, maybe? Carrying her wine into her office with her, she settled in her chair and picked up the receiver on the fourth ring. "Sam Shea," she said into the receiver.

"Samantha is such a beautiful name. Why don't you use it?"

Her pulse jolted as though she'd touched a live wire. Carefully, she put her glass down. "That's a long story. And just at the moment, I'm more interested in *your* name, since you have me at a disadvantage in that department."

"Ah, of course. How rude of me. Aiden Afflack."

A dozen thoughts ripped through her mind. Why was he calling? Where was he calling from? And oh shit, was it safe to talk to him? What if he did the hypnotizing thing over the phone?

Tape the conversation! That's what she needed to do. Her fingers scrabbled with the answering machine.

"Sam?"

"Sorry, you said Affleck? Like Ben Affleck?" Ah, there! She'd hit the right button. It was recording.

"No, not like Ben. It's Afflack with an A, like the duck says."

Yeah, and he was cute and harmless as that duck. *Right*.

"To what do I owe this pleasure, Mr. Afflack? It seems like you were in a hurry to hang up the last time we talked."

He laughed. "Didn't you get the memo, Sam? Always leave 'em wanting more."

"You know what I mean. I needed ... I still ... Dammit, it's hard to integrate the whole thing when I feel like I'm only seeing a little piece of it. I want to understand."

"I know. That's why I'm here."

Here? As in Sioux City? As in right outside her door on a cell phone or at a phone booth around the corner? She shot a look at the alarm panel, which glowed a reassuring confirmation that it was armed. "You're in town?"

"I am."

"Why?"

"Because I find you fascinating."

Sam's pulse leapt again, with a distinctly feminine thrill, but she caught herself. *Get a grip, Sam. He's a vampire; a creature who subsists on human blood. A killer. You don't want him to be attracted to you.* Besides, men who looked like that — even the ones without supernatural powers — didn't pursue women like her. They liked their women more beautiful, dreamier around the eyes, softer around the mouth.

"Right. I have that effect on all the men I meet."

"You might if you put that camera down and let a man —"

"Oh, God, please spare me."

"I'm sorry?"

"Tell me you weren't about to say that I hide behind my camera, observing life through a lens rather than participating in it."

"Ah, but you know what they say about truisms."

She bit back a rude reply. It didn't matter what he thought. What mattered was getting some answers. "You'll really answer my questions?"

"I will."

"What are you?"

"A vampire hunter."

She sucked in her breath. "But I thought ... I mean ... aren't you ... ?"

"A vampire?"

She clearly heard the smile in his voice, and in her mind's eye, she saw his lips curving, blue eyes glinting with humor. "Yes."

"Yes, I am a vampire. Look, do you think we could talk about this face-to-face?"

Her pulse jerked. "The phone is fine."

He sighed. "Okay. But it seems ridiculous, considering we're in the same house."

"In the same —" Jesus, he was in her house!

Her mind shrieked at her to get out, but her legs threatened to buckle under her.

"Samantha?"

This time, his voice came both from the phone and from the top of her stairs. And this time, her legs obeyed her mind's order. Cordless phone still clutched in her hand, she raced for the door. From the corner of her eye, she caught a blur of motion on her left. Then he was there, barring her exit.

She skidded to a stop just short of colliding with him. The gun! Dammit, it was upstairs. She'd never beat him to it. Never get it out of the safe and loaded.

But she had to try.

He let her reach the base of the stairs before moving in to block her path.

"Oh, Jesus."

Chapter 4

GOD, HE HATED this part. The fear streaming off her was palpable. "I'm not here to hurt you," he said roughly. "Please don't be frightened."

"That doesn't seem to be an option."

A pulse beat frantically in her throat. Despite himself, he felt the lust stir. He reined it in ruthlessly. "Of course it is. Just take some deep breaths and relax those muscles."

"Relax? You broke into my home." The pitch of her voice rose as she went. "You hid yourself away upstairs while I puttered away down here —"

"I thought you might appreciate having a meal after your trip."

She made an odd noise. "Thank you for your consideration, but I'm afraid that meal you allowed me to eat is threatening to make a reappearance."

He scowled. People. Ignore their need to graze like cattle and they called it deprivation. Let them fill their stomachs, and they bitch at you. "I just wanted to talk to you face to face. Clearly that wasn't going to happen unless I made it happen."

"So that makes it okay that you broke into my home?"

She held her right hand clutched to her chest, as though nausea really might be rearing its head. Or perhaps she did it to quiet her racing heart? It was certainly pounding hard enough. He could hear its thunder from where he stood, not to mention the more subtle whoosh of her blood surging in her veins.

He smiled. "I do a great many things you probably wouldn't consider okay."

"Like murder?"

She lifted her chin to look him straight in the eyes, putting the lie to her claim of abject terror. Of course, this was the woman who faced down tornados and electrical storms regularly. She was scared, but she had a solid core of courage.

"Exactly so." He met the challenge of her gaze evenly. "But there are many thousands of men, women, and yes, children, alive today because of the *murder* I do."

The look she gave him was skeptical, but he heard the slowing of her heart. Still too fast, but better. He glanced around.

"Could we sit down? There are things we need to talk about."

A broken laugh escaped her. "Of course. By all means, let's sit and chat. I mean, how else would a home invasion be expected to progress?"

He felt another sigh rising, suppressed it. "If you'd prefer we leave here and walk to the park, fine. I saw some benches that were well lit. Wanna grab a cab to the nearest café? Dandy. If a change of venue would make you feel better, then by all means, let's do it. But we *are* going to have an in-person talk."

He watched her weigh her options, practically tasted her thoughts, saw her reach the inevitable conclusion. Any sense of security she might gain from moving to a more public place would be a false one. She'd seen how fast he could move, knew how useless her security system was. He could find her — *reach* her — wherever she chose to go.

"Here's fine, I guess." She crossed her arms over her chest. "Should I make coffee? Or can I offer you a can of soda? Glass of wine?"

"If it helps, I'll have whatever you care to serve, but I don't really have need of food or drink."

"Never?"

"Never."

Despite the fear, he saw interest stir in her eyes. She gestured toward the living room, to their left. "In there."

He motioned for her to precede him. She obliged, taking a seat in the room's only chair, leaving him to take the sofa a good six feet away.

She cleared her throat. "So, what did you want to say?"

"I'm here to answer your questions. What do you want to know?"

She held herself pressed back into the cushions of the chair, her hands clasped together in her lap. "So … you're really a vampire?"

"In the flesh."

He saw her ponder the word flesh, and waited for it.

"You're not … um …"

He arched an eyebrow. "Undead?"

"Yes."

"Absolutely. In exactly the same way you're un-dead. I didn't rise from the dead. My heart beats like yours. My skin warms and cools. My flesh stirs. I'm as human as the next guy. Just genetically altered."

She leaned forward, so slightly he doubted she noticed the change in her own posture.

"Altered how?"

"Viral infection." At the flash of alarm in her eyes, he hastened to reassure her. "Not to worry. It's not contagious like a cold or the flu. I would have to take very specific, very deliberate steps to infect another person."

"By biting them?"

"Feeding alone carries no risk. At least, no risk of infection."

"That creature … isn't that what he was doing? Feeding?"

"Yes, he was feeding, but without permission and with intent to kill. However, in a consensual exchange, feeding is not a health hazard for either party."

"Consensual exchange?" Her eyes widened. "People actually let you *suck their blood*?"

He smiled at her astonishment, ignoring her use of the word 'suck', which was completely off base. She hardly needed to know about the technicalities. "Hard as it may be to imagine, yes, there are plenty of people who are only too happy to consent. It's an incredibly intimate — and pleasurable — act, much like sex. In fact, it usually takes place in conjunction with sex."

"I see."

He rather thought she did, judging from her suddenly rapid respirations. "To continue the metaphor, taking blood without permission is tantamount to rape. It's an assault of the most grievous kind, condemned by civilized vampires. Unfortunately, a vamp who forcibly takes blood doesn't usually leave his victims alive to complain about it."

"Are there many like that? Killers?"

He frowned. "Too many. Yet they're a small fraction of the vampire population."

"But you said you were a hunter?"

"Oh, I'm making inroads into their numbers, all right. But the truth is, there's probably a new rogue created every day."

"Holy mother of God. Every day?"

Lord, she had beautiful hair. And those eyes ... He offered her his crooked smile, the one that never failed. "Maybe it just seems that way."

He saw appreciation register in her eyes, then saw her brush it away with insulting ease.

"And how big is it? The vampire population?"

He shrugged. "Big enough. Mainly in cities, where people have more anonymity, but there are vamps in rural areas, too."

"Are they here?"

He nodded. "In modest numbers. In fact, you've got one on your street, in the old Victorian house with the peeling paint."

"*Edgar Salazar*? But he drives taxi."

"At night, I'm guessing."

She blinked. "So that's true? The sun thing?"

"We're not sun worshippers, that's for sure."

"But do you ... I mean in the sun, do you ..."

He didn't finish her question for her this time, even though he knew where she was going. He lifted an eyebrow. "Do we ... ?"

She had the grace to blush. "You know, like on Buffy."

He grinned. "No, not like on Buffy. No crumbling to dust or exploding in pillars of fire or any of that stuff. But good TV, Buffy."

"Stake through the heart?"

She was leaning forward now, gripping her knees. Yeah, he'd figured her right. Smart enough to be scared; hell, only a fool wouldn't be. But stable enough not to freak out. And fascinated as hell. He was another mystery, another freak of nature like her wild skies.

"Honey, a stake through the heart would kill anything."

She tilted her head. "Silver bullets."

"Nah." He leaned back, brushing a speck of imaginary lint from his black jeans. "That's werewolves."

Her face went lax. "Werewolves?"

He laughed. "Sorry, I couldn't resist. I was just messing with you there. No werewolves. At least, not that I've encountered."

"Well thank God for that, I guess."

"Thank God indeed."

"What about regular bullets?"

"Sometimes."

"They *sometimes* kill regular people. Sometimes not."

"Good point. If you look at it that way, I'm much less likely to die from a gunshot wound than you are. We're fast healers." He leaned back on the couch. "Anything else we haven't covered? *No* to flying, in bat form or any other. *Yes* to sun. *Sometimes* to extreme violence. *No* to food and drink."

"Except for blood."

Actually, they didn't *drink* the blood per se, but that detail didn't signify. "Except for blood," he agreed. "And most of us are productive workers and responsible citizens, just like you. A handful are predators."

"And then there's you."

Her jab took him by surprise. He threw back his head and laughed, but she'd already moved on.

"Your teeth . . . I mean, how do you . . . do it? They look normal."

"Ah, yes, the fangs." How had he managed to skip over that? He ran his tongue over smooth, even teeth, from one gently pointed upper cuspid to the other. "The cuspids telescope into pointed fangs when the occasion requires."

Her gaze dropped to his mouth, as he intended it to, and when she spoke, her words came out at a slightly higher pitch. "Can you do it on command?"

He let his smile widen, let his cuspids partially emerge. No need for full extension. It tended to scare the bejesus out of the uninitiated.

She drew back, pressing into the cushions again.

"Sorry." He retracted his teeth, a tougher task than she probably imagined, considering the arousing images he'd just pictured in order to excite the eruption. Pictures involving her yielding up her silky white throat. "I know it's unnerving to see, but you strike me as a *show-me* kind of gal."

If she were flattered by his assessment, she gave no indication. What he could see was that her brain was racing a mile a minute.

"That man back in St. Cloud . . . he had no marks on his neck. You knew he would bear no traces of the attack."

From the narrowing of her eyes, he figured she was recalling her experience with the cops on the riverbank. Try as he might, he couldn't entirely suppress a smile. "I *did* warn you to go light on the details."

"How did you do it?"

"Remember I told you we were fast healers?

She nodded.

"We can secrete a substance into the wound to heal the artery, stem the bleeding, and ultimately erase the punctures. Essentially, we lend our own healing powers to the donor, albeit on a very temporary basis."

She snorted. "Donor?"

"Donor," he repeated, holding her gaze until she dropped hers. "But victims of vampire assaults get this treatment, too, for the most part. Their wounds are made to disappear, but they die of catastrophic blood loss. That's how these predators cover their trail. No one really looks very hard at the death of a vagrant."

She blinked. "Of course. If they left the victims with evidence on their bodies, it would set off mass panic."

"Not to mention make the killers infinitely easier to track."

She seemed to ponder that a moment, but when she spoke, he saw that her thoughts had taken her in another direction.

"What were you doing at Chief Michaels' house?"

So, she was going to fess up about being there. Interesting. "What were *you* doing there?"

"Taking pictures. Answer my question."

"Visiting with the chief, of course."

"Not a friendly visit, I'd say, judging from the case of gastric upset he seemed to be experiencing the next day."

Holy shit! She'd talked to Michaels. "You're right." He spread his hands in a gesture that said *Okay, I'm busted*. "It wasn't a friendly visit. But I didn't hurt the guy." *Well, not seriously*, he appended silently. "I was merely carrying a message to him."

She cocked her head, an appraising look in her eye that made him a little uncomfortable.

"Is he a vampire?"

"Chief Michaels? Good God, no! He's a worm."

"I thought you were a vampire hunter."

"That's right."

"So terrorizing non-vampires is what? A hobby?"

Was she *baiting* him? For all she knew, maybe he *did* terrorize people for sport. Or police chiefs for favors, or high rollers for cash. Why would she risk aggravating him?

Then it clicked. She knew.

"Ah, Michaels spilled his guts, didn't he?"

Her lips curved in a smile so quick he almost missed it. So quick, it could only be real amusement, not the sustained, blinding white veneer-baring that passed for a social smile these days.

"He assured me he'd never lay a hand on his wife or kid again, and that the movers would be there that very day to pack up his stuff."

Aiden chuckled. "I'm pleased to report the lesson seems to have stuck. But just in case, I drafted a few comrades in fangs to pay him a visit now and again. So long as he thinks they're stone cold as I am, he won't backslide."

"Is that what you are?" She pinned him with her gaze. "A stone cold killer?"

Oh, shit, she thought, managing not to shrink even deeper into the cushions as she watched his face change. Way to go, Sam. Way to tweak the tail of the world's most gigantic tiger when you're completely at his mercy. When you're virtually his hostage!

Gone was the affable, charming man of the last few minutes. In his place sat a man — oh, help, a *vampire* — who scared the crap out of her. Not that he looked angry, exactly. He just looked ... well, like a man who could kill without compunction. Like a man who had no illusions about what he was at his very core.

"I begin to understand how you managed to capture those photographs in all manner of dangerous conditions," he said softly. "You just step right into situations that would send a sane person running in the opposite direction."

She grimaced. "I guess I've heard that before. For what it's worth, I'm sorry."

"Don't be. It's a legitimate question."

She arched a hopeful eyebrow. "One you intend to answer?"

That almost drew a smile. At least, she thought so. But he was still grim-faced when he spoke.

"I assure you, Samantha, that no one has anything to fear from me, until and unless they cross the line and start preying on defenseless victims. Once they've done that, they leave their humanity behind. And when I go after them, I leave mine behind, too."

She shivered, half wishing she hadn't raised the issue. But it was too late now. No backing down. "Does that go for non-vampires, too?"

"Vampires only," he replied in a clipped voice. "You have your own share of predators, to be sure, but you also have a justice system to deal with them. I don't presume to substitute my own judgment for that of the police or the courts."

"But you don't hesitate to be judge, jury and executioner for vampires?"

He shrugged. "Someone must." He leaned forward and it seemed to Sam that she felt the energy around him brush her skin. "Now, if I may, I have a few questions for you."

Questions for her? Her pulse jerked. "What do you mean?"

"What took you to St. Cloud? What took you to Chief Michaels' doorstep? And the next night to the riverbank?"

She didn't entertain the idea of telling the truth for even a second. Venturing within range of a tornado was one thing. Talking about her visions was something entirely different.

"I'm a photographer." She offered him one of his casual shrugs. "I do a great deal of traveling in pursuit of a dramatic photograph. You just never know when you're going to be in the right place at the right time."

He smiled. While she was relieved to see the grim expression erased from his face, she wasn't thrilled at his reaction to her answer.

"What's so funny?"

"How old are you, Miss Shea?"

"Excuse me?"

"Twenty-five? Twenty-six?"

She lifted her chin. "Twenty-seven, if you must know."

"Twenty-seven. And yet your body of work is so impressive."

"Thank you."

"Very impressive," he repeated. "In fact, I think it's safe to say most nature photographers in a lifetime of work do not achieve even a fraction of the success you've encountered at your tender age."

Dismay pushed aside the initial blush of pleasure at his praise. "Just luck, I guess."

"Not luck. Prescience." The grimness was back around his mouth. "You knew where and when to find those tornados and lightening strikes and dust storms. And you knew where to find me."

"That's ridiculous."

"I don't think so. Perhaps I could buy coincidence for one encounter, but the second one? And you can't possibly have tracked me using conventional methods. No reflection on your skills. You'd have to be a vampire, and an exceptional one at that. So the only logical conclusion I can draw is that your psychic ability guided you to me.

"I am not *psychic*!" God, she hated that word! "I can't tell you whether there'll be a traffic snarl on the freeway. I wind up stuck in them like everyone else. I can't tell you which horse is going to win the Preakness or what Wall Street company is going to do a share split. Okay? I don't know what's going to happen tomorrow."

"Ah, but I think you do channel certain information. Or rather, certain energy. The electrical storms, the tornados, the meteor showers, the aurora borealis ... it's all energy. You somehow tune into it. And now I think you're tuning into a new kind of energy."

"Oh, God, are you going to suggest ..." She forced a laugh. "You're very attractive, Mr. Afflack. I'll give you that. But if you think I went to St. Cloud in search of you —"

His lips curved in a smile. "Thank you for the compliment, but I didn't mean me specifically. I think it's the vampire energy that draws you. Or rather, *vampire violence*. I think you're tuning into the violence the same way you tune into the impending violence of nature."

"I think you give me too much credit, Mr. Afflack."

"Aiden," he corrected.

She inclined her head. "Okay, Aiden, you're jumping to a hell of a conclusion. To capture film of a tornado doesn't require pre-science when you park yourself smack in the middle of Tornado Alley in the spring. It doesn't take psychic talent to get sensational shots of the aurora borealis if you're in Fairbanks in October. Or a dust storm in the desert, or a nice meteor light show during the Perseid shower in August."

"Yet you manage to get to so many."

"I guess I work harder than the rest."

"I find that hard to believe. Not your industriousness; I don't doubt that. But it's your sheer productivity. Normally one would expect to have to do a lot of waiting around before that severe thunderstorm cropped up or that tornado touched down. As far as I can tell from reading about storm chasers, no one else seems to enjoy quite such an impressive success rate."

"As I've said, I've been very lucky."

"Hmmm."

"Look, Mr. . . . Aiden, we seem to be at a stalemate. You think I've got some kind of crystal ball that I can peer into to see the future. As I've assured you, I do not. So why are we still talking about this?"

"Because I think you can help me."

Help him? Anxiety sent another jolt through her nervous system. No. There was no way she was getting involved with this. With him. "No, I'm sorry. I can't help you."

"Because you disapprove of what I do?" He regarded her steadily with those impossibly vivid blue eyes. "Is that it, Sam?"

"Do I disapprove of vigilantism? Of course I do! Any civilized person would."

His eyes hardened, sending a shiver down her spine. Yikes! She was provoking him again.

"Ah, yes. Civilized society. Ironic, don't you think, that these civilized people are the very ones I'm trying to protect?"

"But there are rules —"

"Yes, there are. Which is precisely why these creatures will never be apprehended by your criminal justice system. They will never be stopped or contained, never be punished for their crimes."

"But you *kill* them. That's summary execution."

"Agreed," he admitted. "But, Sam, there's no alternative. A rogue cannot be reformed. Recidivism is one hundred percent."

"But —"

"Remember Justin MacKellar from St. Cloud? The rogue I dispatched before he could kill that homeless man?"

She blinked. "You knew his name?"

"By the time I track them down, I usually know a whole hel-luva lot more about them than just their names. For instance, I can tell you that the night before he died, young Mr. MacKellar murdered two elderly men in a nursing home about five miles west of St. Cloud. Their deaths were no doubt chalked up to natural causes. A nurse finds them in the night. A doctor comes by the next morning and pronounces death, and they're shipped off to the funeral home without benefit of an investigation."

"Dear God."

"And the night before that? The victim was a 34-year old drug-using transvestite in the same city. The local medical examiner has since ruled that death an accidental overdose of heroin. The night before that, approximately 40 miles southwest —"

"Enough!"

"Are you sure? Because I could go on. I can attribute at least 20 kills to him in the last month with certainty, and it's safe to assume that given how long he's been doing this, his kill total is in the thousands. Perhaps tens of thousands."

"Okay." She leapt to her feet. "I get it. You're performing a valuable public service. I just don't —"

He surged to his feet, his eyes flashing, face flushed. "You're mocking me?"

She fell back a step, a completely involuntary reaction to his raw, bristling energy. To compensate, she turned her chin up. "Not at all." The words came out sounding amazingly self-assured. Too bad her heart was pounding so hard he could probably have heard it from the next room. "I was merely conceding the point you just made so eloquently. As dangerous as it appears to be out there, I can't begin to imagine how bad it would be without you, or people like you."

His expression didn't change, but some of the tension had gone out of his posture. "But?"

"But I still can't help you." She squared her shoulders. "What you want me to do ... I just can't do it."

He held her gaze for what was probably only a few seconds, but felt like minutes. And God help her, she couldn't have looked away if her life depended on it. Finally he sighed and stepped back.

"Very well. If that's your decision."

Relief turned her knees to water. "It is."

"Then I guess I'll be on my way."

An entirely different emotion gripped her. It felt like ... what? Regret that he was leaving? That she would likely never see him again?

No. Un-uh. No freaking way. He was a vampire. A self-confessed assassin. Hell, she'd *seen* him kill a man. Well, okay, a mass-murdering vampire. Still, he moved in a world she wanted no part of.

As he moved toward the door, she followed him.

"Thank you for answering my questions. You filled in a lot of blanks that were driving me crazy."

Hand on the doorknob, he glanced back at her over his shoulder. In profile, the masculine beauty of his face struck her afresh. If things were different, if *he* were different, she might have dared to touch him ...

"Like the erupting into a pillar of fire thing?"

She smiled. "Yeah, like that. Or the needing an invitation to enter the house thing. You blew that one right out of the water."

The grin he flashed her made the breath stall in her lungs. "Tell you what — next time, I'll ring the doorbell."

A second later, he was gone and she was standing there staring at her front door.

Next time?

A thrill forked through her belly. And not the sensible kind of thrill.

Dammit, Sam. Why do you have to be so perverse?

Chapter 5

SAM TURNED TO face her date, a young novelist she'd met three months ago at a party. In the yellow light cast by her front porch light, he was just as gorgeous as the first time she'd laid eyes on him, with his warm Jake Gyllenhaal eyes and gleaming black hair. She'd invited him to catch a movie with her tonight, hoping that the initial spark of attraction could be fanned into something hotter. Anything to distract her from the hell her life had become. Unfortunately, the spark had fizzled. For him, too, she thought.

"I had a great time," she said. "Thanks for hanging with me."

"Hey, happy to do it." He leaned in and kissed her forehead in what could only be called an avuncular fashion. "Call me anytime. If I answer, it means I'm dodging the work-in-progress. In that event, I promise you I'll say yes to anything short of root canal work. If I don't answer, I'm working. Zero risk of rejection."

She grinned at him. "So you say now. We'll see what the answer is when I ask you to join me for a rousing afternoon of lawn bowling."

"Ha! You underestimate my fear of the blank page."

She laughed. "We'll see." Since he was clearly no more interested in coming inside than she was in inviting him, she gave him a peck on the cheek. "Good night, Conor. And thanks again."

"'Night, Sam."

She slipped inside, relocked the door and dealt with the alarm. At least that was coming automatically now, just like the security consultant had promised.

Too bad nothing else was coming so easily.

She kicked off her shoes and headed for the kitchen to put the kettle on. She'd try the valerian root herbal tea she'd bought earlier today. If that didn't work to buy her an undisturbed night's sleep, she'd call her doctor tomorrow. After two solid weeks of waking two and three times a night with the names of places burning in her brain, she was ready to check out of her mind for a while.

And oh, man, not heeding the calls was *killing* her. But what choice did she have? Every last one of them involved a nighttime location. She couldn't remember the last time that had happened. They were usually pretty evenly mixed between day and night. Which led her to believe she might still be tuning in to some kind of vampire wavelength instead of the usual weather stuff. Which meant she dared not respond to the call for fear it would literally kill her.

And why the devil had the chemistry had to be so damned absent with Conor tonight? Getting hot, sweaty and mindless was just what she needed to take the edge off. And he'd be a good lover. Funny, inventive, adventurous.

Too bad all she saw in her fantasies was a stern, starkly beautiful face, all planes and angles, the skin tightly drawn over hard bone. More Heath Ledger than Jake Gyllenhaal.

Her doorbell rang just as she pouring the hot water over the tea bag in her favorite cup.

Aiden.

Later it would occur to her to wonder why her first thought wasn't that Conor had come back. If dread of the blank page had driven him out tonight, perhaps he'd decided to postpone going home a little longer.

Except she knew it was Aiden, maybe even before he'd pushed her doorbell button.

She went to the door and peered out the viewer. Aiden Afflack stood on her doorstep, his head turned in profile as though scanning the night streets. Heart pounding, she disarmed the alarm and opened the door.

She looked tired, he thought, as she swung the door open. Still beautiful, of course, but tired and nerved-up and edgy. Good. She'd been having the dreams.

"May I come in?"

"Good of you to ask, since we both know you could have been inside waiting for me."

Oh, yeah, she was definitely feeling chippy. But she stepped aside and let him enter.

She locked the door and leaned back against it. "By the way, how *did* you get in here last time without setting off the alarm?"

"Second story window. They're not wired into your security system."

She lifted an eyebrow. "You're sure you can't fly?"

He grinned. "No flying. But I can jump pretty high."

"Of course. Jump two stories," she muttered, then pushed away from the door and headed toward the kitchen.

Without waiting for an invitation, he followed. She must have expected him to, because she tossed her next words over her shoulder.

"I'm fresh out of O negative, I'm afraid, but I can offer you some tea or coffee, if you'd like."

"How about a whisky?"

That brought her head around. "Really?"

"If you've got it. It doesn't give me a buzz, unfortunately, but it still burns going down. I like that."

Something flickered in her eyes — compassion? She bent to open a lower cupboard. "How about vodka?"

"That's fine."

She put the bottle on the counter and got two old-fashioned glasses down from an upper cupboard. Guess that meant she was abandoning the aromatic tea steeping in the mug by the sink. Probably a good idea, given the conversation to come. No doubt she had an inkling.

She poured two neat vodkas and handed him one. "I presume straight up is good if you're looking for the burn."

"Perfect." He accepted the glass and took a sip. Ah, the woman knew her vodkas. Ketel One made most everything else seem rough as jet fuel. He leaned back against the cupboard. "You look tired."

She almost spewed her vodka. "Wow. Does that line work any better for the next-to-immortal than it does for regular guys?"

He grinned. "I didn't know you wanted me to use a line on you. I can do better."

She blushed. "That's not what I meant."

"I know. Can we sit down? I have some things I'd like to talk about."

"Does this have anything to do with why I'm on the verge of asking my doctor for an Ambien prescription?"

"I think so."

She sighed. "The living room, I guess."

He followed her through. She took the same chair she had last time, he the same sofa.

"You've been having visions."

She glared at him. "I have. Every night since you were last here, in fact."

Her words carried a certain amount of venom, but he had no trouble cutting her slack. She hadn't asked for this. He pulled a paper from the pocket of his jacket, unfolded it and passed it to her. Her fingers trembled, he noticed, as she took it.

She glanced at the sheet, then back up at him. "It's a list of locations and times."

"Do any of them mean anything to you?"

"Not the first one. Not the second." Her finger paused on the third.

"Familiar?"

She looked up, her eyes huge. "What happened there?"

"Another homeless victim. The next one, too. Is that familiar? The locations are very close."

Her grip tightened on the paper, wrinkling it. "Yes."

"Keep going," he urged.

"This one ... Union Street in St. Louis?"

"There were two there, actually. A meth-addicted prostitute and yet another homeless man."

The paper shook visibly now. "What about this rural one ... ?"

"Lexington area?"

"Yes."

"Migrant workers. Two of them in the same night."

She swallowed hard, but kept her eyes on the paper. "Was there something involving a train? I can't think of the place ..."

"Warrensburg?"

"That's it."

He whistled. "I wasn't sure about that one. Modern-day train hopper found at the bottom of a gully. I figured it could have been an accident. It's a dangerous hobby."

She laughed, a short, sharp bark of a sound. "More dangerous than he knew."

"Yes."

She folded the paper and tossed it on the coffee table between them. When she lifted her gaze to meet his, he saw that her eyes glittered. "Okay, Aiden. Why?"

"Why?"

She rubbed at her right temple. "Why is all this vampire crap coming to me now? Until I went to St. Cloud and bumped into you, all I found at the end of the line were tornados and anvil clouds and dust storms. What's happened to me?"

"Were you in Montreal recently? Say about four weeks ago?"

Her eyes widened. "An exhibit opening at a gallery on St-Paul. They were showing some of my stuff."

"Is that where you had the St. Cloud dream? The one that sent you to Chief Michaels' house?"

She'd paled. "Yes."

He held her gaze. "I was there, too, in Montreal, to see a friend. He's the one who asked me to straighten out Chief Michaels' thinking vis-à-vis his stalking habit."

She was still looking at him, but her eyes had lost focus. He could almost hear her thoughts tumbling, see the puzzle pieces falling into place.

"So we were both in Montreal when I had the St. Cloud dream. And both in St. Cloud when I dreamed about the second location there, the riverfront."

"Yes."

She focused in on him again. "And you've been here in Sioux City these past two weeks, haven't you?"

"I have. At Edgar Salazar's place just down the street, actually."

She leapt to her feet. "It's *you*! Dammit, you're the reason this is coming to me!"

He resisted the urge to stand, lounging further back into the sofa's cushions. "I think so, yes."

"Then the solution is pretty straight-forward, isn't it?"

She moved closer to loom over him, fists clenched, tears of anger ready to spill. Like one of her rain clouds, he thought.

"Sam —"

"Just stay the hell away from me! That's all you need to do."

"I could do that," he agreed.

"Could do? You *will* do it. I won't have my life highjacked like this. I won't!"

"But what of the victims?"

The tears spurted. "What about *me*?"

"Sam, I caught up with the rogue who'd been cutting a swathe through Missouri last night. Even with computers and access to databases that are supposed to be off limits, it took me that long to sift through the reams of information to put a pattern together. But if we'd been working together, I might have been able to stop him after the first night."

"It's not my —"

"Fault? No, it's not your fault. It's no one's fault but the killers'. But we could stop them."

She pressed her hands to her temples. "I can't."

"Do you want to know how old that prostitute was in St. Louis?"

"Oh, no. Please, Aiden. Don't."

Her eyes begged him not to tell her, but he couldn't afford compassion. "She was sixteen. A runaway. Granted, the meth-amphetamine addiction probably would have killed her in a few years anyway, but as long as she was alive, there was always the possibility that she might get off it."

A moan escaped her.

"And the second homeless victim? He would have been twenty-one next month. The migrant workers? They had families, Sam. Wives and children and one of them with a baby on the way."

She covered her face with her hands and cried silently, her shoulders shaking.

Jesus, she was killing him.

He stood and pulled her into his arms. He half expected resistance, but her arms went around him and she pressed her face into his chest. His heart did a weird tripping thing.

Oh, Sam.

He put her away long enough to shrug out of his jacket, then pulled her down with him onto the couch. She turned fully into him and cried, dampening his shirt. He shushed her and stroked her hair and otherwise did what he could to provide the proverbial shoulder.

But dear God, all he could think about was licking those exquisite, salty droplets away, which would lead to nuzzling her earlobe, then her throat where her pulse throbbed. And then his unsheathed fangs would be buried deep in her delectable neck and she'd be writhing beneath him in a sexual bliss such as she could never imagine.

A moment later, the sobs subsided, but she made no move to draw back.

"I hate you for this."

He stroked her hair, ignoring the unexpected pang under his breastbone. "I know. I'm sorry."

She pulled away, wiping her damp cheeks with the back of her hand.

He fished a clean handkerchief from his pocket and handed it to her.

She moved further away on the sofa's cushions to finish the mop-up operations. "So, what now? How do we ... work together?"

He released a breath he didn't realize he'd been holding. He hadn't relished the idea of repeating this laundry list of victims every week until she acquiesced, but he'd have done it. There could be no room for mercy.

"I'll stay close. I think you need my proximity to make you zero in on the vampire activity. You report your visions to me as soon as feasible. I'll investigate. Easy."

Easy? *Easy?*

"Close, huh?" Now that the tears were gone, the only emotion she could access was anger. She balled the handkerchief up in her fist. "How close are we talking about? *Here*? In my house?"

His eyebrows drew together in a frown. "That's not necessary. And perhaps not very wise."

Of course it wouldn't be wise. It would be downright fool-hardy. But right now, that didn't seem to matter. Making him suffer did. And she had a suspicion how she might accomplish that. "Why not?"

He let his gaze travel down her body and back up again, coming to rest on the pulse that beat in the hollow of her throat. "I think you know why."

She ignored the thrill that forked through her belly. "I see. You're afraid you'll lose control? Take me against my will? Or maybe you're scared you'll drain my blood and wind up destroying your newest and best weapon in this war against thugs?"

He snatched her wrist, pulling her close to his furious face. "In all my years, both before and after I was turned, I have never taken a woman against her will. *Never*. Are we clear?"

She looked down pointedly at the hand gripping her wrist, and he released her instantly.

"I'm sorry," he said, his face flushing. "But I need you to know you would have nothing to fear from me. I have taken blood without explicit consent exactly once. *Once*. And that was last month, from Chief Michaels, to persuade him to stop stalking his wife. And I have never, I repeat *never*, killed or seriously harmed a non-vampire."

Part of her brain warned her to back off; it was a bad idea. But the rest of her was intent on extracting her pound of flesh for what he was taking from her.

"But would it be hard, staying here with me? Would you suffer?"

"Sam, I understand that you're angry about the tactics I used, but I don't think —"

"Just answer the question. Would it be hard?"

His eyes narrowed to blue chips. "It's hard right now. Literally. Is that what you want to hear, Sam?" The cords in his neck stood out. "It's hard every time I see you, smell you. Do you know I can distinguish your scent from every other? I seem to have committed it to memory that evening on the riverbank when you called the cops on me. And when I stand close enough, I can hear the beat of your heart. That vein pulsing so close to the surface in your throat? I can almost hear the surge of blood through it from here."

Oh, yikes, Sam. Call off the dogs. He's way more than you can handle.

Except that's just what he wanted her to do. What his words were calculated to do. And this once, she didn't want to do what he wanted. She shouldn't be the only one adversely affected by this arrangement. He should suffer, too, dammit! After dragging her into this, after commandeering her whole frickin' life, he really, really should suffer.

"But you wouldn't ... force the issue?"

He held himself stiffly, affront written in every line of his body. "I believe I've already answered that."

"That settles it, then." She stood, dusting imaginary lint from her trousers. "You can fetch your things and I'll get a room ready."

By the time Aiden rang her doorbell again, Sam had had more than enough time to cool down. Enough time to regret her insistence that he stay here. She started apologizing before he dropped his bags on her floor.

"I'm sorry, Aiden. I don't know what got into me. You don't have to stay here. In fact, you probably shouldn't."

He paused in the process of shouldering out of his leather motorcycle jacket. The same one he'd worn the first night she'd seen him in St. Cloud, she thought.

"You doubt your safety? After my assurances?"

"No! No, I believe you. I just . . . I regret the other stuff I said. That's not me. I'm not a tease. I was angry and . . . well, just angry, I guess. But I've had time to think about it. You're not making me do anything. You just opened my eyes to what's going on out there. After that, it was my choice."

He lifted an eyebrow. "Not to sabotage my success here, but you had it right the first time. I *did* foist this on you, once I figured out my proximity was the trigger. If I'd continued on my way and left you in peace, you might never have had another inkling of vampire activity."

"*Might* being the operative word. And who knows what I might have blundered into out of sheer ignorance."

"But —"

"Look, if you must know, I have a deeply-rooted aversion to being used, okay? I've already committed to working with you, and if I want to frame this whole thing in more . . . palatable terms, well, that's my prerogative. All right?"

"All right."

His reply sounded solemn enough, but Sam thought he might be suppressing a smile.

"So you can go back to Edgar Salazar's."

He shucked off his jacket, dropping it on top of his bag. "I don't think Edgar wants me back."

"You're that bad a house guest?"

"Nothing like that," he assured. "Vampires just aren't much for the company of other vampires."

"What? Everyone wants to be the alpha vampire?"

He grinned crookedly. "Something like that. And vampires really aren't much for the company of vampire hunters. Edgar's one of the good guys, but he was still glad to see the back of me."

Her face sobered. What must his life be like? A monster of Hollywood horror flick proportions for regular people, and boogieman to his own kind.

"Surely Mr. Salazar appreciates what you do? I mean, if you didn't do it, wouldn't the risk of exposing the existence of vampires skyrocket?"

"Absolutely." He shrugged, rolling up the cuffs on his soft blue shirt. "But I can't say I blame him. You might champion a woman's right to choose, but no one would expect you to want to share your living quarters with the abortionist."

Her stomach did a flip at his analogy. Or maybe it was the way he seemed to be getting so comfortable so fast. "Somewhere else, then? Maybe you could sublet an apartment or rent a hotel room?"

He shook his head. "I already checked before I imposed on Edgar. Nothing available in the neighborhood, and the nearest hotel is so far away, I'd only wind up coming over here and camping out on your roof or in your back yard each night to ensure sufficient proximity while you slept."

"But if you stay here —"

"If I stay here, I'll be on my best behavior. Scout's honor."

She lifted a skeptical eyebrow.

"Okay, so I was a hundred years early for Baden-Powell's first Scout camp, but I'd have made a good Scout."

"Jesus," she breathed. "A hundred years?"

"Nah. I exaggerate."

"Oh, thank God!"

"I think the first scout camp was in the early 1900s, so I was only ninety years or so too early."

"But that would make you ..."

"I'll never tell. I started getting coy about my age when I hit 200." He regarded her steadily with those vivid blue eyes. "Does that freak you out?"

"I guess I figured you were older than you looked. I mean, you told me that you don't succumb to injury easily, that you heal fast, and all that." She grimaced. "Yeah, okay, I guess I am a little freaked out. Especially when I stop and think about how a phrase like *freaked out* would have been received in your day."

"My day?" He threw back his head and laughed, a rich, rumbling sound, drawing her eyes to his throat, to the spill of glossy blond hair on his collar. "Sam, every day is my day. Or rather, every night. That's the benefit of being perpetually twenty-nine."

She blinked. Lord, he was a sight, with his eyes crinkled like that and his stern face relaxed in laughter. And overlying it all was an aura of robust good health and vitality so powerful, it could almost be described as a visible glow.

This could work out after all.

"Okay, you can stay here ... under one condition."

That crooked grin again. "Just one?"

She couldn't help but respond to that smile. "Okay, a couple."

"Name them."

"The first one I think we just covered."

"The no raping and pillaging rule?"

She laughed. "Yeah, that one. Second, you clean up after yourself."

"Naturally."

"You'll fend for yourself in the ... um ... alimentary department."

"Strictly B.Y.O.B. Gotcha."

She frowned.

"Bring your own blood," he clarified.

"Ah, of course."

"Are we getting to the real one now? The one you meant when you said *on one condition*?"

Smart ass. "I want to photograph you."

His grin disappeared. "It won't show."

"What won't show?"

"That extra little whatever it is that you see. That thing that draws your eye to us in a crowd, even though you don't know what you're seeing or why you're drawn to it. On film, it's just not there."

If he thought to dissuade her, he'd taken the wrong approach. Dangling a photography-related challenge like that … well, he ought to have known better. Of course, maybe he did. Maybe he was trying to hook her more solidly than he'd already done. Either way, she couldn't resist.

"Maybe that has more to do with the photographer than the subject."

"With all due respect for your talent — and believe me, I have a great deal of that — I don't think it'll make a difference."

"Thank you," she said, although she took the compliment with a grain of salt. He'd likely browsed her website for all of a minute when he was tracking her down. "But what do we have to lose? We're bound to have a certain amount of downtime."

"There would have to be some rules." His eyes were serious now. Stern. A little intimidating.

"Like what?"

"The results would not be for public consumption."

"Of course not," she agreed readily.

"I won't be photographed engaging in any kind of vampire activity. No fangs, no taking of blood."

"God, Aiden! You think I'd ask you to do that? You think my aim here is to portray you as some kind of freak?"

He shrugged. "You seem to specialize in the freakish."

"I *specialize*," she said, feeling a blush climbing her neck, "in capturing the power and uncontrollable wildness of nature, which is something entirely different."

His eyes dropped to her throat and she remembered what he'd said earlier about being able to hear her blood surging in her veins. She took a reflexive step back. When he lifted his gaze back to hers, his expression remained unchanged. Nevertheless, she knew that he'd noticed the excitation of blood beneath her skin. And he knew that she knew he'd noticed it, which only sent a fresh wave of blood to her face.

Dammit. Too bad she couldn't control her blood.

Oh, well, if he could ignore it, so could she. She lifted her chin.

"Though why you should be so concerned, I don't know," she said. "Even if I *did* photograph anything like that, who'd take it seriously? They'd think I'd engaged in some serious digital editing."

The grin was back. "It's not that."

"Then what is it?"

"It's the equivalent of not just asking a guy to pose nude, but to do so with ... um ... wood."

"Ack! Vampire porn?"

He laughed. "Not to worry. You couldn't know."

"I'm sure I can add that to a whole host of things I'm going to learn over the next while."

His smile spread, wickedly, unapologetically sexy. "With any luck."

Oh, yikes!

"So, how about I take the attic room?" he said. "I took the liberty of scoping it out when I was here last. There's a perfectly-acceptable looking sofa bed up there, and the whole no-windows thing works very well."

Change your mind change your mind change your mind.

"Okay," she heard herself saying. "If you don't mind the cobwebs, it's all yours. I'll get you some bedding."

Chapter 6

AIDEN STRETCHED OUT on Sam's couch in her den, watching a really bad Ninja movie he'd found on her surprisingly basic cable. The alleged star of the movie sported a bad haircut and couldn't act for shit, but it was good for a few laughs. And of course, lots of Ninja action. Not that he was paying it a lot of attention.

Mostly, it was just background sound while he relaxed and regrouped.

Sam had hovered for the longest while, unsure what to do about him once they'd gotten the attic room squared away for occupation. Eventually, he'd shooed her off to bed, since it was well past her bedtime, and since he was well past ready to slap a bag of blood in the blood warmer. His second unit of the night, no less.

The problem, of course, was that the lovely Samantha presented temptation enough when he was fully sated. Not being particularly masochistic, he had no desire to torture himself with her company when the blood lust was rising. Which meant he'd have to ensure he stocked plenty of the red stuff to knock the edge off.

Not that he was particularly keen on bagged blood. His preference leaned decidedly toward warm and willing donors, when possible. But here he was, and here he'd stay, so he'd better get used to the PVC-packaged fare.

He cocked his head, listening. Sam upstairs. Getting out of bed. Washroom trip, or getting up? He heard her cross the landing and start down the stairs. He trained his gaze on the television again. No need for her to know he could practically hear her turning in bed or punching her pillow.

"Aiden?"

"Sam." He glanced up as though he didn't know she'd been standing there. "Did you catch something hot?"

The question was rhetorical. He'd told her that unless she had a vision that was time sensitive, she should just write the information down and they could talk about it the next evening. But if it involved the next 48 hours, she was to come find him.

"Tomorrow night," she said. "Just before 3:00 am, outside Mansfield Township, in western Quebec."

An international border to cross and probably a lot of driving after his private plane touched down. He'd almost have to leave now. Have Geoff file a flight plan, reserve a rental, book a day room in a hotel for tomorrow, another day room for Friday, and then the flight back Friday after sunset.

"I don't have a route number," she was saying, "but I have a sense of the direction, and the house will be easy to identify. It's one of those old Normandy-style cottages, but really tumbledown. Abandoned, I think."

"Great." He picked up his cell phone from the coffee table, flipped it open and hit the speed dial combination to reach his pilot and right-hand man, Geoff Shepherd. "I want you to write down a description, everything you can think of to help me identify it while I make my travel arrangement."

"Hey, wait a minute!" She grabbed his arm as he started to lift the phone to his ear. "I'm coming, too. It could be a lightning storm or a tornado."

"It isn't."

"How do you know?"

He could hear Geoff's voice on the line. Removing her hand from his arm, he lifted the phone to his ear. "Hang on a minute, Geoff."

"If you want to be standing in the right place at the right time, you'd better take me along, because I'm not telling you anymore."

He lifted an eyebrow. "So you *do* believe it's a vampire?"

She colored. "I don't know what we'll find. And neither do you. But I know this — Quebec's weather seems to be growing more extreme. Severe thunderstorms, violent winds, torrential rains, flash floods, hail. Lots of opportunity for great shots. Or it might be a show in the sky, a meteor shower, maybe. I'm not going to sit here at home and miss those opportunities."

"But all the visions you had last week were vampire related," he pointed out.

"Not all."

He frowned. "What do you mean? You identified with nearly every date and place I showed you where a vampire attack had occurred or was suspected to have occurred."

"Agreed, but if you'd asked to see *my* list, you would have seen a handful of other dates and locations that weren't on your list. Who knows what happened in those places? Who knows what amazing photos I missed? And all because I was too scared to go there. But if we go together, you can take care of your business if it's a vamp, and I can take care of *my* business if it's nature gone wild."

Dammit. Did she have to be so … logical?

"You're ready to travel right now?"

She grinned. "I can be in ten minutes."

He pressed the phone back to his ear. "Sorry about that, Geoff. And sorrier still about this next part. I need you to file a flight plan ASAP. I have to get to …" He looked at Sam.

"Mansfield Township, in western Quebec," she provided.

He repeated it into the cell phone, along with his motel and car rental requirements. "Is all that doable on such short notice?"

As expected, Geoffrey Shepherd was equal to the task. And as expected, he didn't query the instruction to reserve two hotel rooms instead of one. Aiden grinned. "See you in about forty minutes, then."

They were airborne for a good ten minutes, still climbing steeply, before Sam gave in to curiosity eating away at her.

"So, this is your plane?"

"My jet, yes."

"Of course. Jet."

"It's a Cessna Citation XLS, to be specific. I wanted something with midsize comfort and lots of range, but with light jet cost." He pointed to the ceiling. "It was the headroom that sold me. You realize you can't even *stand up* in some of these things?"

"Imagine."

He laughed.

"How much does a little toy like this set you back?"

"I don't know."

"You *don't know*?"

"It was a gift, actually."

Her mouth fell open. "A *gift*? But it must have cost millions!"

"Quite a few of them, I think," he allowed. "Cool, huh?"

The lopsided grin he offered her knocked the breath right out of her lungs. Holy hell, he was devastating when he smiled.

She cleared her throat. "So, what's the story? You work for some kind of agency with bottomless pockets? Slayers-R-Us?"

Another laugh. "God, no. Just a benefactor."

Oh, man, even his laugh was addictive. It made her want to make him do it again.

"Geez, does he need a personal photographer?"

"Who said it was a he?"

Who indeed? She kept the smile pasted on her face and shrugged. "I assume you would have said benefactress."

He shuddered. "Are you kidding? Append the *e-s-s* suffix, with all the sexist connotations it implies? You *do* think I'm indestructible, don't you?"

She laughed. "Okay, does *she* need a personal photographer?"

"Oh, you were right the first time. It is a he." He glanced around the tiny cabin. "Now, where's that stewardess?"

A sharp, surprised laugh escaped her. Of course, there was no steward*ess* on board. In fact, there was no one on board except the pilot, a slim 35-ish man with a British accent who put her in mind of a young Jeremy Irons, if Jeremy Irons were considerably cuter.

"Speaking of flight crew," she said, "I couldn't help but notice you don't have a co-pilot up there."

He lifted an eyebrow. "Worried?"

"Not if you aren't."

"Good answer." He released his seatbelt, sliding further down into the leather seat and stretching his long legs out. "Not to worry. I can fly this beast myself, or make myself useful up there if Geoff needs a hand."

"You're a licensed pilot?"

"Yep. Although I will confess, it took a great deal of money to buy that license. No reflection on my skills, mind you. They're better than up to scratch, as Geoffrey would attest. It's just hard to get a license the conventional way when you can't log the daylight hours. Know what I mean?"

"I can imagine."

She fell silent. The trouble, she decided, was that she could imagine entirely too much. Every time he revealed a little more about his life, it raised more questions. Questions she had no business asking. Like, *Who is this benefactor and what is your relationship with him? And just exactly how* do *you earn a crust? Is it a vampire-hits-for-hire situation, or more of a general endorsement of your* raison d'être? *Are you on retainer? Do you often have women as guests on your jet? And are they all now members of the Mile High Club? Oh, no, wait . . . should that be Bite Club?*

Ha! *Bite Club.*

She bit her lip to keep from laughing. She was picturing Brad Pitt, but not the Tyler Durden character from Fight Club. Rather, she pictured him dressed as the delectably tortured Louis de Pointe du Lac from *Interview with the Vampire*. She could hear him now: *The first rule of Bite Club is —*

"Do not talk about *Bite Club*."

Shocked that he'd finished her thought, she whipped her head around to find him watching her, laughter sparking in his eyes.

"What did you say?"

"The first rule of *Bite Club*. Wanna know the second rule?"

"Jesus." She tried to leap out of her seat before realizing her seatbelt was still fastened. A second later, she managed to find the release and sprang to her feet. "I didn't say that out loud. I know I didn't. How the hell did you know what I was thinking?"

"Relax," he said, grinning up at her. "All I caught was *Bite Club*, but it didn't take much to fill in the blanks."

"You're a telepath?"

He shrugged. "I like to call it extrasensory perception, and it's no big deal. Everyone has that capacity, to whatever extent they appreciate it."

"You mean all vampires?"

"No, I mean every single living person. You, me, the guy who serves you your Big Mac. They just don't know it, or know how to use it." He gestured to the chair. "Please, sit."

She met his eyes and heard very clearly the bit he didn't say aloud but intended her to 'hear'. *I won't bite.*

"Very funny."

"See?" He beamed. "You read my mind."

"That's different." She shot him a look he'd have no difficulty reading. "That was totally obvious. It's what anyone might have said next, and what a vampire would be even likelier to say. And you put it out there for me."

He snorted. "And *Bite Club* wasn't obvious?"

Since there was little room to pace, she sat down again. "I don't like this."

"If you're worried I'm going to be reading your every thought, you can relax. Frankly, I've rarely encountered a mind harder to get into, which is one of the reasons I find you so fascinating."

He found her fascinating? "Is that true?"

His lips curved in that deadly smile again. "Completely fascinating."

She blushed. "No, I meant the other. You can't ... infiltrate my mind?"

"Honey, you've got deadbolts on the doors and bars on the windows. There's not much gets out of there."

"Well, that's a relief."

"For me, too, actually."

She lifted an eyebrow. "How so? I would think life would be considerably easier if you could cut to someone's bottom line immediately."

"Easier, yes, but not so much fun. With you, I have to rely on what you say, coupled with non-verbal clues."

"Like a regular person, you mean."

"Like a person who is not in touch with their extrasensory faculties," he allowed. "I'm kind of enjoying that."

Sam found she was enjoying herself, too. Altogether too much. She frowned. "So, what's the plan when we get there?"

Aiden sat up straighter. "Geoff will have arranged for a car to be available at the airport. We'll travel to whatever airport motel he's booked us into, and we'll crash until sundown tomorrow night. Or rather, I will. You can go out and about if you like, but these airport motels don't tend to be situated in the most tourist-friendly locations."

"Don't worry, I'll sleep. I'm pretty good at catching rest when I can, since the shoots move from day to night to day again, and I have to be ready."

"Good. Then we'll sleep. I'll knock you up tomorrow night, as Geoffrey is fond of saying."

She rolled her eyes. "Then we drive to Mansfield Township, find our old tumbledown cottage and get into position."

"Precisely."

"What if it's just a meteor shower? Or a lightning storm?"

He shrugged. "Then you will have company on your shoot."

"And if it's a vampire attack?"

"Then you will stay put and let me take care of business."

Now that she was more than willing to do. She sighed. "I think it's weather-related."

She felt him come to attention beside her. "You can tell the difference?"

"Not exactly," she admitted. "But sometimes the feelings I get are more intense than others, which usually coincides with the intensity of the situation I'm going into. I don't know ... This doesn't have a lot of intensity to it."

Suddenly his hand was around her wrist, his fingers biting into her arm.

"Aiden!"

"Promise me you won't go off chasing one of these night-set visions, no matter how innocuous it seems."

She pulled back against his grip. "Let go."

He released her arm immediately. She rubbed it, more to erase the feel of his fingers on her flesh than because it hurt.

"Dammit, Aiden, do you think I'm an idiot? I'm perfectly aware that it may seem less intense for any number of reasons. Maybe what I'm sensing is a failed attack or one that had to be aborted for some reason. In which case if I went there alone, I might be putting myself on the scene just in time to become the alternate victim."

Thank God. Aiden sank back into his seat. "I'm sorry to get all heavy-handed on you, but these creatures ... Sam, they're utterly pitiless. They would drain your body and toss you aside as easily as you might eat an apple and discard the core. And they'd feel no more compunction about it than you would feel for the apple."

She seemed to shrink deeper into her seat, and he felt a brief pang for frightening her. But dammit, she *should* be scared. He hadn't exaggerated. If anything, he'd understated the danger. Some of these rogues would do much worse than just drain her. But in the end, they would snuff out her life without a thought for who she was, for her talent, for the terrible beauty she captured in her photos. They wouldn't waste a moment wondering what her dreams were or who would grieve for her when —

He caught himself and pulled back. Not good. All this emotion ... dammit, he just couldn't afford it. Better to stay on the surface.

"I don't suppose you'd reconsider staying at the motel while I check out the situation?" He turned toward her to find her watching him with an unnerving intensity.

"You know I can't," she said. "If I do as you ask, I'll never take another decent night shot. It's my livelihood, Aiden. It's what I do. All I *want* to do."

He sighed. "I know." Then, because he needed to lighten things up, he said, "We've got another hour or more of air time and no in-flight movie. How about we make out?"

She laughed, the sound spontaneous, real and inordinately pleasing to his ear.

He grinned back, waggling his eyebrows suggestively. "Aw, come on. You know you wanna. And it would be the most amazing sex of your life."

Still laughing, she said, "No ego there."

"Baby, that's not ego talking. That's the plain, unvarnished truth." Her face had sobered, and he held her gaze. "You know what they say: once bitten, twice as high."

She snorted. "Aiden, *nobody* says that."

"Oh, yeah, I forgot. That's the first rule of Bite Club."

"You're incorrigible, you know that?"

"I try."

Not that it took much effort. This was what he was good at. Skating across the surface of things. Laughing and making others laugh. Taking and giving pleasure. And ultimately, moving on to another tomorrow, trying not to notice how much it looked like yesterday and the day before.

"There!" she said. "What are you thinking about just now?"

He blinked. Dammit, he kept forgetting how perceptive she was. He had to be more careful. "I was thinking you're not really taking me seriously." He let his eyes heat, watched her skin color delicately as his gaze glide over her like a caress. "I was playing it for laughs just then, but it really would be incredible. Sexual bliss beyond anything you've ever experienced, beyond anything that's possible with a non-vampire partner."

"That," she said, "was a very good re-direct."

He grinned. "It was, wasn't it?" Despite her words, he could tell she was affected. Hell, he could hear the bump her heart had taken, sense the surge of blood to intimate parts ... "Nevertheless, it's still true. And what's more, it's the safest sex around. No possibility of STDs, in either direction. No possibility of pregnancy."

"Omigod." The word emerged weakly.

He laughed. "Ah, Sam, I can see the curiosity in you. You always want to know about everything. I can hear the *hows?* and the *whys?* buzzing around in your head right now. That's why you let me in in the first place. You needed to know what I was, what I did. And sooner or later, you'll need to know the other."

"Wow." She widened her eyes in mock ingenuousness. "Is that how you talk the other girls onto that bed over there?"

He glanced at the bed in question, which was little wider than the bench of a sofa. What would she say if she knew the custom-made daybed was not so much for sleeping on, but *in*. The top lifted to reveal the real bed, the one he sometimes had to take advantage of if he absolutely had to fly in daylight, or if there were no motel rooms to be had for the layover.

He swung his gaze back to her. "As it happens, I always travel solo, so I've never had occasion to use it. But if I did, you can be sure no words would be necessary."

"Okay, I believe you, but my answer is no. I'm not interested in fooling around at altitude, or at all. Okay?"

He took her hand, rotating it so he could feel the pulse hammering in her wrist. She didn't resist, but she did stop breathing.

"Liar," he said softly.

"Lothario," she shot back.

He laughed and released her wrist. "Okay, I get it. No action. And that being the case, I guess it's hyperalimentation time."

"Hyperalimentation?"

"Taking one's nutrients directly into the venous system."

"Oh, blood. Of course."

"Strictly speaking, we don't require much for basic subsistence, but I always load up before a hunt, if I can." He crossed to the refrigerator and removed two units of blood. "These rogues gorge themselves nightly and reap extraordinary power from it. I need to gorge, too, to level the playing field."

He felt her gaze following him as he lifted the cover on a second appliance and plopped the bags of blood in.

"What are you doing?"

He grinned. There was that curiosity again. No doubt about it, he'd have her in his bed, or rather *her* bed, before long. Wiping the expression from his face, he turned back to face her.

"Just giving it a hot bath. It'll beep in a bit, when it's ready."

"You have to heat it?"

"Unless I want to court hypothermia, yes. To stay vital, blood has to be stored at about 4 degrees Celsius, and not more than 8 degrees. Before I infuse it, I need to raise it to room temperature, but if I have time, it's better to raise it to 37 degrees, or body temperature."

"Can't you just nuke it in the microwave?"

"If I absolutely had to, yes, but it's tricky. All microwaves are different, and if it's accidentally overheated, you get hemolysis."

"Hemo-what?"

"The red blood cells break down and gradually die, rendering little Aiden's lunch not at all nutritious."

"Wow, this whole thing is a lot more … high-tech than I imagined. Do you also have to type and cross match it?"

"No, thank God. Apparently, once you're infected with this vampirism virus, whatever your blood type was to start with, you effectively wind up with AB blood, which makes us universal recipients. Which means we can be transfused with any blood type, positive or negative."

"My God, you mean there are researchers out there studying vampirism? Why haven't we heard about this?"

"That would be researcher, singular. And he got his MD when bloodletting was still widely-practiced as a remedy for almost anything."

He heard her draw in a sharp breath. "A vampire."

"Yes, a vampire," he said. He might have told her Delano Bowen was a vampire no longer, having recently succeeded in reversing his own mutation after nearly 200 years, but decided against it. That would just open up for discussion something he didn't want to talk about. "In fact, he's the fellow I was visiting in Montreal the same time you were there."

"I see." Something flickered in her eyes. Regret, no doubt, that she'd accepted to do that gallery showing that brought her into his orbit in the first place.

"But don't hold that against him. Dr. Bowen is the most important ally we have in this battle. If he can succeed with the anti-vampire agent he's working on, we'll put these rogues out of business once and for all."

"You mean he's working on a weapon? Fill up a bunch of tranquilizer darts with anti-vampire juice and go hunting?"

Aiden grinned. "That works for me, but I believe Delano was thinking more along the lines of inoculating the demographic these vamps prey on — the homeless, the drug users, the mentally ill — with this agent. Then we serve fair warning that preying on these people will most likely be a death sentence."

He watched the thoughts race behind her eyes. "But won't they just switch to a more secure source? Wouldn't they just start hunting in suburban bedroom communities or subways or all-night video rental stores?"

"Probably," he agreed, "but those kinds of victims don't go unnoticed. They'd be front-page news. Which means vampire hunters would be able to track and exterminate the vermin extremely quickly."

"Wait a minute ... there are others like you?"

He offered her his best grin, the one the ladies loved. "Honey, there's no one like me."

She flushed. "You know what I mean."

"I do. And yes, there are other vampire hunters, all around the globe, including about a dozen of us in continental North America. But you have to appreciate that until I bumped into you, it often took weeks of combing through thousands of deaths reported to hundreds of coroners' offices to pick up a rogue's trail. *Weeks*, Sam, and I'm very good at what I do. Imagine the impact we can have if every vampire hunter's efficiency is boosted by six or seven hundred percent."

"You'd soon be out of work."

"I'll never be out of work. There will always be some idiot making a vampire of a psychopath. But the job would be a lot easier." The blood warmer beeped. "Ah, supper."

Chapter 7

Yikes! Sam leapt up. Time to make herself scarce. "I'll just go …" she glanced around the aircraft's small cabin, "to the washroom, I guess. Freshen up while you … um, eat."

He smiled again, that dead sexy grin. "It's okay. You don't have to hide in the washroom."

"But you said —"

"I said I wouldn't permit the taking of blood to be filmed. I don't mind if you watch. Well, with the bagged blood, anyway."

Her imagination immediately flashed a picture of what the other delivery mode would entail. Aiden molding a beautiful woman close to his body, fisting his hand in her hair, drawing her head back to expose her neck, bending toward the tender, white flesh … Abruptly, she cut the image off, but not before a flush burned her face.

She scowled. "I don't remember saying I wanted to watch."

"You didn't have to."

Oh, God, was she that transparent? She met his eyes, expecting to find mockery, or at least amusement there, but his expression was serious.

"I can see the curiosity in you, Sam. That need to see for yourself. I've seen it from the first. I expect that's what makes you such a fine photographer."

"Okay, I admit it. I am curious." Her heart thudded faster. "Does that make me … a little twisted?"

He held her gaze, his eyes still serious, but glittering with banked heat. "Sam, honey, the best things in life generally are a little twisted."

He broke eye contact to go fetch the blood, and she sat down abruptly, mainly to conceal the way her legs had begun to tremble. He came back with a unit of warm blood in each hand.

To her relief, he took a seat directly across from her. She'd half feared he'd stand right in front of her, giving her an eye-level of his ... um, belt buckle ... while he imbibed the blood.

"Want to change your mind?" he asked, challenge glittering in his eyes.

Half of her did want to shy away from this. The other half, the more insistent half, wouldn't hear of it. "No way. Unless you do?"

He grinned. "Cheers, then."

He smiled widely, baring his teeth. Except it wasn't really a smile, she realized with a jolt. He was telescoping his fangs in preparation to take the blood. And omigod, they just kept coming and coming. They were huge!

She'd seen the suggestion of fangs before, that night at her house when he'd explained what he was. But the small points he'd shown her then were nothing compared to the fangs he now unsheathed. A sharp thrill — part fear and part excitement — shot through her, raising gooseflesh on her arms.

Then, before her eyes, he lifted his right hand and sank his elongated cuspids into the unit of blood, then squeezed the bag. Her eyes dropped to his throat, expecting to see his adam's apple bob as he swallowed the blood, but it didn't move. In a matter of seconds, the unit was all but empty, and his throat hadn't moved once.

Of course! He wasn't drinking the blood! He was infusing it. *Mainlining*. With a start, she realized he'd told her as much minutes ago. Hyperalimentation. Taking nutrient directly into ones veins ...

She met his eyes, letting him see the understanding dawning in her own. The banked heat in his eyes leapt into blazing intensity. Holy mother of God!

Their gazes were now literally locked. Sam couldn't have looked away to save her life. Another thrill rippled over her skin as Aiden tore the depleted bag from his mouth and sank his teeth into the other one, repeating the process.

And then ... sweet Jesus ... he seemed to grow in front of her eyes. No, that wasn't right. He didn't actually grow. No Incredible Hulk bulging of muscle and rending of clothing. It was more like he started to ... well, glow. Not that he didn't always exude a sheen of extra vitality.

But this ... *oh, help!* He was pure energy. Pure sexual energy. And she was falling into his eyes. She heard her own breathing grow as ragged as his.

He was the one who broke the connection. He pushed to his feet and crossed the cabin in a blur. By the time she'd focused on him again, he'd disposed of the empty bags.

"Wild, huh?" he said, wiping his mouth with a napkin.

She blinked. Just like that, he seemed to have mastered himself. She, on the other hand, was still trying to slow her pulse and the rise and fall of her chest. That aura of energy still crackled around him, but he'd reined in the raw lust. Of course, he'd had centuries of practice, hadn't he? While she ... she ... oh, damn, that was hot!

She laughed. "Yeah, that was pretty wild, all right." She shifted in her chair, crossing her legs. "Is it like that every time?"

"More or less." He grinned that lop-sided grin. "More if I've got a woman in my arms. Less if it's courtesy of the blood bank."

God, she needed to photograph him. Right here, right now.

"Keep talking," she ordered, reaching for her camera bag. "I'm going to take a few photos."

He rolled his eyes. "I told you, you won't capture it."

"Then you've got nothing to worry about, right?"

She felt his eyes on her while she dug out her digital and adjusted the settings.

He looked into the lens. "What do you want me to talk about?"

She clicked a photo. "I don't know. Whatever you want. As long as it's about you."

"Great. My favorite subject." He grinned for the camera, then went to sprawl in the chair he'd occupied earlier, long legs stretched out before him. "Here's an idea. Why don't you ask me a question? You always seem to have one or two."

"Okay." She lowered the camera. "Vampires get a kind of . . . sexual jolt from taking blood, right?"

"As you've seen, yes."

"And they can get it from taking even a very little from a donor? Is that fair to say?"

"Also true."

"Well, if it's so fantastic, why do these rogues feel they have to kill their victims? Why not just take their pleasure and leave the victim alive?"

"Like rapists, you mean?"

"Exactly. I mean, what's the risk? If they're preying on society's most marginalized, as you've suggested, the authorities would never believe them if they reported it."

She lifted the camera again and focused. *Click.*

"There are some that do that," he allowed, dropping his gaze to his hands, which were clasped across his stomach. It was a posture of sprawling relaxation, but somehow he no longer looked so relaxed. "Some who rarely kill, except by accident in the course of the assault. They could even glamour the victim into forgetting the assault, if they wanted, but they don't. They want to leave the victim with the memory. And you're right; no one believes the survivors. And as awful as that is, those guys are the exception." He spoke into the camera as she clicked picture after picture, displaying no discomfort. "Mostly, a rogue will kill his victim, deliberately and ruthlessly, and usually without an accompanying sexual assault. Because even though they most assuredly get a massive sexual jolt from the intake, it's not really about sex. It's about the power. It's the kill that gets them off. Not unlike serial killers of the non-vampire variety."

"Point taken." She tightened the zoom and flipped it over to movie mode to capture him in motion. Maybe that was the key to catching his vitality. Lots of subjects looked great in video where body language said so much, but fell flat in stills. Russell Crowe, for instance. "So, how do you handle that minority who don't kill their victims? Or at least not intentionally."

His face hardened. "Do I kill them, too? Is that what you're asking?"

Sam heard the silky note of danger in his voice, but refused to be put off. It was a fair question. If they were going to be working together, if she were going to be helping him find these rogues, she had to know. "I'm asking," she repeated, "how you handle them."

His lips pressed together in a grim line. "Every job has its grey areas. Now shut that video off, please."

Oh, shit! Video, complete with audio. "I'm sorry." She fumbled to switch the camera back to still mode. "I didn't think... I mean, I wasn't trying to record your answer."

"I know." A smile tugged at the corner of his lips. "But I do love to fluster you. And as an added bonus, you dropped that whole unpleasant line of questioning."

She smacked his arm. "You beast!"

"Hmmmm," he agreed. "So, are we done with the photo shoot?"

"Done? I just got started."

"Okay, how about I tell you some tall tales?"

She lifted the camera and took a shot. "Like what?"

"Like the time I met JFK at a private party at the Waldorf Astoria. For a man in such a public position, he sure —"

"Whoa, whoa!" She threw up a hand. "Say no more. I don't want to know."

He sighed. "Nobody does."

"How about something more recent. It's much more fun to skewer the living, don't you think?"

He shrugged, and she snapped another shot, catching the gesture.

"More acceptable, anyway."

She zoomed closer and took another photo. "Meet any movie actors? Rock stars? Literati?"

"All of the above. And not through particularly diligent efforts on my part. They're just pretty thick on the ground in some venues in the wee small hours."

And no doubt he was in demand in those exclusive venues. Even if he were butt-ugly, that aura of his would ensure that he outshone any movie star. The security guards outside those after-hours clubs probably ushered him inside based on a two-second once-over.

"Give me a rock star story," she requested. "A *living* rock star, please."

He tilted his head, considering. "How about the time I drank, smoked and snorted Mick Jagger under the table at the Waldorf Astoria?"

She lowered the camera, pinning him with a fierce glare. "Is this the JFK story in disguise?"

"Hell, no. I just like the Waldorf Astoria. I'm partial to Art Deco. And unparalleled service."

"Okay, tell your story."

"I should preface this tale by confessing that nothing we vampires drink, smoke or snort has the slightest effect on us."

Twenty hours later, Aiden shifted his position on the cold ground. It was uncomfortable as hell, but as Sam pointed out, the deep shadow of the precariously leaning outbuilding was the only viable concealment. At least, the only concealment that offered them a view of the tumbledown Normandy cottage of Sam's dream.

She'd found the place quickly, after only one false start at the intersection three miles back. They'd turned east in their rental, but before they'd covered a mile, she told him they should have gone west back there. When he asked her how she knew, she shrugged. "I just know."

He glanced at Sam, who sat perfectly still beside him, unfazed by the discomfort or the forced inactivity. Clearly, she'd had some practice at both.

Aiden, on the other hand, had practice at neither. He couldn't abide standing still. Maybe because of the immobility and profound unconsciousness of the day sleep. When he was awake, he damned well was going to feel alive.

But nah. He just had a low threshold for boredom. He'd been a devil as a kid, exhausting everyone around him before he exhausted himself. If he'd been a kid today, they'd no doubt diagnose ADHD and jam him full of Ritalin.

Whatever the reason, he had the damndest time staying still. It was harder yet not to talk. Sam had already shushed him. Twice.

He was about to give Sam's thigh a feel just to see what she'd do when he heard someone approaching. He did tap her leg then, to get her attention.

"Someone's coming," he said softly. "From the east."

He saw her lift her head, straining to hear. "I don't hear anything," she whispered.

"And you won't for another minute. Too far away for your ears." And because he couldn't resist the opportunity, he added, "Now, shush."

She didn't reply out loud, but she *did* put a rude word out there in the forefront of her mind for him to catch. He grinned.

Aiden saw the subject first. A teenager, or a very young man, by the look of him. He nudged Sam, indicating the general direction. She lifted her camera and swept the area, back and forth, back and forth. Clearly, she wasn't seeing him yet. Then the kid stepped into the infrared floodlight zone. Aiden knew this not because he could see the subject any better, but because Sam's camera started to click.

Oblivious of the invisible light laying him bare for Sam's camera, the kid approached the house with caution, but also with a familiarity that suggested this wasn't his first visit. Judging by the fullness of the backpack he was carrying, he was probably planning to bunk in the house for the night.

As they watched, the kid moved to within a few steps of the house's front porch and stopped. Probably listening for voices or other indications that the house might already be occupied.

Having checked every room in the house himself nearly an hour ago, Aiden knew the kid would hear nothing from within, except perhaps from the resident mice.

He heard Sam's camera click some more as the teen climbed the steps of the porch. Again he paused and listened. Then he opened the creaking front door and let himself inside.

Sam lowered her camera. "Now what?" she whispered.

Aiden cocked his head. "Now we wait for whatever's coming through that field behind the house."

He felt her tense beside him.

"Not to worry. It doesn't sound like two-legged trouble."

"Animals?"

"That'd be my guess. Now hush. Critters hear better than you do."

This time, he got no rude mental rejoinder. She was too focused on straining to hear something. A moment later, she put a hand on his leg and squeezed, no doubt to indicate they'd come into earshot for her. Again, Aiden saw them first. Wolves. Dark shapes, gliding like ghostly shadows into the clearing of what used to be a lawn. An indrawn breath from Sam told him she could now see them, too, with the aid of the camera. When she started shooting, the clicking of her camera sounded as loud as thunder claps to his ears, but the wolves didn't react. Of course, the small pack was upwind of them, so sound would not carry to them as well as it would have on a still night. Fortunately, that breeze also prevented the wolves from scenting them.

Aiden, on the other hand, had no trouble scenting the wolves. The breeze carried their musky odor to him, wild and stirring. Amazing. He'd caught sight of the occasional wolf on his travels, but never had he been close enough to *smell* one like this.

There were six of them, two of which looked like juveniles. Or maybe they were just females. One wolf — the alpha? — sat on his haunches. The others milled around. One of the smaller wolves bellied up to him, whining, but Mr. Alpha just looked bored. Another animal yipped.

God, maybe they were about to be treated to a front row seat for a chorus session of howling! Nothing, absolutely *nothing*, sent chills up the spine like wolf song.

But suddenly, the wolves' relaxed demeanor evaporated. Alerted by something — perhaps the minutes-old scent trail of the kid — they lifted their muzzles to the wind. Then they melted away, a subtle stirring in the tall grasses.

"Omigod, that —"

This time, he shushed her by putting his hand over her mouth and cutting off her whisper.

Rogue.

Her eyes widened as she realized he'd pushed the word into her mind.

He also placed a hand on her camera, still clutched in her hand and lifted it. Knowing she couldn't see a non-verbal signal but not wanting to risk another psychic message, he squeezed her camera hand, then drew his hand across her throat in a "cut" motion. A vampire would be able to hear the apparatus.

She nodded her understanding. No pictures. Quietly, she put the camera down and picked up her infrared binoculars.

A moment later, the vampire materialized, coming up the road from the same direction the kid had come. Just as oblivious to the infrared light as the teenager had been, the rogue crossed the lawn and climbed the steps of the porch. His steps were confident and unhurried, but Aiden could feel the other vampire's anticipation rising. He opened the door, making no effort at stealth. That was part of the foreplay, no doubt, to terrorize the kid.

"Honey, I'm home!" he called out in a cheerful, sing-song voice, before stepping inside and closing the door.

Aiden leapt to his feet, but not before he felt the shudder go through Sam. She scrambled to her feet, too. From the pocket of his coat, he took a 9mm SIG, chambered a round and placed the butt of it in her hand, muzzle pointed at the ground. "Know how to use one of these?"

She accepted it with obvious reluctance. "In theory."

"Don't worry. You won't have to use it, but it'll make you feel safer."

"Will it kill him?"

"Only if you were very lucky. But it *will* slow him down real good, especially if you empty the whole clip into him. The safety's off. Just point, shoot and keep squeezing the trigger until all the bullets are gone. Got it?"

"I thought I wasn't going to have to use it."

"You won't tonight, but you never know when a little knowledge will come in handy. Keep it pointed at the ground unless you have to use it. Oh, and for God's sake, don't shoot the kid when he comes out. Now, stay put," he commanded. "I'll be right back."

Sam watched as Aiden streaked across the lawn and slipped silently into the house. *Dammit, dammit, dammit!* What was she doing here, in the middle of Nowhere, Quebec, while a vampire hunter stalked a vampire who stalked a kid? What was she doing standing here with a gun gripped in hands that trembled so badly, she'd never hit the broad side of a barn if she had to use it?

Why couldn't it have been about the wolves?

And what was going on inside the house? It was so quiet. Why was there no noise?

Well, duh, Sam. Because he was making sure the rogue is a rogue and not just a gentleman caller. She'd extracted the promise herself, as a condition to cooperating. He must make absolutely certain they weren't blundering in on a consensual exchange before he interfered.

Interfered. Now there was a nice euphemism for what Aiden did.

It erupted then, the commotion she'd been expecting. A shout — the kid's. A terrified scream. Then the crashing of furniture, followed by silence.

Dammit, what was happening? Heart thundering so hard she could hear it in her ears, she waited. And waited. Four minutes later, the kid burst through the front door, knapsack in hand. He leapt off the veranda and raced for the road. A moment later, the pounding of his footfalls on the paved road faded to silence.

Okay, the kid got away. What about Aiden?

He stepped out of the house, the vampire's body slung over his shoulder.

"Stay there," he called. "Give me ten minutes to deal with this, and we can be on our way."

Shaking like the aspen leaves rattling in the trees behind her, Sam sank to the ground. It was over.

So why was her heart still pounding in these great, booming thuds?

God, woman, get a grip! Ignoring the way her hands trembled, she put the gun down carefully and started packing up her camera and lighting equipment. By the time Aiden came back, she'd regained some semblance of composure.

He crossed the lawn, moving like a regular human being, at human speed and making plenty of noise. She appreciated his nod to normalcy.

"You okay?" he asked, when he stopped in front of her.

"Fine. I'm all packed up."

"Great." He glanced around. "The gun?"

She gestured to the ground near his feet.

He picked up the weapon, ejected a bullet from the chamber, released the clip and stuck the whole works in his pocket.

"Which way'd the kid go?"

She pointed west.

"Okay, let's go."

He took the camera bag from her. She'd learned not to protest. Yes, she could carry her own burdens, but it literally was nothing to him. He'd just carried the dead weight of a man — no, a *vampire* — deep into the woods and disposed of it. Pushing that thought aside, she fell into step beside him.

"Is the kid okay?" she asked.

"He's fine. Thanks to you."

He didn't have to say anything more. If she hadn't agreed to work with him, the boy would be dead by now. She dug her fingernails into her palms. "He's alive, but he's hardly fine, is he? I mean, won't he be traumatized by what happened in there?"

"He won't remember it. Or at least, he won't remember what really happened."

Her stride faltered. "You hypnotized him?"

"I suggested he had a close call with a run-of-the-mill pedophile bent on a run-of-the-mill molestation." He slowed to allow her to catch up. "I suggested he get his ass back home and in school, or failing that, to a group home. I also suggested he accept a lift into town form the nice couple in the Taurus who stops to offer it."

"He won't remember you when we stop to pick him up?"

"Nope. As far as he remembers, there was no one else in the house but himself and his assailant, and he escaped by slugging the creep and taking off."

She felt tears start to her eyes and blinked them back. "Thank you."

"All part of the service."

Of course it was. She thought about that as they finished the trek to the car in silence. Otherwise it would be hard to keep a lid on the whole vampires-walk-among-us thing. No doubt many of the near-victims were already stigmatized by mental illness or instability, but if too many stories started surfacing, *someone* would start paying attention after a while.

They found the kid walking on the shoulder of the road some three miles west. When Aiden stopped to offer him a ride, he hesitated a moment, clearly sizing them up. Then his expression cleared and he climbed into the back seat. When they reached the nearest town, Aiden suggested the kid — he'd introduced himself simply as Josh — allow them to help him find shelter for the night. Josh mumbled something about being able to take care of himself, but Aiden brushed his protests away.

"Look, kid, I spent a lot of years on the road, too, back in the day. It was a dangerous world then, and something tells me it hasn't gotten any friendlier. So do an old man a favor and let me set you up in a motel room tonight. I'll pay the shot, then my wife and I will be on our way."

"A motel?"

"Yeah. You know, big comfy bed, security lock on the door, lots of hot water, cable TV."

"And you don't … um, want anything?"

"Just for you to think about getting yourself off the streets for good."

Young Josh had looked hard at Aiden. "Do I know you from somewhere?"

"Nah. I just have one of those faces."

Twenty minutes later, after checking Josh into a motel and pre-paying his stay, they drove off.

"Is that all part of the service, too?" Sam asked.

He glanced over at her, then flicked his gaze back to the road. "For a select few. The few who have a chance of getting off the streets."

Aiden had to put the pedal to the metal to get back to their own motel. Dawn was maybe an hour off as they pulled into the parking spot directly outside their ground floor units. He carried her camera bags into her unit and deposited them on the bed.

"You'll be all right here alone?"

Sam blinked.

She'd been bracing herself for some sort of come on, worrying about how she would handle it. She knew how she *should* handle it, but her imagination had slipped its leash once — okay, maybe five times — too often. If he pressed her hard, would she have the strength to resist him? Did she really want to? Fabulous, mind-blowing, disease and pregnancy-proof sex? But as it turned out, it wasn't an issue. She'd expected at least a token pass. Thus her voice was a little peeved when she said, "And if I said I wouldn't?"

Oh, God, where did *that* come from?

He smiled knowingly. "Then I'd wake Geoff and ask him to crash on that sofa bed."

She stiffened. "That won't be necessary. Goodnight, Aiden. Or rather, good morning."

She turned away in dismissal, only to have him grab her hand and whirl her around again. Before her startled gasp died, his mouth was on hers, his fingers buried in her hair.

For a few seconds, surprise held her unresponsive. Then her body caught up. Or maybe *caught fire* was a better description.

He tasted like nothing she'd ever tasted before. Like dark fantasy. Like the sweetest temptation imaginable. And his scent! He smelled of cool night air and warm leather jacket and heated male skin. She curled her arms around his neck and arched into him, wanting to absorb him through her own skin. Instead she had to settle for taking his tongue into her mouth, welcoming his invasion.

He broke the kiss to nuzzle her cheek, her chin. "God, woman. You think I don't want you?"

Unbearably aroused by his rough words, she tipped her head back, giving him access to her throat. He groaned, and when he nuzzled her neck, she felt the unmistakable scrape of teeth against her skin. Her blood leapt in excitement.

Yessss! The word escaped her lips. It thundered in her blood. It bowed her body against his in an ecstasy of yearning.

Suddenly, he peeled her arms from around his neck and stepped back.

She found herself swaying unsteadily without his support. "Aiden?"

"Sorry, baby. Bad timing."

Huh? "What's bad about it? We have privacy. A bed. What more do we need?"

"Dawn is too close. Already I feel it tugging at me."

He'd rather *sleep*? Way to go, Sam. Way to drive him crazy with lust. "Of course." She stepped back.

He groaned. "Don't look at me like that."

"Like what?"

"Like I just kicked your puppy. I don't have a choice in the matter, Sam. Of the two biological imperatives at play right now, only one can be deferred."

"You mean ..."

"Yes, I must sleep. It will overtake me whether I want it to or not. Think about it. If you were insulted just now, imagine how you'd feel if I fell asleep at a ... critical moment."

Eek! "That could happen?"

"To a fledgling vampire, maybe. Us long-tooths know better than to start something we can't finish."

She touched her tongue to her upper lip, tasting him there still. "Ah, but you did start something."

"I couldn't have you go to bed mad, now, could I?"

She snorted a laugh. "So you'll send me to bed horny instead?"

"That'll make two of us." He slid a hand behind her nape and pulled her close for a quick, hard kiss. "Sweet dreams, Sam." With that, he was gone.

She touched a hand to her lips, smiling.

Then she turned and caught sight of her reflection in the full-length mirror hanging on the wall, and her smile faded. She hardly recognized the woman whose flushed face, sparkling eyes and freshly-kissed lips stared back at her.

God, was she nuts? Was she seriously considering having sex with a *vampire*?

Considering it? Huh! If he hadn't retreated just now, she'd be *having* it.

But what about when her blood cooled? Would she consider tonight to have been a lucky escape and steer clear of such dark waters?

Not a chance. Because dammit, Aiden was right. She *did* need to know. It was no longer a question of if it would happen, but when.

Chapter 8

AIDEN POURED THE cream sauce onto one of Sam's colorful plates, then transferred the oven-baked salmon onto it. He was artfully arranging the asparagus spears he'd steamed to al dente when Sam walked into the kitchen.

"God, that smells good."

"Yeah? Well, I hope it tastes as good as it smells."

She leaned against the counter. "I can't believe you can cook. Can't believe you *enjoy* cooking. I mean, you don't even eat."

He lifted an eyebrow. "You *do* eat, and yet you don't like to cook. Isn't that just as odd?"

"No way. Your cooking is way odder, if that's even a word. Will you have a drink?"

"If it makes you more comfortable."

She reached up and took a single white wine glass down and filled it with chilled chardonnay.

He took her plate over and placed it on the table, which he'd set with her amazingly decent flatware and a woven rattan charger. If she didn't care for cooking, she did care about presentation.

She followed him to the table, taking her seat.

"So, what are you planning to do while I eat this?"

He grinned, taking a seat opposite her. "Watch you, of course."

"I'm going to exercise my prerogative to change my mind," she said. "Pour yourself a drink."

He obliged, returning to the table with a measure of whiskey in an old-fashioned glass. Whiskey that she'd stocked since their earlier conversation when he'd revealed a taste for it.

They'd come back from Quebec three days ago, but Sam had left again almost immediately for Fort Meyers, Florida, where a hurricane spawned a tornado. She'd come back with glorious photos. Photos that made Aiden's stomach lurch like it hadn't in years. To get so close to the ravening beast as it sucked everything up into its deadly funnel ... God, it didn't bear thinking about, mainly because he kept coming back around to the fact that he couldn't protect her from anything during the daylight hours. Not that she'd welcome him "protecting" her from the job she'd been doing without incident for ten years.

"How's the salmon?"

"Mmmmmm," she said around the food in her mouth. "Delicious. Is that dill and cucumber?"

"With a little heavy cream, lemon juice and some dry vermouth."

She lifted her glass and took a sip. "Clearly you went grocery shopping. You'd never find those things in my kitchen."

He shrugged. "I had to do something with my nights while you were gone."

She put her glass down again. "You didn't ... go out? I mean, of course you went out to get groceries. But to socialize? To see people?"

"Actually, I did. That pesky need for blood, you know."

"I see." She lowered her gaze to her plate and started eating the salmon again.

He grinned. She was jealous. The truth was, the only human he'd sought out was the vampire who ran the local paid collection clinic, to stock up on bagged blood. But he wasn't about to tell her that. It would beg questions for which he frankly had no answers. Why *hadn't* he sought out the pleasure of a woman's arms after these weeks of abstinence?

Somehow, it had seemed more important to get back to Sam's place, in case she called. Or to look through her thousands upon thousands of photos. She was even more amazing with that camera than he'd imagined. He'd found a whole series of otherworld-ly-looking landscapes, eerily lit by infrared. She could be selling them hand over fist.

"Back to this cooking thing." She speared a piece of asparagus. "What's the deal with that?"

"Just because I can't enjoy the effects of a good meal by eating it myself doesn't mean I can't enjoy the effects in a ... how shall I say? ... secondary manner."

She paused with the asparagus half way to her mouth. "Omigod! You can taste it in the blood?"

"Taste is not the right word, since we don't drink blood, but I can appreciate it, yes. And let me tell you, I'll take a woman of a certain age over a young woman any day. The younger ones tend to live on the most atrocious junk. And while it might not show on their breasts and thighs yet, it sure as hell shows in the blood."

"So you make a meal *for* them before making a meal *of* them?"

"Hardly. One meal, or even a week of meals, wouldn't make enough of an impact on the blood of a woman with a poor diet. I prefer a woman who feeds her body well on a regular basis."

Sam speared another piece of asparagus. "So, how do you pick them? Follow them around and watch what they eat? Break into their house and check the refrigerator?"

"Nothing so elaborate."

"Then how?"

"Diet doesn't just show in the blood. It shows in your skin, your hair, your perspiration, even in the air exhaled from your lungs."

"You can *smell* them out?"

He shrugged. "All our senses are much more acute than yours."

"So, how's that work? You go around sniffing them on the dance floor?"

He put his whiskey down. "Facial symmetry is notoriously important to attractiveness. Are the eyes too close-set, or too wide, or is one just a hair higher than the other? Forehead too sloping? Jaw not full enough? Or too full? You'd never whip out a ruler to literally size up a prospective partner, but you *do* do it subconsciously. Likewise, I don't go around 'sniffing' prospective partners, but I could no more stop that olfactory information from registering than I could fail to notice height or hair color or bust size."

"Oh, God, that was incredibly rude of me. This whole line of questioning. I'm sorry."

He picked up his whiskey again and took a sip. "Don't worry, I'd have shut you down if it bothered me. Which it probably would if I didn't know it stems from genuine curiosity. You *do* want to know everything, don't you?"

She blushed, and he knew she was recalling his prediction on the plane, that her curiosity would eventually drive her into his arms.

"Guilty, I'm afraid," she said. "And I take your point. A multitude of factors have to come together for chemistry to happen. You'd no more screen for good diet than I would for height alone. Just because I like a tall guy doesn't mean Jeff Goldblum and Shaquille O'Neal are interchangeable."

"Precisely. And I should point out that even non-vampires rely on scent to pick a partner. When sizing up a prospective mate, women unconsciously seek out men whose perspiration marks them as genetically dissimilar. Genetic diversity makes for healthy offspring."

"Really? How do you know this stuff?"

"I watch a lot of TV." He waited until she lifted her glass for a sip of wine and said, "For instance, did you know that due to the shape of the North American Elk's esophagus, even if it could speak, it could not pronounce the word 'lasagna'?"

Sam pffted a fine spray of wine onto her chin. "You did *not* learn that on *Animal Planet*."

"No, you're right. I learned that on *Cheers*. I think it was Cliff Clavin."

She patted her chin with a napkin. "You timed that purposely."

"Sorry. I couldn't resist."

"I guess I deserved it." She speared the last piece of salmon and ate it, washing it down with a sip of wine. "That was delicious, but you know, you don't have to cook for me. I actually have someone who does that."

"I know. I met her."

She set her wine glass down on the table. *"You met Marlie?"*

"She was letting herself in when I came back with the groceries."

"Oh my word! Aiden, why didn't you tell me?"

"I *am* telling you."

"Well, how did she react? Was she frightened?"

"Why would she be frightened?" He angled a reproving look at her. "It's not like I flash fang every time I encounter someone."

Color touched her cheeks again. "Of course not. But she's been cooking for me for a long time, and she knows —"

He grinned. "Knows what, Sam? That you don't have strange men over?"

"That I'm a very private person and no one shares my space."

"I gathered. But don't worry. She understands completely why you'd make an exception for me."

She groaned. "Oh, great. She thinks we're sleeping together."

He nodded cheerfully. "Of course. I figured you'd prefer that interpretation than for me to explain our joint enterprise."

"But —"

"Besides, she's right. She's just jumping the gun a little. We'll get there, eventually. We were almost there several nights ago."

She sent him a look that patently said a gentleman would not have reminded her. "I see. And is that what this little dinner is about? You're sweetening my blood in anticipation of imbibing of it?"

He threw back his head and laughed. "Honey, I'm definitely anticipating imbibing, but it doesn't need any sweetening."

She picked up her glass and tossed back the last of her wine. "Has anyone ever told you you're an arrogant ass?"

"Fairly regularly," he admitted. "But this isn't about my arrogance. It's about you, Sam. I know that mind of yours is working on everything I told you. You're wondering what it would be like to make love with a vampire. How it would feel to yield up your blood, and with it, your most erotic thoughts, your most forbidden fantasies. You're wondering how it would feel to have *my* darkest desires racing through your veins. How it would feel to know in your own flesh exactly what it feels like to be in mine. Imagine it, Sam. Once I've taken your blood, you'll be able to feel what it's like for me when I pump my cock into your slick heat, but you'll still feel your own vagina being stretched and filled. To fuck and be fucked at once. And I'll feel it, too."

"Omigod, where's my camera?" She leapt up from the table and dashed from the room. He heard her feet on the treads of the stairs as she dashed upstairs for her equipment.

Okay, not quite the reaction he'd been going for.

Sam stepped into her second floor studio and leaned against the wall. Oh, man, he'd done it again. Used her own imagination against her, feeding her those images …

The worst part was he was right. If they continued to work together like this, to *live* together, they'd definitely wind up in bed. But if she had anything to say about it, it would be later rather than sooner. Just because he deserved to suffer a little.

Okay, he deserved to suffer a *lot*, considering what he'd dragged her into, but she doubted she could hold out against this growing need long enough to make that happen. Besides which, he could always go out and find female company when she was away, as he'd just done. Or even while she slept.

A picture formed in her mind of Aiden naked on a bed with another woman, their limbs tangled, skin sheened with perspiration, bodies straining toward ecstasy …

Instantly, her stomach clenched with jealousy.

No, not jealousy, she corrected. *Envy.* Jealousy was a possessive emotion, and she had no claim on Aiden, nor did she want one. She wasn't looking for a serious relationship with *anyone* at this point in her life, let alone with an all-but-immortal vampire. Nevertheless, she'd have to be dead not to feel a pang of envy in the circumstances. Sort of like when another woman beat you to the last pair of size 7 Manolo Blahnik classic Mediterranean mules at the half-price sale.

Except this wasn't a no-holds-barred, every-woman-for-herself shoe sale. She could have her Manolo Blahniks any time she wanted, but for now, she was just going to photograph them.

With a smile on her face, she started arranging the room.

"Hey."

She glanced up to see Aiden standing in the doorway. She hadn't heard him on the steps. Of course, she rarely did. He moved almost silently. But she'd been expecting him.

"I heard you moving stuff around up here," he said. "Anything I can help with?"

"Yes. You can sit on that stool."

"You're kidding." His gaze drifted over her assembly of modeling lamps and umbrellas and lifted an eyebrow. "You're going to take a studio portrait?"

"I did warn you there would be photo shoots. That was the deal."

"Of course. I just thought they'd be more ... I don't know ... spontaneous. Less posed."

"Relax. I know what I'm doing. Now if you'd take a seat."

He obliged, hooking one foot into a low rung on the stool and keeping the other planted firmly on the floor. "I didn't know you were into portrait photography."

"Only for friends these days. But I've had this equipment a million years. I used to do a lot of it when I first started out in the biz. Graduation photos, pet portraits, you name it. Heck, I even did weddings. Whatever paid the bills."

She went to the first modeling lamp on the right and turned on the flash head, then did the same to the second one she'd set up to his left.

"Why is one light pointing at me and the other one away from me?"

"The one that's pointing away will actually be the strongest light source. The light will bounce off the reflective umbrella, casting light on the left side of your face. Meanwhile, the one that's pointing at you will give us a much softer light on the other side."

"Because it's passing through that translucent umbrella?"

"Yeah, and because I'm amping the power down."

"Why not stick one light source right in front of me?"

"Because we don't want you to look flat and two-dimensional."

"Photos *are* two dimensional," he pointed out.

"Yeah, but they don't have to *look* it. And before you ask, yes, I could make you look 3D by lighting from just one side, but then you get big, hard shadows on the other side. Hence the second light to relieve the density of the shadows a bit. But not too much or you're back to a flat look. Now, we're not going to talk about light or f/stops or shutter speeds."

"So what will we talk about?"

She moved behind her camera. "How about your favorite subject again."

"Ah, yes. Me."

He grinned and she took a shot.

"Good God. Am I going to get bombarded with that strobe every time you take a picture?"

"Pretty much. But it beats sitting under hot lights. Now stop whining and start talking."

"Yes, ma'am. What would you like to know?"

She took another shot. "I don't know. Tell me about your family."

"They've been dead for centuries, Sam. What can I say about them? I can barely remember what they looked like."

Her heart did a funny little quivering thing. "Did you have siblings?"

"One sister. She was younger than me by almost five years."

"Did she go on to have children? Do you have great-great-great-grand nephews or nieces running around?"

His face tightened. "No, she died young without ever having married. Nor did I marry. My father *did* remarry after my mother's death, but had no further issue. All of which means I have no close blood relatives out there, being fruitful and multiplying."

She clicked several more shots. "That's so sad."

He angled his head. "Sad, yes. But when you've lived as long as I have, you see there are a whole lot of sad stories out there. Mine is no sadder than the next one."

Well, alrighty, then. Clearly, he didn't want to talk about his family. She'd let him off the hook . . . in a minute.

"Just tell me one thing about each of them, and we'll move on."

He scowled at the camera and she clicked his pic.

"What kind of thing?"

"Any kind of thing."

"Fine. My father was a preacher."

She took another shot. "That's good."

"My sister ... my sister was a hoyden ... a tomboy, as you'd call it. My mother despaired of civilizing her."

Sam took several more shots, certain he had no idea how soft his eyes had become. "She sounds like she was a real firebrand."

"She was," he agreed, "but don't try to distract me. You've already had your one thing for Emma."

Two things, she thought. She now knew her name. "And your mother?"

"My mother." His lips curved in a smile. "My mother loved the two of us altogether too much for our father's liking. He thought she spoiled us horribly."

Click, click, click, click.

"Are we done yet?"

"Not quite." She moved to shift one of the model lamps. "But we can change the subject, now. Thank you for humoring me."

He lifted a shoulder in a shrug.

She checked her light meter again. "Tell me about how you came to be a vampire. Unless you still find it too disturbing."

She glanced up to see him smiling mockingly. "Ah, Sam. Such a tender heart. You imagine I was victimized?"

She straightened. "Are you suggesting it was otherwise?"

"Oh, yeah. Most definitely otherwise."

"You *wanted* to be turned?"

"Quite desperately." His expression now was cold, almost cruel. "What would you say if I told you I chose this life? That I actively sought out a vampire who would turn me?"

Oh, crap. She'd forgotten to shoot him. "Then I'd say you must have had a very good reason." She took a couple of shots.

"I did."

"Shall I keep pecking away with questions, or will you tell me about it?"

"You want to hear my story?"

Though he hadn't moved a muscle, he suddenly looked menacing. Bigger. Harder. More unpredictable. *Dangerous.*

Intuitively, she understood it was for the camera. She was pretty certain that the emotions inside were at odds with the posture. "Yes, I want to hear it."

He inclined his head. "So be it. I wanted to be turned so I could kill the whoreson vampires who killed my mother and sister. I knew the only way I could do that is if I became as powerful as they were."

Mother of God. "Vampires killed your family?"

"My mother and sister, yes. After they'd had their sport with them."

Her stomach lurched. "I'm so sorry. That's awful."

"Yes."

"What about you? I mean, why didn't they kill you, too?"

"Father and I weren't home when they came. We were coming back from the neighboring town. I rode ahead, because I was hungry. We hadn't eaten since the midday meal, and it was after ten o'clock. And frankly, I'd tired of my father's righteous company."

He'd slipped into more dated language, more formal language than he usually favored, she realized. "So you stumbled into the scene?"

"Quite literally."

"But they didn't kill you?"

His face tightened. "Forcing me to watch afforded them more amusement than killing me possibly could have."

"Oh, Aiden! I'm so sorry they did that to you."

"I'm not," he said. "Had they mesmerized me and sanitized the scene, I would have known only that some tragedy had befallen my mother and sister while we were gone. I'd have been stricken by guilt and grief for having left them alone, but I would have had no inkling of the evil that had been done to them. I'd have been left with no thirst for revenge." He looked straight into the camera. "I tried to stop the attack, of course. One vampire caught me, held me down as easily as though I were an infant. I swear he fed on my powerlessness, my impotence. My rage. Sam, you can't imagine. The blood-lust, the despair ..."

"My God, Aiden," she whispered, shaken. "How did you keep your sanity?"

He laughed, a short, sharp sound. "Some would say I didn't. But if I did, I kept precious little else. The man I was before the attack was burned away. Those rogues made a vampire hunter that night. And in so doing, they forged the weapon of their own destruction."

When she made no reply, he glanced up. His eyes sharpened when he noticed she'd abandoned her camera. "You seem to have forgotten to take your pictures."

"Forget it. It doesn't matter."

"Take them, Sam." His smile was grim. "If you can stand in the face of a tornado and take pictures, you can damned well do it in the face of a few words. Go on. Shoot. I'll keep talking."

Hands trembling, she went back to work, not because she wanted more pictures but because she needed the distance. And she wanted him to keep talking.

"As I said, a vampire hunter was born that night, even though it would be many years before I could extract vengeance. It took me almost five years to find a vampire I could trust to turn me rather than kill me."

"Wait a minute ... how did you even *know* a vampire could turn you? Was that common knowledge in your day?"

"Hardly. But during the attack, the vampire who held me down offered to let my sister live. I was desperate to do whatever he wanted if they would spare her, but after giving me hope, he said the only way she could be saved is if they turned her into one of them. God help me, I might have accepted the offer, but Emma wouldn't. She said she'd rather die. She ... she told them to get on with it. And they did."

Sam's stomach squeezed into a tight ball. *Keep it moving, Sam. Move off the sister.* "So after much searching for years, you found a vampire to turn you," she prompted.

"Yep." He cocked his head. "Wanna know how I did it?"

A new light had come into his eyes, one she didn't understand. One that filled her with dread and made her want to say no, it didn't matter. But maybe it did. Maybe it mattered for him to tell it. And maybe it mattered to photograph him as he told it. *Click.*

"Yes, I want to know." *Click, click.*

He smiled. "I found a vampire with a predilection for hand-some young men and I seduced him."

She sucked in a breath.

"Does that shock you?" He lifted an eyebrow. "Because I promise you, I would have done worse. Though at the time, given my fire and brimstone upbringing, I frankly couldn't conceive of much worse. But I figured if I was going to damn my soul to hell by choosing to become a vampire, what could it matter if I allowed myself to be buggered in the process?"

Oh, Aiden. "Stop ... you don't have to say any more."

"Why? Does it turn you off, Sam? Does it kill that lovely, perfect hum of sexual attraction that's been building between us to know that I let a man fuck me? Not once, but many times. Until he trusted me enough ... *loved me* enough to give me his gift."

Of all the stupid ... "Dammit, Aiden. You know better than that." She abandoned the camera to step closer, so he could see the truth in her eyes. "It just ... hurts to know how much that must have cost you."

He laughed. "What if I told you I came to enjoy it?"

"I'd say that unless you've been lying to me all this while, that was pretty much inevitable."

He scowled. "How's that?"

"The whole blood/sex, mind-melding thing." She went back to her camera and took another shot. "Unless you've been feeding me a line of crap, you must have felt what he felt. And I can only imagine he felt pretty damned good." His face slackened with surprise and she took another shot. "Plus, you said he came to love you. If you felt those feelings — his feelings — how could you not be ambivalent about the sex?"

"Maybe I just liked getting fucked up the ass."

"Maybe."

He blinked, and she laughed. "Aiden, you idiot. If I were old and decrepit, with one foot in the grave, I would still, after only one look at you, have no doubts about your sexual orientation. You did the needful, and you got what you wanted. And maybe you eased another human being's loneliness for a while."

"Eased his loneliness?" He snorted. "I came within a gnat's hair of killing him."

"You what?"

"You have no idea what it's like to suddenly have so much power coursing through you. When the change came, I wanted to crush him. I wanted to drain his blood and grind his bones to dust. Because he'd given me so much blood when he turned me, I had more than enough power to do it."

"Of course! You'd lived with all that rage so long, and then when you turned —"

"Background noise." He waved a hand dismissively. "Yes, the rage was there, hot as ever, pumping in my blood with every heartbeat, but that's not why I wanted to kill him. I wanted to kill him for what he'd done to me. Or rather, what I allowed him — no, what I *begged* him — to do to me."

"But you didn't kill him."

"No. I pulled myself back from the brink by reminding myself he was not a killer. Though in retrospect, I think he half hoped I would destroy him. But as he pointed out, killing him wouldn't kill my shame, which is what I really wanted to destroy."

She blinked rapidly. "I'm so sorry."

"Not to worry. My supposed everlasting shame died an amazingly rapid death. It was, as I discovered, a rather small sin in the scheme of things. And no sin at all by today's standards." He gave her a wry grin. "Amazing what perspective a few hundred years'll give you."

Knowing he would not want her sympathy, she took her cue from him and grinned back. "A few hundred years? It's amazing how much societal mores have changed in just *my* short lifetime." She cocked her head. "And you know, by today's standards, it's actually kind of hot."

He lifted an eyebrow.

"I've got just one word for you." Her smile widened. "*Brokeback*."

He snorted. Goddamn, but he *liked* her. A lot. "Great. When I finally get you in my bed, you're gonna be thinking about man-on-man action and what it would be like to have a second guy in there with us."

Her lovely face sobered. "Aiden, when you get me in bed, I don't think there's going to be room for anyone else there, even in my imagination."

Ahhhh, at last. "So you're ready to concede that's where we're headed?"

"I think I conceded that the first time you told me what it would be like." She moved behind the camera again and started shooting.

He looked into the camera and gave her his deadliest grin, the get-Aiden-laid-this-very-minute smile. "Then Sam, honey, what are we doing here in your studio instead of making use of that perfectly nice queen bed in your bedroom?"

She looked up so she could meet his eyes directly, and her gaze held a riveting mixture of emotions. A gratifying wealth of desire, a sobering dose of fear, and even a touch of sadness.

"I bet that smile never fails, does it?" she said.

He heard the bump her heart rate had taken, saw her respiration rate quicken in the rise and fall of her chest. Hell, he could all but hear the rush of blood congesting her loins and breasts. But he also saw her determination to resist. It was both baffling and exciting.

"There's a first time for everything, I guess," he allowed. "And judging by the set of your chin, this might be that time."

"I'm afraid so."

"But why?" His brow knit in genuine puzzlement. "Why deny yourself the greatest pleasure you may ever know?"

She drew in a shuddering breath. "Because I can. For now, I still can."

Oh, Sam. You stubborn woman.

He knew he could change her mind. He could take the three steps that separated them and kiss her, and she would go up in flames. Or he could exercise the silkiest, spider-web thin compulsion, and she would cross that space herself, slide into his arms, and put her beautiful mouth on his mouth ... It would be so easy. And so subtle she'd never suspect she'd been manipulated, even in retrospect.

Goddamn, he wanted to do it. His cock swelled with it. His teeth positively ached to erupt, and his hands burned to touch her. But even more, he wanted her to come to him of her own volition, driven by her own unanswerable need.

True, she'd already agreed to go to bed with him three nights ago, but she hadn't been at her strongest then. She'd been traumatized by seeing that kid's narrow escape, by thinking about what the kid's fate would have been had she not agreed to lend her gift to the hunt.

No, he didn't want her to come to him needing comfort. He wanted her to do it when she was strong. And he could wait for that. In fact, the waiting would be a pleasure. Excruciating, to be sure, but a rare pleasure. Because that was part of her appeal, that she *could* resist him. The last time he'd encountered a female who'd said no to him was ... damn, he couldn't remember. But definitely pre-vamp days.

He shrugged. "Can't blame a guy for trying."

"No, I can't. But I *can* thank you for not trying very hard. I think we both know it wouldn't take much of a nudge." She moved to shut off the lights she'd been using, his cue that the photo shoot was done. "Besides, you're going to need tonight to make travel arrangements."

He perked up. "We're going somewhere?"

"For Friday night. Framingham, Massachusetts. Just outside of Boston."

"I'm familiar with the area. I have a condo there. Boston, I mean. Not Framingham."

Her eyebrows soared. "Really?"

"What? You think Boston is too blue-blooded for me?"

"A little too staid, I would have thought. I see you more in New York or Los Angeles."

He laughed. "I have bolt holes in both those cities. Chicago and New Orleans, too. Vancouver, Toronto and Mexico City. But I like Boston. It has history."

"So will we stay there while we're in the area? Your Boston place, I mean?"

"Absolutely. I haven't been there in months. Six or seven." He moved to help her as she wrestled with a clamp that held an umbrella in place. "Here, let me get that." He made sure the back of his hand brushed hers innocently as she pulled away, and smiled at the resulting hitch in her breath. He could wait, but he wanted to make sure the wait tortured them both equally. "I'll help you put this stuff away, then you can MapQuest our destination while I get Geoff busy filing a flight plan into Hanscom Field."

"Not Logan?"

He shook his head. "Much less hassle to fly into Bedford. But not if I don't get Geoff working on it."

"Go." She flicked a hand. "I think I'm going to leave this setup in place for now, in case I want to use it again. And I'd prefer to use my time working with the photos."

"Great. Just one thing, first."

She looked up from detaching her camera from the tripod. "What's that?"

"This."

He pulled her to him and kissed her, once. Thoroughly. And when he finished, both their hearts were pounding.

Sam squirmed on the cool ground, adjusting her position yet again. This was not going to be a meteor shower or a lightning storm. And on the edges of suburbia, it damn sure wasn't going to be a wolf chorus. It was going to be a vampire attack. Knowing that made it hard to sit still.

By contrast, Aiden, who couldn't seem to sit still on their last outing, sat placidly beside her. Knowing it was going to be a vampire attack seemed to have just the opposite effect on him. But his stillness was deceptive. She felt his energy beside her like a tightly coiled spring.

Suddenly her ears perked up. "I hear a car," she whispered.

"It's been climbing this hill for a couple of minutes now."

Of course, he'd have heard it long before she detected it. "Vamps?"

"In the car? It's possible, but not likely." He turned to her. "You *do* realize what this place is?"

"Yeah. It's a bluff overlooking a disused gravel pit."

The headlights of a car were clearly visible now, cutting a swath through the night as the vehicle moved down the narrow, bumpy lane. It stopped a few hundred feet short of them, and the driver cut the engine. Inside the car, the radio continued to play. The muffled music grew louder a second later, as the driver rolled his window down.

"They're not getting out."

"God, Sam, what planet did you say you grew up on again?"

"What do you mean?"

"This is a make-out spot."

"Oh! Well, no wonder I didn't twig to it."

"You never made out in a car?"

She heard the disbelief in his voice and smiled. "I was focused on other things when I was that age. And by the time I *was* having sex, we didn't need to make out in cars."

"What an appalling gap in your experience. I mean, I was born before the first car was dreamt of, yet *I've* made out in —"

He sat up straighter beside her, and she didn't need the pale wash of moonlight to tell he was listening. And scenting the breeze, she realized.

She touched his leg. He turned to her and nodded.

Vampire.

Quietly, she switched on the infrared floodlight. Lifting the binoculars to her eyes, she adjusted the light so it was trained on the parked car, an older Sunfire or Grand Am or another of those sporty little Pontiacs. It struck her then. The occupants of that car were no doubt teenagers, young lovers wrapped up in each other and their own rampaging hormones. And the rogue intended to prey on them. Her stomach clenched. Then the vampire drifted into the frame. The Thai stir-fry she'd had for supper threatened to make a reappearance.

She shot a hand out to grip Aiden's leg, but he pinned it there, preventing her from scrambling to her feet as she wanted to.

Hold.

The word was a mere wisp of smoke in her mind, but there was no mistaking that it was an order.

Oh, God, of course. She let her breath out as quietly as she could, and drew another lungful of air. The vampire had done nothing. Might yet do nothing. Maybe the extent of his perversion was voyeurism. She was the one who insisted her participation was contingent on making absolutely certain the target was a rogue. That Aiden had had to remind her —

Suddenly the interior light went on in the car. She lifted the binoculars again to see that the rogue had wrenched the door open. He must have reached inside the open window and thrown the electronic locks. Aiden was on his feet in a split second, moving quietly across the grass. He needn't have bothered with stealth, though, because the girl in the car was screaming and her boyfriend was shouting.

Sam's heart thundered. *Stop him, stop him, stop him.*

Aiden was close enough now to intervene, but still he held back. Oh, God, the boy was handcuffed to the steering wheel with both hands! And the rogue was circling the car to get to the girl.

Lock your door!

Through the binoculars, she saw the rogue lift his hand. From his grip dangled the car's keys. The girl screamed again and her boyfriend roared. The vampire smiled and unlocked the door.

Now, Aiden. Now!

Still, he did nothing. What was he waiting for? Her hand tightened on the pistol she'd picked up the moment Aiden started toward the car.

The rogue extracted the struggling girl from the car as easily as another man might lift a stuffed teddy bear, depositing her squirming body on the hood of the car. The boy howled again and hit the horn, the loud blare assaulting Sam's ears even from this distance.

And then — thank you, God — Aiden made his move. Seizing the vampire from behind, he hauled him off the girl. A savage wrench and the rogue's neck was broken. Aiden let the rogue's corpse fall to the ground.

"Get in the car," she heard him say to the girl, and she scrambled to obey.

"Sam?" He lifted his voice to make sure she heard. "Can you come here? And bring that gun with you"

Bring the gun? Her heart pounded even harder. Was there another threat? Another vampire? She raced across the uneven ground, skidding to a stop beside Aiden.

"The kids are hysterical. I want to deal with them and send them on their way before I deal with him." He indicated the vampire with a jerk of his head. "Keep that gun trained on him. If he so much as stirs or groans, shoot him. Head is best, but the heart will do if you're squeamish about a head shot."

Shoot him? "But he's already dead," she protested. "I saw you snap his neck."

"Maybe he's dead. Maybe he's not. I just don't want to find out that he's knitting his spinal cord back together while my back is turned." He put a hand on her back. "Can you handle this, Sam? Because if not, I'll have to take some other fairly grisly measures to make sure our friend stays dead. Frankly, that might be more disturbing than your having to shoot him."

The girl was sobbing loudly now, and the boy was desperately trying to get free of his cuffs.

"Okay." She trained the gun on the dead — at least for now — rogue and shuddered. "I can do it. Take care of them."

Fortunately, the corpse showed no signs of reanimating. She kept a careful eye on him, even as she listened to Aiden talking to the kids in that low, hypnotic tone. Once, the night breeze lifted the collar of the rogue's shirt, and she almost shot him out of sheer reflex. Thank God she restrained herself! Had she fired the gun, poor Aiden would have had to start from scratch putting those kids together again.

Eventually, Aiden stepped back from the car. The young man, his hands now free, keyed the ignition, backed the car up, then drove sedately back down the hill as though nothing had happened.

"They really won't remember?" she asked, as the sound of the car's engine faded.

"Not consciously. But it's impossible to scrub the event away completely. For instance, they probably will never come back to this particular make-out spot again. Or maybe they'll give up parking altogether."

"Maybe they'll break up," she said. "Maybe seeing each other will stir that dark thing at the back of their minds, and they'll be too unhappy to stay together." Oh, God, her heart was breaking, and how stupid was that? Those kids were lucky to be alive, to have a chance to love. If not each other, then someone new.

"I imagine a breakup is inevitable," he agreed. "On some level, he'll feel emasculated and unworthy of her love because he wasn't able to protect her. And on some level, she'll despise him for the failure, even if she can't remember it consciously."

"That's so sad."

"Dammit."

"What?"

"You're crying."

"I am not!"

He touched her cheek and found the incriminating wetness there. "Liar."

To his surprise, she turned her face into his hand.

"I know it's stupid to be so upset," she said. "They're lucky just to be alive. A broken romance in the scheme of things is pretty minor. And how long would a teenage romance last anyway? They probably would have parted within the year, gone on to love other people. So why am I crying?"

Oh, Sam. Aiden pulled her into his arms, and his heart squeezed as her arms encircled him and held tight. "It's just the loss of innocence, baby. Theirs. Yours. It's in our nature to mourn it." He crushed her with a hug. "I'm so damned sorry to expose you to this. I swear, if I knew another way ..."

"Not just their loss of innocence. Not just mine." She pushed against his chest and he loosened his hold so she could look up at him. "Yours, too, Aiden."

"Mine? Oh, pet, don't waste your tears on me." He tipped up her chin and smiled into her eyes. "I can't even remember a state of innocence, so I've nothing to mourn. Honest."

"Of course."

She pulled out of his arms to stand on her own, leaving him oddly torn. He liked his women strong. He sure as hell didn't relish a crying woman. So why was he regretting that she conquered her tears so quickly?

Because she turned to you so easily.

Because her heart was filled with something tender for you.

"What will you do to him?" She gestured to the rogue's corpse. "What do you do to all of them to make sure they don't fight their way back?"

"Sam," he said warningly.

"I can't believe it didn't occur to me. I mean, it couldn't be that easy, could it, just breaking their necks?" She rubbed the last of the moisture from her face with the back of her hand. "So, what do you do to them, Aiden?"

"You don't need to know that, Sam. You don't *want* to know."

"I do," she insisted. "I promise you, it won't make me run screaming. And it's not as though I want to *see* it. I just need to know."

"In case you ever have to finish one off?"

"Because I want to know how bad it is for you."

Oh, God save him. *Pity.* She felt pity for him. Well, he could fix that.

"Bad?" He laughed harshly. "It's a fucking *pleasure.* I just think about the bastard's victims. And if that's not enough, I think about my sister. My mother. "

She looked at him, her gaze steady in the moonlight, seeing way more than human eyes should. "You can sell that to someone else, Aiden Afflack. Now, stop stalling and tell me what you have to do."

Emotion rose in his chest, blindsiding him. He crushed it down, letting cold anger seep in to take its place. *Damn her.*

"Decapitation is the gold standard. I've gotten very good at it. Downright surgical, if I do say so myself. And I bury the head separately, just to be sure. Of course, sometimes I'm too rushed for best practice, in which case I find that the old stake to the heart is quite effective, if clichéd, especially in combination with a stake to the brain."

She inclined her head. "Thank you."

"What? You're not going to wring your hands? Cry all over me?"

"Would you like me to?"

"God, no!"

"Then why don't you take that creature and do what you need to do so we can get out of here."

Biting back a curse, Aiden bent and hoisted the dead vampire onto his shoulder. "Wait for me in the car," he instructed. "I'll help you load your equipment when I get back." As soon as she set off in the direction of the vehicle, he gave the rogue's neck another vicious wrench to make sure he stayed quiet, then headed off into the bush with his burden.

By the time he got back, Sam had brought the rented Escalade out of its hiding spot behind a copse of poplar trees and had loaded all her equipment. He slid into the driver's seat. "I'd have helped you with that."

"I'm used to it."

"Fair enough." He keyed the ignition and the SUV roared to life. "For the record, I'm used to my job, too. I don't feel even a little bit bad about what I did here tonight."

"For the record, neither do I. He was going to kill those kids."

"Yes. And I'm pretty sure I've seen this guy's handiwork before." He guided the vehicle onto the dirt road and began to descend the hill.

"But how can he get away with it? How can you explain the simultaneous death of two teenagers?"

"Suicide pact." He adjusted his seatbelt, which was determined to choke him. He didn't need the damned thing, would never get used to wearing it, but Sam insisted. "After he finishes them, he arranges them back in their seats, attaches a hose to the exhaust system, feeds it into the car, rolls up the windows and starts the engine. And voila, death by carbon monoxide poisoning. With their reduced blood volume, they wouldn't have to inhale too much of it in their dying moments to have a sufficient concentration in their blood for a pathologist to conclude they'd died from it."

"Omigod, those poor parents! Left to believe their children were so profoundly troubled, the only option they could see was suicide."

"I know. I've often thought it must be worse than knowing what really happened."

"How many do you think he's killed?"

"I don't know." They'd reached the secondary road that would take them back to the highway. Aiden turned onto it. "How many clusters of suicides do you read about in the papers? Is the impulse to self-destruction really as contagious among teens as all those shrinks think? Or are there more bastards like this out there?"

She sat back. After several moments passed in silence, he began to think she'd spend the rest of the trip that way, lost in her own thoughts. But then she spoke again.

"Why was this one different?"

He glanced at her, her face in profile more visible to him than she probably imagined. "Different how?"

"You said rape wasn't usually part of these assaults. That they got off on the killing itself."

"For most of them, that's all they want. They feed on the terror the attack itself engenders. It flows into them along with the victim's blood. For them, it would be like mainlining pure, undiluted power. It's only the blackest of souls who need more. Their appetites can't be satisfied with mere shock and terror. They want to taste their victim's humiliation, rage, impotence, despair. In fact, I'd lay odds that that bastard would get more pleasure out of that boy than he would from assaulting the girl. The rape would just be foreplay, a means of evoking the volatile emotions he wanted from the male."

"I'm glad you killed him," she said. "I'm glad I found him for you so you could kill him."

He smiled at her tone. "Me too."

"In fact, I wish he'd stirred so I could have killed him again."

His smile vanished. "No, you don't."

She sighed. "You're right. I don't. "

"Why don't you rest. I'll wake you when we get to my place."

"I couldn't."

"Sure you could, if you let me give you a suggestion. And you'd feel as rested as though you'd had hours of sleep."

"You mean hypnotize me?"

"If you want to call it that. And you needn't sound so horrified. I just thought you might want to get away from your thoughts for the next forty-five minutes."

"I can't say the offer doesn't appeal, but no thanks. I'm not a fan of escapism generally. It never solves anything."

"I figured as much. But the option is always there, if you change you mind."

"Hmmmm."

He sent her a sidelong glance. "What?"

"Change my mind? Interesting choice of expressions, considering you're probably quite capable of doing it."

He grinned. "To get you in my bed, you mean?"

"Would I even *know* if you pulled that Kreskin crap on me?"

"Not if I were subtle about it."

"I don't believe it."

"What are you thinking right now?"

"What do you mean, what am I thinking? I'm thinking you're bluffing."

"Yeah, but what are you thinking underneath that? Underneath it *all*? This very moment. No matter how odd it may seem."

She frowned. "I'm thinking I want an Orange Crush."

"Check the cooler." He gestured to the tiny portable cooler plugged into the SUV's cigarette lighter.

He flicked on the interior light so she could locate the cooler.

"Sonofabitch."

He grinned.

"Dammit, Aiden. How am I supposed to go to bed with you now? I mean, how am going to know if it's my idea or yours?"

"Oh, baby, it's very much my idea. But it's yours, too."

"But how do I *know* that?"

"First, even if I were to enthrall you, I could never make you do anything you didn't already want to do, in your heart of hearts. I can't make anyone do anything fundamentally contrary to their values or desires. When I made those two kids forget their encounter, it's because they wanted to forget it. Desperately needed to."

"But you already know I'm attracted to you. You could just give me a hypnotic nudge and I'd fall right into your bed."

"Absolutely," he agreed. "But I couldn't make you want to have sex with me if the idea were fundamentally repellent. You arrived at this point on your own. I swear it. Which brings me to my second point. From the beginning, I knew we'd be lovers. But I also promised myself I wouldn't exercise any kind of compulsion on you to speed it up."

"But why on earth would you do that?" Her tone said, *Hello, you're a man. Why would you* not *use every weapon at your disposal to get laid?*

"Because I wanted us both to know that when you come to me, it'll be because you choose to. Because your desire to be with me beats in your blood loud enough to drown out that voice of caution in your head. Because your fear of intimacy has collapsed under the force of your need to do join with me, mind and body."

"Aiden?"

He lifted his gaze from the road to glance at her again. "Yeah?"

"How far is it back to that gravel pit?"

He lifted his foot off the accelerator. "Did you forget something?"

"No. I just decided I don't want to wait any longer."

Jesus!

"To have sex with you, I mean," she added helpfully.

He jammed on the brakes.

Chapter 9

SAM'S HEART THUNDERED as Aiden pulled the SUV onto the shoulder without making any attempt to execute a U-turn. Surely he didn't mean to ...

He killed the engine.

"Aiden, we can't stop here!" While it wasn't as busy as the highway, especially at this time of night, there'd be bound to be *some* traffic in an area as heavily populated as this.

"We can stop long enough for this." He leaned across the space between them, slid a hand behind her head and pulled her into a searing kiss.

There was nothing tentative about the way his mouth claimed hers or the way he held her head prisoner so he could take his fill from her lips. There was no halting, *is-this-okay?* question in the hand that raked her shirt open to find her breast.

The urgency of his demand was all it took to blast the sense from her head and unleash the desire she'd been holding in check for so long. Fumbling to find the seatbelt clasp, she released it. The seatbelt retracted across her chest until it caught on his hand. Groaning, she pushed his hand away from her breast so the belt could retract all the way. "Back up," she said, pushing against his chest. "I'm coming over there."

"Great idea, but let me fix the seat first." A hum of an electric motor and the seat slid back a few more inches. Another hum and the seat reclined part way. Then his hands were on her, helping her over the console to straddle his lap. "Better?"

"Better." She lifted the hem of the black t-shirt he wore, pushing it up to expose a muscled, lightly-haired chest and flat abdomen. "Much better." She let her hands skim down his chest, smiling as his abdominals tightened. Then she bent to kiss his chest, reveling in the sweet rush of arousal mushrooming low in her belly as she tasted his skin and inhaled his scent. Oh, God, she wanted to *eat* him. She wanted to lick and kiss and bite her way down his chest. She wanted to free his cock from his jeans and suck it.

The thought sent a bolt of arousal to her groin. As did the knowledge that when he took her blood in a moment, he'd know her thoughts, her every desire, and she'd know his. They would feel each other's sensations. *To fuck and be fucked at once.* She shuddered, then closed her lips on a flat, dark nipple and raked it gently with her teeth.

"Sam!" His hands tightened on her hips and he thrust upward, grinding the unmistakable bulge of a hard-on against the apex of her thighs. Even through their clothing, the contact was electric. She drew herself up and arched her spine, the better to press the heat of her sex against him. He took the opportunity to free her breasts from the cups of her bra.

"God, you're so beautiful," he murmured. He abandoned her hips to cup both breasts. Sam felt her nipples harden in anticipation as his thumbs neared the crests. When he scraped his thumbs over them, they tightened into urgent, aching points.

"Please, Aiden." She leaned into him in an invitation he couldn't mistake. "Use your mouth on me."

He did, to devastating effect. The wet stroke of his tongue gave way to the hot suction of his mouth. As he drew on her nipple, she closed her eyes and felt a corresponding tug on her womb, followed by a growing emptiness. No, not emptiness. A restless incompletion. A need to be stretched and filled and oh, God, *fucked* by the cock that strained inches below her. Then he bit her breast gently. His teeth! She opened her eyes and looked down.

"Aiden?" She put a hand under his chin and tilted his face up. And oh, Christmas, his fangs had begun to erupt! Something darker and even more compelling than the urge to mate seized her. "Oh, God," she said raggedly. "Do it, Aiden. Do it now."

"Wait."

Wait? "What?"

"Car coming."

She glanced both ways. "I don't see any lights."

"Nevertheless it's coming. I can hear it. Now scoot over to your side."

She blinked. "But —"

"Just for a minute. Just long enough to get those jeans off you. It'll be easier from that side."

A jolt of lust rocked her, but she could see headlights now. "What about the car?"

"Cars, plural, and I'll take care of it. You take care of those jeans."

"But —"

"Trust me. They'll hardly slow down. They'll know beyond the shadow of a doubt that there's nothing to see here. No emergency. No hanky-panky. I'm just pulled over onto the shoulder, practicing safe cell phone use."

"You can project a thought to the occupant of a passing car traveling at 50 miles an hour?"

"You'd be amazed how focused I can be when I'm motivated. Now, do you need more motivation to get out of your pants?"

Hand on her zipper, she hesitated. "What if you're wrong?"

"I'm not."

That was good enough for her. She removed her jeans and panties, and shrugged out of her shirt and bra for good measure. The first car passed, illuminating the inside of the SUV for a few seconds before its headlights moved on. The driver didn't even slow. The second vehicle, a truck, did slow, but only momentarily. Before its taillights swept past, Aiden was reaching for her, pulling her into another scorching kiss.

"C'mere," he said, when he let her breathe again. "You're too far away."

"Are you ready for me?"

"Honey, I was *born* ready for you."

She snorted. "Lame line, Afflack. I meant your state of undress. Am I going to have … access? Because as you pointed out, it would be easier now than after I come over — oh!"

He'd taken her hand mid-sentence and placed it on his cock. Her fingers closed over him, and levity fled.

He was enormous! Not scary, porn-star-freak big, but big enough to make her pulse take another leap. And it was all hers. In a moment, she was going to climb onto his lap and impale herself on it, inch by glorious inch. But first she wanted a taste.

She leaned over the console and guided the head of his cock into her mouth.

"Ahhh!"

Smiling, she drew back, using the flat of her tongue on the underside of the glans, and he made another guttural sound. Oh, Lord, the scent, the texture ...

Then it struck her. No foreskin. When she'd imagined this — repeatedly — he was ... intact. She lifted her head. "You're circumcised."

He laughed. "Good eye, there, Sam."

"I didn't think ... I mean, if you're as old as you say you are ... Unless —"

"Nope, not Jewish. My father was a protestant minister, remember?" he said dryly. "No, I was circumcised for entirely different reasons, at the age of three, without benefit of anesthetic."

She winced. "Why?"

"The same reason hundreds of boys were circumcised back then — for masturbating."

"Omigod, that's barbaric!"

"In retrospect, sure. But back then, they thought masturbation was not just immoral, but that it gave rise to any number of awful illnesses."

"But *no anesthetic*?"

"All part of the cure," he said. "It was meant to have a salutary effect on my excessively lustful nature."

"And did it?"

"In the short term, I'm sure. But in the long term, it doesn't seem to have corrected my moral shortcomings."

She smiled. "Lucky for you, I seem to have some moral short-comings of my own." She closed her fingers around his shaft again. "Shall we get back to doing as the devil pleases?"

"By all means." His hand closed over hers and pumped it several times and groaned. "But much as this may please us, it's really not what pleases the devil."

"No?" She lifted an eyebrow. "Then what does?"

"I'll tell you another time, preferably when I'm not a thousand percent focused on getting inside you. Come here." He slid a hand behind her head and pulled her close for a kiss. Then his hands were on her, lifting her over the console again to straddle his lap.

He was still pretty much fully clothed, which she found unexpectedly arousing. The contrast of the rough denim on her inner thighs and the silky heat of his bare erection against her core sent a bolt of excitement through her. Desire pooled low in her belly, liquefying everything.

He palmed both her breasts, lifting them up and together so he could tongue one nipple, then the other. "God, you're beautiful."

She felt the scrape of his teeth on her breast again and was reminded that soon those very teeth would sink deep into her neck, penetrating her carotid artery. A tremor shuddered through her, half desire, half fear. "I can't believe we're doing this," she said. "I mean, not *this*. I knew we'd do this. But in a car, on the shoulder of the —"

"Sam?"

"Yes?"

"Don't take this the wrong way, but shut up and fuck me."

The humor in his voice didn't quite manage to conceal the stark need beneath. The former eased her fears, and the latter fuelled her excitement.

She laughed. "I can do the second part, but I can't promise to shut up."

"Deal."

She rose up far enough to allow him to part the swollen lips of her sex and guide himself to her entrance. Then she was sinking, impaling herself on his thick shaft. And oh God, he was filling her, stretching her impossibly.

A sigh escaped his lips, and he let his head fall back onto the reclined seat. She leaned forward, bracing herself on his chest and moved experimentally.

"Ahhh! That feels good." She tilted her hips at a slightly different angle and did it again. And again. "The friction! It's so different."

"Baby, you haven't begun to see different yet."

"Spoken like a man who's never worn a condom."

"Says the woman who never made love with a man who didn't?"

"Exactly." She undulated her hips again. "Oh, that's nice!"

He reached up and pulled her down close to his chest. For a moment, she thought he was objecting to the *nice* word, but he murmured in her ear, "Car."

She lifted her head and sure enough there were headlights approaching from behind. "Oh-oh."

"Don't worry. I've got it." He pulled her back down. "Just stay down."

"No problem," she said, then kissed him. Only to find — yikes! — his fangs were fully extended. She jerked back, heart pounding wildly.

"Easy," he soothed, pulling her back down. "Baby, it's time."

Her womb contracted sharply even as the hairs on the back of her neck rose. The headlights of the overtaking car illuminated the cabin long enough for her to glimpse the flash of very long white teeth, then plunged the interior back into near-darkness again as they swept past.

She shivered. "Will it hurt?"

"Yes, but you'll like it."

His words sent another frisson of excitement through her.

"Okay. Do it." She arched her neck, feeling frighteningly vulnerable as she offered her throat to him.

He didn't bite her immediately, but rather nuzzled her neck, her ear, her temple. She moved on him restlessly, needing something more. Fearing it yet wanting it more and more with every sobbing breath she drew. Then, when she could stand it no longer, he tipped her chin away and sank his teeth deep into her flesh.

The shock of it — the violence — rocked her to her very soul. His teeth burned going in like the sharp, hot pain of big IV needles, and she was caught as surely as a tiny gazelle might be in the jaws of a lion. Somehow she managed not to scream, but she felt her pulse thudding harder than she thought possible. Pushing her blood into him.

Oh, God, she was flowing *into* him.

Panicking, she tried to pull away, but he held her head in an immoveable grip.

Easy, baby.

She heard the words in her head, but knew he couldn't have spoken them.

Don't be afraid. Almost done. Then you'll feel it.

Several things changed. First, to her immense relief, he seemed to be gradually working his way out of her neck. Healing the wound, she realized, just as he'd described. But her attention quickly turned south, where — omigod — he seemed to be growing and swelling inside her!

She tightened her internal muscles around his cock, gauging just how deep inside her he was.

"Oh, yeah, like that!"

It wasn't until he spoke those words that she realized he'd fully withdrawn from her neck. Which meant that any minute, she'd start feeling what he felt ... The thought made her surge against him once, twice, then — oh, shit, oh, shit! — her calf cramped.

"Ow!"

"What?"

"My leg! It's cramping."

"You're kidding? No, of course you're not kidding," he muttered. "Which one?"

"The right one. Oh, God, it hurts!"

His hand found her calf and massaged for a moment with strong fingers as his voice soothed her. "Better?" he asked.

"I think so."

"Gently flex and point it a few times."

She did, gingerly. "Definitely better."

"Good. Now, lie down on my chest and let me do the work, or that leg is just going to cramp again."

She complied, whereupon he urged her to ease her knees back and down until she could lie fully on him, straightening her legs along the outside of his. With him holding her weight, she was able to make the shift, only to discover she couldn't find any purchase in this new position. "What now?"

"Now I take over."

He did. Hands on her hips, he lifted her easily, then let her slide back down as he thrust up to meet her. Again and again he did it, setting up an insistent rhythm. Before long his breathing began to grow harsh, his movements more intense. He was going to come, dammit, and soon. He was going to get off and leave her like this! If only his hands were free to touch her breasts or cup her ass or something . . .

"Your legs," he said. "Move them inside mine."

"What?"

"Just do it."

He shifted his legs wide so she could draw hers together. Instantly, she understood why he'd wanted her to do it. Her clitoris virtually screamed its pleasure with every thrust and retreat. God, she was so close now. Sobbing, she reached for it.

"Come on, baby. Come with me," he urged. "Now!'

He gripped her hips tightly, surging into her again and again and finally, her orgasm slammed into her. He gave a shout and pumped himself into her a few more times until she felt the hot spill of his seed.

"Omigod, Sam." She felt laughter rumble through him. "That was —"

"Awful," she finished.

"God, yes! Gloriously, awkwardly, stupendously awful. Say you'll marry me."

Before she even knew what she was she was going to do, she curled her fingers into a fist and slugged him. "You bastard!"

Chapter 10

HOLY SHIT! SHE'D *hit* him. And not a *how dare you* slap to the face, either. More like a Boom-Boom Mancini right to the jaw. Before he could react to that, she was scrambling off him, and her inadvertent knee to the groin commanded his attention.

"Ow! Careful."

"I *was* being careful." Back on her side, she fished her jeans and shirt off the floor.

"Sam, honey, what's —"

"Don't even talk to me!" Clothes and runners in hand, she levered her door open and stepped out onto the shoulder of the road, bare-assed, then slammed the door.

Uh-oh. Maybe agreeing that the sex was awful — relatively speaking — hadn't been the smartest move. Or laughing.

He put his clothes to rights, raised the back on the seat to the upright position and stepped out of the car. By the time he rounded the vehicle, she had her jeans and shirt on, although the latter was still unbuttoned as she bent to put on her runners.

"Sam, I'm sorry. It wasn't awful. Far from it. It's just that —"

She stood. "You are a snake."

Her words sliced into him, her obvious disgust doing what her bare-knuckled fist couldn't.

"Whoa, wait just a minute. I don't think I deserve that."

"No, not a snake," she corrected. "A *worm.* You are the lowest, most despicable creature I have ever encountered, and I am so incredibly sorry I fell for your stupid line."

"My *line*?"

"You *lied* to me." She rounded on him as only a pissed-off woman can. "You fed me that crap about a mind-to-mind connection to seduce me because you knew nothing less would work. You must have been laughing up your sleeve all this while."

His jaw dropped. "Jesus, Sam, do you really believe that?"

"What do you expect me to believe?"

"I don't know. Shit, I don't even know what happened. Or rather what didn't happen."

"Right," she snapped. "Next I suppose you're going to tell me it's never happened to you before."

He felt a flush burn his face. This must be what it was like to experience sexual impotence. "I understand your skepticism. Nevertheless, it's true. I just couldn't get into your head."

"Ah, of course." Her fingers moved up her blouse, buttoning it with terse, jerky movements. "It's *my* fault."

Jesus. The impotence analogy just kept building and building. He sighed. "No, it's not your fault. It's no one's fault. Your mind is obviously stronger than most, maybe because of the psychic thing."

"I'm not psychic!"

"Okay, because of your special talents. And I admit I didn't try very hard when the connection didn't come automatically. I was ... preoccupied. Maybe a little distracted, listening for traffic and being prepared to deflect attention. It just wasn't the ideal situation."

"Then why didn't you insist we wait until we got back to your place?"

"Gimme a break, Sam. I didn't know this was going to happen. Hell, I didn't know it *could* happen. I've never heard of it. I'm just saying that in retrospect, it wasn't the best setting."

"Dammit."

The fire seemed to have gone out of her voice. "Sam?"

"That's the truth, isn't it?"

"Cross my heart."

She buried her face in her hands and groaned. "Argh! This is so humiliating."

Humiliating? "Huh?"

"In the history of the world, in the history of the millions upon millions of vampire/human couplings over the centuries, I have to be the first to fail abysmally at it."

"Fail?" Aiden laughed. "Sam, did it seem like I was disappointed?"

She lifted her chin. "You agreed it was awful."

"Awful for you," he allowed, "Comparatively, I mean, after what I'd led you to expect. And it was more good luck than good management that you got off at all. I was frighteningly blank about what you needed, what you wanted. It scared the shit out of me."

"And that's a good thing?"

He laughed. "Oh, yeah. A wondrously good thing. A positively thrilling thing. I mean, do you have any idea how long it's been since I didn't know *exactly* what my partner wanted? What she was feeling?"

"Good God! I'm a woman of mystery."

"Baby, you are *the* woman of mystery. Maybe the only one on earth."

"Great. Just wonderful."

She crossed her arms in front of her, clearly feeling the chill of the night air. And equally clearly, she was not as thrilled with the notion of mystery as he was. Her next words confirmed his impression. "What if I don't want to stay a woman of mystery?"

"Oh, we'll get there, to that shared place I promised. I'm sure of it. If you don't mind ... um, practicing. But I have a feeling you'll always have the wherewithal to slam the door shut again any time you want."

She angled her head, her eyes sparkling in the moonlight. "Well, that doesn't sound so bad."

"Which? The practicing until we break through? Or the slamming the door shut again afterward?"

"Both."

"That's my girl."

"God, I can't believe we did it in a car."

He smiled. "Well, you did say your education was lacking in that area."

"Yeah, but on the side of the road? With traffic passing?"

"Frankly, I didn't intend to take it that far. I pulled over to kiss you, thinking that would hold me until we got home. But you pack quite a wallop, Sam Shea. In more ways than one."

She gasped. "Omigod, I *hit* you! Aiden, I'm so sorry. I've never hit anyone before in my life."

"No problem. It kind of took me back to the old days. Waaaaay back. Of course, they used to use an open palm back then, not a closed fist."

She grimaced and touched his face. "I'm so sorry."

He closed his hand over hers, trapping it against his cheek. "Sam, honey, you could have clobbered me with a baseball bat, broken my jaw, cracked my skull, and I'd still be right as rain after a day's sleep."

"Really?"

"Really." He released her hand.

"Just because I can't permanently hurt you is no excuse for hitting you."

"Ah, but if I'd really done what you thought I'd done, I'd have richly deserved it."

"True."

"So can we kiss and make up so we can get back to my place before sunup?"

She glanced toward the eastern sky, where the rim of the horizon was beginning to turn a blue-black. Dawn was still a safe distance away, but the prospect of being caught out here clearly galvanized her.

"Good Lord, yes. Let's get going."

She reached for the SUV's door handle but he tugged her back. "You forgot the kiss part."

A laugh.

"So I did."

She went into his arms for a surprisingly sweet kiss, and he didn't need to push his way into her thoughts to understand her message. *I'm sorry I misjudged you. I'm sorry I hit you.* When he helped her up into her seat a moment later, they were both smiling.

An hour later, he ushered her into his Back Bay condo unit a good forty minutes before full sunrise. The first thing she saw was her own work hanging in the foyer. Occupying most of one wall, it was a series of nine rectangular panels that together formed a picture of a towering bank of clouds after sunset, the dying light turning the boiling clouds into what looked more like angry molten lava than anything airborne. Were it not for the tiny farmhouse and barn on the horizon at the very bottom edge of the photo, one could easily imagine the clouds were the sulfurous, billowing issue of some volcano.

"What the ... I sold that piece in an exclusive deal."

"And it was worth every penny."

She turned to him. "*You're* the Hunter Corporation?"

"Not very original, I know."

"Hunter ... oh, God! I thought the proprietor's name must be Hunter."

"Actually, it's one of my aliases. Aiden Hunter owns this condo. The jet, too."

She moved into the next room, scanning the walls. "Where are the rest?"

"Not here. I display just one in each of my residences."

She turned to look at him, her face guarded. "So you knew who I was from the start?"

"Not immediately. I've been a fan of your work for years, but I always figured Sam Shea for a man. It didn't really click until I said your full name aloud that first time we talked on the phone, back in St. Cloud. Which is pretty remarkable considering that by then, I'd already seen your gear and your business card. My Old World chauvinism showing, I guess. It didn't even occur to me that a woman would chase storms to get these amazing shots."

"Why didn't you mention it?"

"I thought I'd freaked you out enough already."

"That you did." She lifted a hand to her throat, her fingers smoothing, soothing the area where he'd bitten her. "I guess I got over it, huh?"

"Does it hurt still?"

She dropped her hand quickly. So quickly he was sure the gesture had been completely unconscious.

"No." She lifted her shoulders in a shrug. "Okay, a little, maybe. Just enough to be aware of it."

"It'll be gone when you wake. There'll be not so much as a tingle left to remind you."

She lifted an eyebrow. "Are we sure about that?"

He laughed at her skeptical tone. "Very sure. This particular physiological process doesn't require your active cooperation."

"Good thing for me, since I obviously have a cement head when it comes to this stuff."

"A strong mind," he corrected, "not a hard head. It was just the wrong place tonight, the wrong script. First time in a car. First time with that whole blood thing. You were maybe a little too —"

"Self-conscious?"

"Yeah."

"You're probably right. But right now, I need to be *un*conscious. Can you show me where I'm sleeping?"

Ten minutes later, after having settled Sam in the guest bedroom, Aiden retired to his own bedroom. With the impending dawn tugging at him, he stepped under the sharp, hot spray of his shower. After a hunt, he usually had to scrub his skin to within an inch of excoriating it. Tonight, however, he didn't feel the need.

Maybe because that bastard he'd dispatched to hell was a sexual sadist who preyed on teenage kids.

Or maybe he was just too tired to angst about it.

Or maybe Sam washed you clean by accepting you, by giving up her blood.

He snorted. Clearly, the winner was "too tired".

Except when he crawled between his fifteen-hundred-dollar Egyptian cotton sheets to wait for sleep to claim him, his mind was anything but quiet. It kept slipping back to making love with Sam. What a terrifying thrill, not knowing what his partner wanted, right down to how much pressure she wanted when he touched her *right there*. Horror of horrors, he'd almost come before she had! And he'd been powerless to send her over the edge by feeding her erotic images, or even ramping up the wattage so she could experience his sensations intensely enough that his orgasm became hers.

Yes, they'd get there eventually; he was sure of it. She just had to open that Fort Knox of a head of hers. But pray God, not too fast.

"Aiden, wake up."

Sam stood beside Aiden's bed, watching him sleep. When he didn't respond, she bent to poke him on the shoulder, then shrieked when his hand snaked out to capture her arm. A tug and she landed atop him, his hands breaking her fall.

"Aiden!"

He nuzzled her neck. "Mmmmm. How did you know I was dreaming about you?"

"Aiden, we have to get up."

He found her earlobe and bit gently, sending an involuntary shudder through her. "I *am* up."

She dug her fingers into his ribs. "No, we need to get *up* up. We have to get back to Sioux City. I had a dream. We have to get back right away."

His hands stilled on her back. "Tonight?"

"Yes. Or rather, this morning. About 3:00 am, in the West side. West 14th Street, specifically. A house with a wooden balcony on the front with two rails missing and a window box with dead flowers in it on the ground floor."

"Sorry, Sam. That's more than we can do."

Sam blinked and sat up. More than they could do? "But the location ... Aiden, it's sure to be a vampire attack."

"Agreed, but we're not scheduled to fly until 12:30, and we're looking at what, three hours air time? Oh, yeah. Three hours at least. I don't think it's feasible for Geoffrey to file a new flight plan at this point to get us there in time."

She leapt up. "But someone will *die* if we don't get there."

"Probably. But that may be beyond our control."

He pulled himself up to a sitting position. Despite her anxiety, Sam couldn't help but notice the rippling play of muscles in his flat abdomen.

"Remember, Sam, before I found you, a bastard like this would probably have racked up dozens of victims in a town the size of Sioux City before I found him. This is a vast improvement."

"No." She shook her head. "No, that's not good enough! We have to do something."

"I could get Geoffrey working on it, but Sam, honey, I don't think it's very likely."

"Then we need a Plan B." She paced the room. "Maybe someone else can get there sooner. Edgar!" She wheeled in time to see him hauling his jeans on. Her gaze caught on his bare feet and stuck there. She dragged her gaze up to his face. "You could call Edgar and get him to do something."

"Edgar is a cab driver, Sam, not a hunter. I couldn't send him into a situation like that."

"He could take some friends, couldn't he?"

"He could. And that would probably save the life of the unfortunate victim the rogue would have attacked tonight on West 14th. But once he sensed the presence of other vampires, he'd just drift on to another hunting ground ten minutes away, another victim. In Riverside, maybe. A victim who'll be put in his path not by fate, but by our intervention."

"Oh, God. That would be worse."

"Yes."

She sank down on the corner of the bed. "I hate this. I don't want this to be my life."

He sat down beside her. "I know, baby. I know. It sucks." He put his arm around her and pulled her to him.

The urge to put her head on his shoulder and weep was almost overwhelming, but she resisted. She didn't deserve to be comforted. She didn't want to be kissed or caressed or aroused, knowing an innocent victim would die and they were helpless to stop it.

"I have an idea," he said.

She snorted. "I'll bet."

He laughed. "Not that kind of idea. About our rogue back in Sewer City."

"Really?" For that, she'd overlook the slur against her adopted hometown. "What are you thinking?"

"There's another hunter who's sometimes in the area. If I can reach him, and depending on where his last hunt took him, he may be close enough to get there in time."

Relief stung the backs of her eyes. "Really?"

"I can't promise anything. He might be within driving distance or he might be further away than we are."

She blinked quickly. "But you'll ask him?"

"I will. Though how the hell I'll explain how we know where the attack will take place is another kettle of fish."

"Thank you!"

"Don't thank me yet." He reached for his cell phone, paged through his contact numbers until he found the right one, then dialed. "RJ, it's Aiden. How the hell are you?"

Feeling she should give him space to have this conversation, Sam got up and moved a few paces away. Standing beside the dresser, she studied the car keys, coins, bits of paper and other detritus he'd emptied from his pockets last night. Her attention, however, was focused on Aiden's end of the telephone conversation.

"Better than I deserve to be." A guy-to-guy laugh. "So, *where* the hell are you? Excellent. Listen, RJ, can you do an old long-tooth a favor?"

Sam turned to watch Aiden's face as he talked.

"Yeah, I'd definitely owe you one." He lifted his gaze to meet Sam's, his expression clearly saying Sam would owe *him* one after this. That was okay with her.

"I need you to take a drive into Sioux City tonight. West side. West 14th Street, to be specific. I have information that there'll be a rogue hunting there, around 2:30 or 3:00 this morning, and I'd like *you* to be hunting *him*."

Aiden fell silent a moment, but Sam could hear the tinny sound of laughter, followed by the other man's voice over Aiden's hand-held. Aiden angled another pointed look at her.

Yep. She was gonna owe him big time.

"Just humor me, okay? The tip is solid." Another break while the other vamp talked. "Dude, I'm handing you the easiest hunt you'll ever have. It'll be like shooting fish in a barrel." A pause. "But I'm *not* wrong." Another pause. "Okay, okay, if I'm wrong — which I can categorically assure you I'm not — you can razz me about it for the rest of our unnatural lives. Isn't that worth a little inconvenience?"

Aiden beckoned with his free hand and she went back to sit on the bed beside him.

"Great." He put his arm around her. "Now, don't hang up and blow this off, RJ. If you do, I'll have to hunt you down."

Sitting this close, Sam heard the other vampire's reply: "In your dreams, Afflack."

Aiden laughed. "Catch you later, RJ." He flipped his cell phone closed and looked at Sam. "Happy?"

"Very," she said, meaning it. She put a hand on his thigh. God, she'd made love with this man and still didn't know what he looked like naked. They could remedy that here and now ... She batted her eyelashes. "How evah can I thank you?"

He grinned that wicked, sex-drenched grin. "That depends. How ... *grateful* are you?"

Her stomach did a little flip. "Very, very grateful."

"*Anything-I-want* grateful?"

Her stomach did a series of rapid summersaults. "Pretty much."

"Then get dressed, baby." He stood, pulling her to her feet. "We're going clubbing."

What the hell? "Clubbing?"

"You said anything I wanted."

"But I thought —"

"Yes, but I couldn't possibly take advantage of your gratitude. I mean, what kind of a guy would that make me?"

"Gee, I don't know. *Normal*?"

He laughed. "Don't pout. Just go make yourself pretty."

"But what about our flight? We don't have time to clubbing."

"Sure we do. Just one of the advantages of private jet travel. As long as we're at the airport half an hour before takeoff, we'll have time to spare. Now, go get ready. You won't be sorry."

Chapter 11

THIRTY MINUTES LATER, they pulled up outside a nightclub. A trendy one, judging by the lineup of people waiting for admission. Aiden double-parked the Escalade, then got out and came around the vehicle to help Sam out.

"You can't mean to leave the car here," she protested. "The cops will have it towed away and we'll never make our flight."

"I'll deal with it in a minute, once I get you inside."

Her pulse leapt. Inside? By herself? "It's okay. We can park the car and I'll walk back with you."

He lifted an eyebrow. "Afraid you'll be swarmed by men if you go in there alone?"

She snorted. "No. I'm afraid I'll die of terminal uncoolness if I go in there alone. Look at me." She gestured to her jeans, tank top and tailored blazer. "I didn't exactly pack to party."

"You look great. Trust me."

Yeah, right.

He was similarly dressed in jeans and t-shirt, topped with a leather jacket, but that's where the similarity ended. He positively glowed with vitality and emanated more sex appeal than Eddie Vedder and Daniel Craig rolled together with a dash of Johnny Depp. Next to him, she looked like ... well, just what she was. A perfectly ordinary woman, albeit with pretty good hair.

Of course, it was a moot point anyway. Given the lineup, two people wide and stretching for half a block, there was no way they were getting in, singly or together. So she let him bear her along. But when they got to the back of the line, it miraculously parted. Dressed in their club clothes and chattering boisterously, the would-be patrons stepped back without a word from Aiden and without a single complaint. To Sam's disbelief, the crowd continued to part to allow them passage, then closed behind them. In under thirty seconds, they stood before the bouncer who guarded the door. Vampire mind trick. Had to be.

"Aiden! Great to have you back again," the big man boomed.

"Great to be back. Dave, this is Sam. Sam, Dave." To Sam he said, "Go on in. I'll be along after I've parked the car."

With no alternative, Sam forced a smile. "Thanks. See you in a minute."

The inside of the club was packed, and the air throbbed with a Latin-flavored number. How bad could this experience be, with Latin music?

She spied a table on the upper level that appeared to be empty. It also had the advantage, she suspected, of providing a good view of the entrance so she could spot Aiden when he came in. As she made her way through the crowd, every other man seemed to stop his conversation to turn her way. Several of them made eye contact and smiled at her. She returned the smiles politely but pressed on, feeling their eyes following her. Curious, appreciative, interested eyes. Yikes! What the hell was that about? She was accustomed to drawing a certain amount of male attention, but nothing like this. And certainly not when she was dressed like this. Maybe Aiden owned the place, and had somehow marked her as his guest?

As soon as she sat down, a waiter materialized. She ordered a Grey Goose martini, and the moment the waiter left, she trained her gaze on the entrance, praying for a glimpse of Aiden over the heads of the dancers. The very *young* dancers. She scanned the crowd of halter-topped, midriff-bearing, smooth-skinned women, wondering how many of them were legal.

God, how long had it been since she'd been to a club like this? A loooong time. Hell, she'd probably been about as old as those girls out there on the floor. *Come on, Aiden, before someone recognizes me for the 27-year old fossil that I am and throws me out.*

"May I join you?"

So focused was she on watching for Aiden, Sam almost leapt out of skin when the stranger spoke so close to her ear.

"Oh!" Hand to her chest to slow her pounding heart, she turned to the man who stood beside her table. And oh, double yikes! He was gorgeous. Latino. Hair black as night, dark eyes that burned with amazing intensity in a lean, devastatingly handsome face. "I'm sorry. You startled me."

"Forgive me." His smile flashed whitely. "Perhaps I could make it up to you by buying you a drink?"

Ack! He was looking at her with altogether too much interest, and despite herself, something inside responded in a way it had no business responding. "That's very kind of you, but I'm waiting for someone."

"Of course. I should have known." His gaze held more than a tinge of regret, and his smile was dazzling. "If you should change your mind, I'll be here."

What did a sophisticated woman who was used to being hit on by a Hollywood-worthy heartthrob say to that? Since she had no idea, she inclined her head in what she hoped was a gracious fashion and said, "Thank you. I'm flattered."

The stranger slipped away, and Sam's heart rate finally began to slow.

"How did that feel?"

Aiden! Her pulse took another leap. Dammit, she hadn't seen him come in. She cleared her throat. "How did what feel? Running the gauntlet of nubile young girls whilst wearing the staidest, most conservative outfit this club will ever see?"

He grinned, taking a seat beside her. "No, being hit on by the highest ranking vampire in the joint within two minutes of arrival."

Holy shit! "He was a *vampire*?"

A raised eyebrow. "You didn't know?"

"No, but now that you mention it, I should have." And dammit, she really should have. That knowing look in his eye, that totally self-assured carriage that whispered to her hormones: *Come away with me; I'll make sure you don't regret it.* "I think I was a little rattled by the fact that I'm every bit as poorly dressed for this club as I feared."

"Ah, but I'm betting you turned a few heads nevertheless."

She blinked. "How did you know — oh, God! They're all vampires, aren't they? This is a vampire club."

The waiter arrived with her drink just then. If he overheard her comment, it didn't phase him in the slightest.

Aiden peeled a fifty from his wallet and handed it to the waiter. "I'll have one of those, too." When the waiter left, Aiden turned his attention back to Sam. "No, this isn't a vampire club. It's a club that happens to be frequented by vampires, among other clientele."

"There's a difference?"

"God, yes. Vampire clubs are places where Goth kids and vampire posers hang out. And yes, the mental cases who drink — God help them, actually *drink!* — human blood."

"So those guys that eyed me are vampires?"

"I'm sure some non-vamps eyed you, too, but yes, I suspect they were mostly vampires."

"But why on earth would they look at me? Especially dressed like this. Especially when those girls are dressed like *that*. I mean, look at them."

He did look, dammit. And one particularly rack-taculous young woman in a skimpy halter dress looked right back.

"Yes, they are very attractive and nubile, but you'll remember what I told you about young women."

She frowned. About young women? Then it dawned. Their diets. Junk in, junk out. "Omigod. I *smell* better than they do?"

"Bingo."

"Gah!" She picked up her drink and threw back a healthy swig. "You let me come in here alone, knowing I'd get this reaction?"

"I didn't think you'd believe me without empirical evidence. And frankly, I can't blame you after my spectacular failure to deliver the experience I promised earlier."

She felt a flush burn her cheeks. "It wasn't your fault. I'm sorry if I put you on the defensive."

"You had every right. You thought you'd been conned." His drink arrived and he waved away the change proffered by the waiter. "Now, can we dance? I'd hate to waste this opportunity to make every vampire in the house green with envy, thereby enhancing my status."

She rolled her eyes. "Little do they know I'm the vampire world's lousiest lay."

"Are you kidding?" He laughed. "Baby, if Rey Sanchez knew what I know, he wouldn't have given up so easily. I'd have had to face off with him for the privilege of leaving with you."

"Yeah, right."

He reached across the table to capture her hand. "We're going to have to do something about that."

"About what?"

"Your sexual self-image."

"My sexual self-image is just fine, thank you."

"In the regular world, maybe. Come on. Let's dance." He came to his feet and pulled her to hers.

"This is so strange. I never would have pegged you as a dancer."

"Ah, but I came of age in an era when being able to dance was a critical social skill."

She grinned. "Does this mean we're going to dance a Quadrille to this RadioKillaZ's number?"

"Uh, that would be difficult, since a Quadrille requires four couples."

"Whoops." Her smile broadened. "It's the only historical dance name I know."

"That's enough out of you, young lady. I'll have you know I'm completely current."

Somehow she didn't doubt it.

He led her back downstairs to the dance floor. For the next fifteen minutes, she surrendered to the pleasure of dancing with him, relying on his strength and skill to compensate when her rustiness showed. To her delight, he taught her a Harlem shuffle, which he insisted he'd learned during the Harlem Renaissance of the 20s, not the dance craze of the 80s. The music grew increasingly sensual with every number, as did the interactions of the couples around them on the dance floor. Feeling the music throbbing in all the hollow spaces of her body, Sam surrendered to it, and to Aiden. When he pulled her backside to him to end the latest bump-and-grind number, suddenly dirty dancing was no longer enough. It was all she could do not to turn in his arms and tear his shirt open.

She twisted so she could look up at his face. "Can we get out of here?"

His hand tightened on her hip. "I thought you'd never ask."

Outside, the night air did nothing to cool her desire. If anything, it fed the wild need that had been growing inside her since he'd taken her hand and led her onto the dance floor. His hand was at the small of her back now as he guided her past the long line of people still waiting to get into the club. As soon as they were clear of the queue, he pulled her into the mouth of an alley and kissed her. She laid the flat of her hand on his chest and pushed him up against the stuccoed wall. Or rather, he allowed himself to be pushed, which she found totally hot. He could probably stand his ground against a Category 5 hurricane, but he was letting her take charge. She kissed him, letting her hands roam his body as she pressed him against the wall.

More. She needed more.

Going up on her tiptoes, she rubbed her breasts against him. He groaned and closed his hands on her buttocks, urging her belly into contact with the unmistakable bulge of his erection.

She pulled back, breathing hard. "Where's the car."

"Not the car. Not this time."

She looked around. Intoxicated as she was by her own need, she retained enough sense to know the alley was too public. "Then where?"

"Up. Hold on."

Up? "What do you mean, up?"

"The roof. I've already scoped it out." He lifted her off her feet and her legs automatically went around his waist, her arms tightening around his neck. "I recommend you close your eyes for this part, especially if you're afraid of heights."

She didn't even have a chance to squeak her fear before she felt him bend at the knees, gather himself and leap upward. They landed with a bit of a jolt on the roof of the building in whose shadows they'd just been necking. She tightened her chokehold around his neck.

"Oh, shit! You just jumped a full story, with a passenger on board."

"Impressed?"

"Completely freaked out," she said, but omigod, she *was* impressed. If she got any more impressed, she might come on the spot. She glanced around at the graveled roof and at the traffic — vehicle and pedestrian — passing so close below. "Are we there yet?"

"Depends on how much of an exhibitionist you are. Personally, I'm thinking we don't need the distraction."

"Onward and upward, then. And this time, I *will* close my eyes."

Four jumps later, he lowered her to her feet. "We're here."

She clung to him for a few seconds to let the vertigo pass, then pushed away to get her bearings. They stood on the roof of a building half a block east of the alley where they'd started. And their roof was higher than most of the neighboring roofs, and those that towered higher were clearly office buildings. They could strip off their clothes and make love here, right out in the open. The thought brought a fresh surge of dampness between her thighs.

"So what do you think? Will it do?"

"It's perfect," she said.

In the moonlight, she saw the flash of his teeth and grinned back at him. The roof was flat and featureless, save for what looked like an air conditioning unit squatting in the center and a concrete block that served as a foundation for a tower with satellite dishes mounted on it. The locale could only be considered "perfect" by two people who wanted to get busy.

Well, no point playing demure. She shrugged out of her jacket, then grabbed the hem of her tank top and pulled it off over her head. He stripped quickly, too. When they were both naked, he pulled her close.

"Ah, Sam. I want to make it good for you this time. Tell me what you want. Anything. Whatever you want, I can give it to you."

Another surge of warm wetness between her thighs. Did she dare say what she really wanted?

"Come on, baby. Tell me. It doesn't have to be politically correct. This is a sexual fantasy I'm offering. I won't judge. And I can safely promise you I won't be shocked."

Holy smokes. "Are you *sure* you can't read my mind?"

He laughed. "Just an educated guess."

"Okay." She licked her lips. "I want to be ravished." There. She'd said it.

"Ravished?"

"You've just abducted me, spirited me to this lonely location where you can impose your will on me. You could take me any way you want." She raked her nails across his bare shoulder. "You could fuck me until I come and then make me come again."

He pulled away, and for a few stunned seconds, she thought she'd shocked or offended him, but he was only removing his leather jacket. He dropped it at her feet.

"On your knees," he commanded, looking every inch a dangerous stranger. "I want you to suck my cock."

Sam almost came. Limbs shaking, she did as he bade, finding herself at eye level with his jutting erection. He slid the fingers of one hand into her hair, using his other hand to guide his cock to her mouth. She took over from there, closing her fingers around his shaft and taking the engorged tip into her mouth.

His taste exploded on her tongue, salty and musky, and his scent filled her nostrils. For long moments she worked his cock, which grew harder under her ministrations. He gripped her head with both hands now, reinforcing the fact that he was in control, which only increased her own clawing need. All the while, the cool night breeze swirled around her, stiffening her nipples and reminding her of her nakedness and vulnerability. Even the bite of the rubberized roofing material through the thin cushion of his coat excited her beyond reason.

"Enough," he said, after a few moments, pulling her to her feet.

Chapter 12

SHE STOOD IN front of him, trembling, her breasts gleaming in the moonlight, and he wanted nothing more than to pull her to him and kiss the mouth that had pleasured him so avidly. He wanted a firm bed, soft lights and about six uninterrupted hours to touch and taste and memorize every inch of her skin. But that wasn't her fantasy. At least, not right now.

Right now, she wanted to live out the fantasy of being sexually dominated.

He'd been inside enough female minds to know there was a difference between entertaining that kind of fantasy and actually living it out. With the fantasy, Sam would be in *complete control* even as she allowed herself to imagine having *no control*. In reality, she'd have to relinquish that control to have the fantasy. Under normal circumstances, this kind of thing would be a walk in the park. But with Sam, he was flying blind. He could hardly keep asking, 'Is this okay?' when the point of the fantasy was to impose his will regardless of whether or not it was okay.

"Aiden?"

"You realize there's no way you can escape this roof without my help?"

She shuddered. In a good way, he hoped. "Yes."

"If you fight me, no one will come to your rescue," he said flatly. "Even if they did, they couldn't possibly stop me. I can do whatever I want with you. To you."

She wet her lips. "I know."

He led her to the concrete block that anchored the communications tower and backed her into position against the waist-high structure. "Support yourself with your hands," he instructed. When she complied, he added, "Now spread your legs for me."

She adjusted her stance and he stepped close. Her lips were parted now, and her chest rose and fell on short, ragged breaths. He started to lean in to capture her trembling lips, then caught himself. *No kissing, Afflack. Not part of the fantasy.* Instead, he closed his hand on her sex, dragging a moan out of her. Smiling, he parted her folds and began stroking her tender inner flesh. She jerked against his hand and cried out.

"Don't move," he ordered sharply. "And don't come yet. I want to have my mouth on you when you come the first time."

Then do it, dammit!

Her thought slammed into his brain with all the subtlety of a baseball bat, and he laughed. Looked like she could make herself plain if she really wanted to. Which made his job easier.

He knelt before her, urging her legs further apart. Parting the lips of her sex again, he let her feel the heat of his breath as he inhaled the scent of her arousal. Again, she shuddered. Smiling, he leaned in and stroked her with the flat of his tongue. She made a strangled noise that sent a jolt straight to his rock-hard cock. Instead of teasing her as he'd planned, he closed his mouth on her and suckled her clitoris. She gave a muted shout and came. He thrust two fingers into her wet heat and pumped, tonguing her as she rode out the orgasm. Only when she sagged back against the wall did he let up.

He climbed to his feet, his own breath ragged now. "Turn around." His hands urged her to face the wall. "I'm going to fuck you now while your muscles are still clenched from coming." She pushed her breath out on a moan of what he took for approval. "Keep your hands on the wall." At the same time, with his hands on her hips, he urged her feet away from the wall, obliging her to bend at the waist and present her ass to him. And oh, God, she was beautiful. He wanted to tell her that, but again, not part of tonight's program.

Cock in hand, he stepped close and rubbed the head of it against her drenched sex. She arched her back, giving him better access. Gritting his teeth, he bent his knees slightly and pushed into the scalding, impossibly tight clasp of her vagina. She sobbed but thrust back against him. He stood stock still for a few seconds, fighting down his excitement. Then he closed both hands on her hips and started moving, carefully at first to make sure the penetration wasn't too deep or the thrusting too aggressive. When it became obvious she was more than ready to handle him, he picked up the pace, pulling out further, thrusting deeper. Thank God it was too dark to see well. Just thinking about what it would look like, his cock, glistening from her juices, pumping in and out of her, the shape of her beautiful ass, the graceful arch of her neck as he prepared to sink his teeth into it . . .

Dammit. Think about something else, Afflack.

Except Sam's breathing had taken on a ragged edge again, and he found himself wishing for that soft bed and a mirror so he could see her flushed face as she panted open-mouthed, watch her breasts swing and bob as he fucked her from behind.

Think about something else!

Too late. His fangs erupted. He couldn't hold it off much longer. Just like last time. Dammit, how could that be? Without the extra stimulation of her sensations, he shouldn't have these control issues.

He straightened his knees a little, changing the angle of entry. Maybe if he shallowed up, he might last a little longer.

"Omigod, omigod, omigod, omigod, omigod!"

Ah, g-spot. He pumped harder, faster, careful to preserve the angle.

"Yes, right there! Right *there*! Don't stop."

Within seconds, she started to come. And come and come. He felt her vaginal muscles contracting around him in wave after wave. As the last pulses died, he wrapped his arms around her and pulled her upright. She let her head loll on his shoulder. With his mouth pressed to her ear he said, "I'm going to finish with my teeth buried in you almost as deep as my cock."

He felt her pulse take a wild leap. Fear or excitement? Both? He'd know in a minute, provided he could break through.

Tangling one hand in her hair, he urged her head back further to expose the slender column of her throat, delicate as a flower stem. A hard shiver wracked her, but she turned her torso slightly and angled her neck, affording him the best possible access. This time, he didn't nuzzle his way in. With his own orgasm so close, he leaned in and sank his teeth into her flesh, finding the carotid artery unerringly.

Her pounding heart pushed the first exquisite pulses of blood into his venous system, and he felt his cock swell. She gasped and arched her back, clearly feeling it, too. Closing his eyes, he felt for her thoughts, but all he got back was a kind of white noise humming in his head.

He nudged again. *Come on, baby, let me in.*

She stiffened in his arms, so he knew she heard him.

Having taken as much blood as he dared after having fed from her last night, and certainly more than enough to forge a connection, he started to ease his fangs out.

It'll be good, Sam, I promise. Don't you want to feel what you're doing to me? Feel how close I am to exploding? Without missing a beat, he began secreting the healing agent. Her wounds had to be closed before he could resume thrusting, but it was all he could do to restrain himself. *You could go over the edge with me, feel what it's like for me to pump my cock into you until I ejaculate as deep inside you as I can get.*

Yes!

Then let me in.

He pushed forward again, and this time managed to slip in. He felt her heart thudding crazily, her breathlessness, her excitement. He felt the sensation of her delicate inner tissues stretched by the invasion of his cock. Ah, there! She felt him! She felt how desperately he needed to move inside her again, plunging, thrusting, fucking. She felt ... panic?

Dammit, he'd lost her. Or rather, she'd pushed him out.

He would have tried to re-establish the connection, but she leaned forward again, grasping the concrete apron for support and thrusting her sweet ass against him. Basic instinct took over. He grasped her hips and surged into her perhaps a dozen times, then came hard enough to damn near blow the top off his head.

"You've gone awfully quiet."

Sam glanced across the aisle of the jet's cabin to where Aiden lounged in a leather chair. "I'm just tired, I guess."

"Tired or not, we should talk."

"Aiden, I've done nothing but talk all night." And she had. She'd filled the space between them with laughter, chatter, anything to keep her mind hers, and his his. That whole mind-touching-mind thing had scared the crap out of her.

He slanted her a look. "I noticed. But we haven't talked about what happened."

She angled a narrow-eyed look right back at him. "I believe I already thanked you for the most mind-blowing fantasy sex of my life. What more would you have me do? Pin a medal on your chest? Write an ode to your prowess?"

Incredibly, he flushed. "Thank you for the offer, but no. I doubt you could write me a paean I haven't already heard."

"Exactly!"

He pulled out of his slouch. "What does that mean?"

What *did* she mean? Shit. "Nothing. Forget about it."

He sighed. "Sam, I've been doing this gig for damned near 190 years now. It has few enough perks, and I've generally taken advantage of them when they come along. I never pretended otherwise."

She waved a hand. "You're right. I knew it upfront, and I know it now. It's not a problem."

"If it makes any difference, while I'm with you, there'll be no one else. As long as you'll help me hunt these rogues, and as long as you'll have me in your bed, I have no need of anything more."

Her head shot up. He was offering *monogamy* for the duration of their relationship? "Wow, I guess you must be thinking our partnership will be short-lived."

"Ah." He leaned back in his chair again, smiling. "You doubt my ability to be faithful?"

"Frankly, yes. You don't exactly exude that quality."

"Okay, so I haven't had much practice at the fidelity thing. Or *any* practice," he allowed. "But to be fair, my lifestyle to date doesn't exactly lend itself to cultivating those kinds of relationships. I'm never in the same place more than a few days, and until you, I've always traveled alone. Well, except for Geoffrey, and he doesn't count."

She smiled, but her mind was racing onward. "What about when I go away for a daytime shoot? My work could carry me anywhere in the world. I could be gone for *days*."

"Wow, you really think I'd have a problem going without sex for a few measly days?" He looked genuinely offended. "Thanks for the vote of confidence."

She blushed. "I'm sorry. But you can't take sustenance — not even from a bagged unit of blood — without getting aroused. What am I supposed to think?"

"I don't know, maybe that I'd exercise a little self-control? God, Sam, what do you think I've been doing for these past weeks?"

"What about when I went to Fort Meyers? You told me yourself that you went out to take care of your needs while I was gone."

"Yes, to hook up with the local blood vendor."

"Then you didn't ..."

"I didn't."

"So you haven't ... since you moved in with me, you haven't ..."

"Since I tracked you down in Sioux City and broke into your house, actually."

"But that's —"

"Yes. Whole *weeks* without sex."

She smiled. "Okay, I guess I'll have to give you a little more credit."

He inclined his head. "Thank you. Now what about you?"

Huh? "What *about* me?"

"Do I have your assurance of fidelity?"

Her jaw dropped. "You think I'd sleep with someone else while you and I were ... while we ... Jesus, Aiden."

"Are you telling me you felt nothing when Rey Sanchez approached you in that club tonight?"

Whoops! How did he know that? "I ... noticed him," she allowed.

He laughed. "It's okay, Sam. Your reaction was perfectly normal. But bear in mind, he wasn't trying very hard. He'd have waited to size up the competition before deciding whether or not to make a serious move. And believe you me, he would not have held back on any of his *vampire tricks*, as you call them. And the compulsion he planted in your head would not have been for an ice-cold Orange Crush."

Oh, Christmas! Thank God she hadn't had to deal with that. For Aiden's benefit, she shrugged. "I appreciate the warning. But that scenario isn't likely to arise again, is it?"

It was his turn to shrug. "What about when you travel for your day shoots? Once your eyes have been opened to the presence of vampires, you'll see them more readily. And they will see you."

"And smell me, too, apparently," she groused.

He smiled. "That, too."

"Okay, I promise to resist the amorous advances of all comers, vampire and otherwise."

"Thank you. Now, can we talk about it?"

She blinked. "We've talked about the sex. We've talked about the ground rules for our ... liaison. What else is there to say?"

"Back there on the roof, when I touched your mind, you panicked and pushed me out. Which, by the way, takes some doing. What was that about?"

Oh, yeah. *That.* She looked at the cabin floor. "I don't know. It just freaked me out a little bit."

"Freaked you out how? I know you were in my mind for just a few seconds. I felt you feeling what I felt. Didn't you like it?"

She blushed again, fiercely. "I don't know." God, could she say that one more time? "I mean, it's sort of like when you're twelve years old and the boy you went to the movies with and thought you were crazy about up and Frenches you with no warning, and you've never had someone else's tongue in your mouth before."

Aiden threw back his head and laughed. Not a little chuckle, either. A serious belly laugh.

Sam found herself trying to suppress a smile. "You think that's funny, do you?"

"God, yes." He wiped tears from his eyes. "Priceless."

"Okay, here's what I don't get — how can I be the only woman in the world to find the experience so strange? I know lots of girls who were freaked out by touching tongues with someone for the first time. How can touching minds be that different?"

"It probably isn't that different. Probably most people are a little freaked the first time, but unlike you, they probably wouldn't have the strength of mind to stop it."

"But you've never actually encountered it before?"

"Never. Of course, I've never seduced a virgin before."

She snorted. "Virgin? Me?"

"Vampire virgin," he clarified. "But in case you're wondering, I've never seduced the other kind, either."

"Good to know."

"Also good to know that there's every reason to believe you'll get used to the mind thing just like you did the French kiss thing."

Could she really get used to that? Could she lower her defenses enough to let him in for more than a few seconds? Did she even want to try? Of course, these were the same questions she'd asked herself after Yves Mourant had slipped her the tongue. "Maybe."

"Okay, talk time over." He patted the empty seat beside him. "Now, come on over and join me. All this talk about Frenching, I'm feeling inspired."

She bit down on a laugh. "I am *not* going to have sex with you on this plane with Geoffrey on the other side of that cockpit door."

"Who said anything about sex? I just want to kiss that pretty mouth of yours. Besides, it'll give you a chance to see me exercise that restraint I was talking about."

He opened his arms and damned if she could think of a reason not to go into them.

Chapter 13

SAM WOKE IN her own bed to the smell of something amazing cooking. She glanced at her clock radio. Almost 11:00 pm. Wow, she'd slept late.

Of course, she'd stayed up long after Aiden had retired. She'd been too wired to sleep, for a couple of reasons.

First, she'd actually slept on the plane, in Aiden's arms as they reclined in the big leather chair. After kissing her into a state of achingly sweet arousal, he'd soothed her back down, and she'd fallen asleep with her head resting on his chest.

Secondly, once they got back home, the memory of what had happened on that roof back in Boston kept playing in her head on an endless loop. She'd wound up checking email, returning calls, catching up on some financial stuff, and even doing a little housework. Anything to keep her mind occupied.

Finally, around mid-afternoon, she'd succumbed to the need for sleep, only to have her sleep disturbed almost immediately by a vision. Of course, she'd gotten up to jot down the details, then struggled for the next hour to get back to sleep. Even now, she felt like she could use a few more hours. Her stomach, however, declared it was time to get up and investigate those smells.

Ten minutes later, freshly showered, she walked into her kitchen to find Aiden setting the table.

"Hey, look who's finally awake."

"I didn't sleep all that well." She glanced around. Ah, good. He'd made a salad. "What's in the oven?"

"Stuffed pork chop, with a nice side of roasted Campari tomatoes and roasted onions."

"Oh, yum. I could get used to this having dinner for breakfast."

He made a face. "Breakfast is boring. Besides, what could I make you for breakfast that I could stuff with Pecorino, pine nuts, garlic and capers?"

She nabbed a piece of raw onion from the salad. "What's Pecarino?"

"A cheese made from sheep's milk. It's Italian. You'll like it." He caught her hand and pulled her to him. "*I'll* like it."

She blushed. "Well, that's the main thing, isn't it?"

"Baby, you can have Pop Tarts washed down with diet cola and I'd still want you."

She snorted. "You silver-tongued devil, you."

"Mmmmm, *tongue.*"

He caught her head and kissed her, and her laughter dissolved. God, she wanted him again. And he was all hers, at least for now.

When he released her a few minutes later, they both breathed a little harder.

"Okay, you'd better feed me," she said as she pulled away. "I have a feeling I'm going to need the sustenance."

"My pleasure."

As she ate, he sipped at a glass of scotch.

"Have you heard from your friend RJ?" she asked. "Did he get the vamp?"

"Yep. And now he's driving himself crazy trying to figure out how I knew where that rogue would be."

She paused with the fork half way to her mouth. "You didn't tell him, did you?"

"Of course not. But he was impressed enough to agree to go anywhere I had a hunch he might be needed."

"That's good, right? We can be twice as effective."

He angled his head. "Maybe not *twice* as effective. You'd have to have twice the visions. But it will take some pressure off you and me. And in time, maybe we can recruit a few more hunters so we can really cover the continent."

"Speaking of visions, I had another one."

"Yeah? So where are we off to?"

"Actually, it's right here, very close to the last one." She paused to eat a roasted tomato. Mmmm, delicious. She speared a tiny onion. "Which is why I asked if your friend RJ carried through last night. I admit, my first thought was to wonder if he'd blown off your request."

"No." Aiden shook his head emphatically. "He was telling the truth. No way he'd give me credit for an assist if he hadn't made the kill. But two rogues in two nights, hunting *here*? I gotta say, this is strange."

"Why is it strange? I can think of several areas of the city that would be prime hunting grounds."

"Sure," he agreed. "All cities have them. But Sioux City has never been much of a hotbed for vampires, good or bad."

"What?" Half offended. "Not enough culture for you?"

He laughed. "There's that. But no, that's not the reason."

"Then what?" Another bite of the pork chop.

"Our olfactory senses are very keen. The stockyards, the rendering plants … it's not good."

"Omigod." She finished chewing her forkful of pork, swallowed and washed it down with a sip of wine. "The smell thing again?"

"Hey, vampires want quality of life, too, you know. We also don't much like hanging around in close proximity to petrochemical plants or pulp-and-paper mills." He drained his whiskey and put the glass down on the table. "Speaking of which, why do *you* choose to live here?"

Good question. It's not as though her roots here were particularly deep. Why hadn't she left it behind? She shrugged. "Too lazy to move, I guess. And one place is as good as another when you're on the road as much as I am."

"I suppose. So, what time do we need to be on deck?"

"Around 2:45."

"Perfect. That gives us lots of time for our next naked experiment."

She choked on her wine. "Naked experiment?"

"I thought we'd try making the connection right up front. If it's successful, you'll be introduced to a whole new world of reasons to stretch out foreplay."

Instantly, her mind filled with images of them on tangled on her bed, castaways clinging together on a sea of sensation. A trembling started deep inside, half desire, half fear.

She blinked, shook the images loose. "I wondered about that," she said. "I mean, why you didn't do it right up front before? It would seem to make more sense. I mean, that you'd want to be guided by knowing what your partner really liked and what she didn't."

"That's the usual approach." He gestured to her clean plate. "Done with that?" When she nodded, he removed the plate to the sink. "However, you weren't the usual candidate."

"Right. The vampire virgin thing."

"Precisely. So my thought was to try to make the connection at the point of highest arousal and presumably, highest receptivity. Like I said, I've never messed with a virgin before, but I'm thinking it would be hard to allow yourself to be bitten. I didn't want to do it cold. But now I'm thinking that might have been a mistake. When we did make a connection, the intensity of feeling may have been *too* high."

Amen to that. "That's probably fair to say."

"So, what do you think? Are you game?"

Tendrils of excitement unfurled in her belly, setting her nerve endings to tingling. "Totally."

"Then lead on." He gestured for her to precede him.

She did, a little self-consciously. And when she got to the bedroom, she wished she'd had the forethought to make the bed, which was seriously rumpled. "Told you I slept restlessly."

He glanced at the bed. "Looks pretty inviting to me. But first, a taste of that lovely neck." He pulled her close, but instead of going directly for her throat, he reached for the buttons on her shirt. One by one, he freed them until her blouse hung open, and then pushed it off her shoulders. She shrugged and let it fall. Then he reached for the snap on her jeans, releasing it and easing the zipper down. He bent to work the jeans down her legs, and she caught him by the shoulders to balance herself, lifting one leg and then the other before kicking the garment away to join her shirt. He stood, pulling her loosely into his arms and splaying a warm hand across her chest.

"You know, when we're this close, I can actually hear the bump of your heart and the whooshing of your blood. It's just about the sexiest sound I've ever heard."

She sucked in a breath and let it out on a shaky sigh.

"Now that … *that* is the sexiest sound ever."

She angled her neck for him, and he skimmed his hand up from her chest, skating his fingers over her exposed throat. Her heart pounded harder, faster. If he couldn't hear it before, he surely should be able to now.

"I won't take much," he said. "Just a taste is all we'll need."

As his head came down, she lowered her lids and grasped the waistband of his jeans. He made a little growling sound, then his teeth were searing their way into her neck, but this time, the pain was indistinguishable from pleasure. Almost immediately, he started to work his way out again. She cupped his head to hold him there, anxious to preserve the wild excitement that suddenly licked along every nerve ending, but he pulled away gradually, sealing her wound as he withdrew.

"Noooo!" she protested. "Not enough."

He laughed. "Sam, honey, that's me you're feeling. That's how hard it is for me to pull back when I feel your blood hit my veins. Can you feel anything else?"

She bit her lip. "*Oh, yeah.* I can feel you need to get out of those jeans." Without waiting for a response, she reached for him, touching him through the worn denim. "Omigod! That's amazing!"

Aiden sucked in a deep breath. *Omigod* was right. Feeling her emotions as she fully experienced his sensations, watching the rapt look on her face ... oh, Christ! Maybe there *was* something to be said for this seducing virgins thing after all.

Damn, he needed to feel her hands on his bare flesh.

No sooner did the thought form than she found his zipper and slid it down. The next second, her hands were on him, warm and soft and exciting.

"Oh, Aiden!"

He smiled. "Amazing, isn't it?"

Her response was to kneel before him, dragging his jeans down his legs. His cock jerked and she looked up at him. The smile she wore on her face was absolutely carnal.

"Ah, I see you like that," she said. "Me on my knees."

"Baby, I like you on your knees, your back, your stomach, your side ..."

She squeezed his shaft. "On your cock?"

"God, yes!"

She guided the head of his cock into her mouth, and he felt the savage thrill rip through him, then rock her. She moaned in response, then again when she felt what the vibrations did to him. For the next minutes, she experimented, taking him deeper, then shallowing up to run her tongue around his sensitive glans, cupping his balls delicately in her soft hand, fisting his shaft. He opened his mind, letting her feel every nuance, including the pleasure he took in her own awed response.

Eventually, when his arousal threatened to peak, he stopped her and drew her to her feet. "As good as that felt, it's going to pale in comparison to how it will feel when I get inside you. That first moment, when I sink in —"

She gave a shriek and reeled away from him as though he'd belted her a good one.

"Jesus, Sam." He extended a steadying hand, but she shrank back. Hell and damnation! He felt for her thoughts, only to find she'd shoved him out and slammed the door again. "What is it? What's the matter?"

"You didn't feel that?"

"Feel what?"

"Oh, God, where's my shirt? I need to get dressed."

She was getting dressed? *Now*? What the hell had she felt?

He tugged the lightweight coverlet off her bed and draped it over her shoulders. She clutched the fabric to her body as a freezing man would welcome a warm cloak.

"Sit down." He urged her down on the edge of the bed and sat beside her. "Now, tell me what happened, Sam."

"I don't really know." She clutched the coverlet tighter. "I was so absorbed by what was happening, feeling all those new sensations, and then, *wham*."

"I get that. But what was the wham? What did you feel? Or did you see something?" Of course. That must be it. "A vision?"

She shook her head. "No. Nothing like that."

Damn. "Then what?"

"I don't know how to explain it. It was just ... yucky."

"Wow. *Yucky.* I think that's a first for me."

She blushed. "No, not *that*. I was totally on board with the sex. This came from ... somewhere else. Or maybe it was just inside me."

"Sam, there is nothing remotely yucky inside you."

That drew a wry smile. "Thank you, Aiden. But I'm just like everyone else, with lots of jumbled up junk and fear and conflicted crap crammed into the old attic."

"If you say so."

"I do. But I really don't think it was my psychological clutter." She chewed the inside of her lip a moment. "Okay, this is as close as I can come to explaining it. Once, when I was eight years old, we were visiting my grandmother, and I went into the field across the road from her house looking for wild strawberries. I was barefoot, and I stepped on a snake."

"And it bit you?"

"No. It was just a little garter snake, and I'm sure it was twice as terrified as I was. It just wriggled and wriggled, trying to get away, while I danced around trying to get off it. I'll never forget that sensation until the day I die."

Jesus. He had a good idea where this was going. He got off the bed, located his pants. "So it felt like ... uh ... stepping on a snake?"

"The mental equivalent. I felt like I brushed up against something ..."

"Repulsive?"

"Yes. In the same way the snake was. Maybe not inherently bad, but it still touched an instinctual, cell-deep fear." She turned big eyes on him. "Does that make sense?"

He pulled his jeans on and bent to scoop up his shirt. "It makes perfect sense. And I know what you touched."

She blinked. "What?"

He bared his teeth in a humorless smile. "My soul."

Chapter 14

SAM LIFTED HER night vision binoculars and scanned the urban landscape. Nothing moving, not even the drunken derelict who'd bunked down ten minutes ago in the recessed doorway of a pawnshop, using his backpack as a pillow and his jacket for a blanket. Clearly he'd passed out already. And if anyone else were stirring, they'd be sure to see it. Aiden had mounted her floodlight on the roof of her SUV, lighting the place up like high noon for anyone with night vision technology.

Unfortunately, the terrain hadn't offered much in terms of a feasible hiding place, so they'd set up shop on the porch of a decrepit house owned by an old man who obviously suffered from a compulsive hoarding disorder. Every horizontal surface was stacked high with newspapers, magazines, books, junk mail, and Lord knew what else. Sam had expressed concern about the baldly criminal act of breaking and entering, but he'd just slanted her a look and asked what was a little B&E compared with what would go down later? He'd assured her that the home's owner wouldn't waken, which he'd ensured by murmuring in the old man's ear, seeding his sleep with dreams of youth and love and sunshine.

Sam lowered the binoculars and her view reverted to what her naked eye could see with the aid of a few streetlights and the light that pooled on the sidewalk outside the pawnshop and, further down the block, a 7-11 that had long-since closed.

Beside her, Aiden sat as still as a stone statue on one of the two folding chairs they'd rescued from beneath a mountain of paper. It was too dark in the shadows of the porch to see his profile, but she could close her eyes and picture the beautiful lines of his face, the grim set of his mouth.

She bit her lip. She wanted to apologize yet again, to assure him that the hideous, buzz-killing *yuck* she'd experienced earlier had nothing to do with him, but he'd already threatened to bind and gag her with her various camera straps and stash her in the back of the SUV if she didn't shut up about it.

Besides, his quietness had nothing to do with that fiasco, in all likelihood. He always grew calm and still just before the shit hit the fan.

On cue, he touched her elbow and gestured. He'd heard something.

She lifted her binoculars and scanned the area. On her second sweep, she saw him. Tall and spare and clothed entirely in black, he moved with the same grace and confidence as Aiden. Vampire. Had to be.

Except he walked right by the pawnshop doorway, barely sparing a glance at the vagrant who slept there. He continued down the sidewalk, and Sam held her breath, waiting for him to slow his pace and double back. When he failed to do that, she turned to Aiden. "What's he doing?" she whispered. "He went right by."

"He's reconnoitering. Now hush. He'll be back."

Damn. No rogue had displayed that much caution before. They'd all been too fixated on their victims to worry about scouting for danger. Or too arrogant in their own power to feel vulnerability.

Thank God there'd been no suitable cover outside! No way would they have escaped his notice sitting in her SUV or huddled in the shadow of a building. And had he detected them, the rogue would no doubt have kept right on walking, in search of safer hunting grounds. Their intervention would have spared this victim at the expense of another. Her stomach lurched sickly. God, she hated this.

She put the binoculars to her eyes again and waited. Sure enough, the rogue reappeared in her sights, but this time, he moved with purpose. The rogue drew even with the pawnshop, took one last look up and down the street, then moved in on his unconscious victim.

Aiden was on the move, too, gliding soundlessly out the door, down the steps of the porch and across the street. Heart thudding in all-too-familiar fear, Sam lifted the binoculars. And oh, God, the rogue had his victim already! On his feet now and caught in a deadly embrace, the man struggled almost silently, his cries muffled by his attacker's hand.

Hang on, she urged silently. *Help is almost there. Just another few seconds ...*

Her hands tightened on the binoculars in anticipation, but just as Aiden would have seized the rogue from behind for the patented neck snap, the rogue dropped his victim and whirled to face Aiden. If they exchanged any words, they were too far away for her to hear them. But they were not far enough away that she couldn't see the gleam of a knife that appeared in the rogue's right hand.

She wanted to burst out the door and shout a warning, but Aiden had made her promise never to reveal herself if a hunt went south. He could handle himself, he'd said. He was trained in martial arts and was battle-hardened from fighting other vampires, whereas the only workout the rogues got was preying on the weak. He'd be fine, so long as she didn't expose herself and saddle him with the handicap of keeping her safe.

But how could he protect himself against cold steel?

Then — oh, thank God — she saw that Aiden held a knife, too.

The two vampires circled each other. In the background, the vagrant, hand to his throat, pressed himself deeper into the recessed doorway. Aiden made the first lunge, his knife cutting a swath through the night, narrowly missing the rogue. Again, he struck, this time striking the rogue's shoulder. With a roar of pain and anger, the rogue struck back, moving so fast Sam could scarcely see the blur. Fortunately, Aiden was just as fast. When they pulled back, the rogue clutched a hand to his side. Aiden must have scored another hit. He was moving in to press his advantage when someone else joined the melee.

Sam's first thought was that it was a civilian intervention. A very brave and very stupid civilian. She wanted to scream at him to get away. But then he attacked Aiden from behind, in a blur of speed.

Inhuman speed.

Dear God, another vampire! And he had a knife, too! He struck once, twice. Aiden reeled away, turning to face the new threat. And then — oh shit oh shit oh shit — a third rogue arrived to stand with the second. Aiden seized the first vampire, the one he'd succeeded in wounding, and held his knife to the man's throat. The other two looked at each other as though weighing their friend's life, then lunged. The first rogue roared in fury as Aiden thrust him in the path of the descending knifes. The rogue fell, grievously wounded, and Aiden danced away. But he didn't dance fast enough. One of the rogue's blades caught him in the abdomen.

When he reeled away, Sam saw he was bleeding from his belly, and at least two places on his back.

Before she could form a conscious thought, she was out the door and rushing across the street. Snatching off her binoculars, she swung them in an arc with all her might, striking the third rogue squarely on the side of the head. He fell to his knees, stunned.

"Get out of here!" Aiden shouted, then closed with the second vampire in a hand-to-hand struggle.

The third vampire was getting to his feet now.

Gun. Aiden had left her a gun.

And oh, shit, she'd left it back on the porch, in her camera bag. She'd never make it back before the beast caught her.

Besides, the second vampire was getting the best of Aiden, who lay on his back on the sidewalk with the point of a knife mere inches from his heart. He might be the better fighter, but he was seriously wounded. He couldn't hold off his opponent, who had the advantage of gravity.

Do something! Dammit, Sam. Think!

As the third rogue turned to face her, her hands went to the camera that dangled around her neck. The flash! Dialing up what she prayed was the right setting, she lifted the camera and shot him. The flash exploded in his face. He screamed, dropping his knife to cover his eyes.

Before he could recover his sight or his wits, Sam snatched up his knife and raced to where Aiden held off his opponent in a grim, silent battle. Without pausing to think about what she was going to do, she lifted the blade and brought it down on the rogue's back as hard as she could. He screamed a bloodcurdling scream of rage and pain.

And then, thank God, Aiden was free, rolling out from under his wounded opponent. As the other man tried to rise, Aiden kicked him in the ribs, a sickening, bone crunching blow, and he collapsed in a moaning pile.

"Aiden! Omigod, Aiden, you're bleeding. Let me —"

"No!"

He shoved her hard, sending her sprawling on the pavement. As she fell, she caught a blur of movement, heard the whoosh of a limb through air like in the Ninja movies. The asphalt skinned her hands and knees, and her knife skittered away. She bounced up quickly in time to see Aiden locked in combat with the third rogue, the one she'd koshed with her binoculars and blasted with her flash. The one whose roundhouse swing would have crushed her skull if Aiden hadn't shoved her out of the way.

Aiden who was still bleeding from multiple stab wounds.

The knife! Dammit, where was it? She scanned the pavement frantically. She'd stabbed one man tonight. She could stab another.

An agonized scream dragged her attention back to the fight, and she promptly forgot about the knife. The rogue was holding his right arm, which dangled at an obscene angle. Useless.

Aiden bent and picked up the knife Sam had been searching for. He held it easily, loosely, like someone who knew how to use it. Like nothing would give him more pleasure. Battered and bloodied beneath the streetlight, he smiled, looking like the very devil himself. "Had enough, son? Or do you want to play some more?"

The rogue turned and loped off, his arm cradled close to his body.

Aiden turned to the second rogue, who was climbing to his feet. "How about you, slick? Wanna go another round? Because I can promise you you'll end up like your friend over there." He jerked his head in the direction of the dead or dying vampire. "You won't live to see another moonrise."

The rogue spat blood. "Fuck you."

"Suit yourself."

Aiden moved into a crouch and started forward. The rogue practically fell over himself backing away.

"This isn't over," he snarled. "We'll hunt you down."

Aiden snorted. "I wish you would. It would save me a whole helluva lot of trouble."

"Fuck you," he repeated, then turned his malevolent glare on Sam. "And you, too."

Aiden swayed on his feet, relief draining his limbs of strength. If the rogues hadn't fled, if they'd teamed up to cooperate in any kind of half-assed manner, they might have finished him. Which would have sucked rhino. But he was a hunter. Every time he killed one of these bastards, he looked death in the face. It was like an old friend, after all these years. But Sam ... Jesus. If anything had happened to her ...

"Aiden?" She stood beside him.

Even in the dark, he could see the blood spatters on her shirt.

She touched his side, and even though she didn't make contact with the wound itself, her hand coming away wet, gleaming darkly under the streetlight. Very wet.

"Oh, shit! Aiden! We have to get you to the hospital."

"No," he grated, pulling his cell phone out of his pocket. "No hospital. Not under any circumstance. Unless you want to kill me."

"Aiden, you've been stabbed. *Gut* stabbed. For God's sake, you need a doctor! Surgery."

"It's nothing," he waved off her concern. "It'll heal while I sleep. Now, go fetch your camera bag. I presume that's where you left the gun?"

"The gun." She made a choking sound. "I'm sorry. I didn't even think about it. I just saw him stabbing you, and then the other guy ..."

"If it's any consolation, you probably saved my life with that cute little flash trick. But don't ever do that again. Do you hear me?" At the memory of her vulnerability, a fresh surge of weakness threatened to buckle his knees. "I think I aged a hundred years, seeing you in the middle of the fray." She looked like she might say something, but he headed her off. "This may be a shitty neighborhood, but someone will have called the cops by now. We need to haul ass. Go fetch your bag, now, and bring the car around."

"But —"

"But nothing. I'll wait here."

Reluctantly she left him to do as he asked.

His first order of business was to check the rogue. No pulse, no breathing. Fucker was clinically dead. Aiden found a spot between two ribs and jammed his knife into the bastard's heart to make sure he stayed that way.

The next task was making a makeshift bandage to keep his own innards in and staunch the bleeding, which he'd been doing a half-assed job at with his bare hand. Moving as quickly as he could, he stripped the shirt off the rogue. Removing his own t-shirt, he wadded it up, pressed it into the wound — shit, shit, shit, *motherfucker*, that hurt! — and secured it by tying the rogue's shirt around his abdomen.

In a cold sweat, he speed dialed Geoffrey, then RJ. Less than a minute later, he turned his attention to the vagrant, who cowered in the building's doorway, sobbing, bloodied hand clutched to his neck. Five minutes later, Aiden sank down heavily on his ass beside the now calm victim.

The man had lost a good deal of blood, but not enough to be life threatening, thanks to his presence of mind in keeping pressure on the wound while the fight raged around him. Subduing the poor bastard long enough to heal his wounds had taken the last of Aiden's physical strength. Couldn't blame the guy for struggling, though. He'd just watched Aiden stick a corpse. Wiping the guy's memories of the night's events and planting an alternate scenario sapped what remained of his mental energy.

As Aiden slumped back against the doorframe, the vagrant got up, muttered something about vomiting blood, then went off to flag down help. He'd get a thorough going over at the closest ER, which couldn't hurt. Maybe he'd even lay off the booze and get himself into some kind of program, as Aiden had suggested.

Which still left the piece of shit lying on the sidewalk to be disposed of. Unfortunately, Aiden was in no shape to take care of that little detail himself.

Sam's SUV came roaring down the street and stopped at the curb. Almost before the wheels stopped rolling, Sam leapt out. "Was that the vic I just saw shuffling off?"

"He's fine. RJ's on his way to clean up." He gestured to the rogue's body.

"Oh, thank God! Now let's get you in the car. The front seat. I've already got it reclined so you can lie back."

Aiden had to lean on Sam too heavily to disguise how frighteningly weak he was. By the time she got him reclined in the seat and belted, fat tears were falling from her eyes, burning his bare skin.

"Sam, honey, I'll be all right."

"Promise?"

"Cross my heart." *Shit, you'd do better to cross your* fingers *Afflack.*

"Do you need blood?" she asked. "Because, you know, if you need to … I mean, you can have some of mine."

Her offer pierced him just as surely as the rogue's blade. "Thank you, Sam. I do believe that's the nicest thing anyone's ever said to me. But Geoffrey's bringing the full buffet. I'll need to gorge on it before I sleep. And right now, you need to keep it together if we're going to get out of this. Okay?"

"Okay." She put the vehicle in gear, and they leapt away from the curb. They hadn't gotten a block when the questions started.

"Aiden, what happened back there? Where did those guys come from? I mean, what were they doing here?"

"Good question. Feel like a fool for not watching my back. Never had to." His breath seemed to be coming shorter now — punctured lung, no doubt, from his back wounds — so he kept it short. "Rogues don't hunt in packs. Ever. *Dogs* hunt in packs." He shifted slightly, experimentally, and felt wetness beneath his back. Shit, he was bleeding on her car seat from the wounds in his shoulders and back. They'd probably hurt like a bitch, too, if his brain wasn't so zeroed in on the boiling agony of his belly wound. It had been a long time since he'd been cut, but this felt bad.

"For safety, maybe?"

It took him a second to make sense of what she said. The rogues. Hunting in packs. "Don't see why. They fear nothing."

"They fear *you*," she pointed out.

"Yeah, but they're like smokers. S'always the other guy'll get cancer. Never think it'll be them." It struck him then that he'd better give her instructions. Also, that she was speeding like a demon. "Might wanna slow down. Don't need cops."

"Oh, shit." He felt the car's momentum slow sharply. "Sorry."

He adjusted the packing in his stomach wound and grimaced. Fuck, his guts were on fire. And sweat was trickling down his temples. If he'd had a hand to spare, he'd wipe his forehead.

"Are you all right?"

"Fine," he gritted. "But you needa go north ... meet Geoffrey in the parking garage we passed earlier. You know the one I mean?"

"Yes, I know it. Beside the building that looks like it's all glass windows?"

"That's it."

"But I thought we were going home."

"Switch cars, in case we're being tailed, then to the airport."

"We're flying out of here tonight?"

"Tomorrow night. Don't heal so well at altitude." His vision blurred, and he blinked, but the blurriness remained. Shit. "Spend the day on the jet, in the hangar. Safe there. Fly to Montreal tomorrow night."

"Montreal?" She shot him a look. "To meet with that guy who finances your work, right?"

"Delano Bowen," he confirmed. Delano could help them figure this out. He had the resources to get to the bottom of anything. And he could protect Sam, if things didn't turn out well tonight. Geoffrey had his instructions. He'd see that she got there.

She cornered hard, and his vision grayed. Oh, hell. He was going to pass out.

"Sam?"

"Yeah?"

"Gonna close my eyes. Geoff knows what to do. After he gets me stowed away, take you to a motel. 'Kay?"

"No motel! I'm staying with you."

"Long as Geoff's there . . . watch over you."

She turned anxious eyes on him. "Dammit, Aiden, don't you die on me."

"Wouldn't dare," he said. Then the blackness claimed him.

Sam never figured herself for a claustrophobic, but after fifteen hours cocooned aboard a small aircraft, she was having a hell of a time.

Geoffrey had met them in the parking garage. He'd man-handled Aiden from one vehicle to the other. Then, with the aid of smelling salts, he'd brought Aiden back around long enough to hand him a unit of warm blood, which he'd slammed down before passing out again. Then Geoffrey had taken the wheel while Sam crawled into the back seat to cradle Aiden's head on her lap.

The drive was a blur, as was the transfer from the vehicle to the plane. Inside, Geoffrey lifted the top off what she'd supposed was a bed — the bed she'd imagined he'd had lots of mile-high sex on — to reveal a recessed, well cushioned . . . sleeping compartment.

Coffin, Sam. Call it what it is. It's a fucking coffin, complete with satin lining.

She leapt to her feet and paced the short length of plane's cabin, a path her feet knew well by now. In fact, the whole interior of the jet had taken on a coffin-like feel. Beige walls and upholstery. Shuttered windows. Plush seats. Dead quiet.

God, what if he died? What if he wasn't able to heal himself before the injuries took their toll? What if when they opened the lid, he was cold and stiff, a beautiful corpse whose soul had flown? What if he never opened those ridiculously blue eyes again? What if he never looked into her camera lens again with that look on his face she had yet to decode?

No. He was not dead. He *wasn't*. She'd know it if he were.

And oh, Christ, *that* mental path was as thoroughly beaten down as the carpet on the aisle of this tin bird.

But, dammit, she had to believe he'd be okay.

Geoffrey had certainly done everything within his power to ensure his boss's recovery. He'd calmly applied those huge butterfly bandages to pull together the edges of Aiden's wounds, then pushed two more units of blood into him via IV. He'd seemed so calm and matter-of-fact as he worked, Sam had begun to relax. If Geoffrey figured Aiden would be all right, that was good enough for her. But then Geoffrey had closed the lid with the pronouncement that he'd done all he could, and the rest was up to Aiden.

Shit.

She glanced at her watch for the umpteenth time. Shouldn't he be up by now? If they were home, he'd be up by now.

Geoffrey chose that moment to come on board, announcing they'd be taking off in about twenty minutes.

When he went to turn away, she grabbed his arm. "Shouldn't we ... I mean, could we maybe lift the lid and see what's going on in there?"

"Oh, no, Ms. Shea. We mustn't disturb him. The collapsed lung will mend and reinflate well enough, but I imagine he'll need every minute of sleep he can get to repair that nasty liver laceration. It was a bad one, I fear. Now if you'll excuse me, I have to do the pre-flight safety check."

Too shocked to respond, she just stood there as he left her alone to close himself into the flight cabin.

Although Geoffrey said it would be twenty minutes, she sat down and belted herself into her seat. As they waited for clearance, she willed herself to sit there quietly. As they taxied out onto the runway, accelerated down the tarmac and lifted off, she forced her limbs to be still. A major triumph, considering how wired she felt. Too bad she couldn't exercise the same kind of discipline to still her chaotic mind. It kept going like a hamster on a wheel, as it had all night and all day. If she could just shut it down a while, maybe she could escape into sleep ...

"Sam? Sam, wake up. Sam, are you okay?"

Sam lifted her lids to find Aiden bent over her chair, a look of concern on his face.

Aiden! He was up!

She tried to spring up, but her lap belt was still fastened. The restraint did nothing, however, to prevent her upper body from lunging forward until her forehead cracked solidly against his.

Her hand went to her forehead. "Ow!"

He cursed. "I'm sorry. My fault. You were looking so still and white ..."

She covered her face with both hands and her shoulders started to shake.

He sucked in his breath, cursing himself for his stupidity. He'd scared her out of a dead sleep, and then he'd hurt her with his damned rock of a head. "Shit, Sam. I'm sorry. Let me make you an ice pack for that. I'm sure I can rig something up with a bar towel and some ice from the mini-bar. Just give me a —"

Her seat belt retracted with a thunk and she launched herself at him, her arms going around his neck. He caught her, his heart jumping at the feel of her body plastered to his.

"Sam?"

"You're all right! Oh, thank God!"

His arms tightened around her, returning her fierce hug. Unfortunately, his throat also tightened as he felt her tears on his skin. He had to swallow before he could trust his voice. "Hey, hey, what's this? Of course I'm all right. I told you I just needed a nap."

She pulled back and out of his arms, dashing the tears away. "Yeah, that's what you told me. What you didn't tell me was that you had a liver laceration, at least one collapsed lung and God knows what other organ perforations. And so much blood . . ."

"Speaking of blood, I should take some. I still feel a little weak. Do you mind?"

She blinked. "Of course. Should we sit?"

Good God, she thought he meant from her! "After I've put the blood in the warmer."

"Oh!" She flushed crimson. "Of course. Go ahead."

He turned away to see to the blood. Once that detail was taken care of, he went forward to the cockpit, rapped on the door and opened it.

Geoffrey swiveled his head. "Sir! Glad to see you up and around."

"Thank you, Geoff. Glad to *be* up and around. And thank you for the timely evac and the first aid. I managed to get myself diced up pretty good."

"It's all good now, though?"

"It's all good," Aiden agreed.

"So . . . what happened back there . . . you think Dr. Bowen will have some answers?"

"I sure as hell hope so." He clapped a hand on Geoffrey's back. "How long before we touch down at Trudeau?"

"About forty-five minutes."

"Great. Thanks again, man."

Aiden made his way back to Sam, flopping down in the seat beside her. "We'll be in Montreal in forty-five minutes." He glanced up at her. "How's the forehead?"

"Oh." She put a hand to it. "I have a little bump, I think, but it's fine. The question is, how do *you* feel? Is everything really healed up?"

He lifted his shirt to show her there wasn't so much as a scar, only to find an oversized Band-Aid on his belly. "Good God! Who put this on me?"

Her brows came together. "Geoffrey did, of course. Doesn't he usually patch you up?"

"I don't usually get aerated. I suppose he's responsible for wrestling me into this clean shirt, too?"

She nodded. "Yes, but I don't know why he was so determined. You were out cold and probably didn't feel a thing, but it still looked painful."

Aiden had a pretty good idea why. Rigor mortis in vampires was slow to set in, but lasted a good four days, minimum. Geoffrey would not have relished the idea of trying to dress his stiff ass in fresh clothing before delivering his corpse to Delano, if he hadn't made it.

"Guess he knows how vain I am. Even unconscious, I refuse to look bad." He started peeling the bandage back and hissed when it pulled a few hairs from their follicles. "Ahhhh! See, this is why a bandage should always be fashioned from a torn up sheet." At her laugh, he looked up. "What?"

"You take a Rambo-sized hunting knife to the gut without complaint, and you're whimpering about a few pulled hairs?"

Whimpering? He glowered at her with mock fierceness. "I'll have you know it *hurts.*"

She worked to suppress another grin. "It's best to just yank it off quickly," she advised, then rushed to add, "If the wound really is completely healed, that is."

He peeled it back another half inch, giving an exaggerated wince, then looked down. "Yep. Fully healed." He looked up at her, grasping the end of the adhesive strip. "Are you sure about this?"

"Absolutely."

He jerked his wrist, and the Band-Aid came away, taking a patch of hair with it. Goddamn! He blew a couple of breaths out through his nose. "Well, at least that's over."

"You have two more on your back."

"What?"

She laughed again. "Oh, relax, Aiden. There's no hair back there. They'll come off easily."

He smiled back at her, ridiculously pleased to have made her laugh with his display of wimpiness. And more than a little turned on at the thought that she knew the terrain of his back rather well.

Whoa, down boy.

He stood. "Might as well deal with the others, I guess." He unbuttoned his shirt, pulled it off and offered his back to her. "Care to do the honors?"

He heard her stand and closed his eyes, anticipating the feel of her hands on his back, but she removed the first adhesive carefully, with a minimum of cool, clinical contact. Just as well, he decided. Despite the earlier laughter, quite suddenly he was feeling dangerously close to the edge of something. When he felt the second adhesive come off, he turned his head to thank her, but her eyes were riveted on his back. Then she lifted a palm and placed it squarely over the smooth, unbroken skin where the deepest puncture had been.

Instantly, a current moved through him, stiffening his muscles. Oh, Lord, he *felt* her. He felt her emotions as surely as though he were inside her. As surely as though his fangs were buried deep in her artery, her blood mixing with his. The reverence in her fingertips stunned him. It was like a tactile, wordless prayer of thanksgiving for his recovery. God help him, he wanted to weep.

The blood warmer beeped, startling both of them.

Sam stepped back and cleared her throat. "It looks good. You'd never know the skin had ever been broken."

"Thanks." He reached for his shirt and pulled it back on before crossing to the blood warmer. Damn, had she felt that, too?

"I think I'll go freshen up before we land," she announced, then disappeared into the tiny washroom.

There's your answer. She'd felt the connection, all right. The question was, how much had she felt?

Had she felt his fear?

Growling, he pulled the unit of blood from the warmer, distended his teeth and bit into it.

Chapter 15

An hour and a half later, Sam stood in the express elevator of a Montreal highrise with Aiden and an obviously ex-military man by the name of Eli Grayson, head of Dr. Delano Bowen's security team. The express elevator was carrying them to the 27th floor, where they had to disembark and catch another secure elevator to the 29th floor, where Dr. Bowen occupied the penthouse.

The reception they'd gotten at the airport was just this side of rock star treatment. They'd been met by Mr. Grayson, who escorted them to a waiting limousine and whisked them away. As Aiden and Mr. Grayson — or Eli, as he insisted they call him — talked, Sam sipped her Perrier and studied the stranger. Now there was a man she'd love to photograph. Definitely Native American. High, intelligent forehead, brown eyes that missed little, high cheekbones, sculpted lips. And the body. Oh, baby. Even beneath his suit, it was evident he was seriously ripped. If his jet-black hair were allowed to grow out of that military buzz-cut, she imagined he'd have no trouble finding work in the film industry. And not the Adam Beach variety. More like an Indian version of The Rock.

The second elevator eased to a stop and Eli entered a code to oblige the door to open. Then it was down the hall to another set of doors that required a retinal scan. This place was like Fort Knox. She stole a glance at Aiden, who merely watched and waited for the lock to release. Clearly nothing new to him.

The scanner beeped its approval, and Eli opened the door to the penthouse, before stepping back and gesturing for them to precede him. Suddenly, Sam felt an attack of ... what? Shyness? Anxiety? She was about to meet the man who'd bought Aiden a jet that cost millions. The man who, according to Aiden, owned this highrise building. And a medical degree. And a pharmaceutical company.

No, not a man. A *vampire*. A vampire of extraordinary power, intellect and wealth. And his fiancée, Ainsley. What a woman she must be.

As though sensing her nervousness, Aiden put his hand on the small of her back. She was grateful for the warmth as she stepped across the threshold.

"Aiden! Welcome."

A tall, darkly handsome man advanced on Aiden with his hand outstretched. That could only be Dr. Bowen, Sam decided as the two men locked hands, then pulled together to clap each other heartily on the back.

Dr. Bowen pulled away and turned his attention to Sam.

"You must be Samantha."

His voice was mesmerizing, carrying the hint of an accent, an odd, old world inflection.

"Yes, that's me." She gazed up at him, hoping those lips would move again to say something more.

Aiden laughed. "I'd have said she prefers *Sam*, but damned if she's not developing a fondness for the full-fledged version after hearing you say it, Bowen."

Sam blushed. "Aiden's right. I *do* prefer Sam. And I'm afraid he's also right on the other score. Your voice ... your accent ... it's very ... charming."

A tall, slim blonde woman who could only be Ainsley stepped forward. "Don't let them embarrass you, Sam. The first time I heard his voice — over the phone, no less — I let him talk me into meeting him in an abandoned building in the dead of night."

"Hardly that, my love. I persuaded you to come for a job interview. I believe it was 9:30 in the evening, and it was an office building that had merely been abandoned for the night, not some derelict building."

She rolled her eyes. "He makes it sound so safe. I was bitten by a vampire that night."

Sam smiled. "He moves fast, I guess."

"Oh, not him. A rogue."

Oh, dear God! "I'm so sorry. How did you escape?"

"Del rode to the rescue, of course."

Dr. Bowen cleared his throat. "There's a little more to the story than that, I'm afraid. Suffice to say, I was far from the hero of the piece."

Ainsley stepped forward and took Aiden's right hand in both of hers. "Speaking of heroes, thank you, Aiden. Thank you from the bottom of my heart." She lifted his hand to her lips and kissed the back of it.

Aiden suddenly looked as nonplussed as she'd been a moment ago. No, scratch that. He looked downright horrified.

"Um ... thanks. I mean, no sweat." He pulled his hand away, smiling his most charming smile to cover his moment of discomfort. "After all, that's what I do for a living, right? Thugs-R-Us."

"Nonsense. If there's one thing I'm certain of, it's that you're no thug. And you certainly don't terrorize civilians in the normal course of your work. So ... thank you for making an exception for us. I'm happy to report that Lucy and Devon are back in St. Cloud, and Weldon is leaving them scrupulously alone."

"Happy to hear it."

Ah, yes, Chief Weldon Michaels back in St. Cloud. Aiden had told her once that his 're-education' of Chief Michaels was at his benefactor's behest. He'd also sworn that he didn't normally terrorize non-vampires, something she well knew by now but hadn't been too sure about back then.

"Yes, thank you, Aiden," Dr. Bowen said. "I can't tell you how grateful we are, especially for the child's sake. After that experience ... well, she needed to be able to go home. You made that possible."

Aiden shrugged. "Any vamp could have done it."

"Any vamp could have put a scare into him. Not many of them could have made it stick. Not with a guy like that. But enough about Michaels. Tell me what happened back there in Sioux City."

"Hold your horses, Del," Ainsley interjected. "Let's give our guests time to catch their breath, shall we? I know I'd want a chance to freshen up if I'd just been through the wringer they've been through."

Sam shot Ainsley a relieved look. Geoffrey had brought her a fresh change of clothes to replace the blood-stained ones, but she'd made do with a wash-up aboard the plane rather than leave Aiden. She was feeling a powerful need to step under a shower.

"Of course. Forgive me." Dr. Bowen inclined his head.

"You show them to their rooms, sweetheart," Ainsley said, "and I'll see about some refreshments. Would you like coffee, Sam?"

Sam was going to like this woman. "God, yes. Thank you."

Dr. Bowen led them through the suite, past a sitting room, a library — she caught a glimpse of floor-to-ceiling shelves filled with books as they passed, and a number of other rooms whose purpose she couldn't begin to guess at because their doors stood closed.

"How big is this suite?" she asked when they turned down a new corridor with more doors.

"We occupy the entire top floor."

"Shut up!"

Dr. Bowen glanced back at her, flashing a smile. "I know. Criminal, isn't it, to occupy so much space. But I assure you, I do have my reasons."

Sam heard the words but the sense of them barely penetrated. She was too busy processing what her eyes were telling her about Dr. Bowen. Holy hell! How had she not noticed right away? And what was going on here?

"Here we are," Dr. Bowen announced. "Aiden, this one will suit you, I think." He gestured to the room on the left. "No windows."

"Perfect."

Dr. Bowen turned to her, indicating the door directly across from Aiden's. "I hope this one will be to your liking, Miss Shea, but if not, there are several more you can choose from."

"I'm sure it'll be fine. But you really must call me Sam."

"Okay, Sam it is. And you must call me Delano."

"I will. Thank you, Dr ... Delano."

"My pleasure. I think you'll find Eli has already delivered your bags." He glanced at Aiden. "You can find your way back to the drawing room, I trust?"

Aiden laughed. "I think we can manage."

"Then I'll go see if I can make myself useful."

As their host disappeared back down the corridor, Aiden opened his door, flicked on his light, then turned to her. "I don't suppose I could talk you into sharing my shower?"

She pushed him into his room and closed the door behind them.

"Oh, my, we *are* eager, aren't we?"

"What's going on here, Aiden?"

His eyebrows soared. "Huh?"

"Delano Bowen is no more a vampire than I am!"

"Ah, you caught that," he said, sounding pleased.

"Aiden, this isn't funny. You said he was a vampire. You said you were here visiting him when our paths inadvertently crossed that first time, when I had that first vision about St. Cloud. You definitely said he was a vampire."

He shrugged. "He was."

"*What?* He was a vampire six weeks ago and now he's not? You expect me to believe that?"

"I believe I also mentioned he was working on an anti-vampire agent."

She blinked. "He injected himself with an experimental anti-vampire agent?"

He shook his head. "No, though that does sound like something he might have done eventually. But as it happens, Ainsley infected him through sexual contact."

Her jaw dropped. "But how did *she* get . . . omigod, he injected *her* with it?"

He shook his head again. "You got it backwards, sweetheart. Ainsley is the *source* of the anti-vampire agent. It's in her blood."

"Omigod! And it changed him back? One day he was a vampire and the next, just a regular guy?"

Aiden nodded. "Yep. Well, not a *regular* guy, 'cuz he's still 200 years old and change."

"Was he very angry?"

"Hell, no. He was turned against his will. He's been toiling in his lab ever since, trying to reverse the curse, so it was the answer to his prayers. Although it came at an inconvenient time, when he could have used his vampiric strength."

Aiden's voice went on, but Sam no longer heard the words. Because — oh, yikes! — if Delano could become infected through intercourse, then ... "Wait a minute. You said vampires don't ... they can't pick up blood borne diseases."

"Sam, honey, you can stop worrying about your sexual health. In centuries of debauchery, there's never been a case of a vampire receiving or transmitting a disease, sexually or through the exchange of blood. The only blood-borne pathogen known to affect vampires is what's known in vampire lore as the Merzetti Effect."

"The what?"

"Merzetti Effect, after the family who carried it, I guess. But it hasn't been encountered for so long, most vampires think it's an old wives' tale. So far as Delano knows, it flows in the blood of only two living females, Ainsley and her daughter. And since I'd be a dead man if I so much as looked sideways at Ainsley and since the kid's only seven, I think we that safely removes me from danger."

"Ainsley has a *child*?"

"Oh, shit." Aiden dragged a hand through his hair. "Don't ever repeat that, okay? Delano would shoot me for opening my big mouth."

"But if we're staying here, won't we bump into her? The child, I mean. Unless they're hiding her in a back room somewhere." She glanced down the long corridor at the closed doors they'd passed. Was that the reason they needed so much space?

"Hiding her is exactly what they're doing, or rather what Ainsley did, but it's not what you think. Over the millennia, the Merzetti's have been hunted to virtual extinction by vampires who feared them. According to Delano, the gene is passed on only to daughters. The line survives because somewhere along the way, the instinct was born in the mothers to give their newborn daughters over to foundling homes to protect them from those who hunted them. In Ainsley's case, she bore a child and agreed to give custody to a childhood friend who raised the girl as her own daughter."

Of course! "Chief Michaels' wife!"

Aiden did a double take. "How do you do that?"

"When Ainsley kissed your hand out there ... it's the only explanation." Oh, good God in heaven, Michaels was an abuser and a stalker. No wonder Ainsley had all but prostrated herself before Aiden. Her precious child. "I hope you put the fear of God into that bastard."

Aiden grinned. "I did better than that. When I took his blood and got into his nasty head, I let him think I might come back and make him my bitch. And as you know, I've had sufficient experience in that department to fake a credible threat."

Sam laughed. "Omigod, that's perfect!"

Aiden watched her face carefully. After the major *yuck* she'd experienced during their last aborted lovemaking, he'd begun to wonder if what she'd 'touched' that night was the enduring remnants of shame he hadn't quite eradicated after nearly two centuries. But she didn't seem in the least troubled by his reference to his seduction of the man who sired him.

"I would love to have the chance some day to see you put a fresh scare into him," she said. "Maybe you could catch him at his favorite bar some night and have the waiter send over one of what-ever he's drinking. You could tip your drink at him and smile ..."

Nope. No hang-ups there, he decided as she dissolved into laughter again. "God, you're almost as evil as I am."

Her smile faded. "Easily."

Yeah, right. "So ... how about that shared shower?"

She rolled her eyes. "I am not going to have sex with you while our hosts wait for us."

He gave her that smile, his best sexy, resolve-melting one. "How about after our hosts are finished with us?"

He heard her heart rate pick up and knew he had her.

"Are you sure you're well enough?"

"Oh, yeah." At least he would be after Delano hooked him up with a few units of blood. "I'm good."

"Do you think they know?"

He didn't have to ask what she meant. "Probably." He grinned. "Delano knows me too well."

"I thought maybe because they gave us two rooms —"

"He'd have given us two rooms anyway, and not out of delicacy. As a recently lapsed member of the fang club, he'd know I need to be alone in the day sleep, relationship or no."

"You're kidding! You've never *slept* with a woman?"

"Not technically, no."

"I guess that makes you a virgin of sorts yourself."

"Guess it does. But you haven't answered me. Are you going to get naked with me later?"

She bit her lip. "I don't know."

"You're worried about what happened last time?"

"No," she said quickly. Then, "Okay, a little. But it wasn't you. It was *me*."

Good God. Weren't those words to shrivel a man's ... ardor. Well, a lesser man's. "What if I said we could be sure it won't happen this time?"

"I'd say you sounded like every guy I ever met who wanted to get into my pants."

A smile curved her lips, and it was all he could do not to put his own mouth on hers.

"Ah, but the difference is I speak the truth. If I don't take your blood, you won't bump into anything unpleasant in my dark attic."

Her brows drew together. "But it didn't come from you."

"I'd like to believe that, but it hardly seems likely. We were the only ones there, and I presume you're familiar enough with your own darkness, even the subconscious stuff, to know the difference."

She chewed the inside of her lip again, and he could practically hear her thoughts tumbling.

"Okay, say that would work. What about you? I mean, doesn't the act have to ... you know, somehow incorporate ..."

"No, it doesn't. Yes, the blood lust will be aroused, but I can just take a unit of blood afterward. I promise, I won't have any discomfort."

"But just because you *can* doesn't mean you should." She gave him a hard look. "Frankly, if the best thing you can say about it afterward is, 'It didn't cause me discomfort', then don't do me any favors."

"Favors?" He erupted in laughter. "Sam, honey, I've been burning to do you blind again like that night in the car. Well, not like that because the setting was wrong and it was so anticlimactic for you after the big buildup. But you know what I mean. The idea of not having that deep connection to guide me ... It's like being allowed to finally play an honest game of high stakes poker after years of having the other player's hand telegraphed to me. If you can't go wrong, where's the excitement? Where's the thrill? What's the bloody point where the edge is if you don't have to *feel* for it?"

Sam sucked in a breath. "God, Aiden, why didn't you say something?"

He shrugged. "Everyone wants the trip. Hell, *I* want that trip. It's pretty damned hard to top, after all. But once in a while ..."

"I get it," she said. "Even champagne and caviar pall if you don't get to have the occasional plate of macaroni and cheese."

Macaroni and cheese? "Woman, that is the worst culinary analogy I ever heard. But yes, that sums it up."

"Okay."

He lifted an eyebrow. "Okay, as in you'll come to my room?"

"Okay, as in I accept your rationale. We'll have to wait and see about later."

Dammit, she was going to make him wait and wonder. *And you'll love every minute of it, Afflack.* "You are a hard woman, Samantha Shea."

With a sweet smile, she left his room, crossed the hall and let herself into her own room.

Grinning, he closed his door and headed for the shower.

Chapter 16

Dr. Delano Bowen might no longer be a vampire, but he still had a powerful presence. Once the niceties had been observed and the coffee poured, there was no mistaking who was in charge when they got down to business.

Sam sipped her coffee — God, it was good, even better than she made — while Aiden related what happened in Sioux City. Actually, he started out explaining that attack, but quickly had to backtrack to explain how he and Sam came to be working together. With Sam's help, he explained how her weather visions worked, how they'd stumbled on the discovery that Aiden's proximity seemed to warp the process so that more and more, her location-finding dreams were leading her to vampire violence instead of violent weather. He explained how they'd worked out a system that allowed Sam to take her pictures if it turned out to be weather-related, but allowed her to step back and let Aiden take care of business if it turned out to be a rogue. Once the background was laid, Aiden shifted back to recounting the attack. Delano listened without interruption.

"Well," Delano said at last, "We do appear to have a serious situation on our hands. Very serious indeed." His gaze slid over Sam and back to Aiden. "The question is, did the rogues band together merely for protection as they hunted, having been spooked by the knowledge that their fellow predators are suddenly disappearing at a much accelerated rate? Or was it something more sinister? Was it an ambush?"

"Ambush." Aiden's reply was immediate. "That was my gut feeling last night, and I haven't changed my mind. But hell if I know how they knew I'd be there."

"I've sent a team to Sioux City," Delano said. Turning to Sam, he added, "We'd like to do a forensic examination of your vehicle, if that's all right with you. To rule out the possibility of a tracking device."

A tracking device. On her vehicle. That would mean the rogues would have to know —

"Sam?"

At Aiden's prompt, she shook free of her thoughts. "Yes, of course. Please search it."

"And your house," Delano added gently. "May we have permission to search it, as well?"

Her house! Dear God. How much did the rogues know about her and her connection to the man who hunted them? Suddenly, she recalled the way the last rogue had glared at her before he loped off. *This isn't over*, he'd said. She looked at Aiden, realized that he, like everyone else, was waiting for a response. Again.

The house, Sam. "Yes, you have my permission. I'll get you the access codes."

Delano inclined his head. "Thank you."

"You're welcome." Even as she said the words, she realized that the team he'd sent to Sioux City wouldn't need her access code any more than Aiden had. Nor, she realized, did they particularly require her consent. It was good form of Delano to ask, but given what was at stake, she didn't imagine his investigation would be stalled by a lack of it.

Aiden was the one who stated the obvious. "A tracking device on the car or listening devices in the house would certainly explain how they knew where we'd be, but they'd have to know who we were, *what* we were, in order to plant the things in the first place. And since the demise of your friend Janecek, how many rogues out there have the resources, patience and long-range planning skills to build the kind of intelligence network that feat would require?"

"Not many," Delano allowed. "And I keep very close tabs on those few who I am aware of who do have that kind of potential. I can assure you there's nothing doing with them. But even at the street level, banding together as they did to try to eliminate you ... it's extraordinary."

"I thought so," Aiden agreed. "And if they'd had more talent for cooperation, they could well have succeeded. They were mean sum bitches, but I'd wager none of them had real combat training. But frankly, they wouldn't have needed it if the whole teamwork thing wasn't so foreign to them."

"But why is it so foreign?" This from Ainsley, who'd thus far been quiet, except for a few gasps and murmurs when Aiden had related the tale of the attack.

"Because hunting in packs is for dogs," Aiden supplied. "Vampires don't have to. I'm having a hard time picturing one vamp approaching another with such a suggestion. Too much face to be lost when the other guy sneers at you."

Ainsley put her coffee cup down. "Vampires really feel like that?"

"Absolutely," Aiden said.

"He's quite correct, love," Delano said. "Which is fortunate for us. They're enough of a scourge already, operating singly as they do. I can't begin to imagine how brutally effective they'd be if they managed to subdue their egos and unite."

Ainsley turned to Aiden. "But you're a vampire and you and Sam hunt as a team, right? Do you feel like part of a pack?"

"Sam *points*," Aiden said. "*I* do the hunting."

Sam's eyebrows shot up. "*Point?* God, Aiden, way to make me sound like an Irish Setter."

Delano cleared his throat. "Before this escalates, you should know I'm going to ask you to stop hunting for a while."

"Stop hunting?" Aiden leapt to his feet, tension bunching his muscles and making him look fearsome. "You can't be serious! We're making so much headway. Surely you don't want me to sit idly by and let victims die when we practically have an engraved invitation to the slaughter?"

Delano came to his feet to stand toe to toe with Aiden. While he didn't emanate the same menace as Aiden, he did radiate absolute authority.

"What I *want* is to not lose my most valuable hunter, to say nothing of endangering Samantha's life. You said it yourself, Aiden. Had those vampires cooperated more seriously last night, the outcome might have been different. And had they succeeded in killing you, do you imagine they would have let Sam escape?"

"Jesus, Del, give me some credit. I wasn't proposing taking Sam with me."

"*What?* They're *my* dreams! You think you can just leave me behind?" Sam found herself on her feet, too, hands on hips. "But of course you do. I'm just the *pointer*, right?"

"C'mon, Sam. Be reasonable. No way can I take that kind of chance again."

"Dammit, Aiden, it's what I *do*. You think it's *reasonable* to expect me to abandon my livelihood?"

"No one expects you to give it up forever. Just for a little while until we figure out this new wrinkle. Besides, how many shots could you miss? Eight out of ten are going to be vampire-related. Maybe nine out of ten."

Sam felt her fingernails digging into her palms as she fisted her hands. "That was so the *wrong* thing to say."

"But it's true."

If Aiden was oblivious to the thundercloud that was about to open on his ass, Delano appeared to be very much aware of it. "Um, Aiden, maybe you should —"

"Yes, it's true," Sam said, cutting across whatever Delano was going to say. "But only as long as I keep company with *you*."

Aiden's eyes narrowed. "What are you saying?"

"I'm saying I quit. I'm finished. I'm not going to be your Irish Setter anymore." She turned to Delano. "Thank you for your hospitality, but I'll be leaving tomorrow." Then to Ainsley, "Thank you for the coffee. It was a pleasure meeting you both."

With that, she put her mug down and left the room, head held high.

⚸

"Well, that went well."

Aiden heard the mild censure in Delano's softly-spoken words.

"Dammit, she knows how close we both came to having our chips cashed for us. No way could I take her into a situation like that again. No way would she *want* to be in that position again."

"I'm sure she wouldn't," Delano agreed.

"Then why the drama?"

Ainsley came forward. "Was that true? The eighty to ninety percent thing?"

She was looking at him like he was an idiot. Despite himself, he felt a flush rise. "Somewhere in that ballpark, yes."

"Then you've effectively taken away her livelihood already, haven't you?"

"But she agreed to it!"

"Yeah. After you showed her what would happen to these poor victims if she didn't help you get to them in time. Am I right?"

Aiden scowled. "It was still her choice."

"Right," Ainsley clipped. "You just keep telling yourself that." With that, she swept out of the room.

"Okay, what have you done with Aiden Afflack?" Delano said.

Aiden scowled harder. "What's that supposed to mean?"

"You've just driven two gorgeous women out of the room in under five minutes."

"But I'm *right*."

"As I'm learning, you'd be surprised how little that matters," said Delano ruefully. "Besides, Samantha is equally 'right'. If she removed herself from your sphere, she probably could have her life back, just as it was before you came along and commandeered her."

"Well, she *can't* quit. We can't let her. We need her, Del." He gritted his teeth. "I need her."

Delano's eyebrows drew together. "That's how I justified dragging Ainsley into this battle. I needed her. She had that precious property in her blood, the very thing that might let us end this battle once and for all. The thing I could get nowhere else. So I made the decision for her because I felt I couldn't risk her refusal.

I deceived her and misled her and otherwise violated ever tenet of my Hippocratic Oath, not to mention the free and informed consent requirement for ethical research involving humans."

"But it was necessary."

"I thought so at the time," Delano allowed. "But I removed her *choice*, Aiden. By the time I was forced to tell her what was going on, she was in too deep to safely walk away. My decision almost cost her her life, and that of her daughter and her dearest friend. As you say, perhaps it was necessary. But was it *right*? Absolutely not."

Aiden was struck by the complex interplay of emotions on Delano's face as he talked about Ainsley. Though it shouldn't have surprised him. He'd known his friend was totally gone on the girl months ago, when he'd asked for Aiden's assistance.

The two had, against all the laws of man and vampire, become blood-bonded, a development that was believed could only happen between two vampires. And because vampire unions were rare, blood-bonding was extraordinarily rare. When it did manifest, the couple became united, virtually inseparable until the death of one brought about the death of the other, generally within hours.

But then Ainsley unwittingly infected Delano with that anti-vampirism virus she carried. The result was the answer to Delano's dreams, the goal he'd been chasing for centuries — a reversal of his mutation. Except once he'd reverted to 'normal', their blood-bond dissolved. In the uncertainty of that sea change in their relationship, Delano had offered to be reinfected with the vampirism virus so they could have again the certainty of their blood-bond. Which is where Aiden came in. If Ainsley had so wished, Aiden would have made his first vampire that day. Happily, Ainsley had declined the offer, saving Aiden from having to sire his boss and benefactor. Which would have been … strange.

"Would you do it again?" Aiden asked.

"If the situation were exactly the same? If I didn't know Ainsley from the next woman? Yeah, I expect I'd do it the same way. I'd put the research ahead of any other consideration. But loving her as I do now ... I don't know. I don't think I could do it. I think I'd have to let her carry on with her life, blissfully oblivious of this violent world."

Jesus. "Really?"

"Really."

Shit. Delano was right. He was going to have to let her go.

At that thought, Aiden felt his pulse take a jagged leap. Thank God Delano's ears could no longer detect it. He rubbed his forehead. "You're saying I shouldn't have dragged Sam into this."

Delano sighed. "I'm saying everyone deserves the choice, preferably before all the other options are closed."

He was right. Dammit all to hell.

"If she wants to leave here tomorrow, can you protect her? 'Cuz I'd have to stay away from her. Otherwise, her dreams would still be fucked up."

"I can." Delano's response was immediate, confident. "We can have security on her 24-7, for as long as she needs it. Non-vamp teams, of course, to guard against the possibility that another vampire's proximity might warp her dreams."

Jesus. Why did it feel like his heart was being torn out?

Because you know your effectiveness will drop by ninety percent. Because innocent victims will die needlessly.

Because you'll miss the hell out of her.

He sighed. Time to cowboy up. "Okay, I'll go talk to her."

"I'd give them a while, if I were you."

Them? Ah, of course. That's where Ainsley had gone, to check on her guest. "Great. They'll be able to compare notes about how we exploited them."

"I don't suppose the note comparison will stop there." Delano crossed the room to a mahogany sideboard bearing a tray of crystal glasses and several liquor bottles.

"That obvious, is it?"

"Come on, my friend. She's attractive, female, unattached and working with *you*."

"Okay, pretty obvious."

Delano lifted a bottle of Chivas. "Still like the taste of scotch?"

"Please." But his mind was elsewhere. What was Sam telling Ainsley? Maybe he should go interrupt them ...

Delano returned with two glasses in hand, passing one to Aiden. "I can't imagine why *you're* looking so worried. If anyone is going to come off badly in Sam and Ainsley's little huddle, it'll be me. As you can imagine, I was a little rusty in that department."

Rusty? The man had been celibate as long as Aiden had known him, and that was damned near a century. "Yeah, but I bet you got in on the first try," he muttered.

Delano spewed scotch. "God, Aiden. I'm sor —"

"To her head! You got into her *head* on the first try. Jesus, Del. There's nothing wrong with me. Well, nothing like that."

"You mean, the mind connection didn't happen?"

"Not even a glimmer. Not that I tried all that hard. When the connection didn't happen ... well, the novelty and all. I kinda got distracted."

"Ah, of course." The look they exchanged was vampire to vampire. "But what about since then?"

"Well, it took me a while to talk her into giving me a second chance. She figured I baited her with the promise of mind-blowing sex. Instead, the sex just blew."

Delano choked on his whiskey. Coughing and laughing, he put his glass down. "I'm sorry, Aiden. I shouldn't laugh. It's just that it's you, and, well, I don't expect that's ever happened before."

"Nor is it likely to happen again, but I'm glad I could provide you with a little hilarity."

Delano wiped away tears. "So I take it you had better success after that."

"Yeah, we were able to connect, but not for long. She gets ... spooked. Real spooked."

Delano's eyebrows soared. "She's able to allow it or prevent it, as she chooses?"

"Yep. And she can boot me out as easily as a 300-pound bouncer ejects a brawling drunkard."

"Remarkable!" Delano was completely serious now. "Her mind ... it must be incredibly strong."

"Oh, yeah. I mean, it has to be considerably more developed than most because of the psychic talent, right?"

"Aiden, what a find! I must study her."

"Um, that's not gonna happen. She's got an aversion to talking about that stuff. Refuses to categorize herself as psychic despite prescient dreams. And the dreams ... she really doesn't know what's going to happen when we get to wherever she knows we're supposed to be. I think if she could just get her head around the idea that she *is* psychic and learned to embrace the idea, she'd get a helluva lot more out of those dreams."

"I'm sure you're right about that. Pity. I should have loved to study her."

"Huh. I'da thought you have your hands full with Ainsley."

He laughed. "Now that you mention it, I do."

Aiden sipped his whiskey, enjoying the mossy, smoky flavor and the burn of it as it slid down his throat. "Ever figure out how the blood-bonding thing happened with a non-vamp?"

"I still believe it's impossible between a vampire and a non-vampire, but Ainsley is more than a non-vampire. Genetically speaking, she's anti-vampire. The flip side of the coin, if you will."

"Makes sense." Aiden glanced down into the depths of his glass. "Do you miss it? The bond?"

"Let me see. When we were bonded, I couldn't get enough of her, was loathe to leave her side, and got crazy if another man laid so much as a hand on her." A pause. "No, I can't say I miss it, because that's pretty much how it is now. Except I have enough self-control not to throttle people over casual contact."

"Good deal."

"Yes, very good deal."

"Okay, we're done talking about them. Suppose they're done talking about us?"

"Not a chance. Let's go see if Eli has had a sit rep yet from that team we sent to Sioux City."

Sam had barely made it back to her room — after taking one wrong turn and having to backtrack — when a knock sounded at her door.

"Go away, Aiden."

"It's me, Ainsley."

Shit. How stupid did she look? Throwing a hissy fit, fleeing her host's hospitality, and locking herself in her bedroom. "Just a moment." She fumbled with the lock and opened the door. "Sorry, I thought you were Aiden." She glanced down the hall.

"Don't worry. Del will know enough to keep him occupied for a bit. We all could use a little cooling off."

Sam winced. "Sorry. That was incredibly rude of me to leave like that." She stepped back, gesturing for Ainsley to enter and closing the door behind her when she obliged.

"Not at all. I thought you exercised great restraint in the circumstances. He can be an arrogant SOB, can't he?"

Sam grinned. "Just a little."

"Do you really plan to leave tomorrow?"

Sam dropped her gaze under Ainsley's searching look. "I don't know. I mean, I thought I'd made my decision. I thought I was on board with this whole thing. Lord knows I can't bear to think about people dying if I can do something to prevent it. But then he goes and says something like that, something ..."

"Stupid? Idiotic? Dumb-assed?"

"Exactly."

"Honey, he may be a vampire, but he's still a man. He can put his foot in his mouth with the best of them."

"Clearly."

"Look, Sam," Ainsley said, "I know what it's like to have this vampire war thing take over your life. I know what it's like to be kept in the dark while someone else made decisions for you. I know what it's like to have your emotions manipulated so that you wonder if your decisions are really your own. And frankly, I wouldn't blame you one bit if you do walk away tomorrow."

"I sense a but coming."

"Nope." Ainsley shook her head. "No buts. I just wanted to say I know how it feels, and life will go on if you decide to take your bat and ball and go home. Well, not *home*. At least not yet. Delano will insist on sweeping Sioux City clean before he'll let you go back, and even then, he'll probably send a contingent of bodyguards. But you know what I mean."

Sam groaned. "Oh, crap. I really *can't* go home, can I?"

Ainsley may a wry face. "Not without your own personal army."

"Well, that sort of makes my dramatic little speech look silly, doesn't it?"

"Not at all. You might not be able to go home, but you can go anywhere in the world you'd like to go, and Delano will foot the bill. For your security team, too."

Oh, Lord, the idea was tempting. She could get on a private jet tomorrow. She could fly to … where? Aruba, maybe. She'd been there twice on assignment and loved it. She could lie on a beach, letting the sun bleach this dark vampire world right out of her, while the constant wind drowned out all thought. In the evening, she could take sleeping pills and drift dreamlessly, night after night. No vampires. No victims. No dreams.

She reined in her thoughts. "Oh, no. I couldn't."

"Of course you could, " Ainsley retorted. "Aiden got you into this, and since Aiden is Delano's agent, Delano can damn well get you out of it. And it's not like it would even make a dent in his bank account. As far as I can tell, he's richer than God."

"No, it's not that. I just meant I can't bail after all." Sam looked at Ainsley but all she saw in her mind was that teenage couple in the car at that makeout spot. "The things I've seen … All those people who came so close to dying, who would have died had I not been working with Aiden. Kids. Teenagers." She shook her head to rid it of the dark images. "No, I can't quit. I'm in this until your fiancé finds a better way to do it with his vaccine."

"Oh, honey, I hear you. Your conscience won't let you choose any other course, but once in a while, you just want to scream about how unfair it is that you got drafted into this nasty war."

"That's what happened to you, isn't it? You got drafted?"

Ainsley sighed. "More like hoodwinked. I still can't believe I've forgiven him."

Sam took that as an invitation to pry a little. "Hoodwinked?"

"Mmm. He set me up to be attacked by a rogue, who took the bait and bit me. God, I thought I was dead for sure. Then Delano swooped in and 'rescued' me from the jaws of certain death."

Sam sucked in her breath. That was despicable! "He didn't!"

"He did. Then he allowed me to believe I might be infected with the vampirism virus and persuaded me that if I did have the virus, he was the only one who could save me. Of course, I now know there was no possibility I'd been infected. He just wanted to be able to draw my blood regularly for his experiments."

"And you've forgiven him?"

Ainsley shrugged. "My blood was too precious. He's searched over a hundred years for someone with my DNA. He felt he couldn't risk my refusing to cooperate."

"When did you find out?"

"When his archenemy walked up to us on the street outside this building and told me it was all about my blood. Delano had to come clean."

"Ouch." Sam grimaced. "You must have felt —"

"Stupid? Manipulated? Exploited? Betrayed?"

"But you hung around because you'd experienced first-hand what these rogues could do, and you wanted to stop them."

"Exactly."

"Then Delano seduced you with that sexy voice and promises of mind-blowing vampire sex, and now you're engaged."

Ainsley snorted. "Not quite. He kept bolting like a scalded cat when I tried to corner him. Finally, I crept into his bed one night while he slept."

Sam's eyes widened. "Aiden said vampires never share their beds when they sleep."

"Turns out there's a reason for that. After the deep, unconscious healing sleep, they have a very long, very active dream sleep. It's not an especially safe place to be during that phase.

Lucky for me Delano was having a sex dream and not a fighting dream."

Sam wet her lips. "And you don't harbor any lingering resentment? Distrust?"

Ainsley smiled. "How could I? After I seduced him and unwittingly infected him with the Merzetti Effect, he finally got the cure he'd devoted the work of centuries to finding. But as a consequence of his mutation reversal, we lost our blood-bond, which was this really cool thing that let us communicate telepathically at all times. When the certainty of that bond vanished, it left us floundering a little. Delano offered to go back to being a vampire again, so I'd know how much he loved me, every minute of every day." Ainsley's eyes sparkled with suspicious brightness. "He actually brought Aiden here to turn him, and Aiden was ready to do it, if I but said the word."

Sam dragged in a ragged breath. "Oh, my Lord. That's crazy. I love it!"

"Yeah, me too." Ainsley blinked rapidly. "Though as it turns out, it's highly unlikely Aiden could have turned him anyway. No reflection on Aiden's ... potency. Del's subsequent experiments suggest that once inoculated with whatever this thing in my blood is — this Merzetti Effect — the recipient can't be turned. He hasn't tested the theory exhaustively yet, but he's pretty sure.

Sam blinked, too. "But he didn't know that when he made the offer."

"No, he didn't."

"Wow."

They were silent for a moment while they each contemplated that.

"So, now you know my story."

"Thank you for telling me."

Ainsley's brow puckered. "You know, Sam, it strikes me that you haven't had anyone to talk to about this vampire thing except ... well, vampires. Is there anything you'd like to talk about?"

"Oh, God, yes!" Sam sank into one of the two wing-backed reading chairs and Ainsley followed suit. "In some ways, I think this has shaken me more than I knew. Then I catch myself taking in some new bit of vampire weirdness and not even turning a hair."

"Oh, yeah." Ainsley sat. "Been there. And how about the way you look at the rest of world? Has it changed?"

"Completely. I'm looking harder at everything and everyone these days, taking less at its face value. I mean, if vampires walk among us without my knowing, what else can be other than what it seems? Did you feel like that?"

"Oh, yeah," Ainsley said. "Big time. Still do. Then there was the whole thing about *how does it work*? How do they feed? How do they sleep? What about sex? What about sunlight? What about garlic and silver and holy water?"

Sam's smile widened. "Yep. Asked them all."

"And did Aiden ... um ... answer them all?"

Sam laughed. "The sex, you mean?"

"Of course!"

God, she liked this woman. She found herself wanting to talk about what happened with Aiden. "Doesn't that freak you out just a little bit? That whole mind connection thing?"

"God, yes! It's so intense. Feeling the original sensations, then feeling his sensations, then feeling him feeling you, and on and on. It's ... overwhelming."

Suddenly she had a very clear recollection of what it had felt like — for her and for Aiden — when she'd taken his cock into her mouth. The memory drew blood to her loins, and a blush to her face. "But you get used to it, right?"

Ainsley smiled. "I never really had the chance to get used to it. Apparently one night was enough to infect Del. Now that he's reverted, it doesn't work that way for us anymore."

"Do you mind very much?"

Ainsley's grin broadened. "It was only one night, but it was a long one. We learned plenty about each other and what we like. So no, I don't mind. I'm very grateful we had that experience, but the sex is pretty fabulous as it is." She looked closer at Sam. "How about you? Still getting used to it?"

"You could say that. I mean, that one time, I loved it, but it got a little bit too intense and I pulled back." Sam wrinkled her nose. "And the next time ... well, it wasn't good. Intimacy issues on my part, I guess. I'm not eager to try it again."

"Oh, I'm so sorry."

Sam smiled at the depth of compassion in Ainsley voice. "No need to be sorry. Aiden's completely fired up now about sex without blood, so the mind thing won't come into play."

Ainsley blinked. "Sex without blood? Wow. He must really have it for you."

Ack! Time to dispel that idea. "Nothing like that. It's just the challenge that excites him. That little bit of mystery. Looking like he does ... being what he is ... let's just say he's a little jaded. And I'm the drink of clear spring water he wants to clear his palate."

"Don't sell yourself short. But I take your point. It comes too easily for him." Ainsley's smile was pure female devilry. "My advice is make him work for it, and he'll love every minute of it."

"You think so?"

"I *know* it." Ainsley stood. "I'd better get back to Del. He'll want to know you're okay." She lifted an eyebrow. "Any message for Aiden? I expect I'll find him with Del, and he's sure to ask if you're really bent on leaving."

Sam thought for a moment. "Nah. Let him sweat it out."

Ainsley grinned. "Good girl."

Chapter 17

AIDEN HOVERED OUTSIDE the door to Sam's bedroom, wrestling with a completely unfamiliar sensation. *Indecision.* Christ, was there a more pernicious affliction on God's Earth? Once you let it in the door, it fed on itself.

Worse, it laid bare the fear that begat it.

What if she made good on her threat and removed herself, his most powerful tool, from his grasp?

Worse, what if he couldn't stem the vicious attack of conscience Bowen had precipitated with his talk of choice, and he *urged* her to go himself?

Jesus, what would he do with this hole in his gut that opened up at the mere thought of her leaving?

Before he could decide whether to knock on her door or retire to his own room, her door was wrenched open from within.

"Hello? Mortal here. I'm getting older by the minute while you stand there. So what'll it be — in or out?"

"In." He stepped through the door, feeling his face flush with another unfamiliar emotion. *Embarrassment.* "I didn't realize Delano's walls were so thin."

"They're not. I could practically hear you angsting out there."

His head whipped around.

"Oh, relax. I couldn't literally hear. Your secrets are safe."

He should have been relieved. Hell, he *was* relieved. But suddenly he felt the opposite and equal desire to reveal himself to her. And Christ on a pogo stick, how scary was that?

God, he wanted a drink. Nearly two centuries since he'd caught a buzz from booze, and still the desire persisted. A pretty damned good argument in support of a biological basis for the pursuit of mind-altering substances. Even when conventional intoxication was beyond him, he still craved it.

Fuck it. Just say your piece and get out of here. This is Montreal. You can find a fang-banger on the first street corner and get out of your mind on blood and sex.

"I'm sorry about what I said earlier," he said stiffly. "If you want to go, it'd be okay. I mean, after it's safe. Delano's right. I didn't really give you much of a choice."

She stood gaping at him.

"So, that's what I came to say." *Evidently.* He hadn't known what the hell he was going to say until he opened his mouth. "So ... have a nice life, Sam Shea." He gave her his killer smile. "Keep taking those pictures."

He turned to leave but was arrested by her command.

"Whoa, mister! Hold it right there. What did you just say?"

He turned to face her. "You said you wanted out. I'm telling you you're free to go. I won't fight it. Provided you accept Delano's protection, of course."

"But ... I don't understand." Her brow furrowed.

"Consider it an honorable discharge."

"But what about the rogues? What about the *victims*, Aiden?"

He felt a muscle near his eye begin to tic. "They're my problem. Sam. I shouldn't have made them yours."

"No, you shouldn't have," she agreed.

"So, I'll be seeing you then." He started toward the door again, but she stepped in front of him.

"Damn right you'll be seeing me. Because I'm not going anywhere. I might not have come to the hunt willingly or happily, but I've seen too much to walk away now. I can't let innocent people die if I can prevent it."

Hope caught fire in his chest. "What about what you said earlier?"

"Jesus, Aiden. For a man who has burned his way through thousands of women, you really don't know much about handling them, do you?"

Ah, the pointer comment.

She was right, though. Beyond seducing them and leaving them very, very happy, he knew squat about dealing with women day-to-day. But even he knew comparing a woman's utility to that of a dog — no matter how critical the function in question — was bound to be offensive.

"You're right," he allowed. "I don't have a lot of practice dealing with women outside of hooking up. And what experience I do have in the non-sexual realm is ... um ... dated, to say the least."

"I can imagine."

The edge to her voice suggested jealousy, which he found oddly pleasing. But he couldn't let that distract him. He owed her an explanation.

"I'm sorry if I offended you. I was just feeling incredibly ... inadequate. As a hunter, as a vampire, as a man. When Delano felt it necessary to warn me not to expose you to unnecessary risk until we figure this out ... It was a knee-jerk reaction, nothing more."

"*Inadequate*?" She blinked. "Aiden, you're like the next thing to Superman."

"Some Superman. I couldn't protect you back in Sioux City. You had to come to *my* rescue, for God's sake."

"I don't know about that. After seeing the way you heal, I'm inclined to think you'd have handled all three of those guys just fine by yourself, if you hadn't had to worry about me."

"That's debatable. But what isn't debatable is that you saved my life by evacuating me into Geoffrey's hands. Without the infusions, I'd have been toast." Looking down into her soft hazel eyes, he remembered her offer of blood when he was so grievously wounded. "What's also not debatable is our hunting again before Delano gets to the bottom of this."

Her face hardened. "By which you mean it's not safe for *me*. Meanwhile, you'll go tooling around out there on your own, even though it's likely somebody's figured out how to hunt the hunter."

"No, I won't be *tooling around* anywhere. Delano's determined I take some R&R for a few days while his people investigate."

"And you *agreed*?"

He shrugged. "He's footing the bill. Figured I'd better humor him. Oh, and he's offered us the use of his cottage in the wilds of northern New Brunswick."

"*Us*?" Her left eyebrow soared. "Until a minute ago, you were resigned to my leaving this whole ... partnership behind."

Damned woman never missed a trick. "Until a minute ago, I didn't know I was going to let you go. Delano no doubt assumed I'd coerce your cooperation again."

"I see."

From the way her eyes had softened, he was afraid she did.

"So the offer was for both of us." He raised a hand to rub the back of his neck. "Delano thinks if we get away, have a chance to wind down and concentrate on ... other things, it'll be easier not to hunt." He heard her heart rate take a bounding leap as she contemplated the other *things* they could concentrate on, but since she quickly lowered her lids to conceal her reaction, he pretended not to notice. It seemed the gentlemanly thing to do. And surely he could learn to be a gentleman again, or at least approximate one. "He's got a cottage — a safe house, really — in some remote place on the New Brunswick side of the Restigouche River. Way out there in the woods, I'll never stumble on any action, and maybe you won't get the dreams."

"We're not needed here?"

"Not at the moment. It's all about intelligence gathering right now, and that's not my department." He tilted his head. "Unless you'd rather not go? Because this backwoods rusticating thing is Del's idea. He thinks we both need a vacation, whether we want it or not. But if you really don't like what the doctor ordered, I'm sure —"

"We'd be all by ourselves?"

"Completely. Like we fell off the edge of the world, Del says. But still just a satellite phone call away if we want a pick-up."

"Can we leave soon?" This time, she held his gaze and made no effort to hide the heat there.

Aiden smiled. "Sundown tomorrow. Del says he can have a guide meet us at the local airstrip and take us to the cottage."

"Good. That's settled, then. Now we've got some time before sunup. Want to put it to good use?"

"God, *yes!*"

Sam shouldered her camera bag and reached for her suitcase filled with clothing borrowed from Ainsley.

"I've got it." Aiden took the handle from her grasp and hefted the bag as though it were weightless. "Get the hatch, will you?"

Sam closed the SUV's hatchback and turned worried eyes on the cottage. It looked only slightly less decrepit in the pale wash of moonlight than it had under the full glare of their vehicle's headlights.

"Are you *sure* this is the right place?"

"No," he said dryly. "Delano's man clearly led us to the foot of this goat path and sent us up, over and down this ridge as a joke."

"Maybe he did," she said. "Maybe that old guy is some kind of Norman Bates freak and … oh dear Lord, look! Is that *moss* growing on the lower logs? God, it's probably rotting right into the forest floor."

"Relax, Sam." Aiden flicked on a flashlight, no doubt for her benefit. "Delano warned me it doesn't look like much from the outside. The intent is to keep the locals from getting too curious about what might be *inside*."

"What locals?" she responded. "We must be in the outback of the outback."

"Too isolated for you, Sam?" He gestured for her to precede him up the steps. "Too rustic?"

She regarded the dingy, sun-faded blind covering the window on the front door. "I'll tell you when I've seen the inside."

A moment later, they stood inside a thoroughly modern, if small, kitchen. "Oh, Aiden, it's lovely! And it has *electricity*!"

"You expected what? Kerosene lamps and a woodstove?"

"I don't know. Maybe. Or electrical appliances run on a gas generator or something."

"He has one of those, too. A generator, that is. But I don't imagine it gets much use. The electrical cable is buried, so it's not vulnerable to ice storms and falling trees and such."

Holy shit! "Buried? All the way up this ridge?" It had been miles since she'd seen a hydro pole. She'd known a woman once who'd paid nine grand to lose the ugly wires attached to her house and have them run underground for all of maybe 100 feet.

"Did I mention he has more money than he knows what to do with?"

Sam lowered her camera bag to the slate-tiled floor. "This is incredible. Let's look at the rest of it."

The tour took all of three minutes, most of which was spent oohing and ahing. The style was clean and clearly masculine, but with luxurious touches. The dark hardwood floors were a work of art, as was the Persian carpet under the heavy dining table. The walls were painted throughout in neutral, calming taupes and sages. The window treatments that looked so shabby and uninviting from the exterior were gorgeous, all rich fabrics that pulled in splashes of color to mix with those neutrals. The bedroom was dominated by a queen bed with a simple but gorgeous headboard and footboard in matte-finished cast iron. The bath boasted an old-fashioned clawfoot tub, but it was the very modern open shower that stole Sam's breath away. And it wasn't the exquisite Italian tile or the multiple showerheads that had her heart racing. It was the fact both the tub and shower were more than big enough for two.

Instantly, she visualized the two of them in the shower, doing what they'd done last night.

Ahhhh ... last night.

Aiden had kept her up for hours, intent on learning every nerve ending she had, every nuance of her response when he placed his mouth here, his talented fingers there ... It had been amazing. Never had a man worked so hard to elicit such pure erotic sensation. Never had a man taken her so high.

The third time, she'd woken with his cock hard against her buttocks and his mouth hot on her nape. For a wild moment, she'd thought — *hoped? feared?* — that he'd arch her neck and bury his teeth in her throat. Instead, he'd rolled her over and entered her with no preliminaries, fucking her hard and fast and carelessly. And oh, God, she'd come even harder that time, a long, explosive orgasm that just kept going and going.

"It passes muster, I take it?"

Sam blinked. *The cottage, Sam.* He was talking about the cottage. "Oh, yeah. And then some." She moved out of the bathroom and back toward the kitchen. "But I think Delano is wasting his time keeping the exterior uninviting. With this kind of renovation, the quality of the finishings ... there's no way everyone up and down the Restigouche River doesn't know about this. It would be the talk of the town."

"Not with the contractors he uses. Complete discretion can be had for the right price." Aiden strode to the refrigerator and opened it. "Ah, good. We're fully stocked." He glanced at Sam. "How do you feel about red meat?"

Her stomach growled, a testament to how accustomed she was getting to eating her main meal at night. "Let me at it."

He grinned. "Perfect. Why don't you go have a cat nap while I make you dinner?"

"Is that your polite way of saying I look tired?"

"No. It's my way of easing the guilt for keeping you up last night, and for the fact I plan to do it again tonight."

"Fair enough."

Sam thought briefly about having a soak in the tub, but decided to save that for when she had company. Besides, she really *did* need the sleep. Her eyes were starting to feel gritty. Not even bothering to strip, she toed off her shoes and curled up under the woven throw that had draped so gracefully at the foot of the bed. She'd left the door open, so the sounds of Aiden working in the kitchen carried clearly. As she drifted toward sleep, it occurred to her she couldn't remember the last time she'd felt so ... content. Safe. Cared for. Happy.

Happy? Her eyes sprang open. *Oh, Sam, that is* so *not smart.*

And it was so not changing just because it was foolhardy. So she might as well focus on enjoying this while she could. When he moved on, she'd deal. She always had.

Punching her pillow into shape, she rolled on her side, pulled the throw up to her chin and let go of the worry.

He should wake her.

There was nothing more tragic than an overdone filet mignon. And it would be seriously overdone if it rested much longer. Yet here he was at the foot of her bed as she slept, marveling at the way her brow furrowed as though sleep were something that required tremendous concentration. Watching her lying there like that made something expand in his chest until he felt too big for his own skin. Too full. It was a strange sensation, but not entirely unpleasant.

Sighing, he moved to the edge of the bed and placed a hand on her shoulder. "Sam? I've got your supper ready."

She rolled over onto her back. "Already?"

He grinned. "It's been an hour and a half. C'mon. You have two minutes to freshen up. Any longer and my masterpiece will be ruined."

She joined him in the kitchen a moment later, her face freshly scrubbed and tousled hair tamed. "So what is this masterpiece?" she asked, taking a seat at the spot he'd laid for her.

"*Voila.*" He placed the plate in front of her and watched her eyes widen. "A perfectly grilled filet mignon and asparagus with a roasted shallot and tarragon sauce."

She groaned. "Oh, God, it looks positively sinful. And I love asparagus."

"I know. Dig in and I'll pour you a little wine."

While he was at it, he poured a glass for himself. If nothing else, he could enjoy the smooth tannins on his tongue.

"Omigod, I've died and gone to heaven," she said after swallowing the first bite of beef.

He placed her glass in front of her. "I thought you did that last night."

"Different heaven." She grinned and speared a piece of asparagus. She patted the chair beside her. "Sit down. Talk to me while I eat."

He sat. "What would you like me to talk about?"

She popped a shallot into her mouth. When she finished chewing, she said, "Tell me something about you that I don't know. Something surprising. Something I'd never guess in a million years."

He treated her to a raised eyebrow. "That's your idea of light dinner conversation?"

She shrugged. "Nothing about our relationship has been conventional. Why should we start now?"

"True enough." He took a slow sip of wine, but his mind was racing. "But if I show you mine, you have to show me yours. And it has to be on par with mine. You can't wimp out on me."

She held up her fork. "Wait a minute! You've lived hundreds of years as a vampire! How can I possibly have something to compare with that?"

"Easy," he said. "I'll tell you something from before I was turned. Before I ever knew about vampires."

"Deal," she agreed, returning to her meal. If he hadn't heard the bump her heart rate had taken, he might have thought she was completely comfortable with the idea of revealing herself.

"Okay, but finish your meal first. I did not labor over that hot stove just to have it go cold while we talk. I'll tidy up the kitchen while you eat."

Five minutes later, just as he finished the last pot and put it on the draining board, she called him back to the table.

"Can you top up my wine?" she asked.

He obliged.

She took a sip. "Okay, I'm ready. Hit me."

He sat down at the table. "You'll remember I was twenty-nine when I was turned?"

She nodded. "Of course."

"Well, at that ripe age, I'd finally outgrown my youthful rebellion against my father and by extension, the church. In fact, I came to embrace the church again in a very real way. I was actually preparing to become a lay preacher, under my father's tutelage. He was an Oxford Methodist."

"You wanted to be a *preacher*?" Sam put her wine glass down. "Are you serious?"

"Oh, yes. Completely serious. I could never equal my Father for sheer piety, and let's face it, piety can be a little grating to live with. But I did find a kind of genuine relief in the church. I found repentance and peace and faith in Jesus Christ, and that was the message I wanted to take to other people. I truly thought I'd spend all my days in that little parish, dividing my time between working the farm and preaching, while I grew as stout and complacent as my father."

"Oh, my Lord. That's the path you were headed down before ... before ..."

He glanced up to see she had fingers pressed to her lips.

"Precisely. But there's more. I was engaged to be married. When the vampires struck, I was less than a month from my wedding." He ignored the sound of distress she made. "Of course, I broke it off. I had to. Though she did as I bade and told the village that she had made the break; that I'd gone mad and was no longer safe or decent husband material. In retrospect, that was true enough. She went on to make a much better match. I was glad of that."

"Oh, Aiden, I'm so sorry. You lost everything. Your mother. Your sister. Your fiancée. Your faith."

"Ah, but there's the rub. I didn't so much lose my faith as turn my back on it. I didn't blame God, as so many people seem to do in the face of tragedy. No, I didn't blame God because I knew these creatures for the evil they were. But I couldn't let vengeance wait for the Lord. I wanted to mete it out myself. I still do." He bared his teeth in a grim smile. "I made vengeance mine, and I'll burn in hell for it."

"Don't say that!"

The anguish on her face twisted his gut. "Worried about my eternal soul, Sam?"

"I don't know if I even believe in God, but I don't believe anyone is damned."

"Redemption for everyone? Even the rogues whose souls I dispatch to hell without giving them the opportunity to so much as repent their sins?"

He saw by the look on her face that she instantly grasped her dilemma. He saw it by the quick movement behind her eyes, the indrawn breath. If the rogues were capable of redemption, then dispatching them summarily was itself an act of evil. Yet to say otherwise — that they were beyond redemption — was to acknowledge that salvation was not available to all. No matter what consolation she tried to offer, it had a grim flip side.

"Relax, Sam." He smiled again. "It was just a figure of speech. Forget about it." To make sure she did just that, he gave her something else to think about. "Okay, your turn. And make it good."

"Okay." She picked up her wine glass and took a fortifying sip, then put it down. "I used to be psychic."

He lifted an eyebrow. "That's your secret? Newsflash here, Sam — you're *still* psychic."

She waved a dismissive hand, as though her precognitive dreams were nothing. "Sorry. Wrong word. I used to be telepathic. I could listen in on people's thoughts."

"Now that's a handy skill," he allowed. "How did it work? Did you have to touch them, or something they'd touched, like in the movies? Put your hand on their heads?"

"No, I didn't have to do anything. It all just came at me, from all directions. I could ignore 90 percent of it ... people think the most inane things. *Did I let the cat out? Wow, what a cow. I'm hungry. I wish he'd call. Stupid toothache. God, I'm tired.* But some of it just screams for your attention and you can't shut it out."

"Looks like you figured out a way to stop it, though, huh?"

She shook her head. "Didn't need to. Puberty stopped it."

He grinned. "I guess that's probably a good thing. At least you were spared having to hear the lewd thoughts of men on the street when you started to ... um, blossom."

She snorted. "I don't know about that. It would curl your hair to know how many lewd thoughts are directed at children."

His fist tightened involuntarily around the stem of his wine glass. *Bastards.* "Christ, Sam. I'm sorry."

"Hey, nobody touched me."

"They did in their minds. In *your* mind."

She shrugged. "Worse things could happen."

He forced his fingers to relax. "So, were you disappointed when you lost this telepathic ability?"

"Are you kidding? I was *thrilled*. It didn't come nearly soon enough for me."

"And did this blessed event happen as soon as puberty started, like someone flipped a switch? Or did you have to wait until it finished?"

"Pretty much as soon as it started, I was able to dampen down the noise fairly well. Eventually, it got so I couldn't hear anyone's thoughts even if I tried."

"So you would have been what? Ten? Twelve?"

"Sixteen."

"Um ... isn't that rather ... I don't know ... late?"

She nodded. "Very late for it to not even have started. Late enough to warrant a medical diagnosis of pubertal delay secondary to malnutrition."

Oh, shit. "Eating disorder."

She laughed. "Yeah, it was an eating disorder, all right. An involuntary one."

Something cold and dark slithered in his stomach. "What are you saying? You were mistreated?"

"My parents didn't think so, but fortunately the cops did. They removed me from their custody just before my fifteenth birthday. And I'm the one who reported them."

"What the hell? Sam, how could they do that? Was it a case of poverty? They couldn't provide the essentials? Or ignorance? How could they let you starve to the point you ... failed to develop?"

"That was the point. They *wanted* to stop my development."

Dark dread stirred in his gut again. "They weren't ... they didn't ..."

She blushed. "No, nothing like that. No pedophiles in my family closet. They did it out of greed. You see, I was their little cash cow."

Cash cow? But how ... His blood ran cold. "I swear to God, if you tell me they put you in some kind of freak show, I will hunt them down."

She looked at him, her warm hazel eyes brimming with gratitude. "That might be the nicest thing anyone has ever said to me."

"Sam ..." he said warningly.

She smiled. "Relax, Aiden."

He recognized his own words from a moment ago and knew she was enjoying feeding them back to him.

"They didn't turn me into a circus act or a freak on the TV talk show circuit," she continued. "That wasn't where the real money was to be made. The money was to be made on the stock market. Insider trading, without being an actual insider. We lived in New York City, and five days a week, I spent a big chunk of my day with my parents, having breakfast and lunch and coffee and dinner about a hundred times a day in places where the corporate types hung out. Or rather, they'd have lunch or coffee and I'd have water or diet pop or a salad as I eavesdropped on people's thoughts. If we hung around long enough, there was always information to be gleaned. My parents would sit and chat, and I'd write down what I heard in my book. An onlooker would think I was writing in a diary or a journal, probably. Of course, I'd point out to my parents who was having these *God-if-the-public-only-knew* thoughts. My dad would subsequently investigate them to make sure they really were senior executives in a position to know something and not just junior executives or gophers who merely thought they knew something."

"So your parents would get the jump on the market with the benefit of this insider, non-public information?"

"Exactly."

"But how did they know you'd lose your ability with puberty?"

"My grandmother — my mother's mother — apparently had telepathic skill, too. My mother got bypassed, but she grew up hearing stories about her own mother's experience, and how it went away as soon as my grandmother started to mature. When they recognized it in me, they knew it had a limited lifetime."

"How did they get away with it so long?" His chest ached at the idea of her going hungry, which probably hadn't bothered her nearly so much as failing to develop like the other girls around her. "Weren't there any teachers who noticed your malnourished state? I would think they'd be fairly well trained to spot that kind of thing, with all the eating disorders out there these days."

"I was home schooled, and with the salaries my parents paid those tutors, nobody was saying anything. Besides, it really wasn't an issue until I turned eleven. Until then, I really didn't mind being exploited. We were wealthy, and took lots of vacations to great places while other kids had to go to school. I got to do pretty much whatever I wanted most of the time, and I felt good about being able to please my parents. It was all great until puberty threatened. After that it got pretty bad, but they told me it was for my own good. Purifying my body."

"Purifying your body?"

"At that point, I didn't know about puberty wiping out the telepathy. But I *did* know other girls' bodies were beginning to change and I wanted mine to change, too. My mother told me that this regimen of purifying my body would help, so I cooperated fully with the bizarre diet and rigorous exercise program. It wasn't until years later I overhead my parents arguing about it. My father was beginning to fear I would suffer permanent consequences and that it had to stop so I could grow up, but my mother wanted to score one more big payday."

"Jesus, Sam. They exploited your talent for profit, and they stole your childhood away in the process. That's pretty fucking bad. But to then interfere with —" Dammit. He had to cut off the thought. The thirst for revenge had his cuspids threatening to erupt.

"Yeah. Pretty rotten, huh?" Thankfully, she didn't seem to notice his struggle. "But even then, I didn't do anything right away. I guess not having any rebellious teenage hormones floating around in my system held me back. But eventually I got angry enough that I reached out and called a hotline. They called the police for me."

There. Fangs under control. Much better. "What happened then?"

"My parents hired an expensive lawyer, who persuaded the DA he'd never get a conviction, because there were plenty of people ready to testify that I voluntarily engaged in frenetic exercise and routinely purged. Any idea of pursuing charges was dropped, but I didn't care. I was free. Under the glare of publicity, to substantiate their defense that I had an eating disorder, they had to put me in a treatment program for anorexics. Let me tell you, I am still that hospital's best success story. I proceeded to ... how did you put it? ... blossom at last. My usefulness to my parents was over."

"Did you go back home after you got out of treatment?"

"Yes, I did. I thought about petitioning the court to get emancipated, and force my parents to hand over some of the money I made for them to support myself, but I knew that would never work. No court would believe me over my parents, and they'd never believe the telepathic thing, especially since I no longer had it. Fortunately, just threatening to sue them was sufficient. They settled some money on me, and stayed out of my way. I studied photography, and when I turned 18, I started having the weather dreams. When I turned 19, I started following them. The rest is history."

"Wait a minute. How did you get from New York City to Sioux City?"

She grimaced. "I followed my first boyfriend. Which proved to be a big mistake. But once I'd settled there, I really didn't feel strongly enough about New York to make my way back. I mean, I didn't have any real friends there."

"What about your parents? Are they still alive?"

"Oh, yes, but they've since retired to Florida."

"Do you ever see them?"

She shook her head. "Not in a long while."

They were both quiet for a moment. Then he got up, went around the table and pulled her to her feet. Cupping her face, he touched his lips to her forehead gently, briefly. Sweetly. "Thank you."

Chapter 18

THANK YOU? SHE looked up him. "For what? Telling you this stuff? I promised *quid pro quo*, remember?"

"No." His thumbs stroked her cheek. "For helping me with this vampire hunt thing. I have an idea now what it must have cost you to allow yourself to be exploited again. So, thank you."

"Well, at least the cause is a little nobler." She reached up on tiptoe to touch her mouth against his. Their lips met, clung. "Mmmm, I'm hungry again."

He laughed. "Anything on the menu I can get you?"

She slid her hands up his flanks. God, he felt good. So solid. "I think there might be one or two things you could interest me in."

He pulled her closer for a slow, lazy, tantalizing kiss.

When he finally released her mouth, she was completely ready to go. "In the circumstances, I suppose it would be tacky of me if I said I wanted to play the sinner to your savior?"

She felt his laugh reverberate through her chest.

"Baby, you can play sinner for me any day of the week. As long as it involves the laying on of hands."

"Oh, yes. Lots of laying on of hands. Maybe you could prescribe some penance, too?"

"You are a wicked one, aren't you?"

"I'm trying."

He put her away. "Okay, then. Go wait for me. I have to take care of my own supper, and it'll take the blood warmer a few more minutes to bring it up to temp."

She wanted to say, *"I got some O Neg right here that doesn't need heating"*, but managed to force the words back down. If she let him take blood, they'd be in each other's skins again. She wanted him, but she wasn't ready to try that again. Not just yet.

"Perfect." She smiled brightly. "Where's my bag? I might as well unpack while I wait."

"I left it at the foot of the bed."

She found her bag just where he said she would, and it took only a matter of moments to unpack the contents. Everything was on loan from Ainsley. Ainsley was taller, so the jeans and khakis had to be rolled up at the cuff and the jackets and shirts were a little long in the arm. And Sam definitely filled out the t-shirts and sweaters a little more than Ainsley would. She could have used another couple of bras, but otherwise, she was good, right down to unopened packages of thong panties and a gorgeous satin peignoir set.

She lifted the latter out and looked at it. Made of pale taupe satin trimmed with contrasting cream stretch lace, she knew she'd look more like a virginal bride in it than the sinner she was supposed to be playing. Still, she couldn't resist trying it on. And once she had it on, she couldn't wait for Aiden to see her in it. To take it off her.

Shivering, she reached for the last items in the bag, a bag of basic toiletries Ainsley had loaned her. Together with the lipstick Sam carried in her purse, she was adequately fixed, at least for a wilderness get-away. As she lifted the cosmetic bag to take to the en suite bathroom, her gaze fell on one last item, an autoinjector. Resembling an Epi-Pen, it was marked with the simple initials ME.

Merzetti Effect.

Transferring the cosmetics bag to her left hand, she picked up the autoinjector gingerly. Oh, man, she'd forgotten all about it. Mainly because she didn't want to think about the circumstances under which she might have to use it. Delano had given it to her just before they left, saying, *"This is filled with an anti-vampire agent. If you ever find yourself in a situation where Aiden can't help you, use this to defend yourself. With a little help from my street team, word is already spreading that this serum exists. Hopefully a potential attacker will back off when you threaten them with it, and you won't have to actually use it. Unfortunately, your best hope is its deterrent power, because it won't stop them immediately. It takes a matter of hours to take effect, but when it does, it will reverse the mutation, stripping away their vampiric powers, and possibly worse. In my case, all it did was reverse the mutation, but I can't rule out the possibility that it might be fatal for some. My blood type is compatible with Ainsley's, as it turns out. Maybe that saved me, maybe it's irrelevant. We don't know. We haven't had time to research that angle. But in the meantime, we're doing our best to get the word out there."*

"Well, look at you."

Sam turned to see Aiden framed in the bedroom door. His gaze dropped to the autoinjector in her hand and his face paled.

"Jesus, Sam. Could you put that thing away?"

"Sorry. I was just unpacking." She opened the top drawer of the dresser and dropped it in on top of her underwear and socks.

His face softened. "Shit. *I'm* sorry. I shouldn't have snapped at you. It just makes me a little nervous."

She laughed. "You're entitled. It'd be like me walking in to find you waving a loaded gun in my general direction."

He moved to her side, opened the drawer and retrieved the autoinjector. "Where's your purse? You should keep this in there at all times so you've got it on you if you need it."

"Think I'm going to need it out here?" She retrieved her purse from beside the bed and handed it to him.

"I think it's never too soon to start the habit." He dropped the serum into her bag. "Whoa, what do we have here?" He lifted out a small digital camera, and deposited her purse on the dresser.

"That's a backup. I can't stand the idea that I might be caught without a camera, so I keep one in my purse, one in the dash of my car, one in my luggage in case I get separated from my camera bag." She shrugged. "They're not as sophisticated as the cameras I use on my shoots, but they produce a surprisingly good image in a pinch."

Aiden clicked the on button and the camera whirred to life. Then he lifted it and snapped her photo.

"Aiden!"

He took another and another, as she advanced on him, laughing. She caught his arm and plucked the camera from his grasp. "You're supposed to be the model, not me. Remember?"

"Sorry, couldn't resist. You look so good." He took her hands and held them away from her body for an unobstructed view of her curves under the peignoir. He looked as though he especially appreciated the way the stretch lace gathered under her ample bust. "My God, Sam, you are the most beautiful creature."

His words, and the thickness of his voice as he said them, was all the reward Sam wanted. "Thank you. It's pretty, isn't it? Although I really don't look very wicked."

"That's okay. You can be my angel tonight, and I'll be the wicked man who wants to pull you down off your pedestal and into the dirt with me."

She smiled. "Suits me."

He gave her a mock scowl. "Play along, woman. I'm supposed to be seducing you."

She lifted an eyebrow. "You've been doing that since I saw you on that sidewalk outside of Chief Michaels' house in St. Cloud."

He grinned. "I knew you were watching. I could feel it."

"You knew *someone* was watching," she corrected. "And that much was obvious from the pictures. You were totally hamming it up."

"Do you like to watch, Sam?"

Her pulse took a jagged leap, one that she knew he could hear. "I like to watch you," she allowed.

He turned her in his arms so she was facing the mirror. His hands fastened on her hips, pulling her buttocks into contact with the front of his soft denim jeans. She felt his arousal stir. His gaze met hers in the mirror, and Sam's legs went weak.

"God, you look too good to touch," he murmured against her ear. "But I'm going to do it anyway. I'm going to touch every inch of you."

He skimmed his hands up her midriff until his palms encountered the lace beneath her bosom, and she leaned her head back on his chest, letting her breath escape on a shaky sigh.

"I'm going to stroke you with my hands, with my tongue."

His hands cupped the globes of her breasts, and she closed her eyes.

"Open them," he commanded. "Watch what I'm doing to you."

She obeyed, in time to see him pull the scooped neckline down to reveal both her breasts. Her nipples drew even tighter, an irresistible temptation for his hands.

"Aiden!"

"You like this?"

The combination of the sight of his big hands on her breasts and the exquisite sensations he produced with his touch had her practically panting, but she managed a strangled, "Yes!"

She felt his pleased laughter.

Moments later, when she was on the verge of begging him to put his mouth on her, he dropped his hands to her hips again, where his fingers started gathering the satin, pulling it up, up, up, until he could grasp the hem. Then his right hand slipped beneath the gown and between her legs.

"How about this?" he asked, as he parted her tender, arousal-swollen flesh. "Do you like this, too?"

"Oh, yes, please." She leaned back on him, splaying her legs a little wider to give him better access.

"Look at yourself," he urged. "Look how beautiful you are."

She lifted her head to comply, and sucked in a breath. "I look like a stranger."

"Not to me, baby. Never to me." He let the skirt drop and returned his hands to her breasts, cupping and lifting them. "Take our picture," he said. "In the mirror."

"Aiden!"

"Take it."

She lifted the small digital and took the picture.

He pushed her breasts up and together. "Again."

Again she obeyed.

He turned her in his arms to kiss her, and her arms went around his neck, the better to press her bare breasts against his chest. God, he was still fully clothed. She should do something about that. As his mouth devoured hers, she dropped her free hand to the hem of his black cashmere sweater and started tugging it up.

He got the message, stepping back to haul the sweater over his head. She took a picture.

When he came back to her, instead of taking her into his arms again, he swept the peignoir's jacket off her shoulders. She let it slide down her arms to puddle at her feet. Then his hands were working the gown off her shoulders. It took a little shimmying, but it too pooled at her feet in a pile of satin and lace. She didn't need a mirror to tell her that her naked flesh was flushed and aroused.

She wet her lips with her tongue. "Want some help with those jeans?"

They were gone in an instant, leaving him as naked and obviously aroused as she was. In one stride, he reached the bed, pushed the decorative pillows onto the floor and whipped the covers back. He extended a hand to her. "Come, Sam."

In that instant, standing there with his hand extended in invitation, she saw him as a man. As he might have looked on his own wedding night, if he'd had one.

Suddenly her image of him as a thrilling, dangerous vampire, as a larger-than-life, superhuman lover, collided with the picture she'd formed of his pre-vampire self.

And with it came realization that she'd been treating him like some kind of ... rock star. Just exactly as every other woman — the vampire groupies — must have treated him. Even as they gave up their blood and their bodies, it was all about what they could take from him. A little piece of him, a memento, without thought for what he might need beyond blood and sex. She flashed back to the time on the roof of that club when she'd asked him to play to her fantasy by dominating her. Not that there was anything inherently wrong or shameful about that. And not that she wouldn't enjoy a repeat performance in the right circumstances. But not tonight.

Tonight she was going to make love to the man.

"Sam? You okay?"

"Aiden." She put the camera down and moved into his arms. Pressing her face to his chest, she clasped his back with her hands, feeling the muscle beneath his warm skin, the heavy thud of his heart beneath her ear. She lifted her head and eased away a fraction of an inch. "Aiden, I want to give you something tonight."

She felt him stiffen subtly. "Give me something?"

"So far, it's been all about me. Tonight, I want it to be whatever you want. Anything. However you want it."

She felt his chest expand as he dragged in a lungful of air. "Really?" The word came out on a rough rasp.

"Really."

His fingers tightened on her hips. "What if I said I wanted to tie you face-down, spread-eagled on this nice bed and blindfolded? Use you mercilessly all night long."

Her heart missed a beat, but she wasn't sure whether it was fear or excitement that caused the jolt. "I'd say don't make the restraints too tight. My left wrist is kinda gimpy."

"Dammit, Sam," he growled. "Never consent to something like that."

She smiled. "I trust you, Aiden. Besides, I don't think that's what you really want tonight."

He groaned. "You're right. Tempting as you make it, that's not what I want."

She raked the tips of her fingernails lightly over his back. "What *do* you want?"

"I don't know." He shuddered as her nails made the return trip up his back. "*This*. You holding onto me, looking into my eyes. I want it so slow it kills me. So sweet, it makes my teeth ache."

Intimacy. Her heart took another faltering bound. He wanted her to make love to him for real. It would be the easiest thing she'd ever done. It would also be the most recklessly stupid thing she could possibly do.

She pulled away. He released her immediately, but his eyes were filled with questions. She answered him by climbing into the bed. "Come here, baby."

"Oh, Sam."

He slid into bed beside her. Suddenly, she felt shy, which was ludicrous considering how thoroughly they had already shared each other's bodies. As though divining her thoughts, or maybe because he was feeling a little exposed himself, he drew the sheet up to cover them.

Lying side by side now, he took her face in his hands and kissed her, and any awkwardness dissolved. He kissed her mouth softly, sweetly, then moved on to her nose, her forehead, her eyelids, the sensitive spot behind her ear.

When he came back to her mouth again, she kissed him back with the same tenderness. Her hands shaped his face, memorizing the varied textures before moving on to the hard bones of his skull beneath all that springy hair. God, she loved the shape of his head and face. She drew her hand down his neck, delighting in his small shiver, then continued down along the hollow of his spine to the small of his back, pushing the sheet down as she went.

His own hand tangled in her hair, sweeping down her back, then up her arm, across her upper chest to find the delicate hollows along her collarbone. His mouth followed, seeking out the shadows he'd traced a moment ago with his fingers.

"You're so tiny across the shoulders," he murmured. "I love that about you, but now that I know what your parents did, I can't help but wonder if you were meant to be like this. Are you shorter than you were genetically destined to be?"

"Let it go, Aiden. I have." She traced the frown lines on his forehead. "I may be less than I was meant to be in physical stature, but I think maybe I'm more than I might otherwise have been, if that makes sense."

He smiled into her eyes. "Perfect sense."

Sam's stomach fluttered.

She'd been attracted by his beauty, wowed by his power, stimulated by his coolness factor, and even by his rough edges. She'd been seduced by his blazing sexuality. But she'd never seen this Aiden. This Aiden needed something from her. She prayed she knew how to give it to him.

"I think," she said, tracing his mouth with a finger, "that I've got some catching up to do. After last night, you've mapped every inch of me with your hands and mouth, but I didn't really get a chance to reciprocate."

He groaned. "Oh yeah. I'd like that."

She placed her hand in the center of his chest and pushed. "On your back, mister."

When he'd obliged, she drew herself up onto her knees beside him. For a moment she looked her fill, letting her eyes skim down his chest to the sheet that pooled at his hips. A sheet that was doing a poor job concealing his erection.

"I feel like the luckiest woman in the world right now." She splayed a hand on his lightly-haired chest, feeling the thudding of his heart through the wall of bone and muscle and flesh. "All this, and it's all for me."

"All for you," he agreed. "Every needy inch of me."

She leaned over him, letting her hair fall like a curtain around them, and kissed his mouth. He met her with restrained hunger and, yes, need. It was as palpable to her as though she were right there in his mind. *God, Sam, why hadn't you seen it before?* For all the mind-blowing sex he'd had, he hadn't really been touched by the hand of someone who loved him. Not for centuries.

Her heart contracted with sympathy.

No, with *empathy*. She knew just how he felt. She just hadn't racked up as many years of it as he had.

Well, his drought would come to an end tonight. Because God help her, she loved him. And when she touched him, she was going to make sure he felt it to his soul.

She started with his face. As she skimmed moist lips over his forehead, she thought about how much he'd suffered, how he suffered still, thinking his soul damned. He'd said it was just a figure of speech, but she knew better. She also knew the good that he did outweighed the bad. It had to. But all that death, all that violence ... She kissed his eyelids, his temples, willing peace to flow into his conflicted soul.

With one hand still tangled in his hair, she worked her way down his throat. When she reached his shoulders, she had to release his hair so she could explore that wide, muscled terrain with both hands. Which led to an exploration of his arms, down over rock-hard biceps to the ropey muscles of his forearms, to his big calloused hands. Silently, she praised his strength and control as she kissed first one palm and then the other.

"Sam..."

"Hush, Aiden. Just open up and feel this."

She swung a leg over him so she was straddling his hips with nothing but the sheet between them. He sucked in a breath, and she felt his erection leap. Smiling, she bent to kiss his chest, then turned her head to lay her ear over his heart. His strong, fearless heart. A good heart, no matter what he thought. He'd sacrificed so much to avenge his mother and sister, and the sacrifice was unending. She pressed her lips to his skin lovingly.

"Jesus, Sam," he gasped. "What are you doing to me?"

She lifted her head to meet his eyes. They blazed with a heart-stopping mix of arousal, need and confusion. "Am I hurting you?"

"Oh, God, yes." A big hand closed over her head to press her face back into his chest. "But don't stop. Don't ever stop."

She shimmied down his body, paying loving attention to every rippling muscle of his flat abdomen and the tender, ticklish flesh over his obliques. She skipped over his cock, raking her nails gently over his trembling thighs, the bumps of his knees, the hard swell of calf, right down to the soles of his feet. And back up until she straddled his knees.

"I saved the best for last."

All he could manage was a stifled groan.

Smiling, she took his shaft in hand. God, he was even beautiful here. She closed her mouth over him, her heart overflowing with gratitude for this wondrous manifestation of his desire for her, his need. But oh, God, the scent of him. The taste. And the sounds he was making. She was losing her focus...

Aiden was on fire. His skin. His lungs. His heart. It was like she'd stripped the armor off him with the soft pads of her fingers and the brush of her lips. And now he was twisting in the fire, dying, craving more.

Dear God in heaven, he needed to be inside her. But not yet. Not like this. If she took him inside her now, he'd surely shatter, leaving broken pieces of himself strewn around for her to see. He just needed a few minutes to collect himself. And he knew just how to buy the time. He'd push her onto her back and return the favor, building back his defenses while he drove her out of her mind with his mouth.

He sank his fingers into her hair. "Sam ... Sam, come up here."

She moved up his body until she straddled his hips again, trapping his sex between them. And oh, Lord, she was so wet and hot.

"I want to love you like this," she said. "On top so I can watch your face."

She rose up on her knees and took his cock in her hands, and he knew he couldn't deny her. Couldn't deny himself. And when she sank down on him, he was lost. Emotion rushed in from all sides, like an empty cup pushed just beneath the surface of the water. It flooded him, his heart, his soul, until he was sure he couldn't possibly contain it, but still it came. He was drowning.

She leaned forward slightly, bracing herself as she rose and sank on him, taking him deeper each time. The action brought her thrusting breasts closer. Automatically, his hands left her hips and found those glorious globes. Lord, they were lovely. Full and heavy in his hands, swollen with arousal. The thought of all that blood engorging the tissues had his teeth aching to erupt. He forced the instinct down, thanking God he'd fed so well and so recently. In this fragile state, if the blood lust were stronger —

"Omigod, Aiden. Aiden."

She reared back. He felt her sheath contracting around him, rippling rhythmically, drawing him deeper. Gripping her hips, he watched her, back arched, head thrown back, lips parted. When the sex flush suffused her face, neck and chest with rosy color, he thought his heart might explode.

"Sam ..."

She collapsed on him. "Sorry. I couldn't stop it. I wanted to do that a lot longer. I thought if I went slow ..."

He rolled her beneath him. "Put your arms around me, Sam."

She complied, wrapping her legs around him, too, as though she knew how desperately he needed to be enveloped in the pure sweetness of what she was giving him. He was beyond caring, now. Beyond trying to conceal his need from her.

Propping himself on one elbow, the weight of his body pinning her to the mattress, he sought her mouth with his. Finding his own taste there mixed with her sweetness drove his excitement up another notch. With his free hand, he stroked her breast, the hard point of her nipple, the silky skin of her midriff. When she surged against him, he started moving against her. For long minutes, he tortured himself with slow, full thrusts, rocking the bed beneath them. Another minute of that and she caught fire again, her breath coming in fast, shallow pants, hips angling to take him deeper.

He felt her fingers flex on his back, felt her nails dig in.

Mine, he thought on a savage thrill.

And his fangs erupted.

Shit! He had to finish now and get the hell off her, or he'd break his promise. There'd be no stopping.

"Do it," she said. "Do it now so I can feel you when you come."

Why had he imagined she wouldn't notice? He closed his eyes. "It's okay," he said hoarsely. "I don't have to."

"I want you to."

He opened his eyes to search her face. "But you said —"

"Nothing bad can happen. Not here. Not tonight."

He needed no further urging. Using his free hand to angle her head, he exposed her neck. The world narrowed until all he could hear was the thundering of her heart and the surge of blood in her carotid artery. With a moan, he bit down. He heard her gasp, felt her blood hit his veins like a freight train. Then he was in. In her skin, in her mind, in her heart. Tears sprang to his eyes.

"Aiden! Omigod, Aiden."

Too late, he realized she was feeling in him what he was feeling in her. Not just the physical sensations, not just the mind fuck. The love he'd felt in her fingertips was here. It spilled from her heart, pushed into his veins …

Oh, Christ, he was still taking her blood.

Her hands closed on his head to hold him at her throat. *More. Take more.*

His cock swelled inside her, and he felt her hips surge against him in reaction. But he'd already taken enough. More than enough.

Sam, I have to close your wound. Be still now, or we'll make a bloody mess of Delano's bed.

Hurry. I want to feel you move inside me.

Sweat beaded his brow as he worked his way out, secreting the healing substance. When she was decently healed, he reared back on stiff arms and started thrusting. Slowly at first, to let her come up to speed.

"Omigod, I feel *fantastic* around your cock."

He laughed. "Yes, you do." He shifted his position higher on her pelvis and rocked into her in such a way as to maximize the drag on her clitoris. Ahhhh! "Taking my cock feels pretty fantastic, too."

"God, yes!" She lifted her hands and scraped her fingernails over his chest, shuddering as she felt his response. Reading his desire, she arched up to lick and nibble one flat nipple.

Lost to all but sensation now, he pumped himself into her fast and hard. He felt her orgasm start in her mind before he started to feel the rhythmic contractions in her tightening sheath. It was all he needed to trigger his own release. It seemed to go on and on for minutes, each feeding off the other's ecstasy, until she'd milked the last of his essence.

He thought briefly about breaking their link immediately, but rejected the idea. It was too late anyway. He had nothing left to hide. He'd fallen in love with a mortal woman. With Sam. And she loved him right back, though God only knew why.

She drew a hand down his back gently. The reverence in her fingertips made him want to weep.

"I love you," she said.

He lifted his head to look at her. Her hazel eyes glistened with emotion. "I know," he said, brushing the hair back from her forehead.

"And you love me," she said.

He smiled. Leave it to Sam to declare his love for her. "Yes. Yes, I do."

She smiled back at him. "It's probably a very bad idea."

"Yeah, I know. You'll get old and die and break my heart."

She snorted. "More like I'll get old and you'll move along to the next —"

She flinched beneath him and Aiden caught a whiff of something foreign. Something not him, not her. And he could feel her pulling back, pulling inward again.

"Wait, Sam! I felt that. Stay with me. Stay, dammit!"

She hesitated on the brink of breaking their link.

"Sam, come back into me. Please. That wasn't you and it wasn't me. That was an intruder. If you let me in, let me get a good feel of it, maybe I can figure it out."

Okay. She closed her eyes, bit her lip and let her mind open to him again. And ... nothing. After long moments, she opened her eyes and let the connection drop. "He's gone."

"He?"

"Yeah, I think it's a he. But you felt it this time, right?"

"Oh, yeah. Definitely. And I think I know how they tracked us to set up that ambush."

Her eyes went wide. "I'm a beacon. I'm somebody's goddamn *beacon!*"

Chapter 19

SAM TOOK A sip of the calming herbal tea Aiden had insisted on brewing for her, but there was only so much that chamomile flowers, spearmint leaves and rose petals could do for a gal. A belt or two of whiskey might have worked better, but she was afraid to take anything that might cause her to let her guard down. Nobody, but *nobody*, was getting into her head again any time soon.

She felt a pang for Aiden, for whom nothing he swallowed could help. And he could definitely use the help. He was wearing the kitchen floor out with his frustrated pacing.

He whirled to face her. "You're sure this was the same person who intruded last time?"

"Yes. It had exactly the same feel as before. Remember how I likened it to stepping on that snake? It wasn't that the entity was intrinsically evil. But like the snake under my foot, it was where it wasn't supposed to be. Especially when you and I were ... you know."

"I know."

"I have to let the walls down in order for us to make that connection, and he seems to be right there waiting to slide into my head as soon as the window of opportunity opens."

"Well, that's easy enough to guard against. We'll go back to the bloodless rule."

Sam's face warmed as she recalled how she'd all but begged him to bite her not twenty minutes ago, and the mind-bending sexual bliss that ensued. "Do you think we can do that? You know how scared I was of risking it again, yet in the heat of the moment, I was the one who insisted you do it."

She saw the memory flare in his eyes, but he tamped it down. "That was before we knew the nature of this thing." He stopped his pacing to grip the edges of marble topped island beside her. "No way would I take your blood now, not even if you *begged* me. No matter how badly I might want it. Upon my honor, I will do nothing to facilitate another invasion of your privacy. No one touches you, physically or mentally, without your consent. *No one.*"

She slid from her stool to put her arms around him. Laying her head on his back, she inhaled his scent. "Thank you."

He closed his hand over hers, pressing it into his chest. "I love you," he said gruffly.

She smiled against his shirt, her heart swelling with happiness. "I know."

He turned in her arms. "Yeah, but I figured I'd better man up and say it myself."

She laughed, turning her face up for a kiss.

When he let her breathe again, she asked, "So, what are we going to do after Delano develops his vaccine and somehow manages to inoculate the vulnerable? Without telling them about vampires, of course."

"Oh, he'll get it done. For years, he's had a network of people working in soup kitchens and shelters and so forth, trying to look out for these folks. They'd be easy to immunize, possibly through food. And how hard would it be to pass out free injectibles in a crack house? Or food in a bunkhouse full of itinerant workers? He'll get it done."

"But what then? What will we do after those people are rendered too risky to prey on?"

"We'll still have to hunt for a while, but it'll be much easier. If the rogues lose the fringes of society and are forced to start preying on the more visible mainstream, they'll be very easy to track. There are dozens of hunters out there. I can see us clearing up this plague real quick."

"Okay, but what then?"

"Well, there will always be a few that go bad, but it should never be a full-time job again. In which case, I guess I'll have to look for an honest way to make a living. Or maybe I'll just become your live-in chef."

"So, you plan to ... stick around?"

He arched an eyebrow. "Trying to get rid of me?"

She shrugged. "I was just thinking ... what if that guy never goes away? What if we can never do the blood thing without him getting into my mind?"

"Ah, I think I see where this is going." He pulled away. "You don't think I can be faithful. You don't think I can do without a live donor, or two or twenty, on the side. That's it, isn't it?"

His eyes had cooled, and Sam felt her stomach lurch. "Don't be angry. I just want to be realistic, and you don't strike me as a bagged blood kinda guy."

He looked offended. "I *always* take bagged blood before a hunt. It's the only way to get enough to stay on equal footing with the rogues who gorge on victims."

"But for regular sustenance?"

He rolled his shoulders as though to loosen them. "Okay, I never used to do the bagged blood thing except for a hunt. But that was before we hooked up. Like I told you before, other than your blood, I've taken nothing but the blood bank special for weeks."

"I know. And you have no idea how relieved I was to hear that. When I went away on that shoot, I thought for sure ..." She took a deep breath and released it. "Anyway, I'm glad you didn't. It kills me to think about you with another woman. Not that that stops me from imagining it."

"Now *that* I can understand. Remember that night you brought that pretty boy home?"

"But I never brought anyone ... Wait, are you talking about *Conor*?"

"You kissed him on your doorstep."

"Yeah, on the *cheek*."

He snorted. "It looked like a kiss from where I was standing."

"You were *watching*?"

"I wanted to tear his throat out."

"Jesus, Aiden. You weren't even living in my house yet. He didn't even put his arms around me."

"Hey, I didn't say it made sense. Possessiveness, jealousy ... it had been so long since I experienced those emotions, the concept had pretty much lost its meaning. I wasn't particularly pleased to be reintroduced to them."

"The point being?"

"The point is I would never do to you what I couldn't stand for you to do to me. Simple."

"Really?"

"Really. And if you need proof it can be done, look at Delano. He put in the better part of a century without taking blood from a live donor."

She slanted him a skeptical look. "You can hardly compare your situations, though, can you? From what you've told me, Dr. Bowen looked on his condition as a curse, visited on him forcibly. He would be highly motivated not to indulge his nature, whereas you —"

"Okay, point taken," he muttered. "But it *can* be done. And if Del could do it celibate, I sure as hell can do it with the woman I love in my bed."

She blinked. "Celibate for a century?"

"Damned near."

"Oh, my word."

"Exactly. I can't imagine how he did it. We've been celibate for ... what? Half an hour now? And I'm already thinking about that open shower. Did you notice it has a *bench* in there?"

She laughed at his exaggerated leer. "I did notice, in fact."

"I can think of some uses we can put it to."

"Me, too," she confessed. "But do you think we should call Delano about this other thing?"

"Yeah, I do. Tell you what — you go get the water warmed up, and I'll make that call."

Forty minutes later, Sam slipped into a soft terry robe from the bathroom linen closet. She'd combed out her towel-dried hair and was in the midst of brushing her teeth when Aiden came up behind her wearing a towel around his lean waist.

Sam spat toothpaste and rinsed. "I forgot to ask — what did Delano have to say that kept you so long? I thought the hot water would be gone before you got here."

He reached around her for a toothbrush. "He just filled me in on a few critical details about this place."

"Like what?"

"Like the escape route that will take us through a tunnel to the river and the motorboat moored there, in the unlikely event we should need it."

She watched his reflection in the mirror as he applied toothpaste and started brushing.

"Do you think we will? Need it, I mean."

He removed the brush from his mouth. "Doubt it." He spat and rinsed. "That would be some pretty fine-tuned location skill if that little shit can find us way out here, based on a few seconds of psychic contact. Nevertheless, I always like to leave my options open. Del is resting easier, after I scoped it out and confirmed the escape route is intact."

She turned to face him. "You actually went down the tunnel to the river?" It shouldn't have surprised her. She'd seen him move at superhuman speed a time or two, but it was so easy to forget when he always paced himself to her speed.

"Yep. Boat's there, tank's topped up, and the motor starts on the first try." He replaced his toothbrush. "I should tell you Del was a bit concerned that your psychic intruder would keep pressing until he found us. He was on the verge of ordering us back to Montreal, I think, but I was able to assure him the barriers were back up and they'll stay up."

Sam blushed, knowing that meant Delano must know the circumstances under which the barriers came down. Between what she'd told Ainsley and what Aiden had told Delano, they had no secrets. Such were the hazards, she supposed, when you turned into a psychic beacon when you got your groove on with a vampire hunter.

"I'll take the couch," she said. "You'll need the bedroom. It looks completely sun-proofed."

"You'll sleep with me tonight."

Surprise jolted her pulse. "In the same bed?"

"After that scare … I just want you close."

"I thought that wasn't such a good idea for vampires and non-vampires to share a bed. Dangerous, even."

"The biggest danger is for the vamp." He dropped his eyelids. "I'll be essentially comatose for about five hours, during which I can't be woken. After that, I move into a long period of dream sleep. I can be woken in that latter state, if need be, but it leaves me grouchy as hell to be awake while the sun is still up." He lifted his lids to meet her gaze. "You can appreciate why being completely defenseless like that might make a guy feel a little … apprehensive."

"But Ainsley said …"

His eyes sharpened. "Ainsley said what?"

"Nothing."

"Tell me."

"That's how Dr. Bowen got infected. Or *dis*infected, if you want to look at it that way. As I understand it, Delano neglected to tell Ainsley she was a walking anti-vampire cocktail. She couldn't understand why he was dodging her advances when the chemistry between them was obvious. So she crawled into his bed one day when he was already sleeping, and when he woke up that evening …"

"Good for Ainsley." Aiden grinned. "Well, as I mentioned, it had been a while for the guy. For us, on the other hand, it'll have been hours, not decades. I think I can control myself long enough to get up and take some blood."

She bit her lip. "What if I touch you in my sleep? And what if you're having a hunting dream?"

He tipped her chin up. "Sam, honey, I can smell your scent when you're at the other end of your house, on a different floor. I can feel your heartbeat in my head. Your blood … it's *in* me, Sam, enriched from the meals I cook for you with my own hands.

Believe me, baby, I'll know you're there. And I will never hurt you."

He held out his hand to her.

Tears leapt to her eyes, but she blinked them back and accepted his hand. "Sorry, I'm a little emotional. You're my first virgin."

Laughing, he scooped her up and carried her to bed.

Aiden woke to find Sam's side of the bed cold. Lifting his head, he listened. Ah, she was in the kitchen. He could smell the coffee clearly. Which meant he'd better get up and feed her before she resorted to building another one of those ungodly submarine sandwiches like she'd done the night before last.

In the three nights and days they'd been here, they'd shared the same bed. Sam had taken about a million pictures of him. Once in a while, he got his hands on the camera and managed to get a few of her. Which usually provoked a tussle in which he let her wrest the camera from him. A camera that was quickly forgotten.

The first evening, he'd been the first to waken, but only because her whimpering had cut through his dreams. Thinking it might be one of her visions, he'd tried to wait it out, but when she grew more and more distressed, he wakened her. She'd cried out, then burrowed so hard into his arms, he thought she was trying to disappear inside him. She'd had a nightmare that the psychic invader had been eavesdropping on her dreams. He'd comforted her the only way he knew how, with fierce, passionate lovemaking that tested his promise not to take her blood. Tested it sufficiently, in fact, that they agreed that henceforth, it might be wiser for him to feed first. She wasn't the only one who woke up hungry.

Speaking of hungry ...

He threw the covers off, made a washroom trip, dressed and headed for the kitchen.

"Aiden, you're up."

"Mmmm." He swooped in to kiss her mouth, which tasted vaguely of toothpaste and more strongly of coffee. He pulled back and looked around. A covered pot sat on a lit burner and he could smell bread toasting. "And you're cooking."

She grinned. "I felt like breakfast for a change. I can't remember the last one I had."

"Eggs?"

She nodded. "Boiled. I'll fix them with some of that olive oil mayonnaise, and the toast is whole grain."

He frowned. "Let me cut you up some melon and squeeze some orange juice."

"Already done. I may not have much expertise in the kitchen, but I can do breakfast." She turned the burner off under the eggs and reached for the toast that just popped. "I even fixed your breakfast." She nodded toward the counter next to the refrigerator.

He followed her gesture to see that she'd already put a unit of blood in the blood warmer. "God, woman, I could get used to this."

She went back to preparing her breakfast, no doubt to give him privacy while he infused the blood and dealt with the inevitable aftermath. He was grateful for her discretion. The impersonal sexual jolt the stuff gave him had no place between them. When he came to her, she'd know the voltage was supplied completely by the two of them and nothing else.

"The moon is even fuller this evening." Sam carried her empty plate to the table. "Maybe we could take another walk?"

He'd scoped the property out comprehensively last night. What the nearly full moon hadn't shown him, he'd checked out with the aid of Sam's night vision binoculars. They'd seen all manner of wildlife, from raccoons to a majestic moose, the latter moving through the woods with remarkably little sound. Aiden couldn't recall the last time he'd enjoyed a night so much.

"Good idea. Eat up and we'll go." He sank down on the chair beside her. "So ... any dreams while you slept?"

"Not a one, thank God. No psychic stalker nightmares, and more importantly, no visions." She ate some of the egg and chased it with a bite of toast. "Maybe there's something to this remote location thing after all. Maybe I need a certain population density or certain level of vampire activity to stimulate the dreams."

"Maybe." Well, that was a blessing. At least she wouldn't have to angst about victims who died tonight, since she had no foreknowledge. "And what about me? Did I ... behave in my sleep?"

"You were an absolute gentleman," she said, but her slight blush suggested otherwise. As did the almost-memory niggling at the edge of his mind.

He grinned. "By which you mean nothing you couldn't handle with a poke in the ribs and an order to roll over?"

"That would be accurate, yes."

"Good. Now, are you about ready to venture out? Because if we don't do it soon ..." He leaned in with intent to kiss her.

"It'll wait," she declared, abandoning her chair in favor of straddling his lap.

Aiden couldn't have concurred more heartily.

By the time they dressed again to go out, three hours had passed.

The air was cool when they stepped outside. Again, Aiden marveled at how well disguised the cottage was. The exterior really did make it look very ramshackle. As they walked down the drive, he almost wished they'd come out sooner. Last evening when they'd come out, it had still been early enough that he'd felt pockets of warm air ripple over his skin as he moved through it. Feeling those remnants of the sun's energy rising from the earth ... damn, it'd been good.

The wood smells floated through Aiden's head. The subtle scent of decay from fallen, moss-covered trees and last year's leaves. The more pungent scent of the living forest, with a hint of stagnant water from that boggy area they'd discovered last night. He inhaled deeply, drinking in the scents of the night.

And froze.

"God, Aiden, look at that moon —"

Aiden turned to shush her, but found himself looking at a rogue bearing down on them with preternatural speed. He shoved Sam hard, without even a word of warning, the motion bringing him more squarely into the rogue's path. He heard her cry as she landed, but had to stay focused on the attacker. Unable to get out of the way in time, he ducked low and braced himself. The rogue hit him like a fucking freight train, but his attacker took the worst of it, sailing over Aiden to land on his back where he lay winded and gasping. Aiden was on him in a second, wrenching his neck so viciously, he almost tore his head off.

"Run!" he yelled at Sam, his eyes searching the woods for attackers. There were more. He could smell them.

"I can't!" she sobbed. "My ankle. I can't stand."

Goddammit! He'd hurt her when he'd shoved her aside.

There, from the direction of the road! He'd seen a flash of movement.

He scooped Sam up in his arms. "Hang on, baby. This is gonna hurt."

He streaked back to the cottage, which appeared just as they'd left it in the moonlit clearing. Eyes and ears straining, he dumped Sam on her feet, dug a key from his pocket and placed it into her hands. "Unlock it," he ordered. "I can't turn my back.'

He drew the knife from the sheath he always wore on his right leg and crouched, ready for another attack.

Behind him, Sam's breath came in sobs of pain and fear, but her hands didn't fail her. She had the door unlocked in seconds and stumbled inside. Aiden backed over the threshold and slammed the door, locking it. A groping search of the trim around the door frame and he found the switch Delano had told him about. Within seconds, iron security bars rose from the floor to reinforce the door.

"I like the look of those bars," Sam said.

"I still have to deal with the windows." He put his knife in her hands. "Stay right here by the door," he ordered.

"Oh, God, windows!"

"It's okay, Sam. See?" He hit the first switch and a steel plate slid into place over the glass. "Just stay there and I'll get the rest."

He moved like lightening, hitting switch after switch. But when he reached the last room, the bedroom, a rogue came crashing through the window. Or rather, part way through it. With an extra burst of speed, Aiden met him and drove him back. Back and down, ensuring one particularly jagged fragment of glass eviscerated the bastard's belly on his way out. The rogue screamed and fell backward.

"Aiden?" The terror in Sam's voice twisted his gut.

"It's okay," he called, hitting the switch. "We're good. I got all the windows." When the metal panel slid into place without incident, he hustled back to the entryway. Sam stood on one leg beside the door, back braced against the wall for support, his knife gripped tightly in her hand.

"It's my stalker, isn't it?" Her voice quavered. "The guy who keeps getting into my head."

Aiden gently pried the knife from her hands. "Yeah, I think he's behind it, but he's not alone." He resheathed the knife. "I killed the first one, and the other one who tried to come in the window is neutralized, at least for tonight."

"How many?"

"Judging by what I scented, more than the two I've seen so far. But we'll get a look from the tunnel. Del has a security camera down there."

She sucked in a breath. "Oh, God, I'm so sorry."

"Nothing to be sorry for. This is not your fault."

"But I'm the beacon! I'm the one who led them here."

He took her arm. "Listen to me, Sam. This is not your fault. I'm the one who dragged you into this. And I'm going to get you out." He lifted her into his arms and carried her to the bedroom where he deposited her gently on the bed, angled away from the bloody mess on the carpet by the window. He crossed to the closet, swept Sam's clothing to one side. Quickly he located the lever Delano had told him about and pressed it. The back panel of the closet slid open to reveal a weapons cache.

"Ah, thank you, my paranoid friend." Ignoring an M16 assault rifle — too unwieldy — he took the shorter M4 carbine off its pegs, rammed a magazine home and pocketed a few more. Tossing the weapon on the bed, he helped himself to a 9mm semi. He jammed a cartridge in place and chambered a round. "You've had lessons, right?"

She swallowed. "A couple, yeah."

"Good. Safety's on, right here, see?"

She nodded, taking the gun from him. "Got it."

He loaded a Smith & Wesson .45, shoved it into his waistband and dropped some spare clips in his jacket pocket. He looked at a number of hunting knives, selected one with a sheath that could be strapped to his other ankle.

"So, is this where you call Delano for reinforcements on that satellite phone?"

"Can't," he said as he secured the sheathed knife. "We left it in the truck."

She frowned. "But how did you phone Delano earlier?"

"I went out there to use it, then hung up and tossed it back into the vehicle when you came out to join me for our walk last night. I figured I'd grab it on the way back, bring it inside, but I forgot."

"Oh."

No recrimination in her voice. No trace of disgust on her face when he turned toward her. That was okay. He had more than enough fury at his carelessness for the both of them. "I know. I'm sorry. That was criminally stupid of me."

"Wait! I have a cell phone." She started to get up, but gasped and fell back.

"Stay put," he said. "Is it in your purse?"

"Yes."

He collected her bag for her and handed it to her. "I doubt it will work way out here," he said. "I can't remember the last relay tower I saw."

She pulled the phone out of her purse, tried it and groaned. "You're right. No service."

"No problem. We don't need Delano's help to make our escape by river. It just would have been nice if Del's team could have corralled some of these bastards for interrogation."

She clasped her arms around herself as though she were cold despite the jacket she wore. "It's so quiet. What do you think they're doing out there?"

"I don't know, but it's time to go take a look."

"In the tunnel, you mean?"

"Yep." He took a first aid box from the gun cabinet, then slid the concealing panel back in place. "Got any Ibuprofen or Tylenol in that purse?"

She nodded.

"Good. You're going to need it. I think piggyback is probably best. Let's get you up on your good foot and I'll take care of the rest."

She stuck the gun in her purse and slung the strap around her, then accepted his hand up. He turned and lifted her onto his back. She tried to swallow down a moan. Her body was so stiff, and he could feel she was holding her breath.

"I know it hurts, and I'm so sorry, Sam. But we'll be away from here soon and we'll wrap it. That'll make a big difference. That and some painkillers." He eyed the pillows on the bed. "Can you handle this first aid kit, too? That way I can grab one of these fat pillows to elevate your foot in the boat."

"Good idea."

She took the small box from him and wedged it between her chest and his back. That'd work.

Supporting her with one arm, rifle and pillow dangling from the other, he made his way to the dining room.

"Where's the tunnel access?" she asked, her voice rising. "We don't have to go out, do we?"

He flipped back the Oriental rug beneath the dining table and tapped one of the tiles sharply with the butt of the carbine. A motor whirred to life and a large chunk of the floor, complete with rug, table and chairs lifted up, then slid smoothly sideways several feet to reveal concrete steps disappearing into a black pit.

"I know it doesn't look like much, but wait'll I get the lights." Descending several steps, he hit a switch and a series of fluorescent tubes came to life, illuminating a long corridor.

He felt her twist and knew she was looking back at the gaping hole above.

"Don't worry. It closes from down here." Aiden hit a second switch and the motor whirred again, and the floor above them began to move back into place.

"Thank God! I know you said they can't get in, but I feel better with it closed."

"Me too." He eased her off his back and helped her settle on the floor, handing her the pillow.

She slid it under her injured foot, then looked up to watch the concealed door settle into place with a rumble. "God, that's amazing!"

"Hell, this is low tech compared to how his real residences are kitted out. Most are equipped with a helipad and helicopter."

"You're kidding!"

"Am I? Ask Ainsley to tell you about fleeing St. Cloud when Janacek attacked them."

"I'll do that." Her laugh had an edge of hysteria to it. "Just as soon as we get out of here and back to safety."

He put a hand under her chin. "Hey, it's gonna be all right, Sam. I promise I'll get us out of here safely. It's just damned inconvenient."

She closed her hand over his. "I know you will."

He wanted to say something more, but a thud reverberated from the floor above them.

Her eyes rounded. "What's that?"

"Ramming the door, most likely, but they can do that all night and it won't come down. Not unless they brought a tank with them to knock a wall down. And if they try a power saw to cut through the logs, they've got a surprise coming. An electrifying one." He crossed the hallway and flicked another switch. A bank of small television screens sprang to life, but their screens were universally dark.

Sam groaned. "It's black out there. You can't see anything."

"That's because I haven't hit the infrared." He searched the control panel. "Here. Got it." A flick of the switch and the screens brightened.

"Omigod, they're everywhere!"

Aiden swore softly. They weren't *everywhere*, but he counted nine of them, and that without perfect 360-degree vision of the exterior. There were probably more. And they were circling the house, looking for vulnerabilities.

"It's okay, Sam. They can't get in. But we'd better make our getaway while they're busy trying."

"Look!" she cried, pointing at one of the small screens. "What's he doing, the big one?"

He sucked his breath in on a hiss. "Gasoline. They're going to set the place on fire."

Sam moaned.

"It's okay, baby. They'll all be watching the fire while we're slipping down the river."

"Good," she said. "That's good. I like the sound of that."

He took the M4 off his back and knelt. "Okay, time for a boat ride. Let's get you up and on my back."

She gathered up the first aid kit and pillow and accepted a hand up. "Ready."

He bent, taking her slight weight easily. "You might want to close your eyes. It's one thing to run in the dark at these speeds. It's another in a tunnel. You might get sick."

"Trust me, they're already closed."

He grinned. "Then hold on."

Some distance from the tunnel's mouth, the fluorescent lights left off, to prevent leaking light from betraying its presence. Aiden slowed, pulling up ten yards from the tunnel's end, straining to hear over the pounding of Sam's heart.

"What it is?"

"Hush," he said. "I heard something."

A crash, followed by a splash as something hit the water.

He lowered Sam to the ground. "Stay here," he whispered, pointing to the ground. When she nodded her understanding, he stole forward. When he neared the tunnel's well-camouflaged mouth, he dropped to the ground and inched forward on his belly. Once in position, he lifted Sam's night vision binoculars — the ones that he'd planned to use for watching wildlife on their peaceful woods walk — and scanned the area.

Dammit. One vamp on the floating dock and another on the riverbank on the overland trail leading from the cottage. He'd have to deal with them quickly and quietly. And since he didn't have a silencer, that meant hand-to-hand. Good thing he was well-supplied with knives.

Once more, he swept the riverbank with the glasses, then panned back across the dock. Just the two. He could take them.

Then the motorboat exploded in a ball of orange fire.

So did Aiden's brain.

He dropped the binoculars, forcing back the scream that wanted to rip from his lungs.

Fuck, fuck, fuck!

He scuttled backward.

"Aiden?" Her voice was barely a whisper, barely loud enough for him to hear over the rogues outside, who were whooping and laughing and congratulating themselves.

"What happened? Are you hit?"

"No, but my night vision's fried. I was scanning the dock with the infrareds when the boat blew up."

"*Our* boat?"

"C'mon, let's move back. When they stop celebrating, we wanna be out of earshot."

He boosted her onto his back again. Once again, she stifled a groan at the pain. When they'd gone far enough down the tunnel, Aiden said, "This'll do. That's our only escape route, and I don't want to get too far away. When the flames die down, we need to be sure we can slip out unobserved."

"But without the boat …"

He lowered her to the floor again. "We'll have to swim for it. When we get far enough away, we'll crawl out and find a place where I can take shelter for the day, and carry on tomorrow evening. There's no way we can keep your phone dry, but sooner or later, we'll find a land line we can use, and we'll call Del to haul us out."

"You're kidding! Have you *seen* that river? I can swim, but damn ...

"It's okay. I can swim well enough for the both of us, even with your bad ankle. I promise. We just need to make sure we get away clean." He pulled himself to a sitting position, back resting against the wall, legs outstretched.

"Wait a minute. Won't the fire bring the authorities?"

"I doubt it. Not way out here. Not unless the rogues are careless enough to start a serious forest fire, and I imagine even that would take a while to come to anyone's notice. We're a long way out."

Sam groaned. "I can't believe this is happening." She dragged the pillow around to prop under the calf. "How could they find me based on a short glimpse inside my head? We'd have had our hands full finding this place without a guide, and we had directions."

Good point. Unless ... oh, hell and damnation. He rubbed the back of neck. "Maybe it wasn't such a short glimpse after all."

"But —" She looked at him. "Oh, God, the nightmare I had a couple nights ago! It wasn't really a nightmare, was it? He was really inside my head."

"It seems the likeliest answer."

"*Stupid*. Oh, God, I'm so stupid! Why didn't I see it?"

"Because it had never happened like that before. We assumed it could only happen under specific circumstances, when you let the barriers down to merge your mind with mine."

"But I should have thought of it. For God's sake, when is your mind more vulnerable than when you're sleeping? If I'd realized he'd been in my mind, we could have vacated last night." She pressed her hands to her temples. "I'm such an idiot."

"Hush." He took her hands in his. "If anyone's an idiot, it's me. You hear me? I'm the one who's supposed to be protecting you." He paused for a moment when his voice threatened to break. "Sam, honey, I'm the one with a lifetime of experience with these bastards. I should have twigged to the possibility."

She smiled. "I appreciate the effort, Aiden, but it was *my* mind that creep was in. I should have known it."

"But you were sleeping, dammit." To push into someone's defenseless mind while they slept ... it was despicable. A violation of the lowest kind. He let go of her hand for fear of squeezing it too hard. "Okay, there's no point arguing about who's the biggest idiot here," he said. "We'll have plenty of time to debate that when we get out of here." He tipped up her chin and pulled her face close for a quick, hard kiss. "Wait here. I'm going to the tunnel mouth to make sure our arsonists have lost interest in the burning boat and gone up to watch the burning cottage. In the meantime, you dig out whatever painkillers you've got in that purse and take some."

Sam watched Aiden's crouching form until she lost sight of it in the deepening gloom. She continued to watch, thinking she might see his silhouette against the faint, flickering light from the dwindling fire outside when he got closer to the tunnel's mouth, but he must have dropped to his belly again.

She leaned her head back against the concrete wall and closed her eyes. Now that she was alone, the fear and dread she'd more or less managed to force down blossomed in her gut, pushing out all warmth. Or maybe that was this damned cold concrete floor. She shifted her legs, trying to draw them up for warmth, but her injured ankle sent a screaming jolt of agony to her brain. Breathing in short puffs, she stretched her legs back out again, ignoring the chill from the floor.

Okay, deep breaths now, she counseled herself. *That's what you need.* Hand on her belly, she drew in a big breath, expanding her lungs, stretching her diaphragm. She exhaled, slowly and fully, feeling her tummy flatten again. *Atta girl. Air in, tension out. Breathe that fear right out. Breathe out the pain.*

Except the air she was breathing in was tainted by smoke, because they were stuck in this tunnel and their boat was burning and their escape route was blocked.

Dammit, this was all her fault. Why hadn't it occurred to her that that freak had actually been in her mind? They could have been well away from here by now. They could be safe behind the walls of Delano's penthouse apartment.

Instead, they faced a night in the water, battling hypothermia while Aiden towed her dead weight to safety. Then a day in some fisherman's lodge or maple sugaring shack, or God, maybe a cave! And possibly another night in the water.

Tears sprang to her eyes at the mere thought of what was in store. Her ankle hurt so damned much. How was she going to get through this? She wouldn't be able to sleep, either. Aiden would have to; his biology demanded it. But she wouldn't be able to. If she slept, her stalker might find her again.

She caught the cast of her thoughts and reined them in ruthlessly. For God's sake, Sam! Aiden was going to do all the work. He was going to swim for both of them, carry her overland until they found shelter. He's the one who would push himself to his limits, not you. You'll just be a passenger.

She blinked as a thought occurred to her. How long could he keep that output up without blood? She would gladly give him hers — it was the least she could contribute — but such an exchange would surely turn her into a beacon again ...

Her ankle throbbed sharply, reminding her she should take the meds right away, as Aiden had urged. She flipped open her purse, which she still wore with the strap slung across her chest, and found the Advil. Popping three regular strength pills, she swallowed them dry, capped the bottle and put it back.

She heard a faint scratch and whipped her head around to see Aiden making his way back down the tunnel. Had they gone already? Was it time to take the plunge into the cold river?

"All clear?" she asked when he was close enough for her soft words to carry.

"Unfortunately, no. I heard them talking." He held out a hand. "Come on, let's move further back down the tunnel to cut the risk of our voices carrying."

She went through the drill again, picking up the pillows and first aid kit, and he hoisted her onto his back once more. When he was satisfied they'd gone far enough, he stopped. "This'll do, but we still have to keep our voices down."

She settled herself again, doing the shallow *puff, puff, puff* thing with her breathing until she'd expelled as much of the red-hot pain as she could.

He must have noticed her distress. "That ankle's gotta hurt."

She waved his concern off. "I took some pills. It'll feel better soon. Now, hit me with the bad news."

"It's not *all* bad." He sank down beside her. "The good being they haven't found the tunnel. It's well camouflaged and very hard to see from the outside, but I was a little concerned that my scent might linger from that night I scoped it out. Obviously the rain yesterday has washed it away, and now everything is overlain with smoke."

"The bad news?"

"They plan to keep a vigil all night. They're worried we might somehow have escaped the cottage and will come looking for the boat to make our escape. And there are three of them now, not two."

"All night?"

"Afraid so. And they're none too happy about it. Which is lucky for us. If they'd taken up concealed positions instead of standing around bitching to each other about it, we might have blundered right into them."

"So we're not getting out of here tonight?"

"If it were one or even two, I'd go for it. I could probably pick them off quietly. But three … it would be hard to get away without someone raising an alarm. With the boat, we could've gotten away, alarm or no. But without it … if we didn't get away clean …"

"Tomorrow night, then. We just have to wait them out, right?"

In the pale light cast by the fluorescent fixture further down the tunnel, his face looked grim.

"If they're concerned enough to post guards on the dock until dawn, they'll be back tomorrow night. They'll want to sift through the cold ashes to confirm the kill."

She sucked in a breath. "And find the door to this tunnel?"

"Afraid so."

Her stomach lurched as she imagined the rogues forcing the door, invading the tunnel. There would be gunfire. Blood. Death. She shook the images away. "So we just have to be up sooner then them and slip away before they come back." Her excitement rose as her idea took root "They have to take shelter somewhere, right? We can get away before they get back here."

Aiden shook his head. "They knew they were looking for a remote location, Sam. They'll have brought their own rolling shelter. A cube van, a U-Haul truck, anything on wheels with a windowless cargo space. I'm betting they'll be on site, or close by."

Sam grimaced. Okay, so they wouldn't have a *huge* head start, but surely they could still get the jump on them. "I'll stay awake and rouse you early. You *can* be woken early, right? We can still get a bit of a head start."

"We still couldn't outrun them, Sam. Not with your ankle."

"The SUV! If we can enough of a jump on them to get to it —"

"Forget it. They'll disable the vehicle, if they haven't already torched it."

Her brain raced. There *had* to be a way. "The river! You said you could swim for both of us. Couldn't we get away in the water if we got a head start?"

"If we happen to leave in a torrential rain that washes our scent away during the small window before they come. Otherwise, they'll know exactly what we did. They can hop in their vehicle, drive twenty miles down the road and just wait for us to come bobbing down on the current."

"But what choice do we have? If you're right, they'll come back, find us and slaughter us. We have to make a run for it!"

He held out his hand. "Pass me your purse."

She blinked. "My purse?"

"The anti-vampire juice is still in there, isn't it?"

"Yes, but that's for if we're cornered by a vamp. A *single* vamp. It's not going to work against a horde."

"It's not for them."

"Then who ... ?" She looked at his face. The grim lines around his mouth had deepened, but his blue eyes blazed brighter than ever. "Oh, no, Aiden. No!"

Chapter 20

"It's the only way, Sam. We have to get out of here, together, in broad daylight, while they sleep. And the only way I can do that is to lose the sun allergy."

"You can't, Aiden," she said, hearing how high and thin her voice had become. Taking a calming breath, she continued: "This is your life. Your *purpose*. If you do this, you won't be able to hunt anymore."

He gripped her wrist, leaning close to let her read the determination blazing from his eyes. "The only purpose I have now is to keep you safe. I dragged you into this, and I'm going to get you out. Simple."

Anguish twisted her gut into knots. "But there's no going back!"

He dropped her hand. "Give me the injector, Sam. I know what I'm doing."

"Didn't you hear me?" She pulled the purse close, sheltering it on the other side of her body. "It's *irreversible*. Aiden. I know Delano gave you to understand it could be reversed. Ainsley told me all about it, how he offered to be turned back again, and how he was going to get you to do it for him. But he was *wrong*. It wouldn't have worked! Everything he's done in the lab since then suggests that once you get that stuff in your system, you can't be turned. Or turned *again*, in your case."

A muscle leapt in his cheek. "I know. He told me."

"Then you can't do it!"

"It's our best bet, Sam."

"No." She shook her head. "I can set out at dawn."

"Sam —"

"Listen to me. I know I can't walk out of here. But in the water, in daylight ... Aiden, the river could carry me a long, long way while those rogues are sleeping. And when I'd gone far enough, I could get out and find a phone, and then Delano could send an army to get you. He could get to you before sunset, and get you out of here!"

He cupped her chin in a big, warm palm. "Sam, I love you for formulating that plan, but it won't work, for two reasons. First, our vamp crew will have brought along a handful of non-vamp helpers. Drivers, sentries, thugs, that kind of thing."

"You can't possibly know that."

"Yes I can. Because that's what I'd do in their place. That's what I *do* do. Notice how I never fly without a non-vamp pilot? Never embark on a road trip without a non-vamp who can drive? That's because I have to cover off the possibility that I'll be stranded somewhere and need a non-vamp guardian to see me safely through the daylight hours. These guys will have done the same. No way would they come this far without non-vamp support. They just wouldn't do it."

"Okay, but who's to say they'll be surveilling the dock? Wouldn't they be more likely to stand guard outside the vamps' shelter?"

"How they're deployed depends on how many there are. But if they're *not* standing guard out there and you manage to slip unnoticed into the river, that brings me to the second reason your plan won't work. Honey, that beast would *eat* you. They don't call it the Mighty Restigouche for nothing. The current is swift, and I'm sure there'll be rapids, hydraulic holes ... If I were with you, we could probably body surf them safely. In my current state, that is. I could probably have steered a course. But alone, Sam, with that bad ankle ..."

She dug her hands into her hair, squeezing her head as though she could push back her dread. "But I don't want you to do it!"

"I know, baby. But I don't see any alternative."

"It sounds like the river could kill us anyway." She dropped her hands. "Why not wait and see? Maybe they won't come back. Maybe they'll accept that they got us in the fire."

"They'll come back. Face it, babe. It's the only way we can get out." He rubbed the back of his neck. "And we won't have to risk the river, either. We'll drive out."

Drive? "But you said they'll trash the SUV."

"Yeah, but their vehicle or vehicles will still be operational."

Her eyes widened. "What about the non-vamp guards?"

"I can deal with them."

"But you'll be —"

"Non-vamp, yes. But I won't have forgotten how to use a gun or a knife. I won't have forgotten what I'm so good at. I can take them out, Sam, and we'll drive out of here with a bunch of sleeping killers for cargo." He held out a hand to her. "Give me the injector now. We shouldn't waste any more time, since I'll need to be through the worst of it so we can get away tomorrow while there's still lots of daylight left."

She clutched the purse tighter. "What if doesn't work for you the way it did for Delano? What if it doesn't work at all? God, Aiden, what if you don't survive it?"

That muscle in his jaw leapt again. "Then you will take every one of these weapons and leave here at daylight. You might have to crawl, but you'll have to find their vehicles, because that's the only way you're getting out of here. If you see a sentry, shoot him. Shoot to kill, Sam. I mean it. It's your only hope. Then lay low and wait for others to come. Because there'll be others. When they stop coming, search the dead guys for keys. Someone will be carrying them. As soon as you score keys, you gotta find that vehicle. If there's more than one vehicle, you gotta shoot the tires out of the other one so they can't give chase, which they might do if there are any non-vamps huddling in the woods, hiding from gunfire. But don't do that until you're sure you can start the vehicle you pick to drive out of here. Then get yourself to a phone booth and call Delano. He'll take it from there. Oh, and don't sleep, no matter what."

"I *hate* this!"

He laid a hand on her chin and pulled her face close for a kiss. It was long and full of yearning so poignant that she could no longer hold back the tears. Her cheeks were wet with them when he lifted his head.

He held out his hand. "*Now*, Sam."

She wiped the moisture from her face. With hands that trembled, she retrieved the autoinjector. "Do you know how to use it?"

"Can't be too hard, can it?"

Sam let her breath out on a shudder. "I'll get it ready."

Following the steps Delano had showed her, she unscrewed the tube, removed the auto-injector, and removed the cap. "Hold it like this." She demonstrated the proper grip. "Then drive this end against your thigh at a 90-degree angle, with a fair amount of force. It's spring loaded, and it takes some force to activate it."

"Do I need to bare my leg?"

She shook her head. "No, it's designed to be used through clothing."

He took the device from her, adjusting his grip to mimic the one she'd showed him.

"That about right?"

She swallowed to ease her aching throat. "It's perfect."

"Sam?"

"Yes?"

"I love you."

She managed a smile. "I love you, too." She swallowed to ease her aching throat. "Don't die on me."

He grinned, giving her his wickedest, sexiest smile. "I'm hard to kill. Haven't you noticed?"

She choked back a half-laugh, half-sob. "Go ahead then. Do it."

He lifted his arm and brought it down, jabbing it firmly into his left thigh.

Aiden felt the jab of the needle, then the sting of the serum. He waited a few seconds, then lifted the autoinjector clear.

"Let me see it," Sam said.

He handed it to her, and she inspected it carefully.

"Good. You got it all." She sheathed the injector in its tube again and recapped it. "How do you feel?"

He massaged the area. "Stings like a bitch."

She smiled. "That little poke? This from the man who was gut-stabbed and shrugged it off like it was nothing more serious than a shaving nick."

Ah, but he wasn't going to be that man much longer, was he?

He didn't say that to Sam. Neither did he tell her that he could feel the serum moving in his veins like liquid fire, pushing further and further into his system with every beat of his heart. Instead, he returned her smile. "It's always the little stuff. You can't have forgotten removing the adhesive bandage from that knife wound?"

Her smile widened. "I haven't."

He leaned his head back against the tiled wall, suppressing a grimace. Jesus God, that stuff was nasty! It felt like a creeping toxin, poisoning him by slow, fiery degrees. Maybe Sam's fears were right on the money. Maybe he wouldn't survive this. Maybe his black heart was too far gone, after all these years, after all the kills, all the women he used so casually and forgot so easily. Maybe the only way to get the vampire out was to kill the host.

"Aiden?"

She looked so concerned, he lifted a hand to her face. Or rather, he tried to. His arm refused to obey the command of his mind.

Shit. The day sleep. There were still hours of night left. No way should he be feeling like this. Unless ... ah, crap. Of course. His vampire physiology was preparing to battle the Merzetti Effect, forcing him into the healing sleep so it could 'repair' the perceived damage being done to his system.

He swallowed. "Think I'm gonna need to sleep, Sam."

"What?"

"Shusssh. Not so loud."

"You don't look good."

"S'okay. Need to sleep. Can't stop it."

"You can't leave me!"

She picked up his hand but he couldn't return her squeeze with a reassuring one of his own. Goddamn this paralysis.

"S'okay," he repeated, managing a smile. "Bonus, really. Change'll happen ... I'll be oblivious."

She moved closer to him. "What do I do when dawn comes? How long should I let you sleep? What if I can't wake you? Oh, God, I hate this."

"Mid-morning at latest. If you can't wake me, leave. Do like I told you."

She drew back. "I will *not* leave you."

"Sam?"

"What?"

"Come close."

She knelt again beside him, laying a hand on his face.

He drew in a breath, turning his head ever so slightly into her hand. God, she smelled good. Even with the taint of smoke that had invaded the tunnel, he could smell her skin and the French milled soap she used. He closed his eyes to better savor the scent.

"Aiden?"

He opened his eyes. "Don't mind going to hell. Earned it."

She made a distressed sound, but once again, he was powerless to lift a hand to her face. Her precious, beautiful face.

His lids drooped again. He let them rest a moment while he gathered his strength. He figured he had maybe a minute before sleep took him, and no force on earth could stop its inexorable march. He better talk faster.

"Don't mind going to hell," he repeated. "But I can't go there thinking 'bout those bastards coming down this tunnel and you standing guard over my unconscious body." He forced his lids to open through sheer will, the effort required almost painful. "Don't make me do that. Please, Sam. *Please.*"

She was crying now. The soft sounds were breaking his heart. He couldn't comfort her, couldn't even keep his eyes open.

"Sam?"

"Okay," she said. "If I can't wake you at a decent hour, I'll leave. I'll hijack the truck like you said."

"Shoot anyone gets in your way."

She dashed away tears. "I'll shoot anyone I have to to get to a phone, to get Delano out here."

He might have told her that with that ankle of hers, it would take her so long to execute the plan — *if she could execute it at all* — that she probably wouldn't be able to reach a phone in time to get troops here quickly enough. But it was her only chance. He needed her to get safely away . . .

Instead, he said, "Thank you." At least he thought he got the words out. Then the black vortex claimed him.

The next five hours were the longest of Sam's life.

The first twenty minutes she spent crying, surrendering to the fear and pain. She wanted to wail and lash out at something, but that would only get them found. So she cried silently. It didn't do much to ease the pain in her heart or her ankle, but it did ease the ache in her throat. When it was over, she dried her eyes on her sleeves and turned her attention to Aiden.

He'd fallen asleep sitting up. Very carefully, she got up. Standing on her uninjured foot, leaning against the wall for balance, she manipulated the dead weight of him until he stretched out at the base of the wall. Then she'd taken off her jacket and covered his trunk with it, then emptied her bag and rolled it up to approximate a cervical support pillow for his neck.

When she'd done all she could, she dealt with her own ankle, wrapping it in the pressure bandage she found in the first aid kit. Then she settled herself beside Aiden's head, backed propped against the wall and injured leg elevated on the pillow.

As the minutes stretched into hours, she decided it was worse even than when he'd been stabbed and she'd had to wait it out in that plane to find out if he'd lived or died. This time, if he survived, he would be changed forever. No longer vampire. No more superpowers. No vampire mind tricks, no leaping onto tall buildings, no insanely acute senses, no more moving at hyperspeed. No more vampire-hunting gig.

For a while, the smoke in the underground corridor grew intense, as did the heat. Briefly, she began to think they might perish from smoke inhalation, but as the night wore on, she realized the tunnel must have air exchange. It was keeping pace well enough that they shouldn't succumb to carbon monoxide poisoning. On the other hand, she was certain she would never get the smell out of her sinuses.

When she finally relaxed about the smoke threat, a new enemy raised its head. *Sleep.* If she fell asleep now, her psychic stalker would find her. He'd push his way into her defenseless mind, and the vampire horde out there would know where they were. They wouldn't have to wait for another nightfall to finish what they'd come to do. But with Aiden's slow, shallow respirations lulling her, she found herself on the brink of sweet sleep again and again. Each time, she jerked out of it, jolting her sprained ankle. With every neuron she owned sending screaming pain messages to her brain, she was sure she couldn't possibly nod off again. Until it happened again.

Nod off, jerk awake, *pant, pant, pant* to get on top of the pain …

Four hours into it — probably two hours before she should have — she swallowed two more ibuprofen.

Just when it seemed the night would never end, the impending sunup was heralded by trills of birdsong. Finally, pale light began to show at the end of the tunnel. The new day had come.

Of course, daylight brought a bundle of questions. Would Aiden wake up? Had the injection worked? Was there still too much vampire in him for him to be roused from sleep? Would she be forced to keep the promise he'd extracted from her? Oh, shit, *could* she? Could she kill a man? Several men?

And how long could a body go without peeing?

The morning wore on. Thankfully, she felt more alert. Staying awake was no longer a torture. But her full bladder was.

As was sitting here looking at Aiden. Shouldn't his sleep be getting lighter? Shouldn't his limbs be more restive if he were inching closer to wakening?

Dammit, it was getting late.

She pulled her cell phone from her purse. It might be useless to make a call, but it still told the time. She powered it up long enough to see it was damned near 10:00 o'clock already.

"How late is it?"

Sam started, almost dropping the phone.

"You're awake! And oh — thank God! — alive."

His lips twisted. "In a manner of speaking."

Damn this ankle! She wanted to leap on him. She wanted to close her arms around him as squeeze him as tight as she could and have him crush her right back. That, however, would require her to be able to move freely. Instead, she powered down the phone and stuck it back in her purse. "How do you feel?"

He ran a tongue over lips that looked chapped. "Like death warmed over."

Belatedly it occurred to her that he might not be much more mobile than she.

"Here, let me help you up." She started to get up, but he restrained her with a hand.

"No, don't tax that ankle. I can see from here it's grossly swollen."

He pulled himself up so he was sitting beside her, his back against the wall. Then — thank you Jesus — he draped an arm around her and tipped her chin up with his other hand.

"Good morning, Sam Shea," he said, then lowered his head to kiss her.

She kissed him back with a fervor that betrayed her anxiety, her relief. Rolling her hips, she pressed her breasts into his chest, felt the thudding of his heart against hers. God, if she could crawl *into* him, it might just be close enough.

"Oh, Aiden," she murmured against his lips. "I was so scared. If you hadn't come back to me ..."

"Hush, baby." He angled her chin and kissed her again, sweetly this time.

His touch was so sure, his kiss so familiar that for a wild moment, she began to wonder if he had changed after all. A shaft of fear set her heart pounding. Oh, please God …

She drew back to look at him, and exhaled a sigh of relief. Yes. Yes, he was changed. That extra luster, that air of extreme vitality, was gone. He looked like a regular man. Okay, a healthy, inordinately handsome young man. With a killer hangover.

"It worked, didn't it? The serum worked."

"Judging by this very mortal headache and the cell-deep raging for water, yeah, I'd say it worked."

Sam sucked in a breath. "Of course. We have to get you water."

"There's plenty of it right outside."

"River water?"

"It wouldn't be the first time. Lots of towns pumped water from the rivers."

Sam snorted. "Yeah, but that was then and this is now. I shudder to think what kind of industrial effluents might be carried in that water. Besides, after all this time, I rather doubt your gut still has the flora to deal with the bacterial stuff. We'll find you some clean drinking water." She pulled away and got awkwardly to her feet, or *foot* rather. "Come on. There are two six-packs of water in the back of the SUV, if they didn't torch it." She'd bought the water at a convenience store en route from the Charlo airport, not knowing how rough living conditions might be.

"Sounds like a plan. But we'll have to be careful exiting.

He seemed a little clumsy himself as he got to his feet, but once up, he seemed steady enough. He bent and retrieved the .45 she'd taken off him last night and stuck it back in his waistband beneath his shirt. She did the same with the smaller 9mm while he picked up the rifle.

It took longer to reach the end of the tunnel today. Aiden insisted on carrying her piggyback again, but his pace was considerably slower than yesterday's. Moments later, they crouched at the mouth of the tunnel, watching and listening, in case the vampires had left a non-vamp sentry. Sam strained to catch any sounds of human activity, but all she heard over the sound of the river was the intermittent song of birds and the occasional splash of a fish jumping. Once she heard a skittering noise in the leaves, but it turned out to be a chipmunk. The little creature paused momentarily right outside their hiding place, tail twitching as it scented the air, then scurried on.

"I think we're good to go," Aiden said after a few more minutes, but she noticed he kept his voice down, as though someone might be out there yet. "The birds and squirrels wouldn't be so comfortable if there were someone out there. But let me go first. I'll scout the area." Rifle at the ready, he made to push through the concealing brush into the morning.

"Wait!" she hissed, catching his arm. "What if the sun triggers a reaction?"

"It won't," he said. "I woke up in daylight, didn't I? I couldn't do that if I were still a vamp. Also, I feel like absolute shit. That has to be a good sign, right?"

She smiled, because clearly that's what he wanted her to do. But dammit, she was scared. "Well at least roll your sleeves down. No point exposing more skin than you have to. And wear these." She dug into her purse and produced a pair of oversized sunglasses.

Sleeves now buttoned down, he reached for the sunglasses. "Good God, I'll look like Paris Hilton."

She didn't have to force a grin this time as he contemplated the white plastic rimmed sunglasses with genuine horror. "Don't worry about it. We're literally in the middle of nowhere. No one's going to see you."

He slid the sunglasses onto his face. "How do I look?"

She cocked her head. "More like Beyoncé, actually."

"Just so you know, I plan to deny ever wearing these things." He bent his head to peer over the sunglasses at her. "Okay, stay put a minute. I'll be right back for you."

She swallowed past the lump of fear in her throat. "Okay."

He nodded once, then pushed the brush aside and stepped out into the dappled sun of the riverbank.

Sam peered after him. Why had he stopped? Oh, God, was he having a reaction?

"Aiden!" she hissed. "Aiden, are you okay?"

Aiden struggled to bring his racing heart back under control. God, it pounded like a wild thing in his chest. The sun — sweet Jesus, the *sun!* It touched the back of his outstretched hand now, warming without harming. Relief made his knees weak.

He released his pent up breath and drew another gulp of sun-warmed air. Exhaled again. Still no reaction. *Thank you, Lord.*

"Aiden?"

He turned back to her. "I'm fine. Better than fine." He removed the sunglasses and turned his naked face up to the sky, letting the shifting pattern of sun and shade play over his closed eyelids in an elegant dance. "Sweet Jesus, that feels good."

"Oh, Aiden!" She blinked away tears.

He stepped back into the cave and caught her against his chest, steadying them both. Did her heart pound as heavily as his? He couldn't hear it anymore. He couldn't sense the rhythmic surge or her pulse, nor smell that rich-blooded scent that had driven him crazy. Equally astonishing as the absence of that sensory information was the complete lack of desire for blood. No trace of his vampiric nature remained.

That's right, Afflack. No vampiric power. No speed, no special endurance. It'll take you all day to hike out of here.

He kissed her once, hard, then put her away. "Sorry. I'm wasting time. I'll be right back."

"Make it quick," she said. "I need to pee."

"Of course. Sorry. I didn't think."

"Ah, but you'll be more sensitive to this stuff once we get some water into you."

He came back before ten minutes passed. "No sign of anyone," he announced. "Though I'm not used to relying on these dull senses. We can't let our guard down, okay?"

"Okay."

He helped her into the bushes so she could relieve herself, offering his assistance. She blushingly assured him that with the support of the poplar tree, she could manage by herself.

"Call me when you're done," he instructed, walked away.

As he waited, his focus turned inward again. Oh, man, the *thirst*. It was shredding his concentration. He needed to find water soon if he was going to be even marginally effective protecting Sam. And Sam was all he had left. She was everything.

"Okay, I'm ready."

Aiden fetched her. Hoisting her on his back, they made their way carefully up the hill, from one point of concealment to another. When they'd reached what was left of the cottage, he stopped in the fringe of woods to study the clearing. He eased her off his back, breathing harder than he should be, and motioned for her to be quiet. For fifteen minutes they waited and watched. When nothing stirred, he declared it safe enough to venture into the clearing.

Soot and ash clung to everything, and a few tendrils of smoke rose from the ruins. The SUV was still there in the driveway, looking remarkably intact. Well, except for the paint job. The hood and right fender were bubbled and blackened from the heat. Could they be lucky enough that the damage was purely cosmetic and the car was still driveable? It had been a few decades, but surely he could still hotwire a car.

"Can you stand? I want to check out the car."

She waved him away. "I'm fine, as long as I keep my weight on the good foot and just use the other one for balance."

He rounded the front of the vehicle and cursed. The driveway was littered with essential bits and pieces from the engine and wires from the electrical system. No way were they driving out of here. "Vandals as well as arsonists, I see."

"They wrecked it?"

"I'm afraid so. Pulled everything electrical out of it."

She swore with feeling. "Guess it was too much to hope for that it would still be operational."

"At least the water's still in there." He tried the door handle, then stepped back. Locked. But not for long. "I'm going to knock a window out. But first ..." he scooped her up and carried her over to stand by the vehicle, "I need you to cover me while I'm doing it. We might attract some unwanted attention."

He felt her stiffen as he released her.

"Cover you?"

"Yeah." He pulled her pistol from her waistband, flicked the safety off and put it in her hands. "Safety's off. If anyone comes out of those woods while my back is turned, shoot them and we'll ask questions later."

"Okay," she said, without hesitation.

Damn, what a woman. He wanted to lean in and kiss her. But neither of them needed that distraction.

He took his coat off and wrapped it around the butt of the carbine. It wouldn't do much to muffle the sound of the blow, but it was better than nothing. He lifted the carbine and brought it down with controlled force against the back passenger window. To his chagrin, the rifle glanced off the glass harmlessly. Yesterday he could have smashed that window with his fist and not even strained himself.

Relax, Afflack. It took you a while to adjust the degree of force when you turned vamp. Obviously, you have to reverse the learning curve.

"Let's try that again," he muttered.

This time, when the rifle butt made contact, the window exploded in a gratifying shower of glass. Raking the rifle around the edges, he knocked out the remaining glass and reached in to grab one of the six-packs of water.

He tore one of the bottles from its plastic ring, uncapped it and tipped it up. And oh dear God, the flow of the tepid fluid down his parched throat was as sweet as anything he could remember. Without once lowering the bottle, he drank it dry. His thirst still flaying him, he uncapped another bottle and drank half of it in two swallows, pausing only when Sam touched his arm.

"Take it easy, Aiden. You don't want to drink it too fast and then throw up. You need it to stay down and start hydrating you."

He recognized the wisdom in her words, but it took all his willpower to prise the bottle from his lips. He wiped his mouth. "You're right. But you can't imagine how good that feels."

She cracked her own bottle and took a swig. "Better than sunlight on your face?"

He grinned. "Close, but no. And definitely not better than sunlight on *your* face. God, woman, you are gorgeous. Your hair …" He lifted a hand to touch the multifaceted sable strands, but froze when he noticed a distinctly mechanical sound impinge on the natural sounds of the forest. He looked up, scanning the sky. What the devil was that? "Do you hear something?"

Sam cocked her head in an attitude of listening, but he didn't wait for her to confirm it. Something was definitely coming. "Hang on. This is probably going to hurt. I'm sorry." Water in one hand, rifle slung over his shoulder, he hoisted her onto his shoulder fireman style and raced toward the cover of the forest canopy.

Forty seconds later, lying prone on the ground, panting embarrassingly from the short dash, Aiden scanned the sky. Beside him, he heard Sam doing that huffing thing to channel her pain. The strange, unidentifiable noise increased in intensity until it seemed to beat the very air, sending his heart rate soaring. Then a bizarrely contoured and camouflaged helicopter descended from the sky, hovering over the burned out cottage, sending up a swirling storm of ash and cinders.

Sam groaned. "Tell me that's not an alien aircraft. That would be just the last fucking straw."

He laughed. "No aliens," he said, climbing to his feet. "Just the latest in low observable technology. And our ticket out of here."

As he helped her to her feet, the helicopter landed. Then someone leapt out of the idling aircraft. As soon as the man hit the ground, he bent in a crouch, sweeping the clearing with an automatic weapon. Aiden grinned. Delano's lieutenant, Eli Grayson. He could kiss the man. Maybe he would.

Sam sucked in an audible breath. "That's Eli!"

"It sure is. Come on." He slid his arm around her, supporting her. "Hold your hands up until he recognizes us."

They hobbled into the clearing, Sam with both hands held high and Aiden with his free hand up in the classic surrender posture. "Grayson! Over here!" he called, taking no chances.

Eli lowered his weapon. Aiden picked Sam up started across the clearing.

"Motherfucker!" Eli dropped his assault rifle and ripped off his ammo belt. In the next second, he'd torn off the coat he'd been wearing and was bearing down on Aiden at a dead run.

Surprised into immobility, Aiden put Sam down just in time to get smothered by Eli's jacket. Eli held him fast around the shoulders. "Jesus, Afflack, are you crazy?"

Before Aiden could point out that he was not the one acting like a lunatic, Eli was barking orders.

"Quick, Sam! There's a medic kit in the chopper. We'll need all the epinephrine we can lay our hands on."

"It's okay," he heard Sam say. "Aiden's all right. He doesn't need an epi shot."

Her words loosened Eli's grip and Aiden managed to shove the coat away from his face.

"Hell, Grayson, I'm glad to see you, too, but could you get off a dude?"

"What the hell?" Eli instantly dropped his arms and stepped back, letting the coat fall to the ground. "What's going on here? I've seen vampires dragged into the sunlight before. Why aren't you gasping for your last breath?"

Aiden bent and retrieved Eli's jacket and handed it back to him. "I should think that would be obvious. I'm not a vampire any more."

A pause.

"Holy shit."

"Yeah, we were pinned down in the escape tunnel by a concerted vampire attack. I figured the safest way out was in daylight, so I took the cure."

Eli blinked. "The *cure*?"

Aiden knew exactly was Eli was thinking. The serum had most definitely been a cure for Delano, who'd hated his vampiric nature and sought for centuries to reverse it. But how could a vamp who embraced his nature as enthusiastically as Aiden had done possibly consider it a cure? Good question. As soon as he worked through this ambivalence, maybe he could answer it. For the moment, he ignored the subtext and gave Eli a literal answer.

"Yeah. Delano gave Sam a syringe full of the serum in case she found herself cornered and needed to dissuade an attacker. Since it was no use against the horde, I jabbed myself with it so we could walk away."

"Good call not waiting for nightfall. From my aerial recon, I see there's a short-haul moving truck and a van parked up the road," Eli jerked his head to indicate the direction. "Something tells me that's your vampire horde."

"Gotta be," Aiden agreed, but inside he was quaking. Thank God he'd done the right thing. If he'd shrugged off as pure paranoia the idea that the rogues would hang around, if he and Sam had waited until nightfall to make a break … He saw a flash of himself trying to protect her against impossible odds, and it was like watching his mother and sister die all over again. He pushed the image away and fixed his attention on Eli. "So what are we waiting for? Let's go show our visitors the light."

Aiden started off down the drive, but Eli threw up a hand to stop him. "Not this time, Aiden. We have other orders. Specifically, I'm to take you back to Montreal. Right now, in fact."

Aiden shot him a look. "You're kidding. We have a chance to clean a dozen or more rogues out right now, but instead we're gonna fly off? We're just gonna leave them to drive away and kill another day?"

"Dammit, Aiden, with the possible exception of you, no one wants to destroy those bastards more than I do. *No one*." Eli's skin seemed stretched tauter than usual across the bones of his broad, dark face. "It's all I can do not to march up there and drag them out one by one and watch them die a hideous, painful death. But that's our second priority here, and as such, it's someone else's job. But I swear to you they'll be taken care of. The mop-up crew is less than twenty minutes away, and I already radioed the coordinates."

Aiden glared at Eli, then looked back to the west where the truck must be parked. Goddammit.

"Aiden?"

He heard Sam's voice but didn't turn.

"Let's go with Eli," she said softly. "I'd rather not be here when … I mean, I don't have a problem knowing they're going to die. After all we've been through, all I've seen of these rogues … But please, Aiden, I don't want to be here to hear it or see it. And baby, you don't need to see it either. Not today. You've done enough."

Something shifted deep inside him at her words. She was right. Someone else was coming to do the janitor work. He didn't have to do it. Not today. Probably not ever again. It took a vampire to hunt vampires, and he'd effectively retired when he'd stabbed himself with that injector.

He turned to Sam, feeling exposed and raw, but also lighter. "You're right," he said. "Let's get out of here."

Chapter 21

Minutes later, they lifted off. Sam had strapped herself into a back seat, while Aiden, with his pilot skills, sat up front with Eli. The noise level inside the helicopter was nowhere near as loud as Sam feared it would be. According to Eli, it was all in the rotors. Designed for stealth, the beating of the blades didn't become audible to people on the ground until the helo had closed within a few hundred yards. Still, they needed the helmet mic systems to communicate effectively.

As they rose up above the treetops, Sam dug her nails into her palms to assure herself this was real. Yep. Real as real could be.

Euphoria filled her. They'd gotten away! Against all odds, they were out of the rogues' reach. Safe. A shudder of relief went through her. She closed her eyes and bit her lip, sending a prayer of thanks skyward.

"Take us over the vamps," came Aiden's voice. "I wanna see them."

Sam's eyes sprang open.

"Then look to your left," Eli said. "The short-haul truck is pretty well concealed, but the van sticks out."

Sam saw only the back of Aiden's head as he looked out the window, but when he turned back, the set of his face was grim. "Damn, I'm glad you came along, Grayson. You saved the lives of the three or four men who are probably guarding those vehicles, 'cuz we were going to hijack one and drive out of here. But how'd you know to come?" he asked, voicing the question that was swimming to the top of Sam's mind.

"You remember after that ambush the vamps sprang on you, we sent our forces to Sioux City to find out what was doing? Well, they've been busy, rounding up vamps and cracking heads. One of the vamps gave up a critical bit of intelligence about a psychic who was purportedly tuning into Sam's head."

Sam sucked a breath in. "You know about that?"

Eli craned his neck to look at her. "It's true, then?"

"I'm afraid so. Unfortunately, we only figured it out last night. Otherwise we'd have called for a pickup and gotten ourselves back to safety in —"

"Do you have him?"

Aiden's voice cut across her own. His tone was flat, but something about it made the hairs rise on the back of Sam's neck. Her gaze flew to his face, and holy crap! Forehead pleated, eyebrows drawn down, mouth set … Yikes! He looked every inch as dangerous and deadly as he had as a vampire.

"As of about ten hours ago," Eli confirmed, apparently oblivious of Aiden's cold fury.

Or maybe not. Maybe he was just unfazed by it, soldier to soldier.

"Turns out he's a non-vamp hacker-type geek who lives in his blind grandmother's basement," Eli continued. "Didn't take much to get the story out of him. He couldn't tell us fast enough. It seems he's more than a little scared of his new friends. They found him when he started rambling on one of those Goth vampyre freak forums about a seer teaming up with a hunter to do some serious slaying, and how he'd gotten into the seer's head. It was downhill from there for little Kevin. The vamp boss fastened on to him, and he's been living in terror ever since, frantically trying to get into Sam's head. He was finally able to get in and get a fix on your location, which he fed to the vamp boss."

"A little tidbit that he gave up to your guys?" Aiden said.

"Exactly. I just wish we'd caught up with him twelve hours sooner. It would've saved you from having to —"

"No one's complaining about the timing, Grayson. We're alive. If you'd been twelve hours later, who knows?"

Sam's heart ached as she watched the back of Aiden's head, but he wouldn't turn around, no matter how hard she willed it.

Eli shot Aiden a glance, then trained his gaze back on the instrument panel. "By the way, the plan isn't to kill the rogues back there."

"*What?*" Aiden's head whipped around. "Goddammit! Of all the stupid … Put this bird down, Eli. Now."

Eli kept his attention on the terrain below. "Sorry. Boss's orders."

"Well, he's not *my* boss anymore. I quit. You hear me? Those rogues will walk away over my dead body." Aiden leaned in threateningly toward Eli. "I'm going back there to do the job. You can either turn this bird around and put it down in the nearest clearing, or I'll do it for you."

Sam's racing heart stumbled. "Aiden! No."

Eli laughed. "Christ, Aiden, relax. We're not gonna let them walk. The team that's on its way right now is going in with hypodermics loaded with the Merzetti Effect. The bastards won't fry in the sun like you and I might prefer, but they'll all be taking the same one-way trip you just took."

Aiden pulled back. "Jesus."

Eli laughed again. "Pretty good, huh? They go from immortal rogue vampires to regular thugs, just like that. And in their weakened state, they'll be very cooperative."

"Oh, thank God." Sam sagged in her seat. While she might believe they deserved to die, she was glad no one would have to act as their mass executioner.

Eli cast her a look. "Thought you'd appreciate that, Ms. Shea. Though there's no guarantee some of them won't die anyway. Delano's research is inconclusive. He needs to know if the Merzetti Effect can be deadly all by itself if the rogue is of a different blood type than Ainsley."

"One could only hope," Aiden muttered.

"What we hope," Eli said, "is to have some of these bastards left alive to interrogate. Fortunately, the chances are good. Ainsley is O positive, the most common blood type, so even if the compatibility thing turns out to be an issue, most of 'em should survive to undergo the reversal. And if it's not an issue, they should all survive. And what better way to convince the vampire world that the Merzetti vaccine has arrived than to send these bad-asses back where they came from with their tails between their all-too-human legs. Word'll spread like wildfire."

Sam laughed. "That's *brilliant*! Dr. Bowen is a genius."

Eli cast a grin over his shoulder.

"Brilliant is right." Aiden uncapped his second bottle of water, the one Sam had cautioned him to conserve when they thought they'd be walking out of the woods. Then he tipped it back and drank it down, sighing with deep satisfaction when it was gone. "By the way, if you have trouble making the bastards talk, just tell them you'll withhold water. That'll get them warming up their vocal chords."

"That's what Delano said."

After a few moments, Aiden spoke again. "They'll still be thugs and outlaws, you know. Just because you reverse the mutation doesn't mean they'll be reformed. Once a killer, always a killer."

"Yeah, but we let the cops take care of them. They'll be out of our bailiwick."

Sam saw Aiden's acceptance in the release of tension in his shoulders. She wanted to put a hand on his arm, to communicate her gratitude with a non-verbal touch and a glance, but the interior of the helicopter didn't lend itself to that kind of thing. Nor did the audience.

Nor did the jumbled up feelings in her mind. He'd permanently surrendered his vampiric powers, and with them his whole *raison d'être*, to protect her. He'd irrevocably traded in near-immortality for a very mortal life. If she let herself think about it, the weight of that sacrifice would crush her.

Aiden shifted in his seat, drawing her attention again.

"So if you've got the psychic piece of shit in custody —"

"Kevin Coates."

"So if you've got this piece of shit in custody, you must know who the vamp boss is for that murderous crew back there."

"Yep."

"Let me guess . . . Ramirez? He's one mean motherfucker. Or that prick Stymiest? Or Ng, maybe?"

"None of the above. This is a new crew. And get this, they were a crew before they turned vamp." Eli angled a glance at Aiden. "A street gang, to be precise. The boss hooked up with a vampire chick and persuaded her to turn him. Then he turned the others. You know how it is with the gangs. Those guys are bonded, man. Family. That's why these guys are able to cooperate in a semi-organized way, where other vamps would fall to in-fighting."

Conversation lulled for a while, as everyone considered the implications.

Then Aiden spoke up: "Got any whiskey on board?"

That drew a bark of laughter from Eli. "Nope. Sorry."

"How about more water, then?"

"Dude. Really?" Aiden looked up from the dish Delano set before him. "Plain white rice and poached chicken? That's the best you can offer a man after centuries of abstinence?"

Delano laughed. "That's just for starters, to see how you tolerate it. If you're really good, I'll let you have some sliced banana for dessert."

"Banana? Oh, well then, I guess I'd better tuck in."

"Okay, okay, I'll pour you some wine. But for God's sake, don't tell Ainsley."

Aiden grinned. "Now we're talking."

As Delano retrieved a bottle of red wine and uncorked it, Aiden attacked his meal. For all his grousing, the food was pretty damned good. The rice was delicately flavored with chicken broth, which oddly made it more savory than the chicken itself, which would have fared better in a pan of oil with some garlic and rosemary. The only protest his stomach made was over quantity. He could have eaten a helluva lot more. But Del was right; no point courting a bout of gastritis. There'd be time enough to test richer, spicier fare, like the stuff he made for Sam.

Sam.

He put his fork down.

She'd been so strange since they got off the helicopter atop Delano's towering building. And God, what a sight *that* had been by daylight. The sun gleaming off the glass windows of the other highrises ... He'd turned to Sam to say something about it, but with the aid of the crutch Eli produced from somewhere, she'd made a beeline for the door. So much for hiding behind her for his first public debut as a non-vamp.

And yes, he'd felt pretty damned strange himself. Smaller. Less than he used to be. Downright *shy*.

Not that Delano or Ainsley had made him feel that way. Delano had grasped his hand and hauled him into a bear hug, back-slapping guy embrace. "Damn, Aiden. Just ... damn."

Ainsley had hugged him, too, and when she pulled back, tears glistened in her eyes. "I knew you were a whole lot of man, Aiden Afflack, but I had no idea just how big you were. No idea. Thank you."

He'd glanced at Sam, who'd looked stricken. Then he'd turned back to Ainsley and cracked a joke about how he was getting smaller by the minute, if he didn't soon find something to eat. Everyone had laughed and the awkwardness had passed.

Delano placed a glass in front of him and poured a generous amount of wine into it.

"You get just the one glass," he said, pouring one for himself while he was at it.

"Yes, Father."

Delano rolled his eyes. "Wait'll you finish that glass, hot shot. We'll see if you still want more."

Aiden lifted the glass and swirled it. Beautiful ruby color, full-bodied and leggy, and smelling of ... what? Black cherries? He took a sip and hummed approvingly. Expansive on the tongue. Round. Gorgeous. He took a second, larger sip. "Damn, that's nice."

"Glad you approve. It's only a fraction as old as we are, but by today's standards, it's a classic. A 1993 Leoville Barton."

Aiden snorted. "A wine as old as we are would be vinegar."

"True," Delano conceded.

Aiden took another sip. "Oh, man, I think I'm starting to feel the buzz already. What kind of wine *is* this?"

Delano laughed. "The regular kind, I assure you. Well, as regular as a fine museum wine gets. It's your liver that's out of practice. It'll need some conditioning before you can hold your own again. Even the ladies could out-drink you right now, I'm afraid."

Aiden put the glass down, the exquisite warm buzz threatening to fizzle. "Great. Just what I need. Further evidence of how inadequate I am."

"Hey, careful there," Delano growled. "I went through the same thing, remember? And I'm here to tell you that *adequacy* has nothing to do with it. You're just asking a relatively dormant system to suddenly pick up and start doing its old job again. You'll get there soon enough. Give it a week and you can be knocking back the cocktails like it was the 50s again, if you want to. Though I wouldn't advise it."

"Yes, Dad. And I won't touch that evil reefer I've heard so much about, either."

Delano snorted. "Yeah, you will. But since we're having this *father/son* talk, can I just remind you that if you're not fertile already, you're bound to become so very quickly. So use a condom, okay?"

"Oh, we're having the *sex* talk?" Aiden feigned choking up with emotion. "After all these years, I thought I'd missed out on that."

Delano colored. "Laugh if you like, but it's the doctor speaking now. And it's not just the pregnancy risk I'm talking about. Aiden, it's a different world out there. Some viruses are forever. Hell, some are *fatal*. Some are just … nasty. And some of them even a condom won't protect against, like the human papillomavirus, which —"

"Whoa." Aiden threw up a hand. "You can stop right there, doc. I get it. I'm not invulnerable anymore. But honestly, I don't need a lesson in sexually transmitted diseases. I watch public television, too, you know. Well ... sometimes."

"Okay, then."

They regarded each other for a few seconds, then both burst out laughing.

By the time Aiden got himself back under control, tears streaked his face. "God, I haven't laughed like that in years. Chalk it up to the wine, I guess."

Delano politely agreed.

Aiden looked down at the red liquid in his glass, swirling it to admire its legginess, watching the rivulets slowly descend the bowl ...

Fuck it. If he couldn't talk to Del about this stuff, who could he talk to?

"She hasn't looked me squarely in the eyes since we got on that helicopter."

"Ah, yes. It rather changes things, doesn't it?"

"It changes *everything*. And dammit, I don't even get to make the extravagant gesture by offering to be turned back, like you did. She knows it doesn't work, thanks to you and your big mouth."

"Uh ... excuse me if I'm wrong, but even supposing you *could* be turned back, that kind of offer is only extravagant if you don't *want* to be turned. Correct?"

"I suppose," Aiden grumbled, taking another sip of wine. "If you want to *nitpick*."

"Besides, I'm pretty sure your extravagant gesture beats mine by a long shot."

"It wasn't a gesture. It was a necessity. I couldn't let her stay, but I couldn't let her walk — or rather, crawl — out of there alone either. If anything happened to her ..."

"I know. Believe me, I know." Delano drank deeply of his wine. "So, does she love you?"

Aiden, who'd been in the process of swallowing another sip of wine, choked. Coughing, he put his glass down. "Way to beat around the bush, Bowen."

The other man shrugged. "Hey, we don't live forever anymore. Life's too short for that crap."

Aiden sighed. "You're right. And yes, I think she did love me." He closed his eyes and remembered the way she'd touched him ... "I know she did."

"Then for God's sake, talk to her," Delano counseled. "As a wise man once told me, if she loves you, it won't matter to her that you're not superman."

"But what if it was the whole superhero persona she fell in love with?"

Delano scoffed. "If she were that shallow, that ... empty, you sure as hell wouldn't be sitting here sweating this."

"Right." Aiden tipped his glass up and drained it. "Right."

Delano took the empty glass from his grasp. "So, go get her, hot shot."

Aiden stood and reeled sideways. "Whoa!"

A grinning Delano caught him. "See what I mean about that one glass?"

"Maybe I'd better just chill here a few minutes."

"Good plan. I'll get you a little something more to eat to sop up that alcohol."

Sam sat alone on a chaise lounge in Delano's very new, very gorgeous solarium, her limbs perfectly still, face composed. In sharp contrast to her physical composure, her mind raced. Over and over the same path it sped.

How could she have been so stupid? Why hadn't she recognized that creep when he stole into her head? In the circumstances, how could she *possibly* have dismissed the intrusion as a nightmare? If she had twigged to it, they could have been long gone before those bastards descended. They would have been safe in this apartment, and Aiden would still be his old swaggering self, planning his next hunt. Instead, he'd sacrificed himself to preserve her safety.

He was *so* going to hate her.

Oh, not now. Probably not even tomorrow or next month. But eventually. How could he not? This was all her fault.

A soft knock sounded at the door, startling her thoughts off their hamster wheel.

"Sam? Can you stand some company?"

Aiden. She started to swing her legs off the lounger, grimaced, then lay back. Damned ankle.

"Sure. Come in."

He stepped into the solarium. She thought the novelty of standing in a sunbathed tropical jungle would distract him, but no such luck.

"We need to talk."

Sam's heart thundered. "I know." She gestured to the chair opposite. "But first, how are you doing? Have you eaten? Ainsley said Delano would be getting you something."

"I'm okay. I'm looking forward to being able to eat something with actual flavor. Boiled chicken and rice just doesn't cut it."

He slouched easily in his chair, looking so much like the old Aiden. Except he wasn't. That extra glow was gone.

Sam groaned and buried her face in her hands. "Oh, God, Aiden, I'm so sorry!"

"Hey, hey, what's this? Boiled chicken is boring, but it's not *tragic*."

She laughed. Then to her horror, the laughter turned to sobs.

"Baby, what is it?"

She felt his hand at her knee. Dropping her hands, she saw that he knelt before her now, his forehead pleated in a frown, eyes troubled.

Lord, his *face*. Her photographer's eye had loved it from the first, skin stretched taut over high cheekbones, piercing blue eyes, blond hair curling almost to his shoulders. How had that austerely beautiful face become so much more to her? How had this man become everything she wanted? Everything she hadn't even *known* she wanted.

"Sam?" he prompted again. "What's the matter, baby?" The hand on her knee tightened, and his face hardened. "Is that bastard still getting into your head? I'll kill him. I'll swear to God, if he's —"

"No, it's nothing like that."

His display of protectiveness had her fighting back another sob. That protective streak is what got him here, human and near-powerless by vampire standards. She put her hand over his where it gripped her knee and squeezed it.

He stood suddenly, pulling his hands away. "Is it me, then? Because you can just say so, Sam. I won't hold it against you. Honest. I know I'm no longer what you signed on for."

What she'd *signed on for*? Shock held her motionless. He thought *he* was the problem?

His shoulders lifted in an awkward shrug that made her heart squeeze.

"Look, I know I've brought you nothing but trouble. I forced my way into your life. I warped your dreams."

"Oh, Aiden, no," she said, but he wouldn't be stopped.

"I exploited you, just as thoroughly as your parents did. I introduced you to an ugly world, and I made it impossible for you to refuse to work with me."

"No. We talked about this before, remember? When I threatened to quit? Like I told you then, I might not have appreciated your tactics, but the choice was *mine*."

"And I seduced you." His mouth turned down. "I played to your fantasies to get into your arms, into your bed. And now ... well, look at me. I'm not that fantasy anymore, am I?"

Sam blinked. "Let me get this straight — you think *that* matters to me? You think my feelings have changed because you can no longer jump tall buildings with me in your arms?"

He scowled. "I'm not an idiot, Sam. Since we got on that helicopter, you've hardly looked at me. You can barely look at me now. What the hell am I supposed to think?"

What was he supposed to think? This time, she did swing her legs off the chair to go toe to toe with him, ignoring the shriek of pain that shot from ankle to brain. "How about that it's *all my fault* that you're not a vampire anymore?" she shouted. "How about if I hadn't been so stupid, we never would have found ourselves in that position? You wouldn't have had to make that sacrifice."

"Wait a minute, *that's* what you're freaked about? You're feeling guilty about me leaving the vampire ranks?"

"Of course I feel guilty! You never would have chosen that in a thousand years. A thousand years which you might have *lived* if I hadn't screwed up."

"Sam, I'd have taken the cure eventually anyway." He rolled his shoulders. "So we could ... you know ... be together."

"Would you?" she shot back.

He flushed. "Of course I would. As you pointed out back there in the woods, it's hard to have a happily-ever-after when one of the parties is virtually immortal and the other is not. I'd have changed, Sam, so we could get married, maybe have kids."

The words were a knife to her very heart. It was everything she wanted to believe, but she couldn't. She just ... couldn't. She reached for the crutch propped against her chair, needing its support. "You'd have changed ... *eventually*?"

"Eventually, yes. I mean, there's still work to do, right? I thought I could help Delano, at least until he gets his inoculation program underway."

"And I'd have given you the time." She drew in a shuddering breath and let it out again. "God, I'd give anything to give you back the time."

"Baby, it doesn't matter. Honestly."

He reached for her chin, but she turned her face away. "It does to *me*."

"Why?" He dropped his hand. "Why does it matter so much?"

She met his eyes again. "Because if we'd had more time, I might have been convinced that's what you really wanted."

"But it *is* what I want."

"You didn't say it then." She dashed a tear away before it could slide down her cheek. "You didn't mention that back there at the cottage. You're only saying it now because there's no going back."

"Oh, for chrissakes!" He raked his hair back with a frustrated hand. "I was just getting comfortable with the idea myself. I wasn't ready to say it out loud. Dammit, Sam, I *love* you. I want to marry you."

The knife in her heart twisted savagely.

Damn him! Where did he get off saying that? Where the *hell* did he get off? It was too cruel. He might think he loved her now. Oh, God, he probably *did*. But how could it last? Deep down, he'd resent her for what she'd taken from him, and that love would turn bitter.

She dashed away fresh tears. "I love you, too," she said, "but I won't marry you."

His face went blank for a second, but then his mouth tightened. "Ah, so I was right the first time. I'm not man enough for you anymore?"

She clenched her fists, nails digging into her palms. "Aiden Afflack, I'm not even going to dignify that with an answer. I won't marry you because I refuse to hold you to a rash, impulsive proposal. I won't let you compound one sacrifice with another."

"Sacrifice?" he roared.

"Yes, sacrifice! Aiden, you've spent exactly what? — maybe a dozen hours as a non-vamp? — and you're ready to make that decision?"

"Damn right I am."

"Well, I'm not." She lifted her head. "I think we should go on as we are for a while, enjoy what we have."

"Enjoy what we have *while we have it*, you mean?"

"Exactly," she said, then took an involuntary step back as she registered the twisted fury on his face.

"While I can manage to sustain an interest? While I can still summon the fortitude to be faithful? While I can keep my goddamn dick in my goddamn pants when a beautiful woman walks by?"

"Aiden! Stop it."

"Go to hell, Sam." He wheeled away from her.

Tears spurting, she grabbed for her purse, but somehow managed to upend it on the floor. The contents of the open bag spilled on the carpet. Sucking back a sob, she knelt the best she could and shoveled the mess back in. Thankfully, he made no move to help her. She couldn't have borne it.

She slung the bag over her shoulder and crutched her way out of the room and back to the safety of her guestroom. Where she could contemplate how much he hated her now.

Chapter 22

AIDEN STOOD THERE, chest heaving. The bit of food he'd eaten was churning in his stomach.

He wanted to tear the shit out of something with his bear hands. He wanted a rogue in his sights. He wanted to run at sixty miles an hour, leap onto a fucking rooftop. He wanted to crush and pulverize ... *something*! He looked wildly around the solarium, but everything looked too delicate to take his frustration out on. Except maybe the walls. But if he slammed his fist into that, he'd probably break a dozen bones in his hand.

Welcome back to humanity.

Jesus, why couldn't she believe him? Hadn't he shown her *anything* over these past weeks? Over the past days? Hadn't she been right inside his head, feeling everything he felt for her? Dammit, how could she doubt him?

He paced the room, nursing his anger, until the scent finally sank in. *Her* scent ... that expensive milled soap smell. It clung in the air. Even with these dulled senses, he could smell her.

Just like that, his anger fell away, forcing him to face what roiled beneath it. *Fear.*

What if he couldn't convince her? She could be so damned stubborn! And they wouldn't have that mind-to-mind connection anymore. He couldn't make her *feel* his love, his conviction, the depth of his commitment. All he had to convince her were words.

Not that he hadn't had good success in the past with words. But that was with other women, and he'd been peddling quite a different proposition. Sam, however, had never been a fool for words.

Not to mention that she had some reason to distrust the idea of love. Her own parents had used her unconscionably. Christ, they'd *abused* her with that pubertal delay thing. If he ever got his hands on them ...

And yeah, okay, she probably didn't have a lot of reason to trust him. He'd been the quintessential playboy. But for pity's sake, what choice had he had? Moving from one day to the next to the next, *forever*. Stalking, killing, decapitating. Damn right he bedded women, but never the same one twice. They were honest transactions, but transactions nevertheless. It had never been like that with Sam. It never could be.

He swung his legs off the chaise and put his head in his hands. After minutes of staring sightlessly at the floor, he realized he was looking at a camera, or rather the silver edge of one peeking out from beneath the damask skirting of a chair. Sam's camera, he realized. The little digital spare she kept in her purse for fear she be caught without one. She must have missed it when she'd scooped up the spillage.

He stretched to pick it up. The moment he held it in his hands, he remembered the last time he'd held it. That night at the cottage ... she was dressed in that gorgeous silk and lace thing. He'd taken her picture. Then he'd made her take a picture of their reflection in the mirror.

Don't turn it on, idiot. Don't look. It'll just make you feel worse.

He turned it on, accessed the photos on the memory card. And there she was, in the very first frame. God, she looked so pure and sweet, so untouchable. But he'd touched her ... He advanced the frame, and there they were, reflected in the mirror, her head thrown back on his shoulder, his hands beneath her breasts. He clicked for the next one. Them again, in the mirror. Another click, and he froze.

Jesus, was that really *him*? He was all but unrecognizable to himself. She'd shot him just after he'd peeled off his sweater, but he might as well have peeled off his skin. Goddamn! His heart was there in his eyes, in the yearning evident in every bit of light and shadow she'd captured.

He clicked again, and there he sat on the bed, one hand outstretched.

Oh. My. God.

He paged past it quickly.

More photos of him. In the kitchen, cooking for Sam. Happy. Sitting on a chair watching Sam eat, a completely superfluous whiskey in his hand and a look of such utter peace on his face. How could anyone look at those pictures and not know —

Holy shit! Oh, yeah! That's exactly what he had to do!

He put the camera down, pulled his cell phone out of his pocket and hit speed dial. "Del, I need a favor," he said when Delano answered.

"Aiden? Why are you *phoning* me? Aren't you still here in the penthouse?"

"Yeah, but I don't have time to waste. Do you still have a team in Sioux City?"

"Yes, but —"

"Can you have 'em break into Sam's apartment again? There's something I really need."

A pause. "Then why don't you ask Sam for it?"

"It's kind of complicated."

"I've got time to listen. Where are you? I'll come to you."

He glanced around. "In the solarium. But make that call first, 'kay? I need this yesterday. Here's what you're looking for . . ."

Sam lay on her bed, a cold pack over her eyes. The tears had dried up long ago, but if she was ever going to leave this room, she had to do something about the ugly puffiness. Not that she was going to save any face. Ainsley had already seen her in tears, having intercepted her flight from the solarium. And God bless her for not pressing for answers. Instead, her hostess had sent hot tea and food to her room, delivered by a concerned-looking Eli who insisted on examining her ankle and re-wrapping it with a fresh elastic bandage, but who also did not pry. Later, Ainsley had sent the cold pack, iced tea and fruit.

Everyone had been so kind. But how was she going to face them? How was she going to explain her meltdown and headlong flight from Aiden? *He offered to marry me!* just wasn't going to cut it as an explanation. But she had to explain somehow. Knowing Aiden, he wouldn't defend himself, and she refused to have them think badly of him. She'd have to make it clear it wasn't his —

A knock sounded at her door. Sam tore the cold pack off her eyes and jackknifed up. *Aiden.* She knew it.

"Sam? You in there?"

For a wild moment, she thought about staying silent, feigning sleep. Of course, that would just postpone the inevitable. She had to face him.

Please God, don't let him still be mad at me.

"Just a sec," she called. Shaking her hair out, she checked her reflection in the mirror. Her eyes still looked puffy, but it was a vast improvement. And the best she could do without an application of full makeup. "Come in," she called.

Her heart pounded as he let himself in, but she noticed he didn't close the door behind him. Oh, God, was he leaving? Had he come to say goodbye?

"Your door wasn't locked. Should I take that as a positive sign?" His gaze fell on the crutches leaning against the night table. "Or maybe you just didn't want to be bothered clumping your way over there every time someone knocks on the door."

She smiled. "Both. But I would never lock you out, Aiden." Her smiled faltered. "I don't want to shut you out in any way. I'm sorry for being so ... delicate earlier. It's just that —"

"Can you give me a few minutes? I've got something I need you to see."

"To see?"

"Yeah. Just down the hall to Delano's home theatre." His eyes were intense, serious. "Will you come with me?"

Her pulse jumped. What could he possibly have to show her there?

"Sam?"

"Of course," she said. "Can you pass me those crutches?"

He looked like he wanted to say to hell with the crutches and carry her, but he passed them to her. She had to give him points for that. She needed to be able to move independently. Not that she planned to run out on him again, but not knowing what he had planned, she needed to keep her options open.

A moment later, they entered the home theatre. Sam gasped. It was beautiful! A large screen ... so big it had to be one of those projection unit thingies ... dominated one side of the room. On the opposite side sprawled a large chocolate brown leather sofa and matching leather chairs, with a gorgeous vintage trunk coffee table. The carpet was a pale Berber, and the walls were draped with more dark brown material. Her artist's mind was already projecting images onto the screen.

"Wow! What a great room. Good thing I don't have anything like this or I might never emerge."

"Most vamps are partial to this kind of thing," Aiden said. "If you can make the image big enough and the surround sound true enough, you can almost convince yourself you're that actor, outside in the sunlight."

"Of course. So, what did you want to show me?"

"Have a seat and I'll throw it up there."

She chose the sofa, reasoning that if he were still mad, he'd choose a chair.

He sat with her on the sofa. At the press of a remote control button, the room's lights dimmed and an image jumped to life on the screen.

Sam dragged in a breath of pure pain.

Aiden, larger than life on the 4×6 screen. It was one of the first pictures she'd taken of him, outside Chief Michaels' house in St. Cloud. She'd zoomed as tight as she could. In the frame, his face was illuminated as he touched the flame of a match to a cigarette, which he'd probably taken from Michaels since she'd never seen him smoke another one. And, oh, God, he was gorgeous! Raw, restrained power, and that ... what? ... *dynamism* in stillness. He looked as untamable as any hurricane.

And she'd taken it all from him.

He advanced to the next frame. She pressed a hand to her mouth. If the first shot was gorgeous, she needed to invent a whole new word for this one. A wickedly sensual smile curved his mouth, and he radiated sex appeal from every line and angle of his body. This was still outside Chief Michael's house, but by now he'd sensed her watching presence.

No, not *her* presence, she corrected. He didn't know her then. He'd sensed *a* presence. She could have been any woman — hell, any sexual being — and he still could be confident of the reaction he elicited. The world was his oyster.

But not anymore. Not like that. Thanks to her stupidity.

Next slide. Sam recognized it instantly. It was aboard his jet, on their way to Mansfield Township, and she'd just finished watching him feed. After infusing the blood, he'd exuded such a raw aura of sexual energy, she was certain she'd be able to capture it. Of course, as he'd warned, she wasn't able to catch the full visual impact of that aura on film. But she *did* capture extremely effectively his utter confidence, and that devastatingly easy, careless attractiveness. Looking at these pictures now, she wondered how she'd managed to resist him as long as she had.

And again, she'd stripped that from him.

Okay, yes. He would always be the most gorgeous man she'd ever personally known. If he were the type, he could still easily make his living as a fashion model. But it was a matter of intensity. Aiden *then* and Aiden *now* was like the difference between a 10 million candlepower spotlight and a 150,000 candlepower headlight.

Why was he doing this? Why was he punishing her with these images of all he'd lost?

Oh, God, had it started already? Had the resentment and hatred set in so soon, hastened by anger over her rejection of his proposal?

He lifted the remote to advance to the next slide.

"Stop it!" She tore the remote from his grip. "Why are you doing this? Don't you think I'm suffering already? Do you really think you need to rub it in like this? Aiden, I know what I took from you. I know —"

He took the remote back from her. "Sam, honey, I mean this in the nicest possible way, but shut up and watch, will you?"

"But I don't want —"

"Trust me, baby. Keep watching." He clicked to the next slide.

Aiden on a stool in her portrait studio, one foot hooked carelessly on a wooden rung, the other planted firmly on the floor. The lighting was perfection, and if a Hollywood talent scout ever got his hands on that shot, he'd hound Aiden within an inch of his life.

There were a lot of pictures from that formal photo shoot, and Aiden began advancing them a little faster. Eventually, as one shot gave way to another, Sam's misery was pierced by the evolution she was beginning to see on the screen. *God, yes!* This was the shoot where she'd prodded him to talk about his family, culminating in the disclosure about how he'd become a vampire, and it was all there in this sequence of photos.

Aiden, loosely confident and sexy. Eyes softening as he talked about his sister and mother. Then bristling, somehow transformed into something bigger, harder, more dangerous, as she'd pushed him for the story of how he was turned. Faster now, he clicked through the photos. By the next frame, he'd dropped the posturing, and with each successive photo, his soul was bared on screen as surely as he'd bared it to her with his words.

"Oh, Aiden," she choked.

"Hush, there's more."

The photos shifted location again, this time to Delano's cottage. Aiden in the kitchen, cooking for her. Aiden sitting across the table from her nursing a drink even though he definitely didn't need it and possibly didn't want it, just so she'd feel more comfortable. Aiden looking completely peaceful in the midst of this improbably domestic scene.

Aiden outside on one of their moonlit walks, looking so wholesome and happy, even with the odd infrared illumination.

The two of them in the bedroom, framed in the mirror. Sam looking like a wanton stranger in that peignoir and Aiden with his hands on her midriff, just beneath her breasts. These ones were taken with the little digital, the very one reflected in the mirror, but Sam hadn't yet viewed them. The quality wasn't nearly as good as with the other shots, but what grabbed Sam — once she got over the sexual impact of the shot — was Aiden's face. He didn't look like that man outside Chief Michaels' home anymore. He didn't look like that man aboard the jet, or even the one on the stool in her studio. That man was so far out of her reach, he might as well have been a god. Or Bruce Springsteen.

But this man, the one reflected in the mirror ... maybe, just maybe, *he* could be her man.

A flicker of hope stirred. "Aiden ..."

"Wait. There's more."

The next shot was of him after he'd peeled his sweater off, but sweet Jesus, if he'd cracked his own chest open and showed her his beating heart, it couldn't be plainer.

Tears welled and she covered her mouth with a hand. How had she not *seen it?*

"Just one more."

Aiden, sitting on the bed, one hand outstretched in invitation. She didn't even remember taking that one. But she did remember what she'd thought at the time, that he looked like a man who needed something from her. She'd given him her heart, because she didn't know what else to offer. On second sight, it couldn't be more clear that's exactly what he was asking for. What he needed.

"You *do* love me." She swiveled toward him on the sofa, uncaring of the tears that slipped down her cheeks. "I mean, *really* love me, like I love you."

"I really love you." He closed his hands around her upper arms, and his blue eyes shimmered suspiciously as he looked down at her. "And I really hope you'll stick around to tell me how much I love you every day of our lives."

She snorted a laugh even as she wiped away tears. "Okay, so I stole your line. Again. You'll have to learn to be quicker off the mark."

His hands tightened on her arms. "Does that mean you'll have me?"

She chewed her lip. "Are you *sure* you won't come to resent me?"

"I'm sure. Baby, it was just a matter of time before I turned in my fangs. And before you brush that away as me making the best of a bad situation, think about it. With this serum of Delano's, it's going to be a whole different world. Hunters like me, we'll be rendered obsolete, at least in our current numbers. In the fullness of time, I'd have been happy to cash in my longevity ticket for a chance at a real life with you. The situation back there … it just accelerated the decision by a couple of years."

The hope in her veins burgeoned. She felt it in her chest, her fingertips, in the tightening follicles that raised the fine hairs on her skin.

Careful, Sam. You can't afford this.

She wet her dry lips. "What about … um … you know … the rest of it?"

"The rest of what?" He searched her eyes, and from his response, he'd clearly seen her concern.

"You know — your old life."

"You mean the new city every week? The new fang-banger at the next motel or nightclub? Jesus, Sam, after what we had, you think I can feed my soul on *that*?"

"But you said —"

"Yeah, yeah, I said I was happy with that life. I *was* happy, dammit. I couldn't afford not to be. The sex got me through. Hell, it probably saved my life. And as long as I stayed on the surface, it was enough. But that was before you. I don't want to go back to that. Don't make me, Sam."

Okay, there. He'd laid it all on the line. Hell, he'd literally *drawn her a picture* with those photos.

And she was just sitting there with her eyes closed. Why wasn't she saying anything?

The silence stretched out unbearably, but damned if he'd break it first. He wouldn't beg.

Well, no more than he already had.

Finally, she opened her beautiful hazel eyes. Eyes that shone with a whole new batch of unshed tears. And oh, God, was that hope?

"You're very sure?" she asked softly.

His heart pounded so hard, it hurt in his chest. "Am I sure I want this? Am I sure I want to make a life with you?" He swallowed. "Hell, yeah. I've never been more certain of anything in my life."

"What if you come to resent me? Later, I mean. When you get tired of this. Us."

"Not gonna happen," he said. "Besides, we can ask these *what ifs* till the cows come home. What if *you* get fed up with *me*? I don't know if you've noticed, but I can be a pain in the ass. Or what if I get heart disease and die from all the red meat I intend to eat in the next couple of months? What if you get killed by one of those storms you insist on chasing and break my heart? What if Rey Sanchez comes knocking, and you decide your human lover is too boring?"

"Aiden!"

"Hey, I'm just sayin'. There's no end to the *what ifs* once you start asking them. Hell, what if you decide *being* human is too boring? There's nothing to stop you from being turned."

"My God, you really mean this, don't you? About us, being together?"

"Sam, honey, I want it all. I want to *marry* you. I want to wake up every morning and find you in my bed. Well, when you're not traveling, anyway. I want to cook for you, for *us*. When you're ready — if you want, that is — I'd like to have children with you. I want to plant a baby in your belly and watch you grow round."

"Oh, Aiden —"

"Let me finish. I want all those things, maybe because I thought I'd never be able to have them. But, baby, it's all negotiable. If marriage and parenthood are out — and God knows you've got good reason to distrust both states — then we'll figure something else out."

Her eyes brimmed. "Yes," she said.

His breath stalled. "Yes, we'll figure something out?"

"Yes to everything." A tear broke loose from her lashes and slid down her face. "Yes to marriage. Yes to children when we're ready. And *hell yes* to waking up in the same bed as often as we can."

He pulled her into a crushing hug, pressing her tear-wet face to his shirt. "Thank you, Sam." He pulled back and tipped her chin up. "Thank you for saving me."

She laughed. "Saving *you*? I thought it was the other way around."

"Okay, we can save each other."

"Deal."

He thumbed away the new tears and kissed her mouth. Her lips clung sweetly to his, and he felt a tremor go through her. He gathered her closer, lending her his strength while he took the kiss deeper. She answered with the same well of tenderness she'd showed him last night. When he lifted his head, he was the one who was shaky.

He braced his forehead against hers. "Woman, if I loved you any more, I don't think I could contain it."

"Good, because that's exactly how I feel."

She lifted a hand to his face. He knew she could feel the wetness on his cheeks, but he didn't care. Especially when she lowered that hand to his shoulder and skimmed it lightly, arousingly downward.

"Fortunately," she paused to nibble his ear, "I don't think we have to contain it *all* the time."

He slid a hand down her back to ride the top of her luscious rump. "See, that's why I love you. You're such a *practical* woman."

"*Practical?*" She jabbed his ribs.

"Ow! Did I say practical? I meant *smart*. You're such a smart woman."

"Aiden?"

"Yeah?"

"Stop talking."

Ahhh, yes. A very smart woman, indeed.

Epilogue

SAM LET HERSELF into the church's small gymnasium and took a seat. On the floor, amidst a pile of thick mats, her husband worked with a group of teenage boys. Boys the church might not have welcomed four months ago. Most of them were known to law enforcement. Some of them bore gang tattoos. All of them desperately needed a strong male role model.

Tonight it was martial arts. Aikido, specifically. She watched as the kids grumblingly practiced taking forward breakfalls.

"Why we gotta do this again and again, A? It's stupid."

"It's not stupid. And you have to do it so you don't get hurt when I toss you around later."

The young man hooted. "Yeah? You and whose army?"

Aiden grinned. "I won't need an army. Just a little help from you."

"Like I'm gonna *help* you kick my ass?"

"You'll see. Now give me another roll."

When Aiden was satisfied they'd gotten the idea and could safely be thrown, he invited each in turn to charge him. Of course, he easily flipped each of them to the mat. Sam had seen this before with other teens, so she knew what was coming. The kids didn't.

"Dude! That's *sick*. How'd you do that?"

"I used your own energy, your momentum, against you."

"Are we gonna learn to do that?"

"If you keep coming back. Okay, who wants to be next?"

The charges got more and more inventive, but the result was invariably the same. And the kid always popped up with a grin on his face.

"Man, that's whack! I wanna try flipping somebody."

"In a couple of weeks, maybe. But if you want to do this, you have to learn the theory, too," he warned. "It's not just about learning a few tricks. It's an *art*. You come here, you gotta respect that. Okay?"

More grumbling, which intensified when Aiden made them put the mats away, but Sam was sure they'd all be back next week.

Aiden escorted them all out and came back to the gym. Sam watched him cross the floor and thought what she always thought: *Yummmm.*

He extended his hand and she let him pull her up and into his arms. "Welcome home, Mrs. A."

"Thanks." She kissed him and something inside relaxed. She never felt like she was home until she was in his arms again. When she pulled back, her body was humming. "It was a good trip. I got killer shots of that twister."

"And how did little Kevin like being so close to the roaring monster?"

Sam grinned. "Well, he managed not to wet his pants, but I think it was a close thing.

It had taken Aiden a while to accept the idea of her former psychic stalker traveling with her, but even he couldn't argue the logic. Geeky little bantamweight Kevin was a finely-tuned instrument when it came to detecting vampire activity. And it was the least he could do to make up for the trouble he'd caused. And Kevin was happy to do it. Well, except for the being scared shitless part. Understandably, he much preferred his other role, lending his talent and energies to Delano and his band of hunters.

"And how did you make out with Liss?"

Liss — Melissandre Saint-Pierre by her given name — was the second half of Sam's security team. The half that carried bagged blood and who could handle a rogue almost as well as Aiden used to, so they said. No doubt part of that success had something to do with the fact that she looked like an 18-year-old waif.

Sam smiled. "She's a sweetheart. And you know, I'm almost getting to like her music."

Aiden groaned.

Liss made a ridiculously good living screaming lyrics as the front woman for a punk band, when she wasn't kicking rogue ass.

"How'd things go here?" Sam asked.

"Classes were fine."

Aiden was studying for a social work degree so he could do the work he was so passionate about. She'd been stunned initially when he announced his intention, but the moment she'd seen him with the first group of boys, she understood. He had a talent for it. And something of a history, she discovered. Some forty years ago, he'd taken a painfully thin fifteen-year-old girl off the streets and helped her find self-respect and purpose. That's why he'd learned to cook, he confessed, to nurture the girl. She'd gone on to work with troubled children, and Aiden was now following in her footsteps.

"I got a new crop of boys, as you saw."

She nodded. "They'll all be back."

"I hope so." He pulled her close for another kiss. "Hey," he said when they broke, "we're gonna have company this weekend."

Sam groaned. "RJ?"

"In the flesh."

"We'll have to make good use of tonight, then?"

He laughed. "When do we not?"

She grinned back at him. "True."

"I'm going to have to kick RJ's ass again, though." Aiden's grin turned to a scowl. "He won't quit saying he's coming to sleep with my wife."

Sam laughed. "That's one way of putting it."

This would be the fifth time RJ had come to stay, and a hunter named Garret Evans had been four times, and Liss twice. Each visit had yielded the desired outcome, a vision that pinpointed the activity of a rogue. But the hunters didn't sleep *with* her. They slept in a spare bedroom *near* her. That was all it took, apparently, to trigger the dreams. Thankfully, the requests for sleepovers were growing less and less frequent. Delano and his dual attack with the vaccine and the hunters was having a huge impact.

"RJ's not so bad," she said. "He's actually starting to grow on me."

Aiden snorted. "Yeah, like a fungus."

"He's just a little ... eccentric."

"He's fucking *nuts*."

"Yeah, okay. He's nuts."

"All right, all right, I'll cop to it," he grumbled. "I'm jealous. He's the top hunter now."

Sam dropped her hands from around his neck and skimmed them down his body to hook into his belt, delighting in the way his body tightened. "Yeah, but who's got it better?"

"RJ *who*?"

"Exactly." She went up on tiptoes to meet his kiss.

Note to Reader

Thank you for investing that most precious of commodities — your time — in my book!

If you enjoyed NIGHTFALL, I would be thrilled if you could help me buzz it. You can do this by:

Recommending it. Help other readers find this book by recommending it to friends, readers' groups and discussion boards.

Reviewing it. Please share with other readers what you liked about this book by reviewing it wherever you purchased it, or at readers' sites such as Goodreads.

I invite you to read on for an excerpt from another of my books.

Thank you!

Also available by this author:

Coming September 4, 2012 from Montlake Romance:
EVERY BREATH SHE TAKES
Sensual Romantic Suspense w/Paranormal Element

THE MERZETTI EFFECT, Book 1 in
the *Vampire Romance series*

GUARDING SUZANNAH, Book 1 in
the Serve and Protect Series
SAVING GRACE, Book 2 in the Serve and Protect Series
PROTECTING PAIGE, Book 3 in the Serve and Protect Series
NEEDING NITA, A Novella in the Serve and Protect Series
(sensual romantic suspense)

**As N.L. Wilson (writing partnership of
Norah Wilson and Heather Doherty)**
The Dix Dodd Mysteries
THE CASE OF THE FLASHING FASHION QUEEN
FAMILY JEWELS
DEATH BY CUDDLE CLUB (Coming Fall 2012)
(funny mysteries in the vein of Janet
Evanovich's Stephanie Plum series)

**As Wilson Doherty (writing partnership of
Norah Wilson and Heather Doherty)**
THE SUMMONING: Book 1 in the Gatekeepers Series
ASHLYN'S RADIO
COMES THE NIGHT, Book 1 in the
Casters Series (coming Fall 2012)
ENTER THE NIGHT, Book 2 in the
Casters Series (coming Fall 2013)
(YA paranormal)

About the Author

Norah Wilson lives in Fredericton, New Brunswick with her husband, two adult children and her beloved Rotti-Lab mix Chloe. Norah has had three of her romantic suspense stories final in the Romance Writers of America's Golden Heart® contest until she sold her first story in 2004. She was also the winner of Dorchester Publishingss New Voice in Romance contest in 2003.

Norah loves to hear from readers!

Connect with her online at:
Twitter: http://twitter.com/norah_wilson
Facebook: http://www.facebook.com/#!/profile.php?id=1053773212
Goodreads: http://www.goodreads.com/
author/show/1361508.Norah_Wilson
Email: norahwilsonwrites@gmail.com

Chapter 1

DETECTIVE JOHN QUIGLEY STEPPED inside Courtroom 2, closing the door quietly behind him. One or two people in the small gallery glanced up at him briefly, then returned their attention to the front of the courtroom where a young patrol officer was being sworn in.

Quigg took a seat, glancing around the drab, low-ceilinged, windowless room. *Provincial Court.* Nothing like the much grander Queen's Bench courtrooms upstairs or the Court of Appeal chambers on the top floor. But aesthetics aside, they did a brisk business here. In the fifteen years Quigg had spent on the Fredericton force, he'd been responsible for sending quite a few customers through these doors. Doors that all too often turned out to be the revolving kind, the kind that spit offenders right back out on the street to re-offend.

On that thought, Quigg glanced over at the accused. Clean shaven and neatly dressed, he sat off to the right, beside the Sheriff's deputy. His long hair, drawn back into a ponytail, glinted blue-black under the fluorescent lights. If he were conscious of Quigg's scrutiny, he didn't betray it with so much as a twitch of a muscle. Rather, he kept his flat, emotionless gaze trained on the witness.

"Your witness, Mr. Roth."

At the magistrate's words, Quigg faced forward again.

"Thank you, Your Honour." The Crown Prosecutor adjusted his table microphone and directed his first question to the witness. Mike Langan, the impossibly young looking constable in the witness box, responded, his answer clear and concise.

Over the next fifteen minutes, the prosecutor methodically built his case with one carefully chosen question after another. Constable Langan's manner in the witness box was confident and assured. He referred often to his notebook, which appeared to contain copious, comprehensive notes. Quigg unclenched his fingers and leaned back into his seat. What could go wrong?

Everything.

His gaze slid to the one area of the courtroom he'd so far managed to avoid, the defense table. *Suzannah Phelps.* There she sat, primly erect, all that straight blond hair pulled up into a knot at the back of her head. Even under the black tent-like court robes, she still managed to look model elegant. His pulse took a little kick.

Dammit, why did he do this to himself? He didn't have to be here. He was off today. He didn't have even a glancing involvement with this case, or with Constable Langan.

Because you're a bloody masochist.

"Any questions on cross, Ms. Phelps?"

The magistrate's voice cut into Quigg's thoughts.

"Just a few, Your Honour."

A *few?* Yeah, sure.

"Please proceed."

Quigg glanced at Langan, saw the younger man tense. *Relax man.* He tried to send the thought telepathically. *Don't let her get to you. Don't let her see you sweat.*

"So, Constable Langan, you didn't actually see my client flee the crime scene?"

"No, ma'am. Not from the actual scene. But I did see a man fitting the robber's description running just four blocks from the scene."

"And who provided this description?"

"The shopkeeper."

"And the description was ... ?"

"Native ... er, First Nations individual, average height, stocky build, long black hair worn in a ponytail."

"Were those the shopkeeper's precise words? First Nations individual?"

"Huh?"

"Did the shopkeeper describe the perpetrator as Native? Native American? First Nations?"

"Not exactly."

Quigg sank lower in his seat, suppressing a groan. This was gonna be a train wreck and Langan didn't even know it yet.

"Exactly how *did* he describe him, then?"

"He made it clear that the individual was Indian."

"Those were his words, then? Indian?"

"No." Constable Langan shifted, glancing down at his notebook.

"What were his precise words, Constable?"

Langan glanced at the judge, then back at Suzannah Phelps. "I believe his precise words were, *wagon burner.*"

"Which you took to mean a member of the First Nations?"

"Yes."

Quigg massaged his temple. Ah, Christ, here we go.

"Thank you, Constable."

Her voice was polite, prim, even. Which just served to show that sharks came in all kinds of guises.

Suzannah glanced down at her notes, then back at the hapless witness. "So, Constable Langan, could you take a guess how many males from our Native population would fit that description?"

"Objection, Your Honour. We have eye-witness testimony from the shop owner that the accused is the individual who committed the robbery. He was picked out from a lineup containing no fewer than ten Native men of similar ages and builds."

Finally! An objection from the Crown. Quigg resisted the urge to rake a hand through his hair.

"As my learned friend knows, I could cite dozens of cases where eye-witness identification put innocent men behind bars," responded Suzannah. "And those were cases where the perpetrators' faces were not partially obscured by a kerchief."

"Point taken." The judge leaned forward. "Your objection is overruled, Mr. Roth. You may proceed, Ms. Phelps."

"Thank you, Judge." She turned back to the witness. "Again, Constable Langan, in your opinion, can you tell me how many males of Mi'kmaq or Maliseet descent could answer to that description: medium height, stocky build, black hair?"

A pause. "Quite a few, I would imagine."

"A majority of them?"

"Possibly," Langan conceded.

"Then any Native male observed within a reasonable radius of the crime scene might have fit your description?"

"Maybe. But then again, there aren't a lot of them in this particular shopping district."

Mother of God. Quigg sank even lower in his seat.

"Ah, so my client shouldn't have been there in the first place, in an exclusive shopping district?"

"That's not what I meant." Langan's face hardened. "This particular Native male was fleeing capture."

"Is that so?" She made a show of reviewing her notes. "Was my client running when you first spotted him?"

"No."

"When did he start running?"

"When I cut him off with my vehicle. He was walking fast — I mean, real fast — down the sidewalk, in an easterly direction. I pulled into an alley, blocked him off."

"And then he fled?"

"Yes. He turned and fled back in a westerly direction."

"Were your red and blue bar lights flashing when you executed this maneuver?"

"Yes."

She shuffled some more papers. "Is it conceivable that my client's flight might have been an ingrained response to perceived police harassment?"

"No!"

"No? Constable Langan, are you a member of a visible minority?"

"No."

"Objection!"

The judge held up his hand in the prosecutor's direction. "Overruled."

"Imagine for a minute that you are a member of a visible minority. What might you do if a police cruiser were to suddenly swing into your path like that?"

Constable Langan bristled. "The guy had the money on him. The *exact* amount that was later determined to be missing from the cash register."

"Ah, so now we have a First Nations male, walking where he ought not to, with more money in his pocket than he should have?"

"Money he stole from that shopkeeper at knifepoint!"

Damn, the kid was losing it.

"Ah, yes, the knife." Suzannah flipped the page on the legal pad in front of her. "A knife which bore no fingerprints and which you haven't been able to tie to my client."

"He dumped it down a sewer grate a block from where he was apprehended, two blocks from the scene. He still had the polkad-otted blue-and-white handkerchief in his pocket. Give or take the coins in his pockets, he was carrying exactly the amount of money that was stolen. He was ID'd by the shopkeeper ...."

Quigg closed his eyes, pressing a thumb and forefinger against his lids. Inside his head, he heard the theme from *Jaws*.

"Thank you for that summation, Constable, but I think the Crown was planning one of its own." She flipped another page on her yellow pad. "Since you're feeling so loquacious, maybe you can answer this question for me — do you yourself ever carry a handkerchief?"

Langan blinked.

"Would you like me to repeat the question, Constable? When you're off duty, wearing your civilian clothes, do you ever carry one of those polkadotted handkerchiefs? Shoved in a front pocket of your jeans, maybe, or in your coat pocket?"

Five more minutes. That's all it took to completely decimate the Crown's case. Not that Roth surrendered without a fight. He called the shopkeeper and adduced his evidence. Evidence which the defense challenged effectively. But by the time Suzannah fin-ished her summation, she'd planted more than just the seed of reasonable doubt. No one in the courtroom was surprised when the judge pronounced his verdict without even a short recess. *Not guilty.* The prisoner was released.

Quigg stood and slipped out the door as quietly as he'd slipped in.

⁂

Suzannah stood, turning to scan the gallery. The seats had emptied out, apart from her client's two female cousins. Certainly the owner of the gaze she'd felt boring into her back for the last half hour was gone.

"Congratulations."

She turned toward Anthony Roth, whose lean, dark features were wreathed in resignation. Fiercely competitive, he hated to lose, but he was a good prosecutor. He knew his role wasn't to secure a conviction at any cost; it was to get to the truth.

"Thanks."

"And you made yourself a brand new friend on Fredericton's finest, too. Quite a day."

She grimaced.

When young Mike Langan had finally been excused from the witness box, his body language as he jammed on his hat and tugged at his Kevlar vest had screamed exactly how he felt. Suffice to say he wouldn't be joining the ranks of the Suzannah Phelps Fan Club any time soon.

That's how it goes, Suzie-girl. You didn't get into this business to make friends.

"Couldn't be helped," she said lightly. "You know I had to play the cards I was dealt."

"Of course. I'd have done the same thing in your shoes." Roth swept his briefcase from the desk. "Fair warning, though. It'll be different next time we cross swords over this guy."

"There won't be a next time."

His lips lifted in a cynical smile. "Right."

As soon as the Crown Prosecutor moved off, her client moved in. Gripping her hand in a two-handed clasp, he pumped it enthusiastically. "Thank you, Ms. Phelps."

"You're welcome, Leo." Suzannah withdrew her hand. "You still interested in a job at the graphics studio I mentioned?"

He nodded. "Yeah. Yeah, I am."

She plucked a business card from her briefcase and handed it to him. "Give this lady a call. She agrees you have talent, but you'd have to prove yourself."

The card disappeared into Leo's huge hand. "Thanks, Ms. Phelps. This is great."

"And you'd have to stay clean, Leo. You understand?" She caught his gaze and held it. "Squeaky clean. No more altercations with the police."

"I understand."

"I hope you do. You put a foot wrong after this, they'll be watching."

He cast a sideways glance at his cousins. "Gotcha."

"Good. Now get out of here."

He grinned and was gone.

Suzannah turned back to the desk, her smile fading as she began packing her note pads, law books and files back into the big hard-sided court bag.

Dammit, she'd won, hadn't she? Why didn't she feel better?

Made yourself a brand new friend today… Roth's words echoed in her head.

"Oh, for pity's sake." She was such a baby sometimes. Shoving the last file into her bag, she glanced around the courtroom. Normally, she'd adjourn to the ladies room to remove her court garb, but she could do a striptease in here today and there'd be no one to witness it.

One tug and the white tabbed collar came off. Then the robe, over the head like a choir gown. She ran a hand over her hair to make sure it hadn't come loose. Satisfied, she folded the robe carefully, stuffed it into a blue velvet sack and pulled the drawstring tight. There. Street ready. She smoothed her pinstriped skirt, slung the sack over her shoulder, hefted her bag and headed for the exit.

Despite the quick change, her getaway was not as clean as she would have liked, however. In the corridor, she ran into Renee LeRoy, half-assed reporter and full-fledged pain-in-the-ass. Suzannah searched her mind for the name of the local weekly Renee worked for, but it eluded her. Not that it mattered. She avoided reading her own press if she possibly could, especially anything *this* particular woman might have to say.

Well, at least this explained the sensation she'd felt of being watched back there in the courtroom. Suppressing a groan, Suzannah tacked on a pleasant smile. "How's it going, Renee?"

The other woman didn't smile back. In fact, her face was set in grim lines more reminiscent of a Russian forward in the '72 Canada/Russia hockey series than a female reporter. As soon as the thought crossed her mind, Suzannah chastised herself. Her dislike of Renee LeRoy had nothing to do with the other woman's appearance and everything to do with her attitude.

"I see your client walked away a free man."

Oh, hell, here we go again. The woman was a broken record. "The burden of proof always rests on the Crown, Renee," she said reasonably. "This time, they failed to meet that burden."

"Thanks in no small part to you."

"Why, thank you." Suzannah offered a wide if disingenuous smile. "I'd be flattered, except I think any reasonably competent criminal lawyer would have secured an acquittal under the circumstances."

The reporter's eyes narrowed. "Doesn't it keep you awake at night, Ms. Phelps? Doesn't your conscience ever bother you, knowing you're helping guilty men go free?"

Suzannah's lips thinned, along with her patience. Was a little open-mindedness from the press too much to ask? "What would *bother me* is to see a conviction entered on the quality of the evidence we saw today. My client deserved to be acquitted. Now, if you'll excuse me, I have a schedule to keep."

A minute later, she descended the steps of the Justice Building and crossed the parking lot. The sun had already begun to dip behind the tallest buildings, casting long shadows. Even so, heat rose from the asphalt in shimmering waves.

All of southern New Brunswick had been gripped in a heat wave since the July 1st Canada Day holiday. Like the rest of her pasty-faced compatriots, Suzannah had welcomed the first real taste of summer. Now, almost three weeks later, she cursed the humidity that made perspiration bead between her breasts before she'd even reached her car.

She thought briefly about stowing her case in the BMW's trunk, but decided that would require too much effort. Instead, she hit the button on her remote to release the door locks. She opened the back door on the driver's side and tossed the garment bag onto the back seat. She'd started to swing the heavy bag into the vehicle when a flash of color from the front passenger seat caught her eye. She lost her grip on the handles, and the bag collided with the car's frame and thudded to the pavement.

Oh, God, no. Not again.

⁂

"Can I give you a hand with that?"

She seemed to just about come out of her skin at his words, whirling to face him. Wide blue eyes locked onto him, and for an instant, Quigg saw fear. Not surprise. Not your garden variety momentary fright when someone startled you. This was real, raw fear. Then it was gone, and she wore her smooth Princess face again.

"Thank you, no. I can manage."

Her voice was cool, polite, completely assured. Had he imagined the blaze of fear?

Bending, she righted the briefcase, deposited it on the car's seat and closed the door. She must have expected him to move on, or at least to step back, because when she turned, she wound up standing considerably closer than before. Closer than was comfortable for her. He could see it in the quick lift of her brows, the slight widening of her eyes. But she didn't step back.

Neither did he.

Damn, she was beautiful. And tall. In those three-inch heels that probably cost more than he made in a week, her gaze was level with his. Throw in all that long blond hair that would slide like silk through a man's hands, and a body that would . . . .

"You're that cop."

He blinked. "*That* cop?"

"*Regina vs. Rosneau.*"

"Good memory." They'd secured a conviction on that one, but her client had taken a walk on appeal. Though in truth, Quigg hadn't minded over much. The dirtball had done it, all right, but strictly speaking, the evidence had been a bit thin. One of those fifty/fifty propositions.

"*Regina vs. Haynes.* That was you, too, right?"

Okay, dammit, that one still stung, although the insult was almost two years old now. Two defendants, separate trials, separate representation, each accused managing to convince a jury the other guy'd done it. Of course, Quigg could take consolation from knowing the noose was closing yet again around Ricky Haynes' good-for-nothing drug-dealing neck. Haynes had since moved outside the city limits, beyond municipal jurisdiction, but Quigg had it on good authority that the Mounties were building a rock-solid case against him.

Yes, he could take some consolation in that. Some *small* consolation. Not enough, however, to blunt the slow burn in his gut right now.

"Keep a scrapbook, do you, Ms. Phelps? Or maybe you cut a notch in your little Gucci belt, one for every cop you skewer?"

Something that looked astonishingly like hurt flashed in her eyes, but like before, it was gone before he could be certain he'd really seen it. Then she stepped even closer and smiled, a slow, knowing smile that made him think about skin sliding against skin and sweat-slicked bodies fusing in the dark, and he knew he'd been mistaken. When she extended a slender, ringless finger to trace a circle around a button on his shirt, his heart stumbled, then began to pound.

"Definitely not the belt thing," she said, her voice as husky and honeyed as his most sex-drenched fantasy. "At the rate you guys self-destruct under cross, there'd be nothing left to hold my trousers up, would there, now, John?"

Then she climbed in her gleaming little Beemer and drove off before his hormone-addled brain divorced her words from her manner and realized he'd been dissed.

Against all reason, he laughed. Lord knew it wasn't funny. Certainly, young Langan wouldn't share his mirth.

Of course, the whole thing defied reason, the way it twisted his guts just to look at her. She was rich. She was beautiful. She was sophisticated. She was the daughter of a judge, from a long line of judges. She was ... what? He searched his admittedly limited lexicon for an appropriate term. *Kennedy-esque.*

Meanwhile, his own father had worked in a saw mill; his mother had cleaned other people's houses. Suzannah Phelps was so far out of his league, there wasn't even a real word for it.

She was also the woman not-so-affectionately known around the station house as *She-Rex.* And worse.

Much worse.

Except she hadn't looked much like a She-Rex when she'd spun around to face him, her face all pale and frightened.

Quigg turned and headed for Queen Street, where he'd parked his car. What had spooked her? Not his sudden appearance. He was sure of that. She might not have much use for cops, but she wasn't scared of him.

Maybe it was something inside her car.

He'd reached his own car, which sprouted a yellow parking ticket from beneath the windshield wiper. Great. He glanced up, searching traffic. There she was, at the lights a block away.

What could be in her car to make her look like that? Or was he completely off base? Was it a guilty start, not a frightened start? Hard to say. She'd masked it so quickly.

Damn, he was going to have to follow her.

Climbing into his not-so-shiny Taurus, he fired it up, signaled and pulled into traffic.

Even at this hour with the first of the home-bound traffic leaving the downtown core, tailing her was child's play. As he expected, she headed back to her office. No knocking off early for Suzannah Phelps. She probably put in longer days than he did. Two blocks from her uptown offices, she pulled into another office building's parking lot. Quigg guided his vehicle into the gas bar next door and watched Suzannah drive to the back of the lot where she parked next to a blue dumpster.

Pretending to consult a map he'd pulled from his glove compartment, Quigg watched her get out of the car and scan the lot. Then she circled the BMW, opened the passenger door and pulled something out. The car itself blocked Quigg's view, but he saw a flash of mauvey/pinky floral patterned paper. Then she lifted the dumpster's lid and tossed the object in. Quickly, she rounded the car, climbed in and accelerated out of the lot.

Quigg watched her vehicle travel east along Prospect. When she signaled and turned into her office's parking lot, he slipped his own car into gear. Thirty seconds later, he lifted the lid to the dumpster.

Flowers? She'd been scared witless by flowers?

More likely by who sent the flowers, he reasoned. Maybe they still had a card attached. Out of habit, he patted his pockets for latex gloves before remembering he didn't have any on him. He wasn't on duty. He had some in a first aid kit in his car, but he wasn't about to dig them out. This wasn't an investigation.

Well, not a sanctioned one.

Grimacing, he retrieved the prettily wrapped bouquet with his bare hands. The florist's paper appeared pristine, undisturbed, as though Suzannah hadn't even looked at the contents. Carefully, he peeled the paper back. Then he dropped the bouquet back into the dumpster.

Holy hell! Long-stemmed red roses. Or rather, what he suspected used to be red roses. Now they were more brown than red. Rusty, like old blood. Dead. Probably a dozen of them.

His mind whirled. How had she known? She hadn't even opened the wrapper.

Because it wasn't the first time, obviously.

Because they'd been deposited in her car, right there in the barristers' parking lot, while she was inside defending Leo Warren. While a commissionaire kept an eye on the lot. While her car doors had no doubt been locked.

No wonder she'd been spooked.

He picked up the bouquet again and examined it closer. No card. *There's a surprise, Sherlock.*

Why hadn't she told him? She *knew* he was a cop.

Domestic. The answer came instantly. Had to be. She knew the source, but wasn't prepared to make a complaint because she didn't want to make trouble for the jerk who'd done this, thereby increasing his rage. How many times had he seen that age-old dynamic in operation?

Except he hadn't expected it from Suzannah. She was too much of a fighter. What could be going on in her head?

Quigg tossed the bouquet back in the dumpster and closed the lid. Climbing back into the Taurus, he sat for long moments.

He should leave this alone. He knew it.

He also knew he wasn't going to.

"This, you dumb-ass, is how careers are ruined."

But she'd called him John. Back there, outside the courthouse, she'd called him by his Christian name. Nobody called him John, except his mother. It was *Quigg*, or *Detective Quigley*, or *Officer*, or even *Hey, pig!* But back there, while her index finger had traced delicate circles on his chest, she'd called him John.

Stifling a sigh, he keyed the ignition and slipped the Ford into gear.